Alyzon
Whitestarr

Alyzon
Whitestarr

ISOBELLE CARMODY

RANDOM HOUSE 🏠 NEW YORK

Copyright © 2005 by Isobelle Carmody

Published in the United States by Random House Children's Books,
a division of Random House, Inc., New York. Originally published in Australia
by Penguin Group Australia, Camberwell, in 2005.

Random House and the colophon are registered trademarks of Random House, Inc.

Visit us on the Web! www.randomhouse.com/teens

Educators and librarians, for a variety of teaching tools, visit us at
www.randomhouse.com/teachers

Library of Congress Cataloging-in-Publication Data
Carmody, Isobelle.
Alyzon Whitestarr / Isobelle Carmody. — 1st American ed.
p. cm.
Summary: When Alyzon, the ordinary member of an extraordinary family, develops
enhanced senses, she becomes aware of an evil virus that preys on people's spirits,
and realizes that the sickness and its proponents are aware of her and are a
menace to her family.
ISBN 978-0-375-83938-2 (trade) — ISBN 978-0-375-93938-9 (lib. bdg.)
[1. Psychic ability—Fiction. 2. Family life—Australia—Fiction. 3. Supernatural—Fiction.
4. Australia—Fiction.] I. Title.
PZ7.C2176Aly 2009
[Fic]—dc22
2008033796

Printed in the United States of America

10 9 8 7 6 5 4 3 2 1

First American Edition

For my brother Matthew,
who talked philosophy at seven . . .

Prelude

The sky was a soup of colors swirled together, and the sea was restless under it. Waves lapped the shore fretfully, sighing.

A man and woman walked from their car down a steep curving road to the sea, wearing bathing suits, towels slung around their necks. His shorts were too heavy to dry well. Both wore sunglasses for no other reason than because they had worn them all day. As they rounded the road, they saw the shallow beach.

"Well," the man said, and they both stopped.

There was a naked pregnant woman, wading in the sea; they were both shocked and fascinated. A barefoot man wearing jeans and no shirt prowled the shore, while a big older woman clad in a voluminous dark plum dress and a shawl was seated on a blanket facing the pair. A slight girl with mouse-colored hair seated beside her was almost hidden. The seated woman's brooding presence suggested some ritual in progress—a spell or an archaic binding. The girl might have been a sprite.

"Well," the woman murmured at last, shaking herself

slightly to dislodge an inexplicable premonition of danger. "Let's go down."

Only when they reached the beach did they realize there were others; a plump youth of some eighteen or nineteen years peering into rock pools; a girl sitting on a rock combing her hair, which some trick of the sunlight rendered faintly green. The attention of these young people, like that of the man and the older woman, was focused on the pregnant woman.

As they drew nearer the strange group, the woman with the sunglasses noticed that the man in the jeans was extraordinarily good-looking. When he turned to smile at the newcomers, she felt the charm of the smile and responded.

It was not until they had come to the end of the path that they saw there was yet another girl curled under a bush at the rim of the beach. She was biting her nails. Even from a distance it was clear she had gone too far and was hurting herself. Unlike the others, her eyes were not on the woman in the water but on the handsome older man.

Feeling self-conscious, the couple piled towels, shoes, and sunglasses together. They swam, keeping carefully to one side of the inlet, leaving the other to the pregnant woman. When they were drying themselves, the woman in plum walked past them to an old van parked in the dunes. She returned with a steaming mug of liquid.

"All the comforts of home," said the man.

"It's herbal medicine for her," she said, nodding toward the pregnant woman. "She's in labor."

The couple turned to stare openly at the pregnant woman. She had come into the shallows, and the man was now positioned behind her, supporting her back with his chest. The watching couple suddenly understood. What was about to take place was both extraordinary and utterly commonplace: a woman was about to give birth. At any given moment there must be millions of them in the world.

The woman resumed her sunglasses automatically and, remembering her own labor in a hospital, felt an echo of the pain, the need to push, the excitement of it all that no one had ever told her about. She could see now that the pregnant woman was doing the shallow panting. Her long red hair was lying in damp streamers down her back and across her swollen belly. It made the woman watching feel both afraid and thrilled.

Tonight she would dream of a woman screaming.

The man at her side wondered at a couple who would offer themselves and the woman's pain and their unborn child up to that sunset, that sea. What did it mean in a world of hospitals and doctors and nuclear fission? What was it saying to the world? (To him?) He remembered the rank stench as his own daughter was born. How primal the birth, despite the hospital bed, the hovering doctor.

As the couple left, the sun was setting and clouds saturated with night were beginning to reach long fingers over the sky. Again the woman experienced a stab of unspecified danger, and it occurred to her that her fear was not of the family on the beach, but for them.

The man glanced in the rearview mirror as he drove away. Two girls were leading a skittish brown horse between them across the road. They seemed barely able to control it, and he wondered what would happen if it got away from them.

1

It starts with my family, and in a way that's the whole story.

There's my mother, Zambia. You probably won't have heard of her. She's the artist, Zambia Whitestarr. Then there's my da, Macoll Whitestarr. His stage name is Mac, and he's the lead guitarist in a band you've probably never heard of that plays a lot of improvised music. Then there's us kids: my older brother, Jesse; my older sister, Mirandah; me, Alyzon; Serenity, who tries to make us call her Sybl; and last but not least our baby brother, Luke.

People always raise their eyebrows when I say how many of us there are. "Fi-ve," they say, lifting their voice up at the end to show how they can hardly believe it. I guess we do have a pretty big family by ordinary standards. Mostly people have two or three kids. Somebody told me the size of a normal family is two-and-a-half-kids. I don't know how they figure the half. I mean, what's half a kid? A baby? In that case there's four and a half of us, Luke being the half, only what he lacks in size he makes up for in Starr quality.

Ha ha.

Da always says we have a cast as big as *Ben Hur*, which is this old movie about half-naked muscle men who wrestle lions. Da loves movies. He always says if he had another life, he would be a film director. Not the kind that makes movies about giant dinosaurs or meteors flattening New York; art-house movies where you don't have any idea what they're about, but you can't help watching them because they are sooo weird, and then you come out and the world seems to have shifted a bit while you were inside.

Da says that's the whole point of those movies: to put you off balance; to make you see things from a different angle. I always answer: "We Whitestarrs are unbalanced enough already."

I mean, you get the picture. This is not your common or garden-variety family where Da or Mum goes to work in an office or some place, and you shop and watch TV in the evenings, and go for barbecues on the weekends. For a start, Mum and Da work weird hours. Mum paints at night. She's what's called *nocturnal*. She sleeps in the daytime and gets up and eats breakfast while the rest of us eat dinner. The best part of her being up all night is that if you wake up with a bad dream or you can't sleep, you can go to her studio. She wraps you in her shawls and lets you curl up in the corner of her tatty old studio couch while she makes Vegemite toast and pots of herbal tea, and you eventually fall asleep watching her paint, bathed in moonlight.

Da only works at night when he has a gig. Generally he and his band, Losing the Rope, rehearse four days a week in the afternoons and some nights. He earns a living arranging other people's music and giving music lessons. The rest of the time he's either practicing his guitar or composing his own music.

To say we're not rich is an understatement. There's a few good months, a lot of bad months, and the occasional ugly month when we're not having milk in our tea or butter on our bread and bills with red type and a nasty tone come in the mail because of what Da calls *The Gap*. That means the difference between when you ask somebody to pay you and when you actually get the money.

When I was small I thought The Gap was this big crack in the pavement out front of our place, which had appeared when a truck mounted the curb one night. It was wide enough that little kids needed help to step over it and old ladies with canes were always tutting at it. What used to scare me about it was that you couldn't see how deep it was, no matter how hard you looked. It was too dark, and I was too scared to reach in and see if I could feel the bottom.

One day the man up the road saw me lying on my belly staring into it and he told me to watch out for the bears. Somehow that gave me this creepy idea that there was a dark underworld of bears and the crack opened onto it, but it wasn't wide enough for them to escape, although that's what they wanted to do more than anything in the world. They thought humans were mutant bears whose fur had fallen out, and they wanted to tear out the throats of all us puny, hairless bears living up here in the sunlight. But they couldn't find a way to escape. So they would come to the crack and gaze up at us. Whenever I stepped over it, I could feel their eyes glittering with bloodlust and hate. And whenever Da warned us that The Gap was widening, I would have nightmares about the bears, fearing that they had figured out a way to open up the crack enough to escape.

Of course, I grew out of thinking the bears were down there, but I still get a feeling of unease when Da talks about The Gap. Da says it doesn't matter about being poor because everyone should live on the edge some of the time; it reminds you you're alive. One bit of me agrees with him, but another bit of me feels like it would be easier if you didn't live too close to the edge all of the time.

We kids go to school like regular kids. The truth is I like school. I'd get bored if I was home all the time just doing anything I wanted, like Jesse.

Da tutored us all in music, of course. He taught us piano and guitar, but I'm the only one who doesn't play anything. All that teaching couldn't seem to take hold in me. It just slipped out as fast as Da fed it in, until he said kindly that maybe I took after Mum. That might be OK if it wasn't for the fact that most of the others are artistic as well. Mum says it's because I haven't developed the right side of my brain yet. Da thinks it's because I haven't found my form.

It was different with the others. Jesse plays blues on his guitar, Mirandah plays saxophone in a jazz group with some kids at school, and Serenity plays cello really well. Or she used to, anyway. Da says it doesn't matter about me and

Mum not being musical because somebody needs to be the audience.

What I'm trying to say here is that in a family of extraordinary and talented people, I am the odd one out—the chicken in a house of peacocks. The worst of it is that the others really *are* peacocks. Mum has stunning blue eyes, masses of wavy red hair, and pale, soft skin. Mirandah takes after her, except she's blond. Da, Serenity, and Jesse have thick, wavy, coal-black hair and blue eyes. Jesse is kind of overweight, but he's still really nice-looking. Da is so handsome that some of the girls at school make swooning faces when he goes by, and female teachers always talk to him for longer than any other parent at parent-teacher nights. Luke has only been in the world for half a second or so, so we don't know how he'll end up looking, but right now he has creamy skin, a fluff of inky curls, and opaque blue eyes. I have this pale brown, straight hair that won't grow past my shoulders without splitting, and my eyes are gray. Smoky, Da calls them, but that makes them sound a lot more interesting than they really are. I'm kind of skinny and short, too. Compact, Da says, which makes me sound like the economy size. So maybe *I'm* the half in the Whitestarr family.

I'm a bit ashamed to admit that, although I never minded having no talent, I did mind being plain *and* untalented. But who could I blame? Mum and Da can't help the way their genes worked together to make me. I guess even genes have their off days.

* * *

That was how I thought of us all before the accident. I had everybody all worked out and filed away. Mum was full of impractical romantic visions that made her inattentive to the real world; Jesse was lazy and absentminded; Mirandah was bossy and superior and tactless; Sybl-Serenity was moody and getting moodier. Luke was sweet, but just a baby. And Da? He was kind and generous and easygoing and filled with integrity. And he loved music.

2

When I think back, I always come to this thing that happened just before everything changed forever. Our English class went to the office of the *Coastal Telegraph,* our local newspaper, on a field trip that had been arranged by our English teacher, Mrs. Barker.

First the editor told us what his job was, then he passed us on to a sad-looking man called Eddie, who took us downstairs to look at the old part of the building where they used to set some of the print by hand. Eddie explained that people used to fit every letter of the headlines into a metal box, which was fixed onto rollers and inked; then paper was pressed against it. Sort of like a huge stamp set.

We saw these enormous wheels of paper in a machine that used to roll them over those inked metal plates. It was exactly like you see in the movies when something happens and they supposedly show the front-page headlines being rolled out. Except it was all frozen forever, like dinosaurs in a museum.

"That's not how newspapers get put together now,"

Eddie said, sounding wistful. "All the typing and laying out—that's the way the stories and photographs are organized on a page—that gets done on computers now."

Eddie abandoned us in the staff cafeteria, where we were to have lunch. Marilyn Bobbit whispered loudly to Sylvia Yarrow that gray Eddie seemed a bit like one of the components of those old machines. Sylvia giggled and agreed he looked just as obsolete.

I spent lunchtime pretending to eat and covertly watching Harlen Sanderson flirt with the elderly cafeteria attendant. It was so sweet to see her blush when he gave her a flower he'd plucked from a vase.

After lunch, a cheerful guy called Clarry showed up and took us to where the advertising was laid out. He told us that newspapers were really only there so people could advertise things they wanted to sell. Journalists were too silly to know any better. He grinned when he said that, to show he was joking, but you could see it was what he really thought.

He took us to a tiny room where there was a typewriter-like machine called a teleprinter. He said it used to spit out news from agencies all over the world, but now they had the Internet. He left us with a girl called Riley—I don't know if that was her first or last name. Her job, she told us, was to sift through the mass of stuff on the Internet for backfill. This was information that journalists might use to compile other stories, or for research, or it might be stories that were about our region. She printed these out and filed them, or passed them on to anyone who might be doing a story and could use them. Sometimes journalists would ask her to track down information for them. She showed us the computer room where news was coming in and said that she often knew first when some big news story was breaking. Then we had a look at the photo file before going to the boardroom, where a journalist was going to give us a talk to finish up the day.

We had been waiting about twenty-five minutes when in walked this guy with dark-brown, restless eyes, short black hair, and a loose way of walking and moving, as if he wasn't properly screwed together at the joints. He wore a dark gray suit that looked expensive, although he wasn't all that old. He told us his name was Gary Soloman and that he was an A-grade journalist. Then he launched confidently into this talk about journalism as a career. It sounded like something he had memorized and you got the feeling he was just unwinding a spool. But when he said a journalist couldn't afford to get emotionally involved, Jezabel Aster broke in to ask him if he'd ever done a story that got to him.

That seemed to stump him, and we all waited to see what he would say. I thought he was probably just going to jump back into his prepared rave, but he frowned and said in a slower, less confident voice, "It's funny you should ask. You need to be detached, but I guess every journalist has stories that get past the barrier you try to set up. For me it was something that happened when I was on court rounds the first time. There was a case about a teenager who had murdered his ten-year-old brother. It wasn't an accident. The older brother had written in his diary that he wanted to murder his brother and described how he would do it, and then he did it. He took the kid to this bit of track, saying they were going to flatten coins on the rails, and when a train came along, he pushed him under."

The whole room was so silent that anyone entering might have thought it was empty. I glanced around and saw how stunned people looked. All the sarcasm and laughter had been wiped away.

"Why did he do it?" Jezabel finally asked.

Gary Soloman nodded. "That's what I wanted to know. That's what the court wanted to know. The guy who did it was eighteen. He didn't seem that bright. I kept thinking he just didn't understand that when he pushed his brother under the train he'd stay dead. Maybe he thought his brother would get up like the coyote after the train runs over him in the cartoon. That was the tack the defense took."

"But didn't the guy say why he'd done it? Didn't someone ask him?" Jezabel demanded.

"The defense came up with all sorts of reasons. He'd been depressed. His father was out of work. He was in trouble at school. But when they asked him, he only said he'd thought of doing it and then he did it. He got a suspended sentence because the judge decided he wasn't responsible, that he needed psychiatric treatment. But what got to me was that I didn't believe this kid was crazy. And if he wasn't, then why had he done it? I guess that's why I'm a journalist in the end. Because I want to know the real reason."

He looked so intensely at us that it made me uncomfortable. It was like he really expected us to tell him why that guy had murdered his brother. I noticed Harlen Sanderson had this funny look on his face, and I thought he was going to make one of his smart-serious summing-up statements and get us all off the journalist's hook. But instead, Nathan Wealls, who was sitting next to him, waved his paw in the air and asked whether the journalist wore boxers or briefs. It was the stupidest thing to say, but everyone cracked up, mostly out of relief at having that demanding silence broken.

Mrs. Barker came in then, looking like she wanted to ask why we were laughing. Gary Soloman went back to lecture mode, saying he had gone to university and had majored in journalism and communications, all the while bombarding the *Coastal Telegraph* with applications for an internship until they offered him a job.

Then Sylvia asked in her slightly sneering voice what use newspapers were anyway. "Only old people read them. You see the news on television about a minute after it happens, so why would anybody bother with newspapers?"

Gary Soloman answered, his voice cool and confident. "Newspapers offer some very specific advantages over television. The main thing is that you can take your time reading a newspaper story and think about what you're reading. Television journalism mostly offers news as entertainment. It's the news via Steven Spielberg."

One of the boys said loudly that it just meant he wasn't good enough for television, and another boy said, "You mean he's too ugly."

"That's enough," Mrs. Barker snapped. She thanked Gary Soloman for his time and herded us out, her face set in a stony expression.

 3

That night I caught the bus home with Mirandah because we came out of the school gates at the same time. I was late because of the detention Mrs. Barker had given the class, and Mirandah had been practicing in the gym with the jazz kids. We didn't bother waiting for Serenity, who was always late but wouldn't be seen dead coming home with anyone, let alone her sisters.

Mirandah was in purple; she even had a purple rinse through her hair. *Amethyst,* she called it. She said it was a healing color, though I don't know which part of her she thought needed healing. Before purple, it was green.

I only wore dark colors, except for my jeans, mainly because you can't see dirt on them, and also because I didn't have to try to figure out what colors to wear together. Serenity wore black, but she wasn't a Goth. She was just in mourning for the world.

"What do you think of when I say *evil*?" Mirandah asked as we got off the bus.

I shrugged and switched my bag to the other shoulder. "I guess it's when people do things like kill one another." I was thinking of the case the journalist had told us about, wondering if Gary Soloman would have been satisfied with the idea that the guy who had killed his brother was evil.

"You think of murder as evil?" Mirandah sounded disappointed.

"Well, I don't think evil exists as a force. I think *deeds* can be evil—"

"But what's the difference between a bad or wrong thing and an evil thing?" she interrupted.

"I think it's evil when you know it's bad and it will cause harm, and you want to do it anyway."

Mirandah shook her purple hair impatiently. "So are loggers evil when they push aside protesters and chop down an ancient tree?"

"Mostly I think they just feel they're in the right, and they want to let people know they're angry."

"But can a person be evil?" Mirandah asked, sounding frustrated.

"What, like a vampire or something?" I asked. The annoying thing about Mirandah in this sort of conversation is that you know she has the whole discussion mapped out in her head and when she asks a question it's only to get the answer she expects, so that she can draw the conclusion she has already come to.

"Idiot," she said, sounding disgusted. "Vampires aren't real."

"That's what I mean. I think only fictional characters are evil. I think there are evil actions, not evil people."

"What about Ted Bundy, that serial killer?" Now she sounded triumphant.

I mulled over that. "I think Ted Bundy was an anomaly. He was human, but some bit of him was something else and that was the bit that did all of the murdering."

Mirandah was silent for a while. Then she said, "The band says purple's not the right look for jazz. They say I should wear black or sequins."

"What's that got to do with evil?" I asked.

She looked at me as if I were a fool. "What are you talking about?"

I sighed and let it drop, although I thought the conversation about evil was a lot more interesting than the one about clothes. "Tell the band you'll wear what you want. Where are they going to get another sax player as good as you?"

She nodded. "Yeah. But I don't like to take such an aggressive stance."

"Why don't you ask Da?" I suggested.

"Poor old Da," Mirandah said, shaking her head fondly. "He's not exactly with it musically."

"You shut up," I said. "His music is great."

"Like you'd know," Mirandah couldn't help saying. I walked faster. "I'm sorry," she said, catching up. "Stop galloping."

I slowed down, but I was still mad. I hated it when she talked that way about Da.

"I said I was sorry," she said impatiently. "Don't be such a grump. I can't help it if Da's music's just not where it's at."

"Where *what's* at?" I asked coldly.

"Oh, come on, Aly. I just mean Da might be your knight in shining armor, but he's never going to rock the world, that's all."

I said nothing because we'd reached our front-yard gate. Mirandah pushed it open and went through. I lingered to close it, wanting to be away from her. By the time I climbed the steps and came through the door, Mirandah had gone upstairs to her room. I went down the hall to the kitchen to find Jess sautéing mushrooms in pesto and Da talking to Mel and Tich from his band about a gig they had been offered. He was feeding Luke, who was gurgling happily in his arms.

"Well, I guess it's a break for us," Mel said in his usual gloomy way.

"Fronting Urban Dingo is more than a break!" Tich protested. "Everyone's saying they're the next big thing. I can't believe they'd ask us."

"Cost-cutting," said Mel.

"Giving local bands a go," said Da. He noticed me and smiled. "Hello, Alyzon."

"Hi, everyone." I felt angry at Da all of a sudden. Maybe Mirandah was right about him never breaking into the big time. He gave music everything he had, but it gave so little back and we had to live with that. How could he smile when he was a failure?

"Bad day, Alyzon?" Da asked, as if he read my thoughts.

I sighed. "Detention after school. An hour of watching the boys throw spitballs at the roof."

"What was the detention for?" Mel asked, pushing fluorescent orange dreadlocks out of his eyes.

I shrugged. "Some of the kids were messing around on a field trip."

"Some of the kids?" Da asked gently.

"I might have laughed a bit," I admitted. We smiled at one another.

"Typical," Mel said. "Schools are outdated, fascist institutions. It would be much better if there weren't any schools. We should all be teachers and students our whole life long. . . ."

"Do you want me to have a word with the teacher?" Da asked.

I kissed Luke. " 'Course not. I'll take Luke up and see if Mum's awake," I offered, shedding my bag.

I scooped Luke up, feeling amazed all over again at how little he weighed. If I didn't know better, I would think I was holding a bundle of blankets. I smelled his head, loving the milky, soapy scent of him.

"He'll be asleep if Zambia doesn't hurry up," Da said, giving me a smile.

* * *

I was in my room after dinner writing a report for science when Serenity came in loaded with library books. I don't know how many of them she reads, but Mirandah reckons it's so we can tell her biographers how she used to lug around masses of heavy books.

Serenity and I share a bedroom, so half of the room is

decorated by me—which is to say, is *not* decorated. The other half of the room is painted black, and Serenity's bed is draped in black satin. There are no pictures other than a magazine clipping that shows Sylvia Plath doing a reading. The mirror on her half of the room is always turned to the wall, and she has a vase with a single white lily on her bedside table.

She put her books away and changed from her school uniform into black home clothes, then took out her cello and tightened the bow. Then she began to tune the cello. When she was satisfied, she laid the bow beside the cello and started gnawing ferociously at her nails.

"Do you have to do that?" I asked, disgusted. I could actually hear the little thunk as she chomped through another bit. "Much shorter and you'll officially be a cannibal."

"You are such a nothing," Serenity hissed, and stalked out of the room.

Which left me feeling glum because it was pretty much how I saw myself.

* * *

I was reading an hour later, and daydreaming that Harlen was giving a flower to me, when Mirandah came in and gestured at me to come downstairs. As soon as I got into the hall, I heard snatches of a woman's high-pitched voice: ". . . stupendous . . . reaction . . . marvelous . . ." The voice and the superlatives belonged to Mum's agent, Rhona Wojcek. I grimaced.

Jesse padded out of the bathroom still wearing his pajamas—and carrying his guitar. He played in the shower nook because, he said, the acoustics were good. Despite the fact that he could play well and practiced all the time, he always refused Da's invitations to join the band, and he never tried out for any others.

"Who is it?" he asked.

"Rhona," I said, wrinkling my nose. "She's come for Mum's paintings for the exhibition."

He rolled his eyes and went to his bedroom.

Rhona was sitting at the kitchen table when I went in, incredibly tall, frighteningly skinny, with collarbones that stuck out far enough to stack books on. "Brilliant," she was saying. "Such a wonderfully moody new series . . ." She glanced up from the sheet of slides as I entered and gave me the faintly puzzled look everyone gave me, as if wondering what I was there for.

I wondered that, too.

"Hi, Rhona," I said, blinking a bit at her skintight pink dress and turban, thinking that if I had been a buyer, I wouldn't have listened to a word she said about art. The only good thing about Rhona was her continued faith in Mum, which Mum treated as if it were a sort of slow wasting illness that she would probably die from someday.

"That's a stunning ensemble," Rhona told Mirandah, who entered wearing purple boots, purple tights, and a violet tie-dyed petticoat with ragged lace. She looked at me. "You ought to wear a bit of color once in a while, Alyzon. It would brighten you up."

I ate a tomato, cheerfully thinking there was definitely hope for me if Rhona disliked how I looked. A picture of

Harlen Sanderson crept into my mind and I felt my face grow hot. I felt Harlen was way out of my league in the human attraction stakes. But that didn't stop me from daydreaming.

Mum came into the room. No, strike that. Mum *glided* into the room wearing a long floating shift of green chiffon over black leggings. She had caught her hair up in a jeweled comb, but red curls were spilling artistically in all directions.

"Daaarling," Rhona shrilled, rising and holding her arms open wide. Da and I grinned at one another covertly as Mum went forward and allowed herself to be enfolded in long, thin, pink arms. It looked like some sort of carnivorous stick insect consuming a butterfly. "You look marvelous, Zambia."

"That's very pink, Rhona," Mum said. Luke started to fuss so she took him in her arms and rearranged her clothes to feed him. Rhona averted her eyes. She thought artists had no business breeding. Their work ought to be progeny enough, she had told Mum the previous year when she learned of the new pregnancy, thirteen years after the last. Then she had hinted about abortion.

"Oh no," Mum had said, blissfully dismissive. "But this will be the last. I sense it."

"I hope you sense yourself using contraception in the future." Rhona had been shattered enough to be slightly acerbic, but it was wasted on Mum.

"This one is needed in the world," Mum had said dreamily.

"Serenity. So much black," Rhona said now, as Serenity came in.

"Sybl," Serenity corrected her coldly.

We all trooped out to wrap and pack the paintings, leaving Mum in the kitchen feeding Luke. Rhona came along behind us, poking holes in the lawn with her stiletto heels.

"She should use professional movers," Rhona said, as usual.

"We can't afford it," Da said, also as usual.

It took almost an hour and there were just a couple of smaller paintings left to be fitted in when Mum asked me to take Luke and put him in his car seat in Rhona's hatchback. It was just starting to rain as I came out carrying him. I noticed the back of the van was open and went round to see if the rain was getting in.

That's when it happened. Our cat, a monstrously overweight gray tabby called Wombat, jumped from the roof of the house onto the uplifted door of the van. It was designed to stay open, but once it started to close, it fell like a guillotine.

I felt the rush of air, and some instinct made me step forward rather than back, so the door smashed down on my forehead with all the force of a falling piano—instead of on Luke's. A rocket exploded with incredible, painful intensity inside my skull, and all the strength went out of my knees.

"Luke," I whispered fearfully as the darkness ate me.

4

"Alyzon?" Someone shouted my name so loudly that it hurt. And I could smell roses so strongly it was as if someone had shoved them up my nose. Depression crawled like a mass of black beetles inside the smell. I wanted to speak, but it was too hard.

* * *

"Alyzon Whitestarr." The same voice shouted at me, yelling my whole name like an incantation, stinking of flowers and wet dirt, pushing sorrow and roses down my throat and into my ears. I tried to open my eyes, but they were glued shut. I tried to speak, but I couldn't find my mouth to let the words out.

* * *

"Alyzon. Come on, now. Wake up." A hand lightly slapped a cheek that might be mine, if I could ever find it. The voice tasted of snot and tears and despair.

I felt a finger on my eye, lifting the lid. Light speared into my brain, but the touch was worse. Despair leaked from the fingertips and burned into me. There was a flashing image of an older man lying in a bed, pale and emaciated. I tried to pull away, but the movement started an earthquake that threatened to tear my head apart.

"Better not to move," the rose-scented stranger shouted, taking the hand away. Then: "She's awake."

"Alyzon."

Da's voice. He was yelling, too. I turned my eyes toward the voice and was enveloped in the smell of fresh coffee grounds, which was weird because Da didn't drink coffee. Mingled in with the smell of coffee was a sharp ammoniacal stink that filled me with a sick, tense apprehension. I opened my eyes properly, and the skull-splitting brightness resolved slowly into white faces around the edge of a suspended light. I didn't understand until it occurred to me that I was lying down and they were leaning over me; Da and a woman with short dark hair.

"Good," the woman yelled, leaning nearer and touching my hand. The smell of roses and wet earth pressed in on me, along with a feeling of terrible exhausted grief. "Alyzon, you're in the hospital. Do you remember what happened?"

Fear gouged into my heart, sliced through the anxiety and grief and the oppressive smells. "Luke . . ." It came out as a rusty creak of sound.

Da gave a sobbing, bellowing laugh. "He's all right, love. You managed to fall with him on top of you." Pride and love blazed out of his eyes at me, and the smells of coffee and ammonia were swallowed up by the smell of caramelized sugar and the pungent tang of pine needles.

"Who is Luke?" the woman shouted.

"Luke is our baby, Dr. Reed," Da yelled at her. "She was holding him when it happened."

Of course, a doctor, I thought, as the woman leaned over me. I was afraid she would touch me again. I shrank back, and she frowned, a pulling together of black brows. I realized I could see all the hairs coming out of her skin as if I were looking at her through a magnifying glass. The pores on her face looked like gaping mouths. The smell of roses and wet earth pushed at me. I turned my head away from her to escape it. But I found myself looking at a row of other beds with patients in them, and doctors and visitors around the beds in little clots. A tidal wave of muddled smells flooded toward me, forced its way down my throat, up my nose, through my eyes, my fingertips, choking me, blinding me, suffocating me. My stomach revolted. It punched the world out of me in a great vomiting gout, and I fell back, empty, into the silent darkness.

* * *

"Alyzon?" The woman's voice again. It reached into the dark, caught me, and dragged me up out of the peaceful void.

I opened my eyes in fear, but this time the room was dim and quiet. The doctor was seated in a chair beside my bed. I could still smell her wet earth and roses perfume, but nowhere near as strongly.

"I'm Dr. Reed," she said softly, and I relaxed slightly, relieved she wasn't going to shout at me. "Do you remember hitting your head?"

"Yes. Luke—"

"Your little brother is fine," she said. The slight smell of cloves drifted to me. "Your family will bring him in to visit as soon as I let them know you've woken."

"What . . . what's wrong with me?" I asked.

"Just a concussion from a very hard bump on the head." She paused. "Alyzon, it seems as if your memory is intact. Can you tell me what happened just before you blacked out last time?"

"I . . . I'm not sure. Everything seemed so bright and loud, and there was so much shouting and crying and all of these weird smells. . . ."

She nodded as if she had expected the answer. "A hard bang on the head can cause your senses to become confused and magnified, and produce a lot of odd sensations. How is it now?"

"I can still smell a lot of stuff that . . . well, that doesn't seem to come from anything. But it's not as bad as it was. No one is yelling."

"I had the nurses give you a drug to dull your senses slightly when I thought that might be the reason you were not waking up. But don't worry, they will gradually go back to normal."

"How long have I been here?" I asked.

Another silence, this one longer and as heavy as a block of metal. The smell of cloves grew stronger, but there was also a peppermint smell. "You have been here a month," Dr. Reed said.

I was so shocked I didn't know what to say.

"It's somewhat unusual for a blackout caused by concussion to last so long, but not unheard of; in any case you are awake now," Dr. Reed said briskly. She stood up. "Well, I'd better let your father know the good news. He's walking the grounds." At the door, she hesitated. "Try to rest and don't worry about anything."

After she had closed the door behind her, I felt limp with exhaustion.

* * *

"Alyzon?"

Da's voice groped for me, and I let it lift me gently to wakefulness. The room was still dark, and Da was kneeling beside the bed. Again I could smell coffee grounds but, as with Dr. Reed's scent, it was weaker than when I had first woken. Oddly, the pine-needle smell seemed stronger than when I had first smelled it before. Then I reminded myself that I wasn't smelling any of those things. It was my confused senses making them up, and it would be a lot worse without the sense-numbing drugs Dr. Reed had prescribed.

"Da, Dr. Reed said I've been asleep for a month," I whispered. "What's wrong with me?"

"Nothing permanent, I swear," Da promised. The pine-needle smell seemed to get stronger. "Dr. Reed says you can come home in a couple of days. They just want to do a few tests first."

"What sort of tests?"

"They're a bit puzzled about why you slept so long."

Maybe I looked scared, because Da touched my hand lightly,

and at once I seemed to feel his fear pressing against me like a hot panting dog.

I shifted my hand away. "What happened about Mum's show?"

Da gave a breathy laugh. "The last thing Zambia has wanted to think about is exhibiting."

"You didn't miss the gig with Urban Dingo?"

He laughed incredulously. "You remember that? It's coming up. I wanted to pull out, but the band would have lost the gig. Now I don't have to worry. Maybe you'll be well enough to come along and cheer your old da on."

"Maybe," I said, thinking: *He is telling me he wasn't sure I would wake up.*

* * *

That evening, early, Dr. Reed came with another doctor and they did a series of tests. The next day I had a CAT scan and some other tests that involved electrodes being glued to my head and connected to beeping machines. Nothing hurt, but the doctors' presence was the hardest thing to endure because of how the concussion had affected my senses. I was drained by the smells and the bursts of emotion I felt whenever they touched me.

At one point I tried to tell Dr. Reed about how the smells seemed to be associated with people, but a doctor I had not seen before had come in to mess with the machines and he snapped at me: there were no smells; I was just imagining them because of the concussion. Then he started talking to Dr. Reed about prescribing a stronger sense suppressant. He came over to the bedside as he spoke, and I nearly gagged because he stank horribly. Weirdly, when I looked at Dr. Reed, I could only smell roses and dirt and a sort of disinfectant smell, and even though her expression was politely interested, I had the strong impression that she didn't like the other doctor. She said that she preferred to phase out the sense suppressants altogether. He started to argue, and Dr. Reed gave a pointed glance at me and they left the room. I was glad because, whether or not his smell was imaginary, it was really revolting.

I listened and was surprised to find that I could make out some of the words the two doctors were saying, even though the door was closed.

". . . hysterical . . . typical schoolgirl . . . these drugs could be . . . ," the other doctor said.

"Dr. Austin, I don't . . . not necessary . . . ," Dr. Reed murmured.

I stopped listening and went back into the darkness, exhausted.

 5

I probably sound stupid because I didn't recognize what had happened right away, but finding I had been in a monthlong coma was a shock, and for a while I was always so tired that it was hard to think. I was discharged a couple of days later, after a whole lot more tests that showed nothing.

I felt fine except for the fact that my senses went on bringing me weird and unwanted smells and surges of feelings, even with the sense suppressant. I was beginning to dread the thought of it wearing off: what if I was bombarded with input like the first time I woke, and went into a coma again? If it hadn't been for the odious Dr. Austin wanting to keep me on the stuff, I might have asked Dr. Reed if I could keep taking it. But as it was, Dr. Reed gave me one last pill before Da took me home, telling me the drug would work its way out of my system over a week, and that my own senses would gradually readjust.

On the drive home Da told me they had organized a little welcome-home party for me. I think he wanted to make sure it was all right. I didn't know if it was or not. I could smell coffee grounds on him and also a little bit of the ammonia stink, but there was also the lovely caramelized sugar smell. It was as if Da really did smell of those things.

Of course, the first thing I noticed when I went inside the house was how it smelled. I stopped inside the front door, sniffed, and gave a sigh of pleasure. It wasn't just that my family had cooked a feast of all my favorite things, or that they had filled the place with flowers. It was like the house itself gave off one of those not-real fragrances my senses had got into the habit of conjuring up in response to people. The sweetness of it seemed wonderfully familiar, and I tried to figure out what it was as Da ushered me gently along the hall.

They were all sitting around the kitchen table smiling, even Serenity, and I had to work really hard to keep the smile on my own face, because for a second I nearly staggered back under the force of their attention. It seemed to push at me like a strong wave at the beach. Then there were the smells: cut grass, hot strawberries, expensive perfume, violets, licorice.

A pot began to boil over. Jesse raced for it, and Mirandah yelled at him not to use the tea towel but to get a dishcloth. The minute they turned their attention away from me, I felt as if a truck that had been bearing down on me had pulled back. I sat down on the nearest stool, my legs shaking.

Before I could begin to think about what had happened, Mum put Luke into my arms. Still dazed, I looked down into his face. He smelled of the same scent as the house, and he had changed so much while I had slept. He had been an unopened bud, and now his little hands waved around and reached out for things, and the cloudy blue of his eyes had become a lovely greenish gray. He was looking at me, just as the others had done, but I didn't get any feeling of pressure from his gaze. It rested on me with the same sticky, light innocence as his fingers, asking nothing, saying nothing.

Gradually, I grew calmer. It was as if a tiny stream of quiet was trickling into me from him, and the longer I looked, the deeper the pool of quiet became until, eventually, it soothed all the tangled taut nerves and sinews in my body. I was fascinated to find that, whenever I was forced to look up to answer a question and the pressure of my family's combined attention became intolerable, I had only to look down at Luke to feel soothed and gentled again.

I ate a bit, but the meal tasted as bland as hospital food because of the drug in my system. I didn't have that much appetite anyway, and it was awkward to eat holding Luke, but I didn't want to let him go. I followed Mum's lead, smiling a lot without saying much, and pretty soon, everyone dropped back into their usual roles. Mum stared dreamily into the candle flames and smiled at me from time to time. Da served and laughed and broke into little bursts of song. Jesse strummed his guitar and talked about some complicated article he'd read in the papers. Serenity chewed her nails and stared out the window. And Mirandah talked about her boyfriend, Ricki, while she sewed the hem on a yellow skirt. She had shifted from purple to yellow while I was unconscious, and her wardrobe was going through an overhaul.

I sat, happy to be among them, although it seemed to me

the whole family had grown louder. And not only them. The radio was turned down, but I kept being distracted by its low babble; then there was the phone ringing, people chewing their food and laughing or grunting, Jesse strumming his guitar.

Within an hour I started feeling really exhausted, and Da, who must have been watching for it, said I should go to bed. I didn't argue. Jesse stepped forward to take Luke. I gave him up reluctantly, my hand brushing against Jesse's. The cut-grass smell instantly became very strong, and I got this stunning jolt of static electricity and the feeling of something enormous and dreadfully cramped seething and churning inside Jesse, wanting to get out.

When he glanced into my face to say good night, I could tell from his expression that he had felt nothing.

* * *

Fifteen minutes later I was in bed, and although I wanted to think about what had just happened with Jesse, I was asleep before my head hit the pillow. I didn't wake up again until the following afternoon, and everyone was worrying. Over breakfast, which still tasted bland, I told them I was fine. Jesse said I just needed to get used to being awake again.

I held Luke and stayed up for a little, but soon I felt tired and went back to bed and slept some more. And that's how it went for a week, the noises and smells growing stronger each day as the sense suppressant wore off.

Da said I didn't have to think about going to school until I was ready. The truth was that school seemed like it belonged to another life. I couldn't imagine ever going there again. I couldn't imagine having a normal life.

Then one day, I woke up and saw on the bedside clock that it was only ten in the morning. I hadn't woken that early since before the accident.

I just lay there for a while. The bed seemed so soft and warm, and I let myself sink into the feeling. How had I never noticed what a perfectly wonderful bed it was? The way the pillows were exactly the right height and softness, and how beautiful the rich red of the quilt cover was, like sleeping wrapped in a cotton dusk.

I turned to snuggle deeper, and my eyes fell on Serenity's side of the room.

I had never much liked Serenity's mortuary decor, and since the accident all of the blackness she surrounded herself with seemed almost tangibly heavy, like huge lumps of jellied night. Whenever she was in the bedroom, I heard this sinister whispering—obviously another trick of my haywire senses, but even so, it fit. I shuddered and turned onto my other side, but I could still feel her half of the room behind my back, the white of the death lily glowing in the midst of the blackness like some ghastly fang.

"Get a grip," I muttered.

I noticed how silent the house was. I thought of *The Day of the Triffids,* where the main character wakes up one day and can't hear any of the normal things he would have heard and that's the signal that the world as he knew it had ended. Only I could still hear cars and even the air brakes of trucks on the highway that ran past the other side of our neighborhood. The silence was *inside* the house, and it was an incredible relief to hear nothing nearby but my own breathing and the ticking of my bedside clock.

I padded downstairs barefoot and found I was the only one home. I felt an incredible surge of relief, and something in me that had been coiled tight finally unwound. The minute I relaxed, I realized that I was ravenously hungry. A box from the health-food shop was sitting on the table. Once a week, when she remembered, Mum poked a list under the door of the shop, and they delivered the next day. Among the supplies were fresh mushrooms. I decided to make mushroom risotto for dinner as a way of signaling to the family that I was on the way back, because suddenly it seemed that it might really be so.

I melted butter and chopped garlic and mushrooms to fry in it, then I stirred in brown rice and vegetable stock. I hadn't cooked since the accident, and the scent of the fresh mushrooms and garlic was almost intoxicating. I took a long, deep breath and felt like I had never smelled mushrooms before that moment; that all the other mushrooms in the world were pale shadows of these; this garlic, the blueprint for all garlic. I wanted to laugh, but I couldn't jolly myself out of the intensity of what I was feeling. It occurred to me, as I dished out a bowlful of risotto, that for the first time I wasn't resisting the new intensity of my senses.

I sprinkled on Parmesan cheese and ate a mouthful, concentrating on the taste. The flavor was like a small but potent explosion in my mouth; it made me dizzy for a moment. I felt like I could eat that risotto and die, because it was so complete in every way that it contained the meaning of life. It was not just the taste of the sauce and the nutty flavor of the cheese. The feeling of soft mushroom and grains of buttery rice against my tongue filled my whole body with pleasure.

I ate three mouthfuls, and then sat panting, drained by the vividness of what I'd felt and wondering if I would have the energy to get upstairs again. Then I heard music from one of the neighbors' houses. It was a piece Serenity had played over and over on her cello when she was learning it a few years back.

I closed my eyes and focused until the music seemed to grow louder. I felt like I had never heard that song properly before. Every note sounded itself out separately, just as the rice grains had done in my mouth. It was like I was going into the song and it was being magnified in me tenfold, a hundredfold, a thousandfold its usual self. I felt like I could listen to the music forever and ever, it was so complex. Following every nuance and flourish, I was on the edge of understanding why Serenity had loved it so much, and the thought drifted into my mind that, if I understood, it would tell me something about Serenity and the darkness she was building around her.

The music ended, and an announcer introduced the latest hit track from the Rak. Electronic music chewed into the bright day, ratty and savage. It was like something alive trying to gnaw its way into my skull. It made me think of a phobia

I used to have when I was little. An older kid had told me that earwigs got their name because they liked to crawl into a person's ear and gnaw at their brain to make a little cave for an egg sac. I used to stick plugs of Plasticine into my ears at night, until one melted and the doctor had to remove it.

The memory had taken me away from listening for a few seconds, and the music had faded, but as I listened again, it grew louder and more brutal and vicious until I began to feel sick.

I put my hands over my ears, but the music came through, earwigs of sound devouring my brain.

Abruptly, the song ended. I was sweating and half slumped against the wall, a headache bashing around inside my skull and my jaw hurting from clenching. My upper lip felt wet. I reached up and touched a finger to it and was shocked to see that it was red. The music had made my nose bleed.

"What the hell is going on?" I whispered.

I washed my hands and face in the sink. When I was sure my nose was no longer bleeding, I put the pot of risotto in the fridge. I sat down to think through what was happening to me. Because being hypersensitive didn't explain how music could affect me so strongly. Or why I kept smelling things that were not there, or why I associated those smells with certain people. I had been telling myself the smells were coming from some sort of scent bank in my brain that had been damaged and was randomly spilling its contents. But I suddenly felt absolutely certain that the smells were real, even if they were not coming from real things. Maybe whatever had happened to my brain had made my sense of smell so acute it could detect things that people normally couldn't smell—intangible things.

I thought of Dr. Reed's dirt-and-roses smell and her air of distracted sadness, wondering if I was smelling whatever it was that she was thinking of that made her sad—or the sadness itself. The coffee-grounds smell I experienced when I was close to Da seemed to be permanent, so maybe it came from something in his essence that didn't change. But his pine-needle scent came and went, as did the smells of ammonia and caramelized sugar, so they might come from things he was thinking or feeling at certain moments.

It was wild to imagine that thoughts and feelings could give off scents, let alone that a person's essential self might have a definite odor, but the more I thought of it, the less crazy it seemed. Dogs always seemed to know when you were sad, and how could they know? It had to be that they could smell your sadness because their sense of smell was much better than a human's.

I began to feel excited, because if I could come up with a scent dictionary that connected feelings and thoughts with smells, it would almost be like having the means to read people's minds. But my elation faded when I remembered that overload from my extended senses had put me back into a coma. And look how a bit of bad music had affected me.

Obviously, I was going to have to find some way to protect myself or at least to control what I was taking in, and not just from my sense of smell. I had been able to use Luke as a buffer, and I figured he affected me differently because he hadn't grown into judging things yet. But I couldn't carry Luke around with me all the time, and even if I could, he was going to grow up and change.

I got up to make myself a cup of tea, being careful not to concentrate on the scent. The rich, sweet steam plumed up into my face, and as I blew and sipped, I debated ringing Dr. Reed to tell her what I had figured out. But I was pretty sure I would just sound like someone who sees martians and has this whole rational-seeming theory about why no one else can see them. Because if there was something going on in my brain that a test would show, she would already have found it.

Anyway, I wasn't sick, so why talk to a doctor? I was positive that the accident had done something to the part of my brain connected to my five senses, extending them in some way. All I had to do was to find some efficient way of controlling input before I blew a fuse.

 6

By the time anyone came home, I had discovered that I could use one sense to distract another. For instance, I had forced myself to listen to more earwig music on the radio, and used mouthfuls of apple to shift my attention from hearing to taste just when it was getting unbearable. But it was a bit of a balancing act, because the minute I started focusing on the apple, I started to swoon into *that*.

More useful was the accidental discovery that if I imagined Luke, I could induce a milder version of the calmness I felt when I gazed into his face in reality. The only problem was that I ended up pretty well cut off from all other input. It wasn't that I couldn't see or hear, but I couldn't concentrate on anything else. I needed a more selective technique.

When I heard the car pull up, I was pretty weary. I didn't want to face anyone, so I went back upstairs and climbed into bed. Fatigue rolled over me.

* * *

I woke again when Serenity came to bed. It was dark, and from the silence of the house I guessed it must be late. She switched on the bedside lamp, draping her black scarf over the side of the lamp nearest to me to cut the glare. She undressed in the reflected glow from the white lily, and before she pulled on her nightdress I noticed how skinny she looked. I could see all the knobs of bone along her spine and the delicate lines of her ribs. She seemed suddenly to feel my gaze and turned to look at me.

"Are you OK?" She stepped toward me and brought the scent of fresh, wet violets with her. I was a bit surprised, because I couldn't smell the licorice that I had decided was her essence smell.

"I'm fine," I said. "How was school?"

She shrugged and climbed into bed.

"What do they say about me?" I persisted, wanting to stop her switching off the light.

She rolled over so she could face me, like she used to do when we would talk into the night. "There are a lot of rumors. Some of the girls are saying you've forgotten everything. Sylvia Yarrow claims you've lost your marbles."

"She would. What about the boys?"

"Anyone in particular?" Serenity asked.

I shook my head, deciding I wasn't ready to share my daydreams about Harlen Sanderson. We lay there looking at one another for a while.

"What was it like being in a coma?" she asked at last.

I had the strange feeling that this was not the question she wanted to ask. But I answered her anyway. "Like . . . nothing. I was awake, then I was asleep, and then I was awake. Bang-bang-bang, like that."

"Did you dream?" she asked in a queer, too-casual voice and, just like that, I felt the darkness shift and quiver about her, and the violet smell faded into licorice and a sort of burnt-oil smell.

"I don't remember any dreams," I managed to say, wondering what she could be thinking or feeling that would so radically change her smell.

Serenity reached over to switch her light off. I wanted to ask her not to, but I couldn't think of a good enough reason. Instead I lay in the dark, listening to her breathe more and more slowly until she slept.

I was on the verge of sleep, too, when I heard a door slam. I guessed that Mum was going for a walk. Or maybe she was going to the all-night supermarket. I pictured her walking along the street, hands pushed deep in Da's big coat, her hair a wild reddish tangle in the streetlights, spangled with little spits of rain. I wished I had the energy to get up and go after her, because I loved those surreal night trips where nothing was required of you but to wander along in Mum's dreamy wake.

* * *

I woke, this time to daylight flooding into the room and to Jesse playing his guitar in the shower. Serenity's bed was empty, and my clock said it was just after nine. I got up and went downstairs. Da was washing the dishes and talking, with the phone cradled between his head and shoulder.

"Two vans would be better," he said. He hadn't yet noticed me, so I allowed myself to focus warily on him. I smelled his coffee smell and also the smell of molasses and new rope. I could also smell the real smells he was giving off: sweat from his morning run and dishwashing detergent.

I reached out and got an apple from the fruit bowl in case I needed a distracter, and I jumped when Da suddenly gave a great burst of laughter. I glanced at him, his back still to me. I smelled fresh-stewed plums, tart enough to make my mouth water.

It was funny, but before I had figured out what had happened to me, I had felt no fear about dealing with anyone; now that I knew what I was going to face, my palms were sweating at the thought of Da turning around to talk to me. It was like being in some horrible experiment where you never knew where or when they were going to give you an electric shock.

I tipped some muesli into a bowl and poured in the milk, keeping my eyes on the food because the movement was sure to catch Da's attention. As I felt him turn my way, I flashed him a quick, unfocused smile and spooned up my muesli. When I looked up again, he had turned to the window, still talking.

There was a rusty squeak, and I turned to see Wombat ooze through the cat flap. I crooned to him, and he glided over and started to weave circles around my legs. When he brushed against me, I distinctly smelled tuna, and to my amazement I understood that he was producing the smell to let me know he was hungry. I laughed aloud and knelt down to pat him, fascinated to find that when he looked at me, I wasn't overwhelmed by his curiosity or feelings or thoughts. I felt quite simply his insistence that he needed feeding, clear as a statement and absolutely connected to the smell of tuna.

I got out a box of crunchies, wondering if the focused attention of humans overwhelmed me because they were unwittingly sending everything they thought in a loud unfocused jumble, whereas Wombat used his scent with the same precision as humans used words. He had probably always given off his specific scent statement when he wanted food, but we humans had only responded either to our knowledge that he had not been fed for a time, or to the insistent meow he had come up with to get our attention. No doubt he thought we were totally dim.

This whole idea of animals using scents to communicate in the same way humans used words seemed tremendously exciting, because it suggested that maybe what had happened to me wasn't a damaging of my senses, but the jolting to life of a section of my mind that humans had used at some point in their evolution but had stopped using when they started to rely on language.

I set down Wombat's food and stroked his head, noting the rich salty smell he was now giving off and understanding that it communicated affection for me—or maybe for his food.

"Why not?" Da was saying as I went back to sit at the table. "It's nothing to us how many guests come as long as the Urban crew don't set some sort of limit."

I realized then that he was talking to one of the band

members about the upcoming gig. He started to give off the ammonia smell, and I saw that he was frowning. "I'm just saying we shouldn't expect too much." A listening pause. "Yeah . . . OK then." Da put the phone down, but to my relief, he went back to the dishes as he asked how I was feeling.

I said tensely that I felt good. He flashed a smile over his shoulder, then started drying knives and putting them into the cutlery drawer. He seemed distracted. I got up, deciding I had been brave enough for the morning. But before I could take a step, Da gave a soft exclamation and reached into his pocket to pull out a long envelope. He tore it open, and as he read, the ammonia smell grew so strong that it almost blotted out the coffee smell.

"What's the matter?" I asked.

"Just a bill," Da said lightly. Pushing the letter into his pocket, he went back to drying the silverware. But the ammonia smell stayed strong. I crossed to the fridge and made a big business of putting the milk away, getting out orange juice, and pouring myself a glass.

"School rang this morning," Da said. "How do you feel about going back? You don't have to until you feel up to it." Now there was a pine scent winding through the coffee grounds, but the ammonia persisted.

I took a sip of juice, trying to ignore the flavor, then I turned and looked at a spot on the wall just left of Da's ear, telling him that maybe it was time to go back. I felt afraid of facing all those kids and teachers, but at the same time I wanted to get my life back to normal.

"Why don't you wait until next week? Start out fresh on a Monday," Da said.

I drank some more juice. Then I said, "I guess I could call the school and ask them to give me some work to help me catch up." Da had gone back to the sink, and I went on more easily without him looking at me. "Mirandah or Serenity could bring it home."

"Sybl," Da corrected, obviously wanting to make me laugh, except I no longer felt like laughing at Serenity's desire to become Sybl.

"I don't like that name much," I said.

Da frowned a little. "Me neither, but we have to respect her wishes."

Do we? I thought. Even if I felt that there was something weird about her being so determined to change her name?

Da's frown deepened as if I'd spoken out loud, but he didn't say anything and neither did I.

 7

The next week I went back to school.

I had prepared myself as best I could, practicing quick shifts of focus and being careful never to look right at someone who was looking at me. I had a pocketful of fast-dissolving mints. And I could always use Luke's image if it all got too much, although I was determined not to resort to a total blockout unless I had no choice.

I was pretty nervous, but the worst part would be those first few minutes in class when everyone focused their attention on me. I told myself that if I could get through that, the rest would be easy.

I dawdled deliberately to avoid the early morning locker crush in the hallway because the one thing that really scared me was the thought of being touched, and it would have been unavoidable in the scrum between classes. I had not found any way to lessen the impact of physical contact, and I couldn't imagine what would happen if a few people bumped into me at once. Maybe my brain would explode like in some science-fiction movie.

I took every book out of my locker and put them into my pack. It would be a pain to lug them all from class to class, but I didn't dare risk going back during the day.

I hesitated outside the door to homeroom, heart racing and palms sweating. I told myself I didn't have to go in if I didn't want to. Everyone would understand if I changed my mind. The problem was, if I backed away now, I doubted I would be able to bring myself to try again.

I took a deep breath, stuck a mint in my mouth, and entered the room.

Everyone stopped what they were doing and stared, and I had to grit my teeth to keep from reeling backward. Even looking down and concentrating on the mint I was sucking, I felt like I had been pounded by about twenty pillows simultaneously.

Fighting nausea and panic, I managed to nod my head apologetically at the teacher without actually looking at her, then I all but fell into the seat nearest the door. It was vacant, but Sylvia Yarrow was in the next seat and my hand brushed her bare arm. I felt the burning surge of her corrosive nastiness, which was boiling out of a black lake full of despair and self-loathing.

I don't know what I looked like in those seconds after I brushed against her, but Sylvia must have thought I was going to throw up on her because she drew back hastily. Now that I was looking at her, I could smell the sharply unpleasant stink of burning plastic that she was giving off. Rather than being repelled, I felt a great surge of pity for her. It was this that allowed me to get a grip on my senses. I concentrated on the mint and said, "Are you all right?"

For a split second her face screwed up like she was going to burst into tears. Then she snapped, "Of course I'm all right, you idiot. You hardly touched me." She flounced off to sit in another seat.

* * *

"What did you say to Sylvia just after you came in?" Gilly Rountree asked, moving up one seat to take Sylvia's spot after the homeroom teacher left. "She looked like you punched her in the stomach."

"Nothing," I said. Gilly was giving off a wonderful sea-breeze scent, which vanquished the clammy despair left over from my glimpse into Sylvia.

"Are you OK or not?" Gilly asked doubtfully.

"About half OK and half not," I said. She was looking at me, so I pretended to riffle through my books, asking whether the schedule had changed while I was away.

Gilly sat back in her seat with a sigh. "It's like *Days of Our Lives* in this place. You can miss months, and then you see one show and pick up where you left off. Nothing changes."

Mrs. Barker came in then. She made no more comment on my presence than a swift nod, before outlining the work we were to do that period. I hardly heard her. There was still a roaring in my ears and I felt queasy, but I also felt shakily triumphant at having managed such an ordeal. My aim for the rest of the day was to be so dull and uninteresting that any curiosity about me would die an untimely death.

Once I calmed down, I was able to concentrate on the class. I had always liked English, and it went pretty much as usual except I didn't answer any questions or make any comments. I was too scared of drawing anyone's attention.

The next class was math, and I was surprised to discover that I enjoyed it. It was not just because everyone left me alone so they could concentrate on what the teacher was saying; it was the numbers themselves. How perfect and complete they were! Mathematics, I saw, could be like building a house out of light or music. I had always struggled before, because numbers and calculations had seemed to have nothing to do with anything I cared about, but now I saw that numbers were literally the fabric of life.

I was so absorbed in an equation that I didn't notice the class had ended until I dimly registered Gilly saying: "Earth to Scotty!" I saw then that everyone was packing up, and I reluctantly closed my notebook.

"So, what was it like?" Gilly asked. I glanced warily sideways, but I didn't feel trapped or hammered by her regard. The mathematical calculations I had been doing seemed to hang in my mind like a web, absorbing the rush of information from my extended senses.

"Hello!" Gilly called with laughing exasperation.

"Sorry. What did you say?" I asked, trying to hold the web of calculations in my mind. But like a spiderweb in rain, it was breaking and fraying.

"I said, how was it being in a coma?"

"It was like a long sleep," I said distractedly.

"Ahh, but in that sleep . . . what dreams may come?" crooned Jezabel Aster.

I forced myself to look at her, but her attention did not hurt me, either. Even though the web of calculations was falling apart, it was still absorbing the pressure of her regard. I remembered that Jezabel was the class clown, and thought if I wasn't careful, the next day the school would be doubled up over her imitations of me acting weird. So I said more firmly, "I was just asleep, and then I was awake."

Luckily, the bell rang and Mr. Rackett marched in, right on time as usual, sending Jezabel scurrying back to her seat. Mr. Rackett is the most punctual teacher in school. It's what history does to a man. All of those dates have made him scared he'll miss his own historic moment.

The class was only a single period, but I was too elated by what had happened in math to concentrate. It seemed to me that I had stumbled on the perfect way to screen the input from my extended senses. I was too exhausted to try doing complex calculations, but I tried counting and then simple equations, and both worked to lessen the sensory input, although not as effectively as the web of calculations had.

Other than what had happened in math, the most interesting thing about the whole day was realizing how little I had really known people before the accident. I kept seeing things that I hadn't been capable of seeing before. A thousand details of body language, from fingers twitching or hands shaking to laughter hidden from anyone but me; a sudden sweat that told me someone was scared; the slightest telltale intake of breath.

I felt like some sort of super Sherlock Holmes who could see evidence and make connections that other people were unable to make. Then there were the phantom smells. Mostly I had no idea what they meant, but they made me curious about the hidden aspects to people I thought I knew.

For instance, one of the class troublemakers smelled a lot like Luke after a bath, while a girl I had admired smelled so strongly of paint thinner that just being near her made me feel nauseous. Then there was Gilly, who I had always quite liked, but whose delicious sea smell now so strongly attracted me that it was all I could do not to follow her around like a puppy.

The biggest shock happened at the end of the day.

I had dawdled packing up in the last class to make sure that the hall would be relatively empty when I got there. So there was no one nearby to see me open my locker and find a note from Mrs. Barker asking me to see her. I was wondering why she hadn't just spoken to me in class that morning, when I heard someone call my name.

I looked up and my heart did a total flip, because coming down the hall was the incredibly handsome Harlen Sanderson.

I dropped some books and bent to retrieve them so that I could buy some time to start counting.

"So how does it feel to be back, Alyzon?" Harlen asked, coming to stand beside me. My knees shook as I straightened and looked into his beautiful green eyes, half obscured by the silky black fringe of his hair.

"I'm . . . ," I began, then a hideous stench hit me so hard

54

that I stopped counting and reeled back against the locker in shock and revulsion. I could feel darkness fluttering at the edges of my vision like a ragged black bird, and I saw Harlen's eyes widen in puzzlement.

"That's the old charm, Harl," laughed a boy who had stopped at a nearby locker.

I dropped my books again and knelt down, ostensibly to collect them. Now that I was not looking at Harlen, I couldn't smell the awful rotten stench he had given off. But I could not stay grovelling on the floor. I struggled to my feet and turned to look at my locker.

"Are you all right?" Harlen asked.

"I just . . . f-felt a bit dizzy," I stammered. I had finished putting my books away, so I had no choice but to turn back to him.

He looked sympathetic and said something, but I didn't hear it; the ghastly stench he emitted was growing stronger. Desperately, I pulled open my bag and began shoving books back into it from the locker. Now that I was not looking at him, I was free to listen.

". . . gave me something to give your sister," Harlen was saying.

I had no idea what he was talking about. "You want me to give something to Mirandah?" I hazarded, throwing him a quick look, then zipping up the bag.

"The other sister," Harlen said. He took out a generic-looking CD in a clear blank case and held it out. I all but snatched it and thrust it into my pocket. Then I shut my locker and babbled something about Mrs. Barker wanting to see me right away.

I made for the staff room, stopping at the bathroom first to rinse my mouth out with water. Even so, it still felt like my tongue and throat were coated in the slimy reek that had emanated from Harlen. It was only then that it struck me that he had smelled even worse than Dr. Austin at the hospital. But how on earth could handsome, charming Harlen Sanderson, whom I had yearned after for a year, smell so bad?

I was so rattled that it took all of my self-control to act normal when a teacher finally condescended to answer the staff room door. I guess I didn't quite succeed, because when Mrs. Barker came out, she gave me a searching look.

"I didn't mean you had to see me the second you got the note, Alyzon," she said. "You ought to have gone straight home today. You look pale."

I stammered that I was fine, but she ushered me to a bench outside the staff room and sat beside me, giving off the yeasty bread smell of her essence. It seemed so wholesome after what I had smelled in the hallway.

"The reason I wanted to speak to you was to tell you that you've missed a couple of important tests," Mrs. Barker said. "I can't rerun them for you because they're through the Department of Education, but I can request makeup tests. The only thing is that you'll need to take them outside of school hours. You could come in one day on a weekend and do both at once. How does that strike you?"

I didn't answer straightaway, because she had patted my

arm. When her skin touched mine, I felt how much she liked me; not just as a student, but as a person. I was startled because, while Mrs. Barker was my favorite teacher, I had never imagined she felt so warmly toward me. Certainly it didn't show in her expression. But now I suspected that if she wasn't a teacher and I a student, we might have been close friends.

"What is it, Alyzon?" she asked gently.

"It's . . . uh, I'm fine." I didn't dare look at her until I had managed to start counting again.

She said with a frown in her voice, "Another alternative is that I could ask for an averaging of your previous tests."

"No . . . no, I want to do the tests," I told her firmly, looking into her face but reciting the nine times table to myself so her attention would not overwhelm me. "But I'll need a bit of time to prepare."

She looked pleased. "Of course. It will take a week or so to set it up anyway." She looked me over. "Are you sure you're OK? Your father said you were still suffering some reactions to your accident."

I smiled to think of Da preparing the way for me and felt better. "I think it's just getting used to being around so many people. I ought to be used to it, with my family."

"You have a pretty special family," Mrs. Barker said warmly. She might have said more, but another teacher stuck her head round the staff room door and said there was a call.

* * *

I had intended to phone Da to pick me up so I could avoid the crowded home bus, but coming out of the school, I decided that what I really needed was some space to think about what had happened with Harlen Sanderson. I set off to walk along the bus route, knowing I could hail the next bus if I needed to.

The yellow afternoon light made the walls of houses and buildings look like biscuits saturated in honey, and there was a slight, sweet-scented breeze. I breathed it in and told myself that it was impossible Harlen Sanderson had smelled like that—meaning, I must have been wrong to think smells were only associated with feelings and emotions or people's essences. Perhaps other things gave off smells, too. Maybe Harlen had been thinking of a really awful sight. Or he might even be sick and that was what I had smelled. I tried to focus better on what had happened by the lockers, but I was frustrated by my inability to think clearly about my changed senses. I just didn't seem to have the words to describe my impressions.

It was like this book Da had read us one winter, called *1984*, about a future where the authorities were trying to control everything. One of their methods was to cut words out of the language. This was very clever, because without the words people found they couldn't think about the things those words had expressed. The word for love was taken out, and people stopped being able to love. The book was saying that the most basic things were hard or impossible to do without the words to express them.

I felt I wouldn't be able to think properly about what had happened to me until I could find words to think with. At the simplest level I could see, hear, smell, taste, and touch a lot better than other people. But smell and touch had gone far beyond what those words usually meant. If I had to describe it to someone, I would say it was as if you'd always had really bad eyesight, only you didn't know it. Everything would be unfocused and blurred, but you'd think that was how it was meant to be. Then one day someone handed you glasses that gave you twenty-twenty vision. For the first time you'd see what people looked like. You'd see their expressions and you'd realize there were a whole lot of things people said in body language, rather than in words, which you hadn't seen. So you would understand people and what they were about much better than before. It wasn't like you had suddenly become wise, but only that understanding people better was a natural consequence of seeing better. The world itself would be more clear and precise, and therefore more complex, but you would be able to handle it because seeing better would mean that you could respond better and more accurately. It would tire you to begin with, seeing so much more than before. But after a while you'd get used to it.

That's what I told myself.

 8

Da and the others had been on the verge of panicking when I walked in so late. I felt pretty bad because I hadn't thought that they would be concerned, and I should have.

I told them I was going to walk home every night for a while, that I needed the exercise, and they accepted it, although Da reminded me to call if I got tired. I could tolerate the morning bus rides, I had decided, because I could get in a corner seat before the bus filled up and stare out the window the whole time, then get off after everyone else. But the night bus would kill me, with all those jostling kids bumping up against me. Especially after being around people all day at school.

The walk also allowed me to experience inanimate things with my enhanced senses. One night I caught sight of a leaf waving in the wind, and another night it was a patch of ivy growing up the side of a building. Both times I had been able to indulge my senses as I had done with the risotto, without anyone noticing me standing transfixed by such a small thing. Of course, there were no small things now; that was the point.

It was like everything had an immense story to tell, and suddenly I was listening.

It didn't only happen when I was alone, though. Midweek, I got a stone out of my shoe in class. As I looked at it, I began to feel I was understanding the stoneness of the stone. It was incredibly alien but also wonderful and somehow thrilling. Then I realized that the teacher was shouting at me for not paying attention. She had started out mildly, Gilly told me later, but I had acted like I was deaf, and she had got mad because she thought I was mocking her. Teachers hate to be mocked. Some of them are so paranoid you have to make sure not to do anything they might think is mockery.

The weird thing was that on some level I *had* been paying attention. Walking home that night, I realized that I could vividly recall anything that happened since the accident. As far as classes went, I could remember anything that had been said, any passage that had been read, any question that had been discussed, just by thinking about it. The trouble was that remembering an event in this way took almost as long as the event itself—it was like reliving it from start to finish.

I had been really nervous about bumping into Harlen after what had happened the first day by the lockers, but at the same time I wanted to see him again just to prove to myself that I'd been mistaken. I couldn't believe I had to have some sort of meltdown the one time he had spoken to me and shown an interest. I hoped that Harlen had put my peculiar behavior down to nervousness, because, nice as he was, he had to be aware of how he affected girls. Especially mousy girls like me.

But I didn't see him the whole week, even in class, and by Friday I thought he must be sick and that sickness really could be the reason for the awful smell. He had always been away a fair bit, and although rumor said his rich parents traveled a lot and took him along, hiring tutors to keep him up with his schoolwork, it might be that he was having some sort of ongoing treatment. When he didn't come to school my whole second week back, I was even more certain I was right.

I had given Serenity the CD, telling her Harlen had passed it on. She had taken it without surprise, but when I asked who it was from, she told me to mind my own business. So much for sibling communication.

Friday of my second week back, I had gym. The school had advised against it the first week, but I had said I was fine when the school nurse asked, so I was given permission. I knew that was a mistake, though, when Coach Ekbert announced that we were playing a game of tag.

After twenty minutes of being tagged by other students and having their emotions and weird images hammer me whenever they touched bare skin, I felt as battered and bruised as if the whole class had run over me in combat boots. Each time someone bumped me, I had to clench my teeth to stop from crying out. I could not even protect myself from their direct attention, because it was almost impossible to count in my head with Coach Ekbert shouting out our individual numbers as he yelled instructions or admonishments.

In the end I said I had a terrible headache and asked if I could go to the nurse's office. Coach Ekbert was famous for refusing to accept kids' excuses to cut his classes. He had told us at the start of the year that more kids tried to get out of gym than out of math or science, and that students would cut his class At Their Own Risk. He glared at me suspiciously for a long minute, as if I might suddenly break down and confess that it was all a hoax. Then suddenly Gilly said, "Sir, she was just in a coma."

He didn't look at her, but he waved me away. I stumbled gladly to the nurse's office and palmed the aspirin she gave me, feeling guilty about her candy-scented concern. Just before the lunch bell rang, I slipped out and went to the library. I couldn't face the thought of the halls and school yard seething with lunchtime crowds.

I meant to do some catching up, but I couldn't keep my mind on my books. I kept thinking about the failure of my plan to come up with a dictionary of smell. I had discovered that different people gave off different scents even when in similar situations. I wondered if I had been wrong to assume that all people feeling sadness, for example, would give off the same smell. Maybe every single person had their own unique and individual set of scent responses. It made sense, because no two people reacted in exactly the same way to a situation. Wouldn't one person's happiness be different from another person's? The only correlation I had noticed was that good or innocuous scents appeared to be given off by people feeling positive emotions or thinking good thoughts, while bad scents were given off by people with negative thoughts or feelings. But I couldn't figure out if this also worked with people's essence scents. It seemed too simplistic to imagine that good people would smell good, while bad people smelled bad. A lot of scents couldn't even be categorized as good or bad because it was all so subjective. Some people liked the smell of cigarette smoke or hot tar.

Despite not being able to come up with anything like the dictionary I'd planned, my extended senses were helping me to understand people more than I could have imagined possible. Every minute that passed, I saw and felt and smelled and heard details that showed me how amazingly rare it was for people to actually say what they meant. Words were like bubbles on top of the water; the truth was a shifting current beneath the surface, powerful and silent. No wonder the world was in such a mess, because even if you didn't count the people who were actively deceptive, it must be almost impossible for anyone to really agree on anything, what with everyone hiding what they felt and trying to guess what the other person was hiding. Add in different motivations and cultural backgrounds and religions, and it was a miracle that we hadn't all murdered one another eons back.

I might have been depressed by all that, except that the better I got at reading scents, the better I was able to pierce the evasions and pretenses, and my understanding of the people around me deepened.

For instance, there was Jezabel Aster, who was always kidding around. I was drawn to her now, because, like Gilly, her essence scent was delicious: a mixture of fresh straw and hot honey. And the second I started paying attention to her, I noticed all sorts of things—like she knew the answer to just about anything any teacher asked, although she hardly ever volunteered it and her grades were average. It didn't take me long to figure out that she was super bright. Of course, my insight didn't help to explain why she would want to keep her cleverness secret.

Then there was Nathan Wealls. I had thought of him as a complete Neanderthal because he was always messing around and driving the teachers crazy with his antics. But the sweet bath-soap smell he gave off made me look at him more closely, and I soon saw that he was as soft and gentle as a baby underneath. That was why he let himself be persuaded to make trouble. Anyone who was nice to him could get him to do anything. Yelling at him was exactly the wrong way for teachers to make him behave, because he hated being yelled at, so he messed around all the more, trying to make them laugh. There was nothing I could do, because no teacher would listen to me, even if I could explain how I knew what I did about Nathan. Besides, I wasn't sure it was my business.

My thoughts shifted to numbers, and my growing ability to use them as a screen. The more difficult the mental calculations, the more dense the screen, but it was hard to regulate. It might be possible to build a permanent screen, which I could summon up at any moment. My idea was that the screen would have sections of varying complexity, and that would enable me to use whichever bit of the screen was appropriate, depending on what I had to block. I meant to work out a series of complex calculations and memorize them, then attach some simpler calculations. Sort of like how you learned lines for a play or the way you created a quilt.

Most aggravating were the things I could perceive that were far harder to pin down than smells. For example, the whispers I would hear in the air—sometimes soft and sometimes loud, but never clearly. I hadn't the slightest idea what they meant, but I would hear them just as often when no one was around as when I was with other people, and I had the feeling they were like a sort of imprint on the air left behind by people living and speaking in that space. Then there was a distortion that happened to the air around certain people. I could see it as a vague shifting and shimmering, which was visible only because of what was behind it, like the air over a desert.

Despite my frustrations, the one thing I was now sure about was that I didn't want my senses to go back to normal. Whenever I imagined waking up one morning and finding I was my old self, I remembered a film I saw about a man who had been virtually a vegetable his whole life until a doctor found a way to rouse him using some sort of experimental drug. The guy woke up and was like a child to start with, but he ended up being really brilliant—a genius and also a really good person. The tragedy of the film was that the effect of the drug didn't last, and so he started to regress—and, worst of all, he realized it was going to happen.

It wouldn't be that extreme for me to revert to normal, but even so, I wasn't sure how I could bear it. It would be like living in a world with all the lights switched off, and having them suddenly switched on, then off again. You would be used to the dark, but unlike before, you'd know how things looked with the lights on, so you'd be forever longing to see clearly.

* * *

The third week back at school went pretty much the same as the first two except that between classes I spent a lot of time with Gilly Rountree. Harlen was still away, and I was beginning to wonder if he would ever come back. It was awful to imagine there might be something really wrong with him, but when I asked around, there was only the old rumor about him traveling with his parents.

I went to classes, listened and took notes, read and joined in, always being careful not to draw too much attention to myself. I walked home every night and slept a lot. Whenever I had a quiet hour, I created another piece in my number screen. At home I studied, cooked, and played with Luke. But by the end of the third week, everything was overshadowed by our excitement about Da's looming gig with Urban Dingo.

There were actually going to be two gigs: one on Friday and another on Saturday. Both were already completely sold out. Da and the band were rehearsing in the shed every day, and then they would spend half the night arguing in incomprehensible musical shorthand about the set list. Excitement spread out from them like a whirlpool, and we were all caught up in it.

Mirandah, Jesse, Serenity, and I were going to go to the Friday show. I had got enough of my number screen built that

I felt confident I could cope with anyone talking to me. But the gig would still be a test, because it would be packed and I still hadn't found a way to protect myself from physical contact.

It was not knowing how I would handle myself at the gig that stopped me mentioning it to Gilly. That and a secret fear that Losing the Rope would bomb. I was ashamed of having so little faith in them, especially since the gigs the band had done till now had always been great. But this was a whole different league, because Urban Dingo had just hit it big. Never in my wildest imaginings had I thought of Da's band being mentioned in the same breath as a top-ten mainstream band.

I caught the bus after school on Friday, because I wanted to get home in time to wish Da luck before he left. The show wasn't due to start till late, but bands always had to set up and do sound checks for about ten hours before they went onstage.

Da was in the kitchen when I got in, having tea and buttered bread—his standard pre-gig fare. "How do you feel?" he asked when he saw me come in with Mirandah.

"I caught the bus to save energy for tonight," I told him. I could meet his gaze now, because of my number screen, but I was using a thinner bit of it because there was no point in having extended senses if I dared not make use of them.

Da finished his food, drained his teacup, and said, "Take it easy."

"You take it easy," I quipped, and he laughed, giving off coffee grounds and caramelized sugar and the new-rope smell that always seemed to come up whenever the band was on Da's mind. I was close enough to notice the air distorting intensely around him, as it often did. But tonight the effect seemed much stronger. The air bulged and billowed around him, as if he were sending out invisible rays.

Mum came in wearing a green silk wrap, her hair piled in this loose, casually perfect tumble secured by a giant red plastic chopstick. She was yawning, because she had got up after only a few hours' sleep to say goodbye to Da. But her eyes sparkled with pride as she hugged him, and the drifting clouds that floated and hazed the air about her cleared for a moment when she put her arms around him.

I turned away from them because they were now staring into each other's eyes in this romantic but terribly embarrassing way. I looked at Jesse, who was totally oblivious to Da and Mum. He was shredding lettuce, his concentration so deep that he might have been cutting the facets of a diamond. Da had to wave a hand in front of his face to get his attention a minute later. Jesse looked at him blankly for a second, as if he wondered who Da was, then he laughed and hugged him, wishing him luck.

That was when it hit me that I had been a fool to imagine Jesse was lazy. He looked lazy, because he did things slowly and seemed so absentminded. But there was something going on inside him, inside his mind. That was what I had felt when I brushed against him that first night home from the hospital. And whatever was going on with him had reached the point where it needed to come out, but Jesse wasn't letting it. I focused all of my senses on him and let myself really take in the green, wild smell of his essential self. I could feel how poetic and intricate the shapes of his thoughts were, as well as how urgent they had become.

"You should write them down," I said, without thinking.

My words fell into silence, and they all turned to look at me.

"Huh?" Jesse said.

"I . . . I said you ought to write down some of the things you think about."

"Jesse? Think?" cried Mirandah, who had just walked in the door. Everyone laughed.

Not Jesse. He just went back to shredding lettuce. But I had the feeling he was mulling over what I had said, because the green-grass smell got stronger, like a freshly mown lawn.

Mirandah frowned at me. "You know something? I am beginning to understand why you're getting a reputation as a weirdo." She was painting her nails gold to match her toenails and her dress and the current color of her hair. Gold, she said, was an evolved form of yellow.

"Seriously," she went on. "Sylvia Yarrow told everyone at the pool that Alyzon has been taken over by an alien."

"There's a deeply intelligent theory," Da said, getting a bottle of water out of the fridge.

"Well, you must admit she's been different since she came back from the hospital," Mirandah said.

I had always thought Mirandah bossy and abrasive, but these days I realized she was kind of blind about how people reacted to the things she said. And that made me pity her, like some sort of lame puppy you suspect is never going to be able to walk properly.

"Mirandah—" Da began.

I cut in. "It's OK. She's right about me being different. Knowing I was asleep for a whole month makes me feel like I'm seeing things properly for the first time, and maybe that makes me act differently."

"How do you mean, you're seeing things differently?" Da asked, but the phone rang. It was Serenity saying she'd missed the bus and asking for a ride from the public library. Da looked at his watch and said he had just enough time to get her and bring her back. He pulled on his coat, kissed Mum, and hurried out.

"How come Serenity went to the library tonight of all nights?" Mirandah complained to Mum.

But Mum was gone, back into the vivid clouds of her imagination.

9

It was nine when Jesse drove Mirandah and me to the venue. Serenity had announced that she was not going when Da dropped her home from the library. Da told her it was up to her, but I smelled a seashell sort of odor from him that I felt certain was hurt.

I could have strangled Serenity, whose only reason had been that it would be too loud. The old Serenity wouldn't have let that stop her from seeing Da. That was one of the things I disliked most about how she had changed. It was as if we didn't matter to her at all anymore. Not even Da, whom she had once adored as I did.

Fortunately, the night was too full of promise for me to brood for long. And Mirandah was talking nonstop about some argument she was having with the long-suffering Ricki, which had resulted in him deciding not to meet us at the gig.

The Dome was a huge concert hall made of steel and plastic. Its front was plastered with posters for Urban Dingo. Millions of neon lights were strategically positioned to cast a ghastly orange and purple glow over the throng of people lined up at the gate, making it look like a sort of end-of-the-world scenario. If anyone had doubted it, the crowd was proof that Urban Dingo had made it. The thought of all of these people seeing Losing the Rope made me feel breathless with excitement and nerves.

Da's band had come up with their name soon after they started jamming. There was this Swiss guy, who had looked like a ski instructor, staying with Mel. Whenever he became confused listening to people, which was pretty much all the time since he knew about ten words of English, he would shout: "Stop! I am losing the rope!" It was so funny that Da and the others started saying it whenever things got muddled. Then one day the drummer, Neil Stone, said it would make a good name for their band.

Neil is this really huge guy like Meatloaf, only he dresses a lot better. He says he has to be big, because Stone is a heavy name to carry. People always say drummers are dumb, but he's really smart and nice, and I love him, although sometimes I worry he might have a heart attack carrying all that extra weight around.

It was Neil who had told me that while I was still un-conscious, Urban Dingo's manager wanted to break the con-tract with Losing the Rope because his band was suddenly getting so much attention that they could probably have asked a bigger name to open for them. But Urban Dingo had refused.

I had never been inside the Dome before, but I knew it hosted everything from old-time dance marathons to Jell-O wrestling. Having Urban Dingo play there was a definite coup for the venue. Outside, it looked like a smooth silver dome, but inside, it was a great circular cave of a place, with tiered seating around the edges and a vast central floor. The stage was set up at one end where seats had been removed, and it was swarming with roadies. Quite a few people were down on the floor dancing in demented clots to the house music coming over the PA system, while others were talking and drinking and smoking near the bar.

The music from the PA sounded to me like something alive that had gone crazy from being trapped in a box and was now trying to eat its way out. I recognized the band: the Rak, with its awful earwig music. I put my hands in my pockets to stop myself from putting them over my ears, and intensified my number screen.

Then someone took out a cigarette and lit up. I wrinkled my nose, because using the screen only dulled the extended part of my senses, not the normal bit. I wished there could be a music scene without cigarette smoke. If you wanted to hear a band live, you had to put up with it; and I don't mean the odd whiff, I mean a regular fog of smoke in Cancer City. Of course, it looked great because of the orange and purple laser lights playing over everything and the flashes of light being thrown from huge suspended pieces of smashed mirror on the stage. I tried not to think about what was happening to my lungs.

Before long the place was bursting at the seams with crazed Urban Dingo fans, who showed their solidarity by howling like dingoes every other minute. I was OK because we had wedged ourselves into a corner formed by the side of a booth and the back of some toilets. It offered a good view of the stage, and I didn't plan on venturing out.

"This is so great," Mirandah screamed in my ear. The hot strawberry of her essence was spiced up with cinnamon and coconut oil, and I held myself rigid, afraid she would suddenly grab me or even hug me. But she just hugged herself instead. Which made me wonder whether I was sending out touch-me-not vibes, because I couldn't remember the last time any one of my usually very tactile family had deliberately touched me.

Mirandah grinned at me. "I guess I was wrong," she said. "It really looks like Da's going to rock the world after all." I smiled back at her, because she was as bluntly sincere with her apologies as with her unfavorable opinions.

Jesse went off to get drinks and came back with a sheepish-looking Ricki just as an announcer stepped onstage. I didn't hear the first bit of what he said due to a shouted post-mortem of Mirandah and Ricki's earlier argument. Then it occurred to me to see if I could use my abilities to tune in on a particular sound. I concentrated on hearing the announcer and suddenly I could hear his words perfectly. My delight lasted for about three seconds, because I realized that he was practically apologizing for the fact that Losing the Rope would be opening. The disgruntled manager must have got to him.

"After tonight you'll be able to say you were one of the

lucky few who saw the Dingoes before they went nova," he screamed. "But first, our little local band who lucked out tonight. Here they are. Losing the Rope! Weird name for a way-out band!" He backed off, making conjuring gestures at the empty stage.

"Jerk," Jesse muttered.

Mirandah said nothing, because her lips were now glued to Ricki's. I wished they would go somewhere else and do that, but the one time I had suggested it, Mirandah said haughtily that I was a prude. She didn't see anything wrong with putting your tongue in someone else's mouth right next to your little sister. I hadn't actually kissed anyone except Peter Cos next door, and that hardly counted since we were both five and I had been pretending he was a frog. But in the unlikely event a guy ever kissed me again, I would rather it be in private. Then it occurred to me that with my extended senses I might never be able to kiss anyone, and that depressed me.

The piped-in music stopped suddenly, and my heart sped up as Losing the Rope came onstage. Da and the others didn't put on a dopey production like a lot of bands do. They just walked on in ordinary jeans and shirts. They took up their instruments with a minimum of fuss and a maximum of dignity, and, as Da slid the strap of his guitar over his head, a few people actually booed.

"Idiots," Jesse muttered, but he was grinning with excitement.

Da started to play then.

It's funny, I'd heard him practice a hundred times and I'd

heard him in gigs before, but he had never sounded better than on that night. It wasn't just my new senses. I mean, they made a difference, but mostly it was like Da'd come to some sort of peak in himself. At home I had seen the air shimmer and bulge around him, but now, to my amazement, I could see sparks coming off him, tiny beads of light that flew out and into the audience.

"Who is that guy?" I heard someone yell after about five minutes.

Mirandah and I exchanged a look of perfect glee, and even Jesse pinched my arm with the thrill of it. I jumped at the sudden jolt of his excitement and pride in Da, but since it aligned with my own reactions, it only boosted what I was already feeling.

It wasn't just Da, of course. There were Mel and Tich and Neil. But even though it wasn't the sort of band where everything revolves around this charismatic and egomaniacal lead, Da was the pulsing red center of the stage that night. All of the energy, all of the music's glamour came from him. I don't mean glamour in the dull, small sense in which it's mostly used. I mean glamour in the sense of being some sort of ensorcellment.

After one song the audience was hooked. From then on, they were almost too quiet while the songs played, then at the end of each one they went mad. That announcer had said the audience was lucky to be seeing Urban Dingo, but if Urban Dingo was a nova, that night Da was a supernova.

Listening to that strange, beautiful, difficult music he

played, I realized, maybe for the first time, what Da had been trying to do with it. He was trying to make people see the world differently, just like the people who made those arthouse movies did. And that bending of the air I had noticed at home grew and grew until everyone in the audience must have felt it. It was like, for that bit of time, everything was altered slightly. Anything you felt bad or unhappy about was measured against this blissful sense of space and timelessness Da and the band were projecting, and you could see your troubles from this high lovely vantage point.

Mirandah and Ricki dived in and started dancing, flinging their arms around and swaying and leaping in a way that would usually have mortified me, except that half the audience was dancing wildly by now, as if they just wanted to be part of the music.

"You want to do that?" Jesse asked me, obviously reluctant but willing enough.

I shook my head, yelling into his ear that I'd rather listen and watch. He nodded and turned back to watch the band.

When Losing the Rope finished its set and went offstage, the audience screamed and thumped and thundered for more, until the organizers came out and announced Urban Dingo. A lot of the yelling died away then, but even when Urban Dingo was coming onstage, some people still called out for Losing the Rope. We stayed for the start of Urban Dingo's set, but I was glad when Jesse shouted that we ought to leave. The music seemed gloomy and pompous to me, although at least it wasn't earwig music or dopey pop. Jesse and I left Mirandah and

Ricki, who wanted to say goodbye to friends and said they would meet up with us for hot chocolate at a nearby cafe.

* * *

As we were making our way toward the exit, I saw the announcer who had put down Da's band talking to a tall man in a designer tracksuit and green sneakers and a big white-haired guy in a sleek suit. They looked like they were arguing; at least, the announcer and the guy in the green shoes did. The big guy in the suit was just listening. Then I saw a movement beyond them and recognized the journalist who had spoken to my English class before my accident: Gary Soloman. He was at the bar, but instead of watching Urban Dingo on the screens set up, like others waiting for drinks or food, his attention was riveted on the big white-haired man, Mr. Tracksuit, and the announcer.

The journalist turned his head and looked right at me. He was too far away for me to get a hint of his scents, but I saw puzzlement flicker across his face and guessed he was trying to remember where he had seen me. Before he could figure it out, a little crowd of people came, yelling and shouting and waving their tickets, and he and the others were all lost to view.

* * *

Sitting in the cafe an hour later, we were all so excited we could hardly sit still.

"Your da was awesome," Ricki enthused.

"Urban Dingo must feel kind of upstaged," I said. "I mean, how often does an unknown opening band outshine the stars?"

"Exactly," Mirandah said. "It's practically illegal. Like the bride being outshone by her old maid."

"Old maid! You mean maid of honor," I said.

"Whatever," she said, tossing her gilt hair.

"Da must be so happy," I said, smiling to think of it.

"I think he found himself tonight," Jesse said softly. "It was like he just hit his stride."

"Oh man, can you imagine having someone really famous as a father?" Mirandah said.

"You'll have to have security systems and bodyguards. Hey, maybe I can be your bodyguard," Ricki told her. She giggled and said it was him her body needed guarding from.

Jesse frowned. "I wonder if that's what Da wants. Fame like that. It can be a pretty fickle thing, and Da's a deep kind of guy."

"Don't be a moron," Mirandah snapped, but I thought Jesse had a good point.

"I wish he was here," I sighed.

"He won't be back until dawn, I reckon," Jesse said. "The band'll celebrate and hobnob."

"We ought to go home and tell Mum what happened," Mirandah said.

So we slurped down our hot chocolates and Mirandah went into a ten-minute farewell clinch with Ricki that wouldn't have been out of place on the *Titanic,* then we headed off. Mum was up, of course, although Serenity had gone to bed. We told her what had happened, eating Vegemite toast in her studio and watching her put a base coat on a newly stretched canvas. The clouds around her were this interesting green color shot through with rose streaks, and I wondered if it was her aura I was seeing and if other artists would have one like that, too. Then Luke woke up wanting to be fed, and I suddenly felt overwhelmingly tired.

My last thought in bed before I dropped off was of the *Coastal Telegraph* journalist, the way he had suddenly looked over at me. I would once have dismissed it as coincidence, but it seemed to me that Gary Soloman might have felt my attention, like two fingers pushing lightly against the side of his head.

* * *

"Ah well, I guess that was my five minutes of fame," Da said cheerfully over breakfast on Monday. He was still radiating a few sparks. He had said enough about the second gig for me to guess it had been even better than the first.

As for the rest of us, we had jittered and reveled in his success all weekend, but Monday morning was Monday morning, and so we were pretty much back to normal.

I looked out at the rain-washed pavement as we trundled out for school and thought how empty streets looked in the rain. We could have been the only people in the world. I suddenly felt melancholy. I thought it was probably because no matter how exciting the weekend had been, that was basically that.

10

As if we had made some sort of agreement, none of us mentioned Da's gig at school. The funny thing was that I heard a couple of kids at the lockers talking about Urban Dingo being upstaged by a local band. That drove away the glum feeling that had come over me in the morning, and I started wondering how it would be for our family if Da's band actually started getting regular work. Maybe even a recording contract.

It was hard to imagine Da being famous, though, because like Jesse had said, Da didn't care about fame. He thought it was stupid to care if a lot of people knew your name and face. But maybe I was wrong about Da not wanting that kind of success, because over the past few weeks my abilities had shown me something about him I hadn't known before: Da worried a lot about money, no matter what he said about it being good for us to live on the edge. Whenever he got a bill in the mail, he gave off the ammonia smell, and sometimes he smelled of it when he was talking about not having a gig for a few days.

Gilly hadn't arrived by roll call, and I was disappointed because I'd been looking forward to telling her about Da's triumph. But she turned up halfway through third period and explained to Mr. Rackett that she had been to the dentist. He grunted in disbelief and told her to sit.

"How come teachers always act like everything you tell them is a lie?" she whispered as she slid into the chair next to me.

"They think everyone is trying to put something over on them," I said, opening myself to her gentle sea smell.

Mr. Rackett shot us a look, so we fell silent. After a while he turned to fiddle with the computer so he could show us more historical documents, and Gilly said softly, "I've heard a rumor about you."

"What did you hear?" I whispered, stepping up my number screen slightly.

She leaned closer. "I heard that you can read people's minds."

"OK, I confess. Who told you?"

"Can't you read my mind to find out?" she asked. Then she burst into soft laughter. I laughed, too, mostly out of relief that she had been joking. "But seriously," she said, "Sylvia told me you're possessed by a witch and that you're trying to find other people for your witch friends to take over."

"Great," I said dryly. "What comes next? Witch burnings?"

Gilly shrugged. "It's just that everyone's noticed how you've changed since . . . well, you know."

I sighed and tried to look as though my heart was not doing a war dance. "Being asleep for a month kind of alters your perspective."

"I can imagine," Gilly murmured. Mr. Rackett was cursing, which meant that any minute he would lose his temper and go stomping off to shout at someone in the audiovisual department. He had been warring with the A/V people all year. He thought they deliberately gave him the worst equipment. The truth is he's just one of those people who can't deal with technology. Once, when I was passing the staff room, I heard him shouting at the coffeemaker.

I realized that Gilly was still looking at me, so I said, "I don't think about being in a coma until someone mentions something that happened before the accident, then I remember I was asleep for a month." I kept my voice low because it was a bad move to give Mr. Rackett a human target for his anti-technology frenzy. "It feels...I don't know..." I stopped, realizing that I still hadn't completely come to terms with the lost month. Maybe because a sleep that deep was a little too like being dead for a while.

"When it first happened, they announced it in school," Gilly said. "Everyone thought you'd be back in a day or so. Only it went on and on, and someone said you were on some sort of life-support system."

We didn't say anything for a while, then Gilly asked if I wanted to do something outside of school sometime. I grinned and asked if she wasn't scared I would drag her off to be possessed by one of my witch buddies, and she said she'd take the risk. Then Mr. Rackett lost it, but instead of stomping out as usual, he told us he would hand out photocopies next class. Maybe he had started therapy or something.

He began talking about the American Civil War, and I let myself focus on the way the sun was lighting up some motes of dust in front of my chair.

"You can borrow my notes," Gilly said dryly, after the bell rang. I blinked at her stupidly. "For the Civil War questionnaire. You didn't take any."

"Oh. I . . . I have a good memory," I said.

"But you didn't even listen," Gilly objected.

"A little bit of me was listening," I told her.

* * *

On my way down the hall to the last class of the day, I caught sight of Harlen coming out of the front office. He looked taller and more handsome than ever, with his hair shining dark as the pelt of a mink and his slow, delicious curve of a smile directed at the principal. If he had been sick, he looked perfectly, wonderfully healthy now.

The principal went back into the office, and Harlen turned to speak to a beautiful, stylish woman wearing a suit and carrying a briefcase, whom I had not noticed standing behind him. I thought at first that she must be his mother, because she had the same dark, sleek hair, but as I focused in on her, I saw from her lovely hair and her almond-shaped eyes that she was probably Asian. She was listening to Harlen with a remoteness that did not look at all motherly.

"Dream on and join the queue," Gilly whispered into my ear.

I made a face at her, and we went on to our next class.

* * *

That afternoon I caught the bus home because it was raining hard. I soon bitterly regretted it because it was packed, and I spent the whole trip jammed too close to other people. I screened hard, of course, but the boy nearest me was horsing around with two others and I was scared his flailing, dirty hand would hit my bare skin.

By the time I got home, I was so wound up that I knew I wouldn't be able to do my homework right away. I decided to make toasted sandwiches for dinner even though it wasn't my night to cook. The activity worked the kinks out of me so that by the time Jesse came down, having smelled food, I felt calm and ready for conversation. But Jesse seemed totally distracted as he ate his sandwich, and the second he finished, he went up to his room again. I was still staring after him, wondering what the matter was, when Da came in the back door with Neil, Mel, and Tich. They didn't stay either, but collected their sandwiches as I made them and trooped out to the shed. Mirandah came down and talked to Ricki on the phone while jiggling Luke in his bouncer. But when I'd finished cooking, she hung up and took Luke up to Mum, and then we carried our plates out to the front veranda.

It was a cool night, but the air smelled sweet and we ate while watching people go by. There were more walkers and joggers than usual, because everyone who had been cooped up all day on account of the rain was making use of the sliver of time before night set in.

Mrs. Frizzel from up the street wheeled past the gate, her fat little pug close by her heels. She nodded when she caught sight of us, and, curious, I focused my attention until I could just smell her vinegary odor. She looked disapproving, and I guessed she thought it was uncouth to eat on the veranda.

"The thing is," Mirandah said suddenly, "if Da does become famous, it doesn't have to mean all the things that being famous usually means. I mean, Da isn't like other people who get famous and can't handle it so they take drugs."

"Da would never take drugs," I said.

"That's what I mean, you idiot," she laughed. "I mean famous people go off the rails because there's something about so many people watching them that messes them up. A lot of famous people kill themselves."

"Is this from those dumb magazines you buy?" I snapped.

"I never buy dumb magazines," she said slyly. "I'm just saying that Da won't go crazy if he gets famous, because it would just have happened to him by chance. He wasn't trying to get famous. It's the people who *want* fame that are in trouble."

"You think wanting fame makes people insane?" I asked, trying to figure out her logic.

"I think the reason they want fame can make a person crazy. I mean, people want it because they feel insignificant. They want everyone to know them and be interested in them. They don't realize that being stared at so much will turn them into actors in their own lives. Nothing will feel real anymore. They'll feel less real when they're famous than when they were nobody."

"You think they kill themselves to make themselves feel real again?" I thought that was a surprisingly interesting conclusion for Mirandah. But she just rolled her eyes at me.

"I'm just saying some people can't handle being looked at all the time. It's not what they thought it was. But I think Da would be fine. He would still grow his own tomatoes."

* * *

Tuesday was a blur of preparations for the looming school play. I hadn't had much to do with it, first being in a coma for all that time and second being totally deficient in the area of artistic ability. But now that sets and costumes were being assembled and actors were working up to the dress rehearsal, anyone vaguely willing was co-opted as a gofer. I fetched and carried until the dismissal bell, then went to catch a bus. I was tired from all the running around, and I knew the bus wouldn't be crowded because kids on a field trip that day had been dismissed early. I took a seat in the middle of the bus.

Just as the door hissed shut, an old man in a dirty suede coat reached it and knocked insistently. The bus driver hesitated, and I could tell he was thinking of ignoring the old guy. Then he relented, and the door swished open. The man got in, grumbling under his breath. The bus filled with the noxious reek of unwashed body, rancid food, alcohol, and old sweat. His hair looked like birds would reject it for a nest, unless birds have slums. The trousers and coat he wore were so greasy that they shone like waxed wood in patches at the knees and elbows, and when he sat down, I heard the faint crackle of newspapers that told me he had wrapped them around himself under his clothes. He sat a few seats in front of me but, suddenly, without any warning, he swung round and looked at me. I was wide open, not anticipating any attention, so the savage, sour reek of him leapt at me like a tiger. I was struggling to pull up my screen when the woman in the seat between us shifted. The old man's baleful red gaze flickered to her, and with a gasp of relief, I switched my gaze to her, too. Because I was still wide open, her smell flowed at me next: musty old carpet mixed with some sort of sickly air freshener. She was not looking at me, though, so I was able to turn away.

I was shaken, because I had begun to think I had a good amount of control. But I had been careless to sit there on a bus with my senses unprotected, and I knew I must never do it again. What would have happened if he had gone on staring at me, and I had been unable to call up a screen? Maybe I would have gone on magnifying and swallowing information until I fell into another coma just to escape.

I shuddered, realizing that my confidence and self-control were an eggshell-thin crust over a giant void of ignorance. It was not enough just to be able to create a mathematical screen in my mind. I had to understand more about what had happened to me.

The bus passed a billboard advertising a circus and a small neon monkey waved its little black paw at me. It made me think of Wombat, with whom I definitely seemed to have established real communication. He sought me out now whenever he wanted anything, and a couple of times I had sensed he was trying to transmit something more complicated than his immediate needs.

I thought about animals and how they used their scents and body language. Maybe the old man and his unpleasant personal odor were an echo of the lion who used his urine to mark the borders of his kingdom, or the dog that peed contemptuously into the territory of another dog. Maybe the old man's mind was so corrupted by alcohol that he had regressed into a state similar to his animal ancestors, so that consciously or unconsciously, he was using his odor to reject and lash out at other people. That brought me back to feeling that what had happened to my mind might simply be the accidental uncovering of something buried by evolution—something that might not be gone completely in us humans, even if it wasn't being used consciously.

11

That afternoon when I got home, I stopped at the gate because there was an unfamiliar clacking sound coming from the house. It took a minute for me to recognize that it was the ancient typewriter Mum kept for typing stuff on cards to go with paintings at exhibitions. It's so old Da keeps joking that it's probably an antique and the most valuable thing in the whole house, but he can't sell it to pay bills because Mum is a Luddite who refuses to use a computer. I grinned, walking up the path, because Mum hates naming paintings almost as much as she hates computers. She says when you name something, you pin it down like a butterfly; it doesn't live anymore.

"Reality is elusive," Mum told her agent Rhona once. I had liked the phrase so much that I wrote it on the front of my notebook.

I was half expecting to find Rhona inside waiting, because why else would Mum be up so early? But as I came down the hall, men's voices were coming from the kitchen. I opened the door to find a stranger sitting at the table with Da. He was older and much bigger than Da, almost big enough to qualify as fat, only he wasn't. He was solid under a slippery metallic-looking suit that accentuated a chest like a barrel. His bottom lip was very full, but his upper lip so thin as to be almost nonexistent. His face was hairless and cleanly pink, and his hair was a white meringue swirl. The hair was exaggerated and odd enough that it tweaked my memory. I realized that I had seen this man the night of the Urban Dingo gig. He had been talking to the snide announcer and the man in the green sneakers.

Da noticed me. "Aaron, this is my daughter."

The big man turned so swiftly that I barely had time to strengthen my screen before his gaze was pinioning me. Even screening hard, I was shocked to feel something like a stream of tiny invisible fish surging at me from him. Only the fact that I had plenty of practice at not reacting to unexpected things in the past few weeks kept me from yelping as I felt the man's attention nudge and push against me as if it were trying to get inside my skin.

He turned to Da and said oddly, "This is not Serenity."

"No. Serenity is my youngest daughter. This is Alyzon. Honey, this is Aaron Rayc," Da said. "He helps to manage Urban Dingo."

"Just Aaron, please, and I do not manage the band. It is merely that I take an interest in them and perhaps I have been of some small use to them from time to time in offering advice." He had a formal voice with just a hint of something rich and foreign. He smiled at me, and it was the sort of smile people give when they have been directed to notice you by someone whose opinion they care about. He had lost interest in me after learning that I was not Serenity, which made me wonder what Da had told him about her.

"The name is a version of Alison," Da was explaining. "It was the name of my wife's grandmother."

I went over to the bench and began to make myself a mug of chocolate, because I was very curious about Aaron Rayc. When I was sure he and Da were paying no attention to me, I dropped my number screen.

I was looking at both men. I smelled the familiar coffee-grounds scent of Da mixed with tobacco and rope and a slight linseed odor. There was nothing from Aaron Rayc. Puzzled, I focused on him, leaving Da out of my vision. I smelled after-shave and deodorant, the very faint odor of sweat and mint toothpaste and a touch of garlic—but I could not smell what I had come to think of as an essence scent. Nor could I smell any of his thoughts or feelings. It was unnerving—like meeting someone who didn't have a shadow.

I extended my other senses and saw that the pinkness of Aaron Rayc's skin was actually a slight irritation, as if he had scrubbed himself too hard when he bathed. I listened to the thick, quick *drub-drub* of his heartbeat and the strong pull of his breathing and understood that the big man was excited and trying not to seem so.

"You say your wife is an artist?" he asked, and his voice boomed painfully. I winced and raised the screen.

Da's face lit up the way it always did when he was talking about Mum. "Her name is Zambia Whitestarr. Maybe you've heard of her, if you're a patron of the arts." He refilled their teacups and got some more milk.

"I am interested in artists of many kinds," Aaron Rayc said, following Da's movements with his eyes. He had a voice like thickened cream, all smooth flow and rich blandness. No sign in it of the eagerness I could see in his body language.

"Those drawings are Zambia's." Da nodded to the wall by the door as he passed it. Aaron Rayc got up to look at them, and that was when I noticed the air around him was distorting the way it did around Da. I had the impression there was some difference, but it was hard to make it out against the busy background of the kitchen.

"Your wife's work is very unusual," Aaron Rayc said. "But I have to say that, in general, I am more drawn to mainstream art because it has a wider appeal. It is accessible and, as such, it is democratic. Much so-called high art and, if you will forgive me saying it, fringe art like your wife's is too introverted. Very often its elevation owes itself to elitism; the desire to have a work of art that only some are able to understand inevitably sets up cultural haves and have-nots."

As he spoke, he had a habit of lifting his big hands and waving them about elegantly to emphasize whatever point he was making, then dropping them suddenly and limply into his lap, as if they had fallen dead.

"Whew," Da said. "What you're saying sounds very much like you see art as a form of political expression."

"Like anything creative, it is both a form of expression and a potential force. Think about it. Used properly, painting, music, writing—all of the arts—can be forces for change in society. Haven't all the greatest musical artists changed the world? Elvis, the Beatles . . ."

"Maybe," Da said. "But I'm afraid I don't think it's the business of an artist to *want* to change the world."

"No?" Aaron Rayc looked weirdly delighted. "What about your 'Song for Aya'? That is virtually a protest song."

"You've heard that?" Da laughed in disbelief. "I don't think of it as a protest song, though. I wrote it for someone, because I wanted to tell her how I felt about what had happened to her. I guess you could say it was as much a song about me as anything, although I didn't think that at the time. It was my way of trying to bear what was happening to her. My helplessness . . . but maybe you know the story behind the song?"

Aaron Rayc made a gesture that might have been a nod.

"Anyway, I don't write songs to protest about things," Da said. "I write to understand things more deeply."

"But surely there is an outward urge as well as an inward one?"

"Of course, but it's secondary. If you want to know the truth, I think of my songs as a kind of howling at the moon more than anything else. Wolves howl because they can't help it, you know. The moon demands it of them, just like the world demands a response in music from me."

"Very poetic. Do you write all of the songs for the band, then?"

"I work with the others to produce the music, but the

lyrics are mostly mine. Neil has written some of them. Of course, a lot of our music is instrumental, and it just evolves."

Aaron Rayc nodded, but his eyes were unfocused, as if he were thinking about something else. I wondered why he was here. Their conversation wasn't giving me any clues.

The entrepreneur spoke again. "You will not deny that regardless of your intent, the music you make requires a response from an audience? Is, in fact, a spiritual call to arms."

Da frowned. "I don't deny that people react to the music. I hope they do. But I don't see it as a call to arms because that implies I want them to do something. And I don't. If I think of the 'outward urge,' as you call it, I see myself and the others as sometimes giving voice to things that can't speak for themselves. Children or animals or the earth—but we are also trying to learn how it feels to be that thing we are writing about. To understand it better."

"You believe that you can understand another species? Is that not an arrogance?"

Da nodded. "Of course, but I don't think it is a bad arrogance if the result rouses people to feel for something other than themselves and their own species."

"So you *do* want to change the world?"

Da laughed. "I wish humans would evolve enough to *belong* to life rather than wanting always to dominate and use it. But the truth is that when I make music, I'm trying to figure out what I think about things. I am not setting out to tell others how to feel or think or act."

"And yet people may act differently because of the way

your songs make them feel. Do you not concede that? And if it is so, then don't you have the duty to use that power actively to make the world a better place?"

"It would be truly arrogant to think that I could tell other people how to make the world a better place," Da said.

Aaron Rayc gave an extraordinarily beautiful laugh, and there was no mistaking his pleasure in Da's words. "I knew you would be a true idealist, Macoll. 'Song for Aya' showed it to me as much as it showed me the power of your music and your persona. But I wanted to be sure."

Da shrugged. "Maybe I sound naive to you."

"Not at all." The entrepreneur glanced at his watch, pushing his thick lower lip out, and got to his feet. "I am sorry to have to end this most fascinating conversation, Macoll, but you can be sure we will continue it at some other time." He stood, and Da stood, too. They shook hands, and the air between them swirled and shuddered.

"What did he want?" I asked Da when we were alone.

"I'm not quite sure," he admitted with a slightly puzzled laugh. He crossed to the sink and began filling it with hot water. "He called this morning. He said he had been at the Urban Dingo gig and he'd like to meet me, and I said what about today. To be honest I was half joking, because a man like that usually has appointments lined up from first thing in the morning to last thing at night for a year in advance. But he just said he would come by. I thought then that he must want to offer to manage us, but he didn't mention it. Maybe he wants us to do a gig. He gave me his card just now."

"He would have mentioned a gig, don't you think?" I asked.

Da shrugged. "He didn't mention the band much at all."

"Did you like him?" I asked curiously, thinking again about the suppressed excitement in the businessman and the way he affected the air around him.

"I didn't dislike him," Da answered finally. "It was like meeting a figure on television. He seemed slightly unreal."

"You think it was about religion? He sounded that way a bit when he was talking about changing the world. Maybe he wanted a donation."

Da laughed genuinely then. "In that case he was really barking up the wrong tree. One look at this place falling down around our ears would have told him that. But enough armchair psychoanalysis. I don't suppose we'll meet again despite what he said. Probably he was just curious."

I went upstairs, wondering what it could possibly mean that I hadn't been able to smell Aaron Rayc's essence. Or what those tiny fish I had felt in the air might mean. That brought me up against the usual problem of finding it hard to think about things for which I had no words. My thinking felt muddled, and it occurred to me that I could take the advice I had given Jesse and write about how I saw the world through my extended senses. I knew from composing essays that you always knew a lot more than you thought you did about things, once you started writing down what you remembered.

I changed out of my uniform into home clothes, got out a fresh notepad, and, sitting cross-legged on my bed with my back against the wall, wrote as much as I could about what had just happened in the kitchen. Then I took a break and read over what I had written.

I hadn't come up with any useful ideas, and the writing seemed uninspired. Maybe I needed some sort of specific form. Stream of consciousness was too loose and floppy. I tried writing like a scientist making research notes, but I hadn't written much before I realized the sort of words you use in science essays couldn't say what I wanted to say.

I decided to try diary mode, although I had always hated the way diaries made your life sound so drab. They seemed to force you to write nothing but mean, brooding rants about people who made you mad, and long, dull shopping lists of all the incredibly ordinary things you did in a day or the meals that you ate. Sure enough, even though I was trying to write about events that were anything but boring, I found myself writing so much detail that I soon ground to a halt.

I made up my mind that a simple journal style would work best, but it might be easier if I pretended to be writing it for someone in particular. It would have to be someone who was knowledgeable but still capable of believing strange things if you presented them well enough. Someone interested and smart and a bit stern. I put in the sternness because I thought that would make me less likely to exaggerate or ramble on. The person I ended up imagining was like Professor Kirke in *The Lion, the Witch, and the Wardrobe*.

Sitting as I was with the blackness of Serenity's side of the room staring me in the face, I began to write down what my senses had been telling me about her since the accident. I wrote fast and left blanks where I couldn't come up with the right word, knowing I could come back and fill them in later. I wrote of the shadows on her side of the room and how at night they almost seemed alive. I wrote about the bleak poetry snatches I could hear in the air, even when no one was in the room but me. I described how the Serenity part of Serenity smelled of violets while the Sybl part smelled of licorice. I wrote about how she had got so thin and pale over the past months and how most of her time was spent in her room or at the library. I wrote about her not playing her cello anymore and biting her nails. I wrote about how she had seemed so much her old self the day after Luke was born, but the very next day she had begun dressing entirely in black, rather than just mostly. I remembered how Neil Stone said that she looked like she was in mourning for the dead, rather than celebrating a birth.

I wrote seven pages straight and only when I stopped because my hand was cramping did I realize that the form was perfect. Maybe I would borrow the typewriter from Mum once she had finished her labels. I couldn't use the family computer. Mirandah was so possessive of it that the minute I got on it she would be hanging over my shoulder, reading what I was writing and commenting on how slow I was or suggesting this or that shortcut. Then she would want to check her e-mail. All she ever seemed to get were reams of forwarded jokes from all over the world sent to her by people too busy to be bothered to send a proper letter. They would send a joke that had been sent to them by someone who was also too busy to be bothered with communicating. What was the point?

I sighed and rested my head against the wall. Fatigue began nibbling at the edges of my consciousness, and I didn't resist. I slipped into sleep and into a queer vivid dream in which I was a wolf prowling through a huge, ancient ruined city. The sky over it was dark and polluted-looking, clogged with clouds streaked sulfur yellow and bruise purple. The city smelled as if there were animals in it lying dead and rotting, but the wolf-me was not afraid or repelled. It pushed aside the stink of rot and caught the scent of humans hiding behind their chipped doors and broken windows.

I woke to the bang of a door and the smell of food.

* * *

Jesse had turned himself into a gnocchi factory, and there were a dozen trays of potato dumplings sitting on every surface in the kitchen, waiting to be dunked in boiling water. Some were colored green with basil, some pink with tomato paste, and some orange with pumpkin. Jesse was so absorbed that he didn't hear me come in, but I knew that any minute he would want to freeze them. Jesse had a mania for freezing things. We were always coming across mysterious packages of stuff so altered by their descent into the refrigerator ice age that even Jesse couldn't figure out what they had once been.

I noticed that in his gnocchi frenzy, he had completely forgotten to make any sauce; perhaps he had even forgotten that he was supposed to be feeding us. I went to the fridge, got out mushrooms, garlic, and tomatoes, chopped them up, and fried them.

"What are you cooking?" Jesse asked.

"A sauce to go with your gnocchi," I said.

"Ah," he murmured. Sometimes Jesse reminded me of those sideshow clowns with open mouths that you feed a ball into and wait a few seconds to see if it will fall into the right slot. He turned back to his gnocchi and smiled peacefully. "I'll just put some of this into the freezer."

Da came through a moment later with a music student, a small, painfully shy girl called Portia Sting. He ushered her through the kitchen, talking quietly to her as if she were a wild doe that might bolt. I was startled to see the air distorting around him and sparking the way it had done the night of the gig.

After seeing her out, he came back shaking his head. When he had gone upstairs to wash for dinner, Jesse gave me a sorrowful look. "Poor Portia Sting," he sighed. We both burst out laughing, although I felt a bit mean, because it must be horrible to be so shy.

* * *

Halfway through dinner, Neil Stone turned up. He turned down gnocchi, and once I finished eating, I played a game of chess with him while Da finished the dishes. We both knew that it wouldn't take long for him to beat me, and it didn't.

"You have to learn to think a few moves ahead," he said, after he had checkmated me.

"You always say that, but I don't see how I can guess what you'll do before you do it," I complained.

"You learn by looking at what I've done before. Chess masters actually study their opponents' previous games before competitions." Neil was packing away the chess pieces carefully in the felt-lined box he carried them in. He had a beautiful chess set that had been carved for him by a friend, and I watched him put it away, thinking that if I were to evoke my new ability to remember, it would not be long before I would beat him. But to use my extended sense in such a way seemed like cheating.

After the meal Neil and Da disappeared into the shed, and Mirandah asked Serenity to take Luke up to bed. I was surprised to see Serenity hesitate. When she passed me with him in her arms, I caught her mismatched scents of licorice and wet violet, but they were tinged with a thick, musty smell that reminded me of a piece of wet clothing that has been shoved into a corner and forgotten.

Mirandah was talking on the phone, so I went out on the veranda to read a novel for English. Usually I read all of the assigned novels over the summer before school started, but I had put this one off because its title, *The Lonely Passion of Judith Hearne,* made me think it might be about sex. It was not that I minded reading about sex; it was the knowledge that Mrs. Barker would almost certainly choose me to read aloud one of the sections dealing with it. She always picked on me to read what she called challenging passages because she thought I was mature and that that was a good influence on the others. Sometimes teachers have the weirdest ideas.

I opened the book with a doomed feeling, but the main character turned out to be this sad old woman who reminded me a bit of an older Portia Sting. Since she was absolutely un-likely to have sex with anyone, I could relax. Judith Hearne was as lean as her life sounded, and I knew right away that her desperate need to have something important of her own was never going to be answered. I thought it was going to be dreary, but instead the book turned out to be strangely riveting.

I would have read on into the night, but it got cold. I went up to the bedroom to find the light already out and Serenity fast asleep. She shifted as I slipped into my sheets, and I focused my senses on her without meaning to. A few seconds was all it took for me to know that she was lying there wide awake.

* * *

It's funny when people change. If you live with them, you don't really see it happening because you're too close. I had only been noticing Serenity lately because my senses had given me a new way to perceive her. Now I found myself wonder-ing why she had changed.

Neil's chess advice about examining the past floated into my mind, and I tried to pinpoint the beginning of the change in Serenity. The first thing that came to me was her an-nouncement the year before that we were to call her Sybl. She had made a speech at the time giving her reasons, which I couldn't remember. Mirandah had promptly announced that it was stupid and she wasn't doing it. Mum never used the name, and after a little while of trying to remember, I gave up. I told Serenity that the name just felt wrong. The truth was I was tired of having her snap at me when I forgot. Jesse still called her Sybl as often as he called her Serenity, and Da managed to remember most of the time, although he called her Serenity to the rest of us. I don't think any of us had imagined that she would go on insisting on the name change after all this time.

I thought how skinny she had gotten and how little appetite she had, and wondered if she could be taking drugs. The thought that anyone in our family would do such a lost thing scared me, but it didn't really make sense anyway, because Serenity always said that people who took drugs were cowards.

A sinister little voice whispered that Serenity might believe that, but who knew what Sybl believed.

* * *

I woke the next morning to find Serenity's bed empty. For some reason it made me feel uneasy, but when I went downstairs for breakfast, Da told me that she had left for school early. I asked if he knew why, and he said that she probably had arranged to meet a friend before class. He was making oatmeal when he said this, so he didn't see me gape. How could he not know that Serenity didn't have any friends?

I realized this was another aspect of the change in her. She used to have friends, but not anymore. I had seen her solitary state as a melodramatic choice she was making. But for the first time I wondered, with a pang of guilt, if the friendlessness hadn't been the catalyst for the other changes. Maybe all that was wrong was loneliness.

12

The school was in chaos with final preparations and rehearsals for the play. It was scheduled to open at the end of the week, and the few classes where teachers were not involved in getting ready for the play—or for the interschool sports tournament that was to happen the following week—were like little pools of sanity in a hurricane of overexcitement. Mrs. Barker's class was not one of them, because she was directing the play. In fact, most of her classes that day were taught by substitute teachers. Our session turned out to be one where there were no spare subs, so the class was to be split and sent to sit at the back of two other classes to do worksheets.

Harlen had already been selected for group A when I came in, and he was standing with some of the others at the back of the room. Mrs. Barker selected me for group B, and I was sent to wait at the front of the class. I did not know whether to feel disappointed or relieved.

Gilly had been put into group A, and being without her made me restless. It was amazing to think that we had hardly spoken before the accident, because I had come to love the clean sea smell of her, which perfectly expressed the honesty and openness of her personality. I felt I was foolish not to have been drawn to her before. But she had always seemed so conventional in her neat stockings, shiny shoes, and perfect, sleek braid.

Once I had completed the worksheet, I asked permission to go to the library to work on an assignment. I was still there, absorbed in a book on the Antarctic, when the recess bell rang. Ten minutes later Gilly came in. She grinned at my surprise and said loftily, "There are people who take refuge in libraries as naturally as lemmings look for a cliff."

It struck me that she was probably, and unexpectedly, my first best friend.

We had science in the afternoon. Usually we did practical experiments, but that day Mr. Stravin had us doing theory, so Gilly and I didn't speak all class until we were washing our hands at the end. Even if we hadn't done any experiments in the class, Mr. Stravin made us wash our hands because he said it was a good habit for serious scientists to have. To him, we were all serious scientists in embryo, which was one of the things Gilly and I liked about him.

"You want to come to the movies on Saturday?" Gilly asked quietly, soaping her hands. "There's an old horror movie marathon."

I sighed and shook my head. "I have my own horror marathon on Saturday. Mrs. Barker told me this morning I'm supposed to sit for the two missed tests then."

Gilly grimaced sympathetically. "You could come along

after. You would still see a couple of the movies. And if not for the movies, you should come because the Valhalla has the world's best stale cookies and soapy tea at intermission."

I grinned. "Do I have to pay for the whole marathon?" A very Whitestarr question.

"No, but it'll be my treat anyway," Gilly said.

I might have refused, but I realized with a burst of pleasure that this was how it was with friends.

* * *

School went on being chaotic as the week progressed, and teachers trying to run regular classes must have felt like they were holding down the lid on a furiously boiling pot. Half of them looked on the verge of nervous breakdowns, and there was a lot more yelling than usual. I didn't see Harlen up close, because English class stayed in two halves for the week.

Then, after class on Thursday, I was approaching the glass doors at the front of the school when I saw him standing by the school gates, talking to a couple of guys in expensive-looking clothes. He was as handsome and perfectly groomed as ever, and his black hair shone darkly in the sunlight. He glanced toward the entrance, and although he could not possibly have seen me through the reflector glass, I felt suddenly certain that he was looking for me. A wave of inexplicable fear flowed through me. Without thought, I turned and went back down the hall to a door that brought me out on the far side of the school. Once outside, I cut across the courtyard, knowing the school buildings would hide my retreat from Harlen. I went through a gate in the fence that led me into a lane that, a few minutes later, brought me to Stapleton Park.

It was only after I had passed into the shadows of the big trees there that I slowed down and thought with incredulity about what had just happened. The weird, powerful fear I had experienced must be my subconscious reacting to the memory of the awful smell he had given off. But why was I reacting to it now? Why not when I had seen him in class earlier in the week?

Even just thinking about what had happened made me feel uneasy, so I forced my thoughts away from Harlen and focused my attention determinedly on the carpet of red and yellow leaves that lay under the trees. I let my senses take me into their delicious fermenting smell, and before long I was kicking through them as enthusiastically as a little kid. By the time I reached the end of the trees, I was breathless but also relaxed. I walked up to the top of a small hill where people were flying kites and let my mind go into the kites. For a while it was as if I was there at the end of those fragile strings, bouncing and jerking and longing to go with the wind that tugged at me.

* * *

I did not allow myself to think again about what had happened that afternoon until I was in my room. Then I wrote, "It was like a documentary we saw at school about a gazelle who scents a hyena and flees. But what possible danger could Harlen Sanderson represent to me? It's not as if he knows about my altered senses, and even if he did, what harm could he cause? In a movie, Harlen might want to sell his information to some shady government group of scientists who hunted down people with abilities that could be used as weapons and performed hideous experiments on them, but in real life he is a handsome, dark-haired guy with buckets of charm and a smile to die for."

I thought some more, then I wrote, "Maybe it was actually the guys with Harlen that set off my danger sense. One of them had a shaved head, which always makes me think of neo-Nazis. They had both emanated a dangerous toughness, even though they were wearing nice clothes. I guess I'll know for sure when I see Harlen again."

I put the journal away and went downstairs for dinner. When I saw Serenity stirring a pot, I sighed inwardly. These days, the food she made was either totally tasteless or spiced with such impossible combinations that it was too peculiar to eat. She glanced up from stirring as I came in, and I caught the strong scent of licorice. Sybl, my mind whispered, and my skin rose into gooseflesh. On impulse, I asked, "Why did you change your name?"

"I told you why," she said coldly.

"Yeah, but that was ages back," I said, and realized that I was holding my hands up as if she was threatening to shoot me. She looked a bit as if she wanted to.

"Too bad," she snapped.

I bit back the words that jumped to my lips and waited. Finally Serenity shot me an irritated look. "That name Mum and Da gave me. That's *their* name. It's their way of claiming me. But I belong to myself, and I want to name myself."

They were good lines, but they didn't ring true. The bit about Mum and Da wanting to own her would have sounded a lot more convincing if they were possessive or controlling parents. I wondered if she was quoting one of her beloved poets but knew better than to suggest it.

"But why Sybl?"

She hesitated. "The name doesn't matter," she answered finally, turning back to the pot. I thought she had finished, but she said in a low forceful voice, "Principles matter. The things you believe in. And they only matter if you act on them."

Da and Mirandah came clattering in the door, and Serenity closed her mouth like a trapdoor.

"Smells good, Sybl," Da said warmly.

Serenity glared at him and flung out of the room, muttering that we could help ourselves.

"That's no fair!" Mirandah said, hands on her hips. "Serving is part of it, Da. Isn't that right?"

13

On Friday, Mrs. Barker was teaching English as usual. I told myself it was a good thing, because it meant I would get near enough to smell Harlen. Of course, I was nervous that seeing him would set off my gazelle instinct, so when I stepped into the classroom, I clamped hard on all my senses to make sure I didn't do anything crazy.

Clamping was a technique I had discovered that allowed me to bring the extended portion of my senses back to normal levels. But I was so rattled that I clamped too hard. The class hubbub immediately faded, and color bled out of everything. It was like I was stepping into a black-and-white movie. At the same time the whispering in the air that I had been noticing since the accident got much louder.

A black-and-white Mrs. Barker looked up and spoke to me, pointing to the seat next to Gilly. I could not hear what she was saying because of how loud the whispering was, but the gesture was unmistakable. I headed for the seat. Along with everyone else in the class, Harlen was looking at me, and to my relief I felt no desire to flee. He smiled beautifully, and

I felt a little shock of warmth as I sat down. Mrs. Barker was still looking at me and talking, but now she had an annoyed expression. I hastily released the clamp, and it was beyond strange to see her skin and clothes and the room behind her suffuse with sudden color.

". . . had better get a new alarm clock, Alyzon," she was saying sharply. "One that will wake you early enough to ensure that you are not still asleep when you arrive late to school."

She swung back to the board without waiting for me to respond. I opened my folder and sat staring at it until I sensed that the other kids had lost interest in me. Only then did I dart a glance at Gilly. She looked worried. I smiled at her sheepishly, and she visibly relaxed.

It was hard to concentrate on essays and books after that, because of my confusion over Harlen. I was almost relieved when, after the bell rang, I heard him call my name. I summoned up the thickest part of my screen as I turned and clamped down on my extended senses just in case they ordered me to do anything stupid. Dimly, I registered Gilly's admiring look as she went out. Harlen was weaving through chairs toward me, his smile delicious. But when he got closer, my heart began to pound. The sick, horrible stench was still pouring off him. It was as if he had been carrying something dead in his pocket that had become even more rotten and decomposed.

"Hi," Harlen said, coming to lean on my desk.

It took an immense effort of will to respond in a normal voice. In my agitation I began to clamp too hard again, turning

Harlen to black and white and his voice to a thread I had to strain to hear above the whispering in the air about us. Despite my efforts to keep smiling, the strain must have shown, because puzzlement flickered in Harlen's eyes.

Careful, ordered a soft, stern voice inside me.

I searched for something innocuous to say and blurted out that I had given the CD to Serenity. Harlen's smile widened. "That wasn't why I wanted to talk to you, Alyzon," he said, his mouth caressing my name. "I was thinking we could partner for the field trip."

"Field trip?"

Harlen laughed, and his hair moved over his scalp, soft and dark as a million spiderweb-thin strands of black silk. "The impressionist writing excursion. Didn't you hear Mrs. Barker announce it in class?"

I could not think of a sensible reason to refuse to partner with him. I could hardly say, I can't partner with you because you smell like you are dying inside.

Careful careful careful, the voice inside me urged.

"So, I'll see you later," Harlen said, and he sketched a wave and walked out of the room.

I leaned weakly against my desk, sick and shaking. The irony was that I loved impressionist writing. It was this thing Mrs. Barker invented where you went somewhere and sat with a partner, watching the world go by, writing without trying to force it. It wasn't stream of consciousness writing, which is more about what you're thinking. It was about recording life without imposing yourself on what you saw. A month ago I would have been in heaven to have Harlen want to partner with me. Now all I knew was that I had to get out of it, even if it meant faking sick and staying home.

I had a free period next. That was fortunate, because I could not have coped with a class just then. I went to the library, thinking that Harlen could not smell the way he did because he was sick, unless he had some sickness that had yet to make an impact on his health. That made me think about cancer. But could Dr. Austin also have cancer?

After I had bidden Gilly goodbye at the end of the day, I found myself thinking about Harlen again; about the perversity of his becoming interested in me now, when I could not bear to be near him.

I reached the Vietnamese greengrocers where I had got into the habit of buying an apple or plum to eat on the way home, but it was late and the neat little man who owned the shop was dismantling the displays of fruit and piling them into baskets. I stopped to watch him work. He was so old that his limbs and face were like lovingly waxed wood, but though his movements appeared slow, they were so precise that he was actually working very swiftly, one movement flowing seamlessly into the next. It was like a dance. When I let my screen fade, it didn't surprise me that he smelled deliciously of lemon-tree leaves.

Mr. Rackett had read to us about the Japanese samurai who believed that all tasks, however small, ought to be performed as perfectly and completely as possible. They would have approved of this old man, I thought.

He turned to look at me, and I saw from his expression that he had been aware of my gaze all along. I was not screening and I ought to have felt the pressure of his attention, but I felt only a continuation of the peace that watching him had brought me. In a way, it was like looking into Luke's face. He tilted his head sideways and squinted, as if looking at me in bright light, then he said something. Of course, I didn't understand, but he went on for quite a while, his voice gentle but insistent, the lemon-leaf smell of him intensifying. Then he stopped, a question in his expression. I shrugged and smiled. He nodded as if I had spoken and took one of the persimmons from his basket, offering it to me with a low bow. Not knowing what else to do, I took it and bowed back. The man smiled and apple blossom infused the tang of citrus leaf. Then he went inside his shop.

I lifted the persimmon to my nose and sniffed at its cool skin. Its fragrance made my mouth water, and as I bit into it I let myself take the flavor in with all of my extended sense of taste. The juice spurted into my mouth and a blissful laughter bubbled out of me. At the same moment, a bird poured a wonderful cascade of notes into the afternoon air. I caught sight of myself in a shop window greedily eating the persimmon and grinning like a village idiot, and it occurred to me that the changes in my senses had given me access to unusual joy as well as to mystery and darkness.

* * *

When I got home, Wombat was lying on the threshold of the kitchen door like a fat welcome mat. I stopped to stroke him, and his purr sputtered loudly to life like a little engine. He gave out a nice leather smell, which told me that he had been waiting for me to come home and stroke him. It was interesting how strongly his scents connected to meaning. I told him aloud how glad I was to see him, too, wondering suddenly if I was giving off a scent that echoed my words.

He gave off a freshly laundered shirt smell, which was a request to be scratched under the chin. I obeyed and sensed his awareness of my contentment as a sweet smell that reminded me of Da's caramelized sugar smell. *Is that how* my *contentment smells?* I wondered.

I was absolutely startled to smell the cheesy fragrance Wombat always used to tell me yes. My pulse began to race at the thought that the cat had actually understood my question far more clearly than he would have understood the words I said aloud. Was it possible that I could make my scent messages as specific as his?

Can you smell this? I thought at him hard.

The cheesy smell! Then a burst of burnt toast.

Too . . . loud? I guessed.

The cheese smell again. Wombat was now sitting up and staring at me expectantly. He twitched his long tail and began to give off a series of smells. I forced myself not to think about what they might mean, but just to take in the smells. Gradually, the meaning was clear. Wombat was telling me that before, my smell communications had been weak and unfocused like those of other humans, then after I had come back from being away, they had suddenly become painfully loud. Just now, they were as precise as any animal's—although still too loud.

I thought at him gently and very calmly, *Pat me with your paw if this is better.*

He patted at my knee at once, purring and giving off a strong fishy smell of approval. I grew hot with excitement and felt like cheering; maybe some bit of me did cheer, because Wombat hissed and sprang away. He would not be coaxed back, but sat by the fence twitching his tail in disapproval.

"Sorry," I called and went inside, hardly able to wait to try communicating with other animals. For the first time I regretted our family aversion to owning animals. Wombat didn't count, because he had just turned up on our doorstep as a full-grown cat and refused to leave. *He chose us,* Da always said.

I wanted to record what had just happened in my journal, but Mirandah was in the kitchen and she said dramatically, "You are not going to believe this! Jesse is writing!"

That got my attention. "Writing?"

She nodded. "Da says he has been at it on and off all this week, but today he didn't even come down for a snack—and you know what a snacker he is. You don't seem that surprised," she complained. I didn't have to respond, because the phone rang and she pounced on it.

I went up to my room, feeling excited at the thought of Jesse finally pouring his intense, bursting thoughts onto a page, and also smug because it had been my suggestion. I heard the *clack clack* of Mum's old typewriter as I passed Jesse's room and realized that it must have been him using it when I had heard it before.

14

Serenity was in our bedroom, sitting on the rug on my side of the room with Luke, who was plucking the strings of her cello. There was a delicate scent of violet in the air, and on impulse, I asked, "Why don't you play anymore?"

"Music doesn't seem relevant," she said, sounding tired and flat.

I sat on my bed. "Relevant to what?"

"To . . . to my life now," Serenity said.

"Relevant to the life you would have as Sybl?" I asked.

She flinched and grew rigid, the violet smell metamorphosing into licorice. "What do you mean?"

"I don't know," I said. "It just seems to me like you're trying to make yourself into something but you don't know what it means to be that thing, and when you do, it'll be too late."

She stood up with Luke in her arms. "I don't have the faintest idea what you're talking about." Her voice was haughty, and aniseed began to infuse her smell. This was what I smelled whenever she was pretending to eat or sleep, and I thought of it as the scent of deception.

But what was she lying about?

Luke was laughing at me from her embrace, opening his mouth in a shape of joy that contrasted so sharply with the tight closed look on Serenity's face that fear jabbed at me. Maybe my expression was too revealing, because abruptly she thrust Luke into my arms and left the room.

Luke gazed at me, and I let my screen fall and was instantly entranced by his smell. I had realized that its similarity to the smell of the house had something to do with how we all knitted together as a family around Luke. It was so delicious and compelling that it left no room for my concern about Serenity. Luke was like a flower opening its face widely to the sun and the rain and the wind. Utterly open, utterly absorbed, endlessly absorbing.

I was still playing with him when Da poked his head in. He dropped to his hands and knees and began to snuffle at Luke like a bear trying to reach up a tree to get at him. Luke gave a squeal of joy and stuck his belly out, and we both laughed.

"He knows he's seeing a Starr in the making," I said slyly.

"I don't know about a star," Da said, "but the manager of the Green Room rang today and asked us if we'd like to play there regularly for a while."

"How regularly?" I asked.

His smile became wry. "You're a sharp one, Aly Cat. Once a fortnight, in fact. But it's better than nothing. It's straight pay rather than a cut of the door, and we can sell discs. Plus, it will save us from the phone bill that just arrived." For a moment ammonia tinged the coffee-grounds smell. "I just wish we had the money to do a proper recording and get the discs printed professionally, but that won't happen without the backing of a company. The ones we have look homemade, and that puts people off."

I was startled, because Da usually said that it was better to do your own discs rather than have them made by recording companies who only wanted to turn music into a product. But even as I opened my mouth to say that, Luke gave a sloppy blurt and we laughed again.

"You know Jesse's writing?" Da asked after we had rolled around with Luke for a while.

I nodded.

Da shook his head. "It's funny that you told him to write, and then he goes ahead and does it as if it was the answer he had never figured out. He won't talk about what he's writing, though."

"I think it's better not to talk about things that you're going to write, because then you start thinking how other people will feel about them and that changes how you think," I said.

Da looked impressed. "That's pretty profound stuff."

"It's just how I feel when I have to write something for Mrs. Barker," I said diffidently. "I just want to *do* it. I don't want to *talk* about doing it."

"You may be right," Da said thoughtfully. "What I love about improvised music is that you don't talk about it at all. It just evolves, and it's a purely musical evolution. It's like jamming, but on a more serious and exploratory level." He nodded. "OK, I'll take your advice and leave Jesse to talk to the white page. I think you did a seriously good thing suggesting it. I've never seen him like this."

Luke trilled with excitement as they went out.

* * *

Saturday morning I got up late and fooled around bathing Luke before I had to get ready and head off for school. I was trying to feel like a martyr for having to go in on the weekend, but it was a beautiful, crisp day, and it felt good to be out in it. I felt pretty well prepared for anything the tests could throw at me, and it was actually kind of nice to have something important to do on a weekend instead of just killing time. Plus, I was looking forward to the movies with Gilly afterward.

I went through the park, trying fruitlessly to send scent messages to birds and squirrels, and ended up coming through to the front of the school just as Mrs. Barker pulled up. I summoned up the screen as I came over to her car.

"You're early," she said, smiling as she got out. "The proctor won't be here for another half hour."

"It's nice to be out," I said, relieved that she was not annoyed at me for being inattentive in class the previous day.

"It's certainly a beautiful day." She rummaged for her keys and unlocked the front door of the school. I followed her down the corridor to the staff room, and hovered outside it.

"Come on in, Alyzon," she called. "It's not an official school day, so I think we can dispense with the usual formalities. Do you drink tea or coffee?"

"Coffee, if there's any milk," I said. I didn't drink it often, but it seemed to go with sitting in the staff room.

"We even have a milk frother," Mrs. Barker said, bustling about and making coffee with the same cheerful competence she always showed in the classroom. Instead of her usual knit suit, she was wearing black boots under expensive-looking jeans and a loose cotton jumper that slid off one shoulder and matched her scarlet lipstick. Her hair was out, too, instead of being tied back, and it made her look younger and more glamorous.

"What are you thinking?" she asked.

"You look different," I said. "Younger . . . more . . ."

"More?"

"I don't know. Just more," I said.

She laughed, and I could smell something like wisteria as she shook her head. "You were always an original, Alyzon."

I could see the warmth in her eyes and realized that the wisteria smell was connected to her liking for me, because she had also given it off in the hallway when she had told me about the tests.

"Now what are you thinking?" Mrs. Barker asked.

"You ask a lot of questions," I countered.

She smiled. "I do. I guess I became a teacher because I like asking questions."

"Questions?" I said. "I thought teachers were about having all the answers."

"Only bad teachers," Mrs. Barker said easily. "Good teachers are about asking questions and provoking them in students." She hesitated, and then she said, "Alyzon, I hope it won't upset you if I say this, but . . . you've been very different since your accident."

My heart lurched into a jerky trot.

"Your work in class has always been solid and occasionally very bright," she continued. "But now there is something new in the things you turn in. A quality that . . . well, I'm not the only teacher to wonder at it. I can even tell you that initially some of my colleagues thought maybe your parents were doing your work for you."

"Your colleagues?"

She understood what I meant. "Not me. The thoughts, though startling, still felt like your own. Also, I know that you and your father are not the sort of people to operate that way. But the suggestion didn't hold water anyway, because the same quality was apparent in work completed during class."

I don't know how I looked, but Mrs. Barker frowned at whatever she saw in my face. "I didn't mean to embarrass you. I really only wondered if you were aware of it."

"I . . . I see things differently . . . ," I began. Then I stopped, because part of me was tempted to tell her the truth.

"That's exactly it," Mrs. Barker said, seeming not to notice that I had cut myself off. "It's as if you are seeing things from some deeper perspective. I don't mind telling you that I have seldom had so much pleasure in reading a student's work."

The proctor arrived then, to my relief and maybe to Mrs. Barker's as well, because she jumped up at once and introduced us, then she made him coffee, too.

* * *

It was after five when we came outside. Night was starting to close in, but the light was really beautiful, all pink and gold and purple. I felt tired but contented.

"How do you think you did?" Mrs. Barker asked after the proctor had driven off. We were standing by her car, and she pressed her key to unlock the doors.

"I think . . . ," I began, and then stopped because she was looking past me with a strange expression on her face. At the same time her lovely bread smell was overlaid with the unpleasantness of spoiled milk. I started to turn to see what had caught her attention, but she grabbed me by the arm and almost pushed me toward her car. Luckily I was wearing a sweater, so she didn't touch my skin.

"Get in, Alyzon. I'll drive you home." Her tone was so urgent that I obeyed, and a moment later we were pulling away from the curb. "Please don't look back," she said quickly, as I was about to do just that. It wasn't until she turned into the next street that the sour-milk smell faded.

"Mrs. Barker?" I ventured.

She bit her lip and gave me a sideways glance that was, of all things, slightly embarrassed. She turned her eyes back to the road and hitched a quick breath. "Harlen Sanderson was on the other side of the street." I felt as if she had thrown cold water into my face, but she didn't see my reaction. "Did you arrange to meet after the tests?" she asked.

"No," I said, trying to make myself look calm despite the pounding of my heart.

Again that quick, searching sideways look. Maybe I wasn't controlling my expression as well as I thought, because she said with obvious surprise, "You don't like him."

I opened my mouth to say that I *did* like him, but realized it was no longer true. The old Alyzon who had hero-worshipped Harlen from afar for months, who had longed for him to notice her, had been supplanted by the new Alyzon, who could smell something terrible in him, and who wanted only to have him go back to not knowing she existed.

"I . . . I don't like him being interested in me," I finally said.

"I see." A long pause. "Do you think he was waiting for you just now?"

I swallowed. "Maybe someone told him about the tests. Don't you like him?"

"I don't think that is an appropriate question for me to answer," Mrs. Barker said stiffly, but she must have realized how silly that sounded after she had just asked me the same question, because she then said awkwardly, "I noticed Harlen speaking to you after class the other day and . . . well, frankly, I wondered if you were ready for that."

"He wants me to partner with him for our field trip," I said, to see how she would react.

"Did you refuse?" The sour-milk smell was suddenly very strong.

I shook my head.

She nodded approvingly. "It's best if you don't humiliate Harlen. I can easily introduce some other format for the trip.

Or I might even cancel it altogether, given that the weather is unreliable." Her face was now composed and teacherly. "As for missing him just now, you will be able to say quite honestly that you didn't see him."

She was trying hard to make our conversation seem normal, but it wasn't. I desperately wanted to ask why the sight of him had made her drive us away in such a panic, because it reminded me all too vividly of my own flight two days before. But she had resumed her teacher persona, and I sensed that any attempt to dig would only make her more tight-lipped.

* * *

When we reached the outskirts of town, I asked her to let me out by the bus stop.

"I'll drive you home," she said firmly. I wondered if she thought that I meant to sneak back and meet up with Harlen.

"I have to meet Gilly at the movies," I told her.

Mrs. Barker pulled the car up by the bus stop and I got out. I didn't know what to say, so I just thanked her and said I would see her in school. She smiled warmly, seeming to have wiped all that had happened from her mind.

After she had driven away, I waited ages for the bus. I thought over everything that had happened, feeling more and more uneasy and confused about Harlen. Mrs. Barker's negative reaction to him had been too strong to dismiss as her subconscious reaction to Harlen's smell. Which meant she must know something about him, and whatever it was made her dislike him and want to keep me away from him. Maybe he had done something wrong, and Mrs. Barker had heard about it. But there was not the slightest rumor about him. Certainly not among the kids, and teachers seemed to like him as universally as students. That meant whatever Mrs. Barker knew must have happened outside of school.

Something else struck me. Rumor said Harlen had gone to a private school before, but wealthy parents did not switch their beloved son from a private school to a public school without some compelling reason. Was it possible that whatever he had done was so bad that he had been expelled, and no other private school would accept him?

Although if only Mrs. Barker knew, it might be something she had learned privately. A relative or friend might have told her something. She wouldn't break a confidence and she wouldn't gossip, but she might keep an eye on Harlen and warn someone off if he seemed to take an interest.

The bus came trundling along, and I was glad to be distracted from the uneasy mystery of Harlen Sanderson.

15

"I thought you'd changed your mind," Gilly said when I came up to her outside the Valhalla. She was sipping muddy-looking tea from a foam cup.

"It took longer than I expected," I said.

"You've missed *Attack of the Killer Tomatoes,*" Gilly said severely.

"Oh heck and damn," I said.

She laughed. "Come on. Let me introduce you to my friends."

The friends turned out to be a handsome older guy of about twenty-four in a wheelchair whose name was Raoul; a super-thin, haunted-looking girl with short spiky hair named Sarry, whose clothes were too ragged to be anything but a fashion statement; and a gray-eyed guy named Harrison with glasses and floppy, longish blond hair.

"After Harrison Ford, can ye believe it?" he asked glumly. He only had a slight Scottish accent, but I liked the way it made his words sound. "Parents are the pits. Why couldnae they call me Leopold after Leopold Bloom, or Pushkin, or something with literary dignity."

"Pushkin isn't a name with dignity. It's a cat's name," Sarry objected.

"Cats have a lot more dignity than some humans," Harrison said.

Sarry stuck out a pierced tongue, then grinned at me. "We'd call him Harry, but then we'd be Harry and Sarry, like some sort of terrible comedy team."

I laughed, liking them all enough to move to a thinner section of my protective screen. Sarry gave off the mingled odors of peppermint and popcorn with a strong, slightly unsettling under-scent of camphor. Her body language told me that she was a lot more nervous and wound up than she pretended to be, and I guessed that the camphor expressed that. Harrison was almost exactly my height and a year younger than me, with a clever, gloomy Woody Allen wit that made him seem older. It was his smell that struck me most, because it was the lovely scent of cedar wood and also pine needles and lavender—all smells I really loved—and of course the pine-needle scent reminded me of Da. Raoul was so madly in love with Gilly that his scents of really good olive oil and lemon and some sort of polish were all mixed up with her sea smell. I had only to look into Gilly's face to see she felt the same, but oddly, they didn't show their attraction to each other. I wondered why Gilly didn't just let Raoul know she liked him. I couldn't believe it was the wheelchair, but it was none of my business, so I filed the question away and drank some tea, which really did taste of soap.

"I told you," Gilly said, watching me.

I grimaced. "I thought you were exaggerating for effect."

We went in to watch *Creature from the Black Lagoon,* and I nearly laughed myself sick at the man in his black wet suit with badly glued-on rubber protrusions, running around as the Creature. The gentle silly innocence of that old movie was the perfect antidote to the strange and alarming things that had crept into my life lately. Especially when they were accompanied by Harrison's hilarious whispered asides, which seemed all the funnier because of his accent. My cheeks and stomach hurt from laughing long before the movie was over, and Gilly kept whispering at me not to encourage him. She was sitting at the end of the row, beside Raoul. Sarry was on the other side of Harrison, her eyes glued to the screen like a kid. She actually screamed a couple of times, which cracked up the audience, although she was too mesmerized to notice.

I listened to the others spar between movies, hearing in their ease with one another the length and strength of their friendship. I wondered where Gilly had met them all, because they each seemed so different and I was certain none of them were from our school. There was something vaguely familiar about Harrison, though, but I couldn't think where I might have seen him.

Everything my new senses told me about them made me like them more, and I found myself wishing I had such a group of friends. It occurred to me only when Harrison elbowed me hard for not listening to him that they were warming to me as easily as I was to them.

At the end of the night, we all came outside groaning and stretching and complaining about our eyes.

"Never again," Gilly groaned. "Five movies is too many."

"You say that every time," Raoul teased her.

"How about a pizza?" Sarry asked. "I have some coupons."

"The last bus I can get home leaves in ten minutes," I said regretfully.

"Me too," Harrison said.

It turned out that we used the same bus line. Harrison said that he sometimes came to visit someone out my way, which explained why he seemed familiar. I must have seen him on the bus.

Raoul, Sarry, and Gilly waited at the stop with us. "To protect you from sundry creatures of the night," Sarry said, and they waved us off with mimed histrionics before heading off the other way.

Besides us, there was only a couple on the bus, locked in a tight clinch. Harrison rolled his eyes at them and headed for the backseat.

"That was so great," I said, sitting beside him and feeling suddenly shy.

Harrison began talking about the movies we had seen in amazing detail, revealing an almost encyclopedic knowledge of moviemaking, and pretty soon I stopped feeling awkward. I always liked listening to people who were passionate about something. It turned out that he had an old super-eight film camera and was planning to be a director when he grew up. I asked why he didn't have a digital camera, but he shook his head dismissively. He told me that he was going to apply for film school as soon as he was old enough. It turned out that he was actually in his final year at some magnet school—two years ahead of me.

When he asked about me, I told him about Da's love of movies, thinking how they would like each other. I was telling him about the wildly successful gig with Urban Dingo when the bus came to his stop. I turned to wave as it pulled away. Harrison was standing under the streetlight, and his pale hair glowed white in the night, but I couldn't see his expression because his face was shadowed.

As I got off the bus, I thought over the evening, relishing it. I hadn't had so much fun in a long time, and never with people outside my own family. The bus pulled away, dragged after its glaring headlights, and it became very dark, because the light in the bus shelter was smashed. Pulling my coat straight under the straps of my backpack, I looked up at the sky. There was what Da called a fingernail moon showing, and there was one bright star beside it. Or maybe it was a planet.

I heard a movement in the shadows of the bus shelter, and my pulse began to race.

"Who's there?" I said, looking into the darkness. I willed myself to see better, but before my vision could extend fully, I smelled burning hair. My danger sense screamed at me to run, and I obeyed, taking off like a rabbit toward home. When I reached the gate and looked back along the street, there was no one in sight.

"Idiot," I scolded, thinking I had probably smelled a rat's contemplation of the night's hunt. I pressed my hand to my chest to feel the hammering of my heart.

Just the same, I was glad to find Da and Tich in the kitchen listening to a recording of their latest jam session. I put the kettle on and sat down and let their music wash the fear out of me. When the water boiled, I filled the coffee and teapots for the others, set out milk and sugar, mugs and spoons, then made myself a milky hot chocolate. But I had barely drunk half before I was yawning my head off. I went upstairs. It was late, but the light under Jesse's door and the muffled *clack* of the old typewriter keys meant he was still working. He must have put something under the typewriter to dampen the sound. I went to my own room, undressed, and fell into bed.

* * *

Sunday morning I woke to Luke screaming.

I sat bolt upright, heart pounding like a voodoo drum. Serenity was sitting up, too, an expression of fright and alarm on her pale face. We were both in the process of scrambling out of bed when Da yelled that everything was OK.

"Luke just bumped his head," he shouted.

"Jesus," Serenity said, sinking back. "I nearly had a heart attack."

I relaxed, too, struck by how like her old self Serenity seemed. She even smelled strongly of violets. As she rolled over, hauling the blankets up around her neck, I wondered if all of my vague, dark thoughts about her transformation were silly and melodramatic. People didn't turn themselves into something else except in movies like *The Fly*.

I got up and went to shower, telling myself that Serenity was probably just going through some sort of stage. That was what teenagers were supposed to do, weren't we?

16

That night I went to the school play because Gilly was in the orchestra. Da came, too, saying parents ought to support the school their kids attended. Mirandah decided at the last minute to go as well because Ricki was busy. The play turned out to be lame in parts, especially when Romeo kept forgetting his lines, but there were a couple of kids who were really good; Juliet was fantastic. She was big and plain, but she had this great voice and when she said the lines you felt as if she really meant them. I surreptitiously wiped away some tears when she said her last lines and died.

"The lead girl was very talented," Da said on the drive home. "I wouldn't be surprised if we see her onstage in a few years."

"Talent is only part of it," Mirandah said, with that authority she always seemed to give herself. "You have to have guts and luck."

Da gave her a wry look and said mildly, "Talent may only be part of it. So is the heart only a little bit of your body, but without it the rest doesn't work."

I loved that about Da, the way he could gently demolish an argument without getting mad or mean.

But Mirandah shrugged. "Whatever. Juliet's name is Ann Humber and she's planning to be a nurse."

"Well, maybe she'll have a talent for nursing, too," Da murmured. Mirandah, who has the attention span of a newt, was already channel surfing to find a station playing a song she liked.

Once in bed, I lay thinking about Romeo and Juliet and how sad their story was. Not because they die, but because no matter how many times you see the story or read it, they *always* die. The directors could change this or that angle or dress the lovers in anything or nothing, but they could never change the dying because it was the whole point of the play. The inevitability of the deaths was what seemed sad to me. The idea that you could be trapped in a web of events whose outcome could not be changed.

But maybe to Romeo and Juliet, it wouldn't feel as if they were trapped because they would only live their lives once.

* * *

I was anxious on the bus ride to school the next morning because I had English first period. I had managed not to think about Harlen much the day before, but now all the strangeness of Mrs. Barker's reaction washed over me again.

"You OK?" Gilly asked, after the homeroom teacher had gone out.

I didn't answer, because Harlen had entered the room. His eyes sought me out immediately, and my heart sank as he started toward me. I braced myself for his awful smell, but before he got close enough, Mrs. Barker arrived and told him briskly to sit down.

He made a graceful bow to her that had the other girls in the class sighing and giggling. Mrs. Barker smiled, too, but knowing how she really felt about Harlen let me see that it was a perfunctory smile that did not reach her eyes. She told him again to sit down, and then she began handing out papers. She had gotten around half the room before she told us that there had been some problem in gaining permissions for the field trip, so it would be postponed.

I didn't look at her when she put a paper down on my desk, because I felt strangely embarrassed by our secret complicity. The paper was a list of questions about a book we had been reading, and when it had been completely distributed, Mrs. Barker went back to the front of the class and said, "Understanding a question is part of what is required of you in tests and exams. It is not just a cattle prod to make you spill what you know on the page. Understanding a question requires you to listen to it before you listen to yourself. If you listen well, you will find that a good bit of the answer is coded into the question."

Explaining this took up most of the period. Then we read through the questions and took some notes on how we might answer them.

When the bell rang, I packed up quickly, but before I could leave the room, I heard Mrs. Barker call out to Harlen. I didn't dare look back, but my neck crawled as I escaped.

Math was next, and I forgot everything in the lovely intricacy of fractals and prime numbers. I was still being careful not to show how I felt or answer questions too enthusiastically, but I noticed the teacher looking at me in puzzlement from time to time.

At lunchtime, Gilly said she would skip eating because she needed to do some research for an art theory assignment. I went with her to the library and started looking for information for a history assignment about codes of ethics, like the Hippocratic oath and the Declaration of Independence. My idea was to research the samurai and see if they had a code, but I was disappointed not to find anything useful.

In the end, Gilly didn't get much of her assignment done either, because I spent half the time whispering to her corny lines from the horror movies we had seen and stifling laughter.

Eventually the librarian told me to quiet down or leave. Gilly whispered that she would stick with me even if I was a bad influence, because everyone knew it was when you split up that the monster got you.

* * *

After school, I decided to try the city library to see if they had anything about samurai. I knew I could get a lift home with Serenity when Da came to pick her up, because she always went on Mondays.

There was the usual collection of types on board the city-bound bus. I kept my screen up but overheard two men discussing an article in the newspaper about a man who had jumped off an overpass to land in the middle of rush-hour traffic.

"That's seven this year so far, and that's only the ones that get reported. My brother is in bridge maintenance and he said they have about one jumper a week," one of them said. "All from the bridge. Like they wanted everyone to know about them dying."

"Makes you wonder," the other said, and they fell silent. *Makes you wonder what?* I thought.

* * *

There weren't any books about samurai in the city library, and I was frustrated enough to ask one of the librarians. He said I should try searching under *Bushido,* which was the name for the warrior code in feudal Japan.

"The samurai were just one rank among the warriors, and not even the highest," he explained.

Sure enough, there were eleven books listed. Probably there were a whole bunch in the school library as well. I wrote down the reference numbers and went to get the four with the most interesting titles. There was no sign of Serenity yet.

I sat down and turned my attention to the books. In feudal Japan, the book explained, warriors including samurai were collectively known as *bushi* and were men of valor and dignity, governed by a special code called Bushido.

Men, I thought in feminist disgust. *Maybe women don't have codes because they don't need them.* Then I laughed at myself for getting mad at history.

I read on. There was a lot about Japanese classes and various wars in which the bushi had figured, which I skimmed. Then I came to a bit specifically about Bushido.

Also called "the warriors' way," it said, Bushido was a

system of guidelines and traditions that concerned justice, courage, benevolence, politeness, truthfulness, honor, loyalty, and self-control.

Justice, or rightness, the book went on, was supposed to be the most important rule of Bushido, which counseled its adherents to loathe crooked and underhanded dealings. Every decision had to be based on what was right or wrong, and you had to be able to do what was right without wavering, even if it meant you would be injured or die doing it. No amount of physical strength or training or learning could make you a true bushi if you didn't care about what was right.

Warriors were also supposed to have courage, but I was surprised to read that courage was only valued if you were doing something that was right. I stopped to think about that one, because *everyone* felt that they were in the right when it came to arguments. I could think of a million cases where one person's right was another person's wrong.

For instance, a person being robbed might feel they were right to wound or even kill the robber, but what if the robber was starving and the victim was rich? You could even argue that in such a case, neither of them was wrong, and that the blame belonged to the society that let one person be rich while another was hungry. Maybe it was a matter of degrees of wrongness, too, because the robber would know they were wrong, but might feel it would be a greater wrong to let their family starve. And the rich person might think it was terrible to have so much when other people were starving.

Of course, in the case of Japanese warriors, they were

part of a rigidly hierarchical society and were sworn to obey the shogun they were bound to, so individual conscience didn't count as much as loyalty to one's master. But how would a warrior of honor feel if his master decided he wanted to murder the shogun next door and steal his wife? Was it enough to be honorable in serving your shogun with courage, even if that shogun was dishonorable? Or if his intentions were bad, and you died helping him courageously, would it be said that you had died a dog's death, the death of a person in pursuit of dishonorable goals?

My head was starting to ache a bit, so I stretched and looked around. There was still no sign of Serenity.

I went back to reading.

Bushido required warriors to have nerves of steel, the book said. They must show nothing of their feelings on their face. Children were trained from a very early age by being taken to places like graveyards or execution grounds, where they must not show their fear no matter how terrified they felt. If they failed, they were beaten, and in the worst cases, expelled from training. Warriors were also supposed to show benevolence, which was regarded as a feminine counterbalance to the masculine traits of rightness and stern justice. Benevolence, the book said, included love, affection for others, sympathy, and nobility of feeling.

I made a face at the idea of women being loving and sympathetic while men had to be just and right. But it certainly made sense that all of that toughness should be watered down with a bit of kindness and compassion.

The book went on to talk about warriors having to be polite, which seemed an odd thing to worry about when the main aim of a warrior was to chop the head off his enemy. But I read on to learn that Japanese warriors were supposed to be polite not because of how it looked, but because politeness meant that you were in harmony with yourself and your environment. Warriors would actually chide one another for being short-tempered, because it showed that you were out of harmony.

Finally the book said that if a bushi broke any part of the code, he was dishonored. If he was badly dishonored, he had to commit *seppuku,* which was ritual suicide. I read a description of seppuku with fascinated horror. The dishonored warrior entered the temple and bowed to the witnesses, then he walked slowly to a raised platform in front of the altar. He sat with a *kaishaku,* who was a servant or another warrior, crouching on his left side. An official would come forward with a stand upon which rested the short seppuku sword. The warrior would reverently raise it to his forehead with both hands and bow again to the officials. He would then take down the top of his clothes, tucking his sleeves neatly behind his knees, and stab himself deeply below the waist on his left side. He would slowly pull the blade across to the right side and upward. By law, in order to restore honor, he must show no facial expression while he was doing this, nor when he pulled the sword out and leaned forward to stretch out his neck, whereupon the kaishaku would stand up and cut off his head with one swift stroke.

I shuddered and closed the book, thinking that my ideas of honor and courage were very different from those of the bushi.

I got up to return the books to their places, then I looked around for Serenity; I didn't find her, which meant this must be the one time she had broken her slavish ritual. Just my luck. There were some phone booths at the side of the library, so I stepped outside. It was cold enough that my breath came out in frosty plumes.

Then I saw Serenity standing on the footpath, under a streetlight. As if she felt me staring at her, she turned. When she saw it was me, her expression darkened. "Have you been following me?" she snapped.

"Of course not," I said indignantly. "I came to do some research. Where were you, anyway? I didn't see you inside."

"I was in there," Serenity said defiantly. She turned back to the street, and right at that moment, Da pulled up.

"I didn't realize you came here together," he said cheerfully as we got in. I left it to Serenity to tell him we had come separately, but she said nothing.

Da asked what we had been studying, and again Serenity said nothing, so I told him what I could remember about Bushido. Da said he didn't see how killing yourself could fix your honor.

"Do you think anyone still commits seppuku?" I asked him.

"I think most people would find less painful ways of dying," Da said.

I thought I heard Serenity mutter something, but when I turned around, her face was blank and she was staring out the window.

* * *

Mirandah was cooking, and the house smelled deliciously of Swiss cheese–and–vegetable frittata. I was hungry enough for two servings, but I noticed that Serenity ate only when Da was looking at her. The rest of the time she fiddled with her food, trying to rearrange it to make it look as if she had eaten more than she had. I wondered suddenly if she could have an eating disorder.

She went to our room after dinner, saying she had a headache. I didn't want to go up and have her glowering resentfully at me, or lying there in the dark grimly pretending to sleep, so I stayed to help Mirandah dry the dishes. Three teaspoons in, the phone rang and she threw the tea towel down and went to answer it. I thought it would be Ricki like usual, but she got an odd look on her face and turned to hold out the receiver to me.

"It's Harlen Sanderson for you, Alyzon," she said coyly.

I managed to contain my reaction, but the effort made me feel slightly sick.

"Harlen?" I spoke pleasantly into the phone.

"Hi, Alyzon," Harlen said, his voice sounding deeper and older on the phone. "I didn't get a chance to talk to you today. You want to come out for a while now?"

My heart pounded as I tried to think how to answer.

"Alyzon?"

"Uh . . . sorry, Harlen, I can hardly hear you. We must have a bad connection."

"Is this better?" he said loudly. "I said, do you want to come out for a while? I'm in your part of town, at the mall."

How does he know where my part of town is? I wondered uneasily. But I only said, "I wouldn't be allowed tonight. I have to look after my baby brother."

There was a long pause, then Harlen said in a friendly voice, "Some other time, then? I guess I should meet your parents first."

"Yeah," I said, trying to sound enthusiastic. "I'd better get off now. My sister is waiting for a call."

"OK, we'll talk tomorrow," Harlen said. When I put the receiver down, I saw that my hands were shaking.

"What's the matter, Aly?" Da asked.

"I . . . I don't know. Maybe I got up too fast."

"That's no surprise, considering who was on the phone," Mirandah said. "I can't believe you just played hard to get with Harlen Sanderson!"

Da asked me, "Who is Harlen Sanderson?"

"Only the school pinup," Mirandah said drolly. "What's your secret, daaarling?" she demanded in Rhona's voice, pretending to poke a mike in my face.

"My underarm deodorant," I said so seriously that it took them a minute to realize I had made a joke. Then they laughed. I was glad to have put them off, but inside I was still quaking.

* * *

That night I dreamed that I was inside a samurai warrior who was preparing for seppuku. I was trying my hardest to stop him, because I would die if he died. I couldn't make his body obey me, and when he lifted the sword point, I felt a sense of helpless terror. Then the warrior glanced sideways, and I was aghast to see Harlen sitting beside us as kaishaku.

"I know what is inside you," Harlen whispered.

The shock woke me.

17

I made sure I arrived so late the next morning that there was no chance of bumping into Harlen at the lockers, but when I saw my name on the notice board for litter cleanup duty, I nearly had a heart attack. I thought Harlen had written us in together. Then I saw it was Gilly's name next to mine.

"Hope you don't mind me nominating you as my partner," she said when we met to collect our bins and spikes.

"Not at all. I'm proud to be the one you want to pick up moldy crusts with."

She laughed. "I thought you might rather be with Harlen. He was looking for you at the bus stop this morning."

I didn't say anything for a while. Then I said, "He called my place last night. He asked me out, but I told him I couldn't go."

She stared at me sympathetically. "Did your da say you couldn't?"

"I didn't want to," I told her.

Gilly thought I was joking, of course. "This is Harlen every-girl-in-school-has-a-crush-on-him Sanderson we're talking about?"

"Yes," I said fiercely and unhappily, and her amusement faded. "I just don't get why he's suddenly so interested in me."

"I know why," Gilly said kindly, and I stared at her. "Alyzon, you were always a nice person, but these days it's like something in you is radiating this . . . energy that . . . oh, I can't describe it. But I bet that's why Harlen suddenly got so keen." She took my expression as puzzlement and elaborated. "I mean, it's like when you walk past a hot bread shop. You want to go in even if you're not hungry."

I managed to say lightly, "You're telling me Harlen wants me because I smell like a bread roll?"

Gilly laughed.

"What are you witches cackling about?" Sylvia Yarrow asked, passing by.

"*Witch* is not the word for her," Gilly said when Sylvia had gone out of hearing range.

"She's angry because she's hurting," I said without thinking.

Gilly gave me a curious look. "How do you know?"

I shrugged, spiked a chip bag, and then told the truth. "I just feel it."

"Yeah, well, what I feel is that she is a prime bitch."

We picked up rubbish in silence for a while, following the line of the outer fence, and I thought over what Gilly had said about Harlen. Could it be that my extended senses were attracting him? Mrs. Barker had commented about the change in me and so had Mirandah, and even the creepy dream I had experienced the night before seemed to suggest Harlen was aware of the change.

"So, you liked Sarry and the others?" Gilly asked shyly.

I was glad to have my thoughts interrupted. "They're great. Harrison was so funny."

"He's really smart," Gilly said.

"I know. He said on the bus that he's a senior, and he's younger than me! How did you meet him?"

She shrugged. "I was doing some volunteer work, helping deliver meals to old people. That's where I met Sarry, too."

"And Raoul?" I asked.

"I was doing a computer programming class, and he was the tutor. We just hit it off so well that we kept in touch."

"Then you introduced him to the others?"

She nodded. "We're all movie buffs, and Harrison—"

"Wants to be a director. I know." A vague plan solidified suddenly. "Gilly, would you like to come to my place for dinner one night this week? My dad or brother could pick you up and then bring you home after."

"It'd have to be your dad, and he'd have to come in and meet my grandmother," Gilly said dubiously.

I knew that she lived with her elderly grandmother whenever her mother was away on business trips, which was most of the time. I didn't know anything about her father other than that he had left his wife and baby daughter and now lived in Paris. Gilly never mentioned him and rarely spoke of her mother. Most often she talked about her grandmother, but the old seaweed smell that infused her signature odor whenever she talked about the old woman told me the relationship was troubled.

Nevertheless, I was confident about Da's ability to charm anybody and said so.

"It helps that he's totally gorgeous," Gilly said. I had introduced her to Da the night of the school play. "Why do you call him Da, anyway?" We reached the big blue Dumpster behind the cafeteria and emptied our bins into it.

"I guess it comes from him calling his own da that." I wrinkled my nose at the smell, and reflected that there was a difference between "real" bad smells, such as the odorous reek of the garbage, and the rotting smell Harlen gave off, but I lacked the words to describe the difference.

"What night shall I say to my grandmother?" Gilly asked.

"You decide," I said as we stacked our empty bins and washed our hands.

"How about Friday? I could stay later then."

I laughed. "Done."

* * *

The art teacher was out sick, so after lunch I had a free period in the computer lab to type a draft of the samurai assignment. Gilly was rehearsing with the school band, so I was solo. It wasn't until the bell rang for the next class that I realized the boy sitting at the next computer was in Serenity's homeroom. On impulse, I asked him if he knew her.

"Serenity?" the boy repeated blankly.

"You know," one of the girls insisted. "She calls herself Sybl."

"Oh, her." The boy curled his lip.

"Do you know who she hangs around with?" I asked.

They all laughed. "Nobody here," the boy said, and they went out.

I finished packing my own papers, wondering if he meant that Serenity hung around with someone outside school. I thought how she had turned up outside the library the night before, claiming to have been inside. Was it possible that she hadn't been inside, but had been meeting someone elsewhere? But why be so secretive about it?

Coming out of the computer lab, I forgot Serenity immediately because Harlen was standing in the hall, filling it with his dreadful rotting stench. "Hiding from me, were you?"

I thought of him in my dream, saying, "I know what is inside you."

Forcing myself to meet his eyes, I said disparagingly, "I suppose I have been hiding out a bit. It's all this catching up I have to do because of being in the hospital. I'm really sick of it."

"Poor baby," Harlen crooned, his voice softening. He came a step nearer, and I fought to hide the shudder of horror that passed through me at the thought of him touching me. "You know, I came to school on Saturday to meet you after those tests," he said softly.

"Oh, I didn't see you," I said, praying someone would interrupt us.

"I saw you go off in the car with Barking," he said.

"She offered to drive me home. Don't you like her?" I asked innocently, because it was suddenly clear that he didn't.

"What's to like?" Harlen asked lightly, but there was a definite edge to his voice.

"She's a good teacher," I managed to say.

"There's more to life than school, Alyzon Whitestarr," Harlen said. I fiercely resisted flinching when he reached out to run his fingers down a strand of hair that had escaped from my ponytail. "You are a little goody-goody, aren't you?" He laughed softly. "But maybe you might like to be a little bit bad sometime with me."

I clamped hard enough on my senses to gray the posters on the wall behind him, and suddenly the air was full of hissing whispers. I was terrified that Harlen would touch my cheek, but he just gave the strand of hair a sharp tug and then went away, saying he'd catch me later.

* * *

That night I told Da about asking Gilly to dinner, and he agreed to pick her up, although he joked about getting arrested for driving his beaten-up old van in the most exclusive part of town. His eyes flashed when I told him he also had to call Gilly's grandmother. "There hasn't been an elderly lady yet who could resist my undeniable charms," he boasted.

"You seem cheerful," I laughed.

"Gig tomorrow at lunchtime," he said. "A well-paying job at an upmarket charity function, courtesy of Aaron Rayc."

"Aaron Rayc?" I echoed. "What's he got to do with it?"

Da shrugged. "He's connected to the charity. But Alyzon, I've been thinking about Jesse and how you suggested he write down his thoughts. Your mother said he came into the studio last night at about four in the morning and talked to her for two hours about his ideas. She didn't understand a word he said, but he was in his room typing again today." He looked at me thoughtfully. "You might just have created a monster."

I felt a thrill of excitement. "Isn't it great?"

Da grinned. "Now if you could take our poor mixed-up Serenity in hand."

* * *

The next day was the interschool sports tournament, and I caught the morning bus, knowing that there would be no need to hide from Harlen because he would be competing at a school across town. Unfortunately, the athletes were just leaving for the competition when I got to school.

Just as I met up with Gilly, Harlen stepped between us, his foul stench swamping her gentle sea fragrance. "Beat it, babe," he told her casually, and she melted away at once.

"Why did you do that?" I asked, annoyance at his dismissal of her overriding caution. He hadn't even looked at Gilly.

"I wanted to talk to you before the bus goes." Harlen leaned close. "Let's get together tonight after school."

"I can't," I said quickly. "I'm supposed to watch my baby brother again."

"Can't someone else take care of the brat? That fat brother of yours?"

His calling Luke a brat and Jesse fat would have angered me if I hadn't been shocked that he knew so much about my family. I babbled something about Da being unhappy about us trying to avoid family responsibilities, then fell awkwardly silent.

"You're too good, aren't you," Harlen said, and this time I heard a sharp spike of impatience in his voice. Then the bus started up and he had to get on board.

* * *

At lunchtime I decided to sit under one of the peppercorn trees growing around the courtyard. Maybe it was because Harlen was weighing so much on my mind that I noticed a kid I had seen hanging around him a lot when Harlen had first come to the school. He was sitting on a bench, watching some little kids play a game of soccer.

"Hi," I said, going over to him, racking my brain for his name.

He nodded at me and went back to watching the game. I hesitated a moment, then sat down and unpacked my lunch. "How come you didn't go to the tournament?"

He shot me a look that asked why I was asking, but because I was older he just said, "I'm not into sports."

"You used to hang around with Harlen Sanderson, didn't you? And he's pretty sporty." His name came to me then. Cole. I had shifted my number screen to a thinner segment and at the mention of Harlen his wet-dog smell thickened and became less pleasant. My heart beat faster, because the smell told me that, like Mrs. Barker, Cole did not like Harlen.

"That was last year," Cole said.

"You don't hang out with him anymore?" I let my eyes follow the ball as it sailed away from the toe of a little kid, as if I was hardly interested in his answer, but Cole sat very still, like a mouse hoping a cat would not see him. I felt a surge of impatience. I wanted to know what lay behind Harlen's smell,

154

and the fact that Cole had liked Harlen and now clearly no longer did made me certain he knew something to Harlen's discredit. And maybe it was the same thing Mrs. Barker knew.

On impulse, I asked, "Do you know what school Harlen went to before he came here?" At the same time I pushed the question at him mentally, hoping a focused scent message would encourage him to talk.

"He went to a private school called Shale something," Cole answered promptly in a jerky monotone. I was startled into looking directly at him and saw that his face had gone chalk-white. His eyes, turned to me, were dark and cowed. He looked, I realized with a sick jolt, completely intimidated.

But I hadn't bullied him, I told myself. It was true that I had mentally urged him to tell me what I needed, but that didn't qualify as bullying!

Did it?

My bewildered silence had given Cole time to collect himself. "Why are you asking me all these questions?" he demanded. "Did Harlen send you to test me? I told him I wouldn't say anything, and I haven't."

I opened my mouth and shut it again, hardly able to believe what he had just said. My danger sense began to thrum and I realized too late that Cole was bound to tell Harlen I had been questioning him. Without even thinking about it, I stared at Cole and said, "You don't need to mention this to Harlen, Cole. Just forget about it." I thought the same thing as hard as I could, feeling sick at the way he paled even further.

Then he looked confused. "Sorry. Did you want something?"

Reeling from what I had done, I managed to stammer that I had only asked what time it was. Cole checked his watch, told me, then got up and walked away.

* * *

I sat there for another twenty minutes trying to understand how I could have willed Cole to talk about Harlen when he hadn't wanted to—had promised not to—and then willed him to forget. I had wished people to do things dozens of times since the accident, and no one had given any sign of obeying me before now. The only thing I could think of was that there was something about Cole that had allowed me to dominate him. I calmed down a bit then, because this fitted my theory that my enhanced abilities had primitive origins. Animals were always dominating one another, sometimes by force, but more often by will. One animal seemed mostly to know if another had a stronger will and would just signal acceptance. It must be that Cole had acceded to me in the same way weaker animals did when challenged by a dominant animal.

I turned my mind to what Cole had said, and a chill ran down my spine as the significance hit me anew. He had promised Harlen to keep some secret, and I was suddenly sure that it was not only the same thing Mrs. Barker knew, but also the thing that made Harlen smell so dreadful. I would not get more out of Cole unless I was prepared to force him to speak. And I wasn't, because even if I had not set out to bully him, that was what I had done. But maybe I didn't need to question Cole further, now that he had told me that Harlen had gone to a private school with Shale in the name. The school had to be in or near Shaletown, which was only a couple of hours' train ride up the coast. I could go there and question some of the kids Harlen's age to see what they knew about him. I knew Shaletown pretty well, especially the bit around the Shaletown Detention Center, where refugees were sent while they waited to find out if they were allowed to stay in our country.

Just over a year ago, there had been a major political upheaval that had brought a stream of refugees to the detention center, and a furor had erupted because the government had insisted on sending all but a few of the refugees back to their war-torn country. There had been endless articles in the paper with some politicians talking about limited resources and quotas and terrorists, and other politicians talking about children and women and terror and compassion. Da had gone to the detention center with some other musicians to help protest and had ended up speaking with a refugee, a girl a year younger than me. Aya and Da had begun to correspond, and from those letters and later visits, he had learned that she had two tiny brothers, a mother, and a father, all in the detention center. They had left their country because her father had disagreed too openly with those in power. Da ended up writing to the newspapers and to politicians, like a lot of other people did, asking why innocent people should be kept in a prison for an unspecified time, after which they would probably be sent back to their own countries.

In her letters Aya had talked of her fears for herself and her family if they were refused permission to stay. The letters had been heartbreaking. Were still heartbreaking, for Da had kept them. Aya had talked a lot about her baby brothers, and you could tell how much she loved them.

Da had taken Serenity and me with him sometimes when he visited, and we had both got to know the gentle, doe-eyed Aya.

It had been a terrible shock when we found that the government had refused Aya's family permission to remain in our country. Da had done everything he could, but in the end, they had been sent back and Aya had never written again. We had no idea what had happened to her and her family, but there had been such awful stories at the time of the fate of refugees sent back. In the days when we had been trying to get the government to change its mind, I had felt as if something was winding tight in me, as one after another avenue proved useless. I had felt helpless and frightened, but Serenity had been utterly certain that something would happen to rescue them, even at the last minute.

It occurred to me that the whole Aya thing had been the last time I had really felt close to Serenity. I could remember vividly how shattered she had been when she finally realized what all the rest of us had figured out some time earlier: that there was no way to stop Aya and her family from being sent back.

She had been so angry at Da.

"You talk about doing the right thing! So do something!" she had screamed at him.

Of course, there had been nothing he could do that he

had not already tried. Aside from writing letters, he had offered to sponsor the whole family and support them until they were on their feet. He had said this in an open letter in the newspaper. But hundreds of people had written making similar offers regarding other refugees. All to no avail. The government only reiterated its determination to take a tough stance, calling the desperate letters of refugees emotional blackmail.

Da had not reproached Serenity for her unfairness. I had been angry at her for so unjustly attacking him, but I had been even more confused that the government had simply dismissed our passionate opposition to its decision. How could it not listen when it was supposed to represent us?

Da told me sadly that there were a lot of voters who wanted the refugees sent back to their own countries. "They don't want to imagine how it is for a refugee, because thinking about people who are poor or frightened makes them feel unhappy and guilty at how comfortable and safe their own lives are."

I knew that Da still wrote letters to the government and to various organizations in our country and Aya's, trying to locate the family and urging that the laws about refugees and political asylum be changed. But nothing had changed except that the newspapers had found something else to write about.

I was no better than the government, I thought, feeling suddenly ashamed. I had not thought of Aya in a long time, and wasn't it this sort of easy forgetting that allowed politicians to get away with their terrible inhuman decisions?

It came to me all at once that perhaps Serenity had not forgotten. That even though she had never spoken of Aya again after she and her family had left the country, this might lie at the core of her transformation to Sybl.

She had been so terribly angry and upset that final day, when we had gone with a lot of other people to make a last protest and stand vigil, to force the media to at least report the result of the government's policy. All of us were there except Mum, who had been very close to having Luke.

Thinking back, it seemed to me that Serenity had not truly understood that we had failed until Da and the band had begun "Song for Aya." I had seen the baffled rage on her face as she watched him sing. Dear gentle sorrowing Da, who was singing the song he had written, because there was nothing else he could do.

The song was not a protest song, despite what Aaron Rayc had said. It was a gentle and terribly sad ballad, and so beautiful that it had silenced the shouts and rage and jeers of the crowd. A helicopter that had brought a last-minute news crew carried away footage that was replayed many times on television in the weeks after the protest. The television cameras had also filmed the police stopping Da toward the end of the song, to tell him he had no right to perform there without a busker's license. Da talked with them for the longest time, and even in the few seconds that made it to air, you could see those police officers found it hard to know how to deal with a man who was so nice and gentle and persistent. They had been trained to deal with people who were angry and wanting to hurt or smash something.

A record company had called Da, wanting to release the song, but Da had refused, saying it was Aya's song, and that only she could decide what to do with it. Mirandah had thought Da was being idiotic, and Neil had said they ought to do it if only to raise awareness about the plight of the refugees. They could donate all the money they made. But Da wouldn't budge. "I wrote the song for Aya," he said, "and until she's safe and free and able to hear it, nothing can be done with it, other than singing it."

Unlike the others, I had felt like I understood. It would have been wrong to make a record, no matter who profited, when Aya had vanished and might even be dead. She and her whole family.

The night after that final protest, I had found it really hard to sleep. The sound of Da playing the guitar drew me downstairs, but when I looked from the doorway, he seemed so weary and hurt that I had not wanted to interrupt him. I had gone back to bed to lie in the dark, thinking about Aya and her little brothers and wondering where they were and what was happening to them; wondering how it would feel if that were my family.

I had called out to Serenity, but she had been asleep. But now, sitting on the school bench by the courtyard in sunlight that would not warm me, I wondered if she had really been sleeping at all.

There had been a week of despair and guilt and anger after the protest, and there had been phone calls from journalists trying to rehash the story, or link it to others. Da had been invited to speak to a few organizations, and there had been talk of a concert to raise money for refugees. But then Mum had gone into labor, and there had been the swift and thrilling trip to the beach in the old van with the midwife, and the long wait until Luke made his entrance into the world; and life had gone on.

Except, maybe it hadn't gone on for Serenity.

* * *

I decided to catch the regular bus home that night because it was half empty. To my surprised pleasure, Harrison was on it. I went to sit next to him, wondering too late if that would embarrass him. He might have read my mind, for he grinned at me and said in a loud whisper, "We have tae stop meeting like this."

A businessman in the seat across the aisle gave us a suspicious look that reduced us both to splurts of laughter. Then he looked indignant, and that made it worse. What is it about laughter that the more you try to repress it, the more hysterical you get?

"How come you're out so far?" I asked when we had got ourselves under control.

Harrison gave me a burning look. "Because I wanted tae see ye again, ma bonny lassie."

I laughed in delight at his exaggerated Scottish accent. "But seriously, you want to come over to my place for a while? You could just get a later bus to see your friend. Is that where you're going?"

He looked as surprised to receive the invitation as I felt to find myself offering it, and I half expected him to refuse, but he just nodded and said, "Why not?" On the walk to my house, I asked him which school Sarry went to, and he said she didn't mostly. "A lot of people think she's a bit crazy, and she is, but only in a nice way."

"Nicely crazy?"

He grinned and shrugged. "I think a bit of craziness is good for the world."

Da was in the kitchen with Mel and Tich. I introduced them and asked Da how their gig had gone that day. He grinned and said it had been great—they had been paid on the spot. Harrison didn't blink at Mel's hair or the fact that Tich looked a lot like a white Stevie Wonder, right down to rocking from side to side like a distressed elephant.

"Good to meet you, Harrison," Da said and shook his hand.

"Harrison? After the *Star Wars* guy?" Mel asked.

"Unfortunately, yes," Harrison answered. "I think ma parents wanted tae make sure I'd have an inferiority complex so they could control me better."

Da grinned, but Mel launched into his If-I-was-running-the-world speech, shifting the focus to attack oppression and injustice within the traditional bourgeois family unit.

"Mel, give us a break," Da groaned. "Harrison, this man is not related by blood to us, so don't worry."

"Oh, he likes crazy people," I said, and hustled Harrison out and up the stairs.

"Very funny," Harrison said. "Now your father thinks I'm a nutter."

"It's OK, he likes crazy people, too," I said.

Mirandah was coming out of the bathroom, her hair wet and dripping and very green.

"Green is a very organic color, don't you think?" she asked in that vague way she has when in the process of changing colors. I think it's like the trance snakes go into before they shed their skins.

"Is she on drugs?" Harrison asked when she had drifted downstairs.

"She's on colors," I said, opening the door.

Harrison stopped in the doorway at the sight of Serenity's side of the room. "What's this? You're schizophrenic, or does that just represent your dark side?"

"I wish. That's my sister's half of the room. Her name used to be Serenity, but she is turning herself into Sybl."

Instead of asking if Serenity was a vampire like Mirandah's friends always did, Harrison asked quite seriously if there was something wrong with her. This was so unexpected that I found myself telling him about her transformation into Sybl, her growing isolation within the family, her thinness, and her strange aggression. I didn't mention the thoughts I'd had that day about her transformation having been triggered by the fate of Aya and her family, but I ended up telling him about how she had suddenly appeared outside the library, claiming to have been inside all along, although I had looked for her without success.

"She accused me of following her."

Harrison turned his gray eyes to me. "Maybe you should.

You said she goes tae the library every Monday. Go after her next time. See where she goes."

"Wouldn't it be kind of sneaky?" I asked doubtfully.

He shrugged, a light lift of his shoulders. "She's your sister, and you're worried about her. What else would a decent person do but be sneaky?"

I laughed, as he meant me to. Then I sobered. "I *am* really worried about her."

"Maybe subconsciously you ken that she's in some kind of trouble. After all, the things you consciously notice are only part of what your mind takes in. A lot of other information comes tae you subconsciously. I believe our senses extend right from our conscious tae our unconscious."

I actually felt dizzy. "Extended senses."

"Aye. A lot of abilities that we call paranormal are probably just extensions of normal senses that work beneath the level of consciousness." Harrison walked over to Serenity's table and reached out to touch a finger to the slightly withered lily. He said softly, "People can be crumbling inside without anyone knowing about it. Ye shouldnae think you have all the time in the world tae do something, Alyzon. Bad stuff can come so fast it'll make your head spin. You'd never forgive yourself if something happened and you hadnae tried tae act."

His words made me feel cold.

"I'll do it, if you like," he offered diffidently. "Less chance of her spotting me."

* * *

As I walked Harrison back to his bus stop an hour later, I told him that Gilly was coming to dinner on Friday if her gran agreed. "Do you want to come as well?"

"Another time," he said. "It's better if your sister doesnae know what I look like if I am going tae follow her. The main thing is that I ken what *she* looks like." He patted the pocket containing the photo that he had chosen from those I had offered. It was actually a newspaper clipping of Serenity and me taken during the Shaletown protest.

I felt amazed at how much I had told him, let alone that I had agreed he should spy on my sister for me. It was what he had said about extended senses that had made me trust him so much. I mean, what was the chance of a person whose senses had been accidentally extended meeting someone who would mention extended senses?

It made me think of this book called *Cat's Cradle,* where one of the characters in it believes that some people—and animals and even objects—are linked into groups, destined to tangle and intersect with and affect one another over and over, because of some central thing connecting them all, which they don't know about.

Harrison and I could be members of that kind of group. It would explain why I had felt so easy with him as soon as we met, and maybe even how we had happened to bump into each other on the bus. The only thing I couldn't figure was what the central focus of our group could be.

18

When I got back home, Mel's van had gone and there was a gleaming white limousine in the driveway.

Inside, Aaron Rayc was seated at the kitchen table on the same chair as before, wearing a dark gray tux and a snowy white shirt. Beside him was a stunningly beautiful woman with a black evening dress so plain and perfect that even I knew it had to be a designer gown worth thousands. Her hair was black, too, and coiled into a perfect lacquered chignon secured with enormous diamond-studded spikes.

"Alyzon, you remember Mr. Rayc?" Da said. "This is his wife, Dita."

I nodded to the entrepreneur, and once again I felt the little fish of his attention nudging and butting at my screen. Afraid the dislike I felt would show on my face, I turned to his wife and was startled by how familiar her face seemed. Then I realized it was probably on account of the perfectly made-up beauty she had, which you saw every other minute on magazine covers.

"Pleased to meet you, Alyzon," Dita Rayc said in a smoky,

caressing voice. I muttered something and slipped out. Mirandah was sitting on the stairs, eating an apple and playing with Luke.

"What's going on?" I asked, nodding back toward the kitchen.

"Who knows," she said. "They just turned up and that guy and Da have been talking up a storm ever since."

"About what?"

She shrugged. "Life, love, and the pursuit of happiness."

"All of them, even the wife?"

"Dita, Dita, on the wall?" Mirandah trilled softly, fluttering her eyelashes, and we both laughed.

"I wonder what they want."

Mirandah said darkly, "Guys like Aaron Rayc don't just drop by to shoot the breeze. Everything they do is for a reason. But if he wants to manage Losing the Rope, why doesn't he just say so? What's with all the pussyfooting around?"

I shrugged, thinking of how my extended senses had shown me Aaron Rayc's concealed excitement the last time he had been here. I didn't know what he wanted, but like Mirandah, I was sure he wanted something.

Aaron Rayc began to laugh and we both stopped, listening to it.

"That's a seriously great laugh," Mirandah mused. "Pity the guy who owns it is such a . . . a . . . *nebbish*."

"All right, what's a nebbish?" I asked.

"It's someone who, when they walk into the room, it feels

instead like someone walked out. I think it's a Yiddish word. Here, take Luke. I better get my act together. I've got a hot date with Ricki."

Luke stretched his arms out to me and I took him, thinking Mirandah had found the perfect description for how Aaron Rayc struck me. A walking absence. Maybe that was why I couldn't smell him.

Mum called out to bring Luke in for his bath, and I carried him into the bathroom where she was stretched out like a mermaid with her hair flowing in wet lines over her white breasts and shoulders. I was struck again by how amazingly beautiful she was.

"Did you meet that Aaron Rayc guy?" I asked, undressing Luke and handing him to her.

Mum lowered him into the water, and he chirruped with delight and splashed wildly. She laughed and began to kiss him all over. She hadn't heard me. But I wasn't annoyed. There was no point in being annoyed with Mum for being who she was.

I watched Luke wriggle and plow the water for a bit, thinking how it must remind him of being inside Mum. I knew it was really cramped in there by the time a baby was ready to be born, but somehow I could only ever imagine Luke lying at the rippled edge of a vast sea under an endless reddish dusk, waiting to be born into the world. Partly it was how Mum's stomach had sounded when she was pregnant that made me think that way. Listening to it had been like listening to the sea inside a shell. But also it was because of how

Luke was born beside a sea that was on fire with a bloody, luminous light from the setting sun.

I left Mum and Luke to their bath and went back down to the kitchen to make myself a sandwich. Da and Aaron Rayc were still intent on their discussion.

"It's true," Da was saying. "Great art comes out of suffering, but you can't suffer at will."

"Exactly," Aaron Rayc said eagerly.

Dita Rayc had curled her legs up under her on the chair, and she was now watching Da like a cat watches birds when it's too fat and full to chase them. I moved close enough to smell her and almost gagged at the weird sickly combination of wet cement dust, overripe banana, and musky incense.

"I'm not saying it's obligatory to suffer," Da was saying earnestly. "But you do have to go down into yourself to see what you're made of, and I don't see how you can do that if you're worrying about changing the world. It's looking outward when you should be looking inward."

"But don't you think that striving toward the world is also a kind of suffering? A generous suffering, because it's less 'I' focused?" Rayc asked.

Da thought about that. "You have a point. Maybe it is possible to be a true artist with integrity and a desire to save the world from itself, but I'm not that kind of artist. For me it's very introverted and very personal."

"I can see that," Rayc said. He turned to Dita. "You can see that in his music, can't you, my dear? I mean," he added to Da without waiting for her to respond, "you could see it better if you were a solo artist, of course, or if you had a band that was more in the background."

"How do you mean?" Da asked.

Rayc shrugged. "Today your striving was a little . . . obscured by all that was going on in the music and on the stage. Each of the musicians in Losing the Rope is so different. I can see what you say about this personal questing with music, but I find it hard to equate that with being in a band, and with this band in particular."

Da frowned. "I think Losing the Rope has an energy that comes from our being individuals as well as from our unity, and from our having a respect for one another."

Rayc made a self-deprecating gesture. "I am only a man who takes an interest. But when I see you onstage, Macoll, I see a band built like scaffolding around a soloist with a vision that gets a little muddied. In any cae, I enjoyed the performance today, and the organizers were very pleased." He laughed that gorgeous welling chuckle. Dita gave him a radiant, strangely avid smile, and Rayc lifted a tailored cuff and looked at his watch. "We'd better get moving, my dear. We have a reception to go to. Thanks for the coffee and the chat, Macoll. Once again it has been edifying."

Da got up. "Well, thanks again for suggesting us for the charity function and, of course, for the Urban Dingo gig. I had no idea that it was your doing until you told me."

They shook hands, and I was aware again of the way they both affected the air around them. I tried to figure out the difference in the effects, but the distortion was too hard to see clearly. Then I remembered how clamping had enabled me to hear the disembodied whispering more clearly, and I wondered if it might not do the same for the distorting air. I tried it, and the sound of Da's voice saying goodbye faded along with the color in the room. The whispering grew louder, but my attention was riveted on the distortions in the air around both Da and Aaron Rayc, which now showed quite clearly. Around Da, the air bent outward, as if he was emanating something; but around Aaron Rayc it bent just as strongly inward, as if he were sucking something toward him.

It was as if they were exact opposites.

I let my senses go back to normal and watched Dita insinuate herself off the chair like she'd taken a course in it. Da went out to their car to see them off, and I gathered my wits and pulled the phone book toward me.

It took me less than a minute to learn that there was a Shaletown Elementary and a Shaletown High School in Shaletown, but no private school with *Shale* in the name. In fact, there was no private school in Shaletown at all, so far as I could tell. I was pretty disappointed, but I wrote down the number for Shaletown High just in case.

Da came back in. "That is an interesting man, but he has some pretty strange ideas about what it means to be a creator of anything."

"Probably because he's not," I said.

Da looked surprised. "That's true. I suppose his ideas are quite legitimate, from the point of view of a manager."

"Except he's not that either. He just—"

"Takes an interest," Da said. He was smiling, but he still had a furrow between his brows as if something Aaron Rayc had said had gotten under his skin. He washed some dishes absently. "I guess we're lucky that he takes an interest, since it turns out the gig with Urban Dingo was his doing. He said he had heard 'Song for Aya' and it had impressed him enough to recommend me. He doesn't realize that the band is as much a part of the creation of that song as I am. But I'm a bit puzzled about where he would have heard it after all this time, since it's never been recorded."

"Someone made a pirate recording, maybe. Da, what do you know about Dita?" I asked.

He slanted me a look of amusement. "I should think all there is to know about Dita Rayc is pretty obvious."

I nodded. "But what does she do? Is she a model? Because she looked sort of familiar to me."

He shrugged. "She shops. Her words," he added dryly. Da threw the tea towel aside and went out, saying he had a new student arriving any minute.

I finished drying the dishes and was wiping down the table when the student arrived. I showed him the path to the shed-studio and went back to the kitchen just as Mum came in with her hair all wrapped up in a towel. She was dressed in her painting clothes, but Luke was dressed for bed in his flannel bunny suit. Mum gave me a vague fond smile and set about making a fresh pot of green tea to take up to her studio, Luke tucked into her hip gurgling sleepily.

I wished I could have talked to her about Serenity, but

Mum had never been the one we talked to about our problems. She was always too preoccupied by whatever it was that kept her painting. Mesmerized by her muse, Mirandah said. Mostly I didn't mind. I was even kind of proud to have such an unusual and talented mother. But just occasionally, I wished she was more normal.

Mum drifted out carrying tray and baby with effortless grace, her expression one of dreamy absorption. I had the feeling that if Rayc and his wife were there, she wouldn't even have noticed them.

* * *

The next afternoon Gilly and I were paired up in science, sorting bones and trying to see how they connected.

"Are these real?" Gilly wondered.

"I hope not," I said.

"I don't mind if they are," Gilly went on. "I just like knowing what is real and what's not real."

I couldn't help making some stupid reference to the horror movies, which led her to do the same, and we were quietly laughing when Mr. Stravin's voice snapped across the room like a whip crack.

"Miss Rountree, I assume you have made some astounding discovery," he said icily. "Perhaps you would inform the rest of the class of your amazing breakthrough."

"I'm sorry, Mr. Stravin," Gilly muttered.

* * *

"Crusty old grump," I said when we were dismissed for lunch.

"He's not really," Gilly said. "It's just that he cares about science, and it must be frustrating for him to be here teaching kids who don't pay attention."

"But you *do* pay attention," I protested.

"That's why he was mad, don't you see? He trusts me to take science seriously and he feels I let him down."

I looked at her in wonder. "Gilly, you ought to have a halo. Do you mind if we sit in the library study room for lunch?"

"What else?" she asked. "I know you're not an outdoor person."

I told her that I was only an indoor person when there were wild animals outside. I had meant it as a lame kind of joke, but she looked serious. "So who's the beast we're hiding from? Harlen?" I stared at her, and she said, "It's funny, when he was leaving on the bus yesterday after he'd talked to you, I saw him looking out the window and watching you go into the school. He looked . . . I don't know. Like a cat watching a mouse. Not the way a guy in love ought to look. You should tell him you're not interested."

"I don't want to make him mad."

"You're scared of him," Gilly said in disbelief. I shrugged, wishing I had said nothing. Gilly went on slowly, "I suppose you feel there's something wrong about Harlen just the same way you sensed that Sylvia Yarrow was angry at herself?"

I said a bit defiantly, "Don't you ever get feelings about people?"

Gilly was quiet for a bit. Then she said, "I found out something about Sylvia that might explain why she's so angry."

"What?" I asked curiously.

"Her father had an affair, and Sylvia discovered them together. She told her mother and there was this big fight and her parents split up. Then her mother had a nervous breakdown, so Sylvia has to live with her father and his new girlfriend."

"How horrible," I said. "No wonder she smells of anger."

"Smells of anger?"

"I mean . . . I mean, she seems so angry."

Gilly gave me a funny look, and I cursed my carelessness. I liked Gilly and trusted her, but I didn't want her to change the way she acted toward me. Wasn't that the whole reason I had decided to keep my extended senses secret? To distract her, I told her about bumping into Harrison, and before I knew it I had also told her about Serenity and my feeling that there was something wrong with her. Too late, I realized that I had brought us full circle back to my mysterious ability to feel things about people. But fortunately, Gilly was concentrating on the subject. Like Harrison, she took my concern more seriously than I expected. I told her half-shyly that he had offered to follow Serenity to see what she did on Monday night.

"It seems kind of extreme. But if Harrison thinks it's a good idea . . . ," she said doubtfully.

"I hardly know him, but I trust him," I said.

"It's because he has integrity," Gilly answered. "It's the same with Sarry and Raoul. Whenever I have any kind of moral dilemma, I try to think what they would do. Sarry with her offbeat way of seeing life, Raoul with his honesty, and Harrison with his intelligence."

Integrity. I thought what a beautiful word it was; but people didn't use it much anymore. Yet it fitted all of them—Gilly as much as the other three. "They're lucky to have you, too," I said stoutly.

Gilly hugged me.

"Am I interrupting anything?" Harlen was standing in the doorway smiling, and I suddenly realized how much I disliked his perfect, ever-present smile.

"I was just congratulating Alyzon on doing so well on her tests," Gilly said too brightly.

"Well, she's a smart girl," Harlen said. "Why shouldn't she do well?"

"Exactly what I was saying," Gilly said.

"So why don't you make like the west wind and blow?"

"Oh, I'd love to, Harlen, but we're supposed to help Mr. Stravin with setting up an experiment," Gilly said. "We should be there now, because he wants it ready for when his next class begins."

Harlen's smile did not falter. "All right, I'll be waiting at the front gate for you after school, Alyzon." We watched him walk back across the library through the windows of the study room.

"Hell on wheels," Gilly said when he had gone out of

sight. She looked at me and her face changed. "You're shaking, Alyzon."

I couldn't help it. I started to cry. Gilly made a soundless exclamation and gathered me into her arms. "Don't worry," she said. "I'll figure something out."

19

Harlen's charming smile did not slip when he saw Gilly glued to my side as we came out of the school gates. "What are you two, Siamese twins?" he asked lightly.

"I know it's a pain," Gilly said in a friendly dithery voice. "I'm really sorry to be a gooseberry like this, Harlen, but Alyzon's coming home to my place for dinner tonight. You left so fast at lunchtime that we didn't have a chance to say. I'll just read my book over here while you two talk. Don't mind me."

She sat on the front fence and opened a book and pretended to read.

Harlen stepped closer, still smiling, and took hold of my arm. His fingers dug through the cloth, seeming sharper than fingers ought to feel. *Like claws,* some crazy bit of me thought.

"So when are we going out?" he asked.

"I . . . it depends on . . ."

"On what? Your baby brother? Your father? Her?" He nodded toward Gilly. "Do you have a mind of your own, Alyzon?"

"I . . . Of course I do," I said indignantly. "I just don't get why you're so angry."

For a moment Harlen's smile vanished, and I realized with a shock that I had never seen him without it. He looked younger and oddly vacant. Then he was smiling again. "I guess I'm frustrated. You say you'd like to go out, but somehow it never happens. How about us setting a date for a real date?"

Be careful, my danger sense whispered, and I remembered Mrs. Barker telling me it would be better not to humiliate Harlen. There was nothing to do but nod.

"So when?" Harlen asked with just a flick of mockery.

"I . . . could meet you on Saturday afternoon," I said, reasoning that I could arrange something afterward to keep the meeting short.

"Where?" Harlen asked swiftly.

"The coffee shop in Eastland Mall? The Quick Brown Fox. One o'clock?" Harlen nodded easily and let go of my arm. As he walked away, he glanced over at Gilly, and maybe it was my imagination, but I thought I saw triumph in his eyes.

"See?" Gilly said when he was out of earshot. She looked so pleased I didn't have the heart to tell her I had been forced to agree to a date. Gilly hooked her arm through mine. "Come on. My grandmother will be wondering where we are."

"What?"

She grinned. "I figured it better have the ring of truth when I told Harlen you were coming home with me, so I called my grandmother. You can OK it with your parents from there. You said they were pretty easygoing."

So I went to Gilly's place for dinner. We were driven

there in an expensive, sober black car by a chauffeur called Samuel.

"It's very short notice," her grandmother said. After we arrived, Gilly had brought me to where the old woman had been sitting and reading in a large, beautifully furnished drawing room right inside the front door. Her smile had more politeness than warmth. "We are only having a tuna casserole and salad, and Gilly mentioned you're a vegetarian."

"Salad will be fine," I said, encouraged by the fact that, despite her unfriendly manner, the old woman smelled of ripe blackberries and rosemary.

Gilly was no less stiff than her grandmother, and it took some time and some subtle smelling and watching to figure out that she believed her grandmother kept her only because of a sense of duty. For her part, Mrs. Rountree thought Gilly resented being abandoned to the care of an old woman. It surprised me that two such smart people could have got one another so terribly wrong.

When we went upstairs to do our homework before dinner, I saw that the house was enormous and perfectly ordered, room after room filled with beautifully polished antique furniture. What stopped it from looking like a house in a magazine were the worn but gorgeous rugs on the timber floors, and all sorts of unusual things set about in every room: a strange little saddle chair, statues that looked African, beautiful old tapestries, ceramic bowls, and enormous but dented pewter jugs. There were also paintings, most of them abstracts, which surprised me, hanging amid family portraits.

Gilly whispered with a grimace that the subjects of the portraits were Rountrees and that explained their sour faces.

As we came up the stairs, Gilly pointed out a picture of her mother and father on the day they had married. They were definitely Beautiful People, and I wondered why Gilly's father had left. I thought of my own family, rich in love and poor in money, and knew where I'd rather be.

Still, wealth definitely had its compensations. Gilly's room had an en suite bathroom and a walk-in wardrobe that was so full it was like a dress shop. There were also shelves of toys and ornaments from around the world. Gilly said bluntly that it was all consolation from her globe-trotting mother. She showed me a pile of fancy clothes still in wrappers and said her mother had bought them on her last trip to Paris.

"They're a size too small. I guess it's been a while since she looked at me," she added with bitter humor.

"Your gran seems OK," I said.

"She does her duty."

"Are you sure that's all it is?"

Gilly didn't answer. She was pulling out drawers full of CDs. I could see she was upset, and so I let her play me the music she liked and we spent an hour trying out dance steps. We finally turned on some softer music and did our homework. We had just finished and Gilly was beginning to expound her theory that Harlen was pursuing me precisely because I didn't want him, when a maid came to tell us that the cook wanted us down for dinner. I couldn't believe Gilly lived in a house where there was a maid and a cook and a chauffeur.

"I didn't think people had servants anymore," I whispered as we followed the maid to the dining room.

"My grandmother calls them her staff," Gilly whispered back. "She says she's old and rich and why shouldn't she employ people to help her when there are so many desperate for work."

My da would have had a lot to say about people who had other people as servants, but there was a leafy smell that flowed between the old lady and all of her staff that seemed to indicate affection and mutual respect. Certainly nobody smelled of resentment or envy or even of irritation. It was a good lesson not to generalize principles.

We sat at an ancient timber table long enough for us and all of the Rountree ancestors to eat with their elbows out. There was a red ceramic bowl in the center filled with flowers and tiny floating candles, the reflections of which gleamed softly on the water and on the old, very beautiful silver cutlery.

"It looks lovely," I said.

Mrs. Rountree looked pleased. "I sometimes think I shouldn't mind eating bread and water, as long as I was eating off nice china and there were flowers and candlelight."

The room had begun to fill up with real scents of flowers and candle wax, which perfectly blended with the old lady's smells of rosemary, blackberries, and peaches. I noticed Gilly watching her grandmother with faint puzzlement and tried to gently will the old woman to go on talking, guessing that her granddaughter did not often see this side of her. I felt her desire to be closer to Gilly, but she had no idea how to go about it, and I reasoned that my willing her to talk was only helping her to do what she wanted anyway.

"There are so many sad and ugly things in the world that I feel I must try to counterbalance them with whatever beauty I can produce," she said. "Setting a pretty table in a world of pain might seem callous, given that people are starving and living in dreadful disease and poverty. But in trying to create islands of beauty and peace, I feel I am honoring the dreams of the world."

"That's a good philosophy," I said sincerely.

Mrs. Rountree flushed a delicate pink. "We all have strengths and weaknesses, but we must do what we can with what we have to make the world a better place."

"My da says we have to live by our standards and beliefs no matter what other people do in the world or even to us. Otherwise we're living by their standards," I said.

She smiled. "It is pleasing to hear the wisdom of a father being espoused by his children. I think there are more and more people in the world who seem completely bereft of conscience or any idea of right or wrong."

"I think that's because people are spending less time thinking about the things they do," Gilly said. Her cheeks were pink, and her sea smell was very strong.

Gilly's grandmother sighed and said, "Everything moves faster and faster, and sometimes I feel just so exhausted with all the running here and there, buying this and that. I want things to slow down. I want there to be time to dawdle and time to dream and, especially, time to think."

Gilly sat forward excitedly. "Thinking is out of fashion," she said. "No one bothers making up their own mind. They can let magazines and talk-show hosts do it for them."

Without warning, Gilly's gran started to laugh.

"What is it?" Gilly asked, sounding offended.

"It's you two, and me," Mrs. Rountree said, giggling like a girl. "I sat around with my friends talking about saving the world when I was your age, and now here I am still at it. It seems I'll never learn."

Gilly laughed, too, then she said, "Isn't it better to spend your whole life trying to improve the world than to give up on it?"

"Absolutely," her gran said fervently. "To try when there is little hope is a beautiful kind of foolishness." They smiled shyly at each other, and I thought how strange it was that in a matter of a few days, I had heard two separate conversations about changing the world. Maybe all over the world, people were having those sorts of thoughts and conversations.

On my way home later I sat alone on the plush leather seat looking at the back of Samuel's head and feeling good. Whatever walls stood between Gilly and her gran had been undermined by our unexpected dinner, and I was gratified to think I had played a part in bringing them together. Gilly admired integrity, and there was no doubt the old woman had it.

I was beginning to nod off when the car pulled up to my house. Samuel insisted on walking me to the front door, claiming that it was at Mrs. Rountree's request. "She's an old-fashioned lady," he said with a grin.

"You like her, don't you?" I asked.

"Very much," he said.

Making my way around to the kitchen door, I almost fell over Wombat, who materialized out of the shadows the way cats do. I stopped to pat him and make a fuss over him, because he had vanished after our "conversation." I thought he might snub me, but he pushed his head against me, marking me affectionately with the scent glands under his chin.

"Hello to you, too," I said.

I went to the back door with him weaving in and around my legs, almost tripping me up, and it occurred to me I might be the first person to learn why cats did that. I opened the door and was startled to find Aaron Rayc and Da seated at the kitchen table again, Da halfway through some story about a musician. Neither of them noticed my entrance, and I had the queer urge to back out, but Wombat pushed impatiently past my legs, insisting on being fed. I stepped inside and closed the door.

Only then did I see Dita Rayc sitting a little apart from them. This time she wore a blue velvet dress and matching cape and her hair was drawn into a complex braid at the back of her head. She was fingering a huge sapphire hanging from one earlobe, and my heart gave a little start because she was watching me, her mouth shaped into a wide frosted pink bow.

"Hello, Alyzon," she greeted me in her husky, confiding voice. I disliked the way she said my name, but I disliked her cement-dust and overripe-banana smell more. I could have clamped my senses or moved out of range, but increasingly I felt that stopping myself from smelling bad things was like an ostrich sticking its head in the sand. If I could smell something bad, then the badness was there, and I had better not ignore it.

I got out a tin of cat food and dished it onto a saucer as Wombat wove around my legs, purring and offering his approval and encouragement in scents that communicated their meaning as clearly as words.

"Hello, love," Da said at last. "How was dinner with Gilly's grandmother?"

"I . . . It was great, but I don't want to interrupt. . . ."

Da shook his head. "You're not interrupting. Aaron and Dita just dropped in on their way somewhere else."

"I am here so often lately you must feel I am wanting to be part of the family, Alyzon." The white-haired entrepreneur laughed his beautiful laugh. "But actually, I came to persuade your father to do another gig for me."

"What kind of gig?" I bent down to pick up Wombat so I didn't have to look at Rayc, because his lack of an essence smell made me feel uneasy.

"Another charity benefit," Da answered.

Wombat struggled in my arms and gave off an annoyed smell. *I want to eat more,* his scent told me. I scratched under his chin, and after a brief grumble he succumbed to pleasure and began to purr. I looked back at Aaron Rayc and saw his eyes were on Da again, the pupils huge as if he were looking into darkness rather than light. A chill ran down my spine, and maybe I gave off a scent because Wombat stopped purring.

"Are you all right?" Da asked me. "You look a bit pale."

"I . . . I'm just tired," I said. "I'd better go to bed. Don't sign any contract until you read the fine print," I added lightly, as if it were a joke, but I willed a mountain of caution at Da.

I let Wombat down and bade them all good night, interested to note that Wombat gave Dita a wide berth curving back to his food bowl. Later I would ask him why he had done that, although I suspected I already knew the answer. He could smell her, just as I could, and he didn't like the smell.

What had happened in the kitchen filled me with an aimless urgency, and suddenly I could not face having to see Harlen at school the next day. I had to know what made him tick. I decided I would go to Shaletown High the next day, and hope that the rumor that Harlen had gone to a private school was just that—a rumor.

When I finally slept, I dreamed again that I was a wolf, sitting on a wide stone sill in a half-crumbled stone wall, looking over the ruined city. The air was thick with scents, but my wolf nose separated them easily; spoiled milk, rotten meat, and the smell of wet cement dust and banana.

* * *

The following morning, I called Gilly and told her that I had a routine doctor's appointment in Remington. I didn't want to tell her the truth, in case Harlen asked about me. Somehow, I didn't think she would be a good liar.

"So dinner at your place is off?" she asked, sounding disappointed.

"No, it's still on. I'll get off the train at the stop near your place and get a lift home when Da picks you up. Why don't you come straight from school and meet me at the station?"

"Your da isn't driving you to Remington?"

"He has a rehearsal," I invented quickly, then said goodbye because someone was knocking at the front door.

It was Rhona Wojcek, and after letting her in, I escaped upstairs, ostensibly to get ready for school. I emptied my piggybank for the train fare, tipped the schoolbooks from my backpack into the bottom of my closet, then packed a light coat and some other things. Then I did my hair and put on my uniform. By the time I got downstairs again, Da and a sleepy-looking Mum were up listening to Rhona talk about reorganizing the exhibition that had been put off. She had found a new gallery that would be perfect, and a new approach.

Rhona gave me a wary look, as if she expected me to suddenly throw a fit and fall to the ground frothing at the mouth just to spoil another show opening. She always took things personally. If a bus was in her way, she felt like the bus driver had stopped there to spite her. She left as soon as she had secured Mum's agreement, refusing coffee or tea.

While I ate breakfast, Da started to tell Mum about Aaron Rayc's offer the previous night. My ears pricked up.

"Don't you want to do it?" Mum asked, in that way she has of seeming to hear things that are left unsaid better than the things that are said aloud.

Da ran his hands through his hair and sighed. "The trouble is that it's just me he wants. He says the whole band is too big for the venue and the occasion, but I just feel it's not fair to the others. I mean, the songs I play are Losing the Rope's songs, even though I write most of them."

Mum spread her hands like two butterfly wings. "Ask Neil."

"Oh, Zambia. He'll say I should do it. They all will," Da said, but Mum was no longer listening. You could see it in the way she had turned her face from Da's to the table, where an ant was excavating a pile of crumbs. It was running all around the edges and waving its feelers frantically as if it were sending out a semaphore signal to other ants.

I looked up and saw that Da had stopped talking and was watching Mum with a combination of longing and, strangely, pity.

 20

Getting off the train in Shaletown, I felt that it must be obvious to anyone that I was skipping school, even though I was wearing my uniform and had a clipboard clutched to my chest.

I didn't know exactly where the station was in relation to anything else, because Da had always driven us there in the past. But I had picked up a map of Shaletown at the station, and once I'd found a quiet place away from the streams of people, I unfolded it and studied it. Shaletown High was about twelve blocks from the station. It looked simple, but I set off with trepidation, because I am a genuine map idiot and I couldn't believe that my enhanced senses would have changed that.

I was right. Somehow I got turned around twice, and both times it took me ages to find my way back to the right road. The day, which had started out gray and dreary, grew steadily brighter and warmer until I ended up having to carry my blazer. By the time I got to the school, I had my sweater off as well, but I smoothed my hair and put the blazer back on before I entered the yard. The neater I looked, the less likely that I would be stopped and questioned by a teacher. I wasn't worried about having the wrong uniform, because there were often kids at our school in different uniforms, either new arrivals or visitors.

Because of my woeful navigational skills, I had arrived later than I intended, and the recess bell was ringing. I gave up my immediate plan of finding a toilet and headed for the door where kids were spilling out into the yard. I calculated that I probably had fifteen or twenty minutes of recess in which to find out if Harlen had attended the school, and why he had left.

A group of girls looked to be my age, but I dismissed the idea of approaching them. They were a flock of golden-haired beauties with snooty expressions and, in my experience, exactly the kind to sneer at newcomers or outsiders and enjoy giving them misinformation. I wandered around the side of the building into a big courtyard in the middle of the school. Some of it was marked into a soccer field, and there were a few people watching a game.

I studied the watchers and ended up settling on two plump girls sitting together on a bench. They both glanced at me as I approached, and I did a double take because they were identical twins.

"Hi," I said brightly. "I was just wondering if someone I know used to go here. His name is Harlen Sanderson."

They exchanged a look, as if deciding who would speak, then the one on the left said, "I don't know any Harlen. What year was he in?" I told her, and she shrugged. "Maybe you should ask Glad."

"Glad?" I echoed.

They both pointed to a tall, fit girl with spectacles who was dribbling the ball along the field. She moved beautifully as she went for a goal, and I drew in a breath of pleasure because it was such a long shot, and yet she managed it. I found myself exchanging a smile with the two girls, who suddenly looked more friendly. "She's good, isn't she?" said the one who had not yet spoken, sounding exactly like the one who had.

I nodded. "That's Glad?" I turned back to study the girl, marveling at the names some kids got.

The bell for the end of recess rang, and the two girls dashed off. I waited until the older girl was leaving the field, then fell in beside her and asked my question again.

She said at once and decisively that he had never attended the school. "I run the school magazine, see?" She shot me a bright glance and saw that I didn't see. "Look, our mag comes out biweekly, and we always feature a few students each issue. We publish a photo of them and a mini interview—their thoughts, dreams, et cetera. A lot of rot, most of them talk, but still. If there had been a Harlen Sanderson here, I'd know because by the end of a year we've done everyone. But if you want to double-check, they have back copies in the library. *The Roving Eye,* it's called."

I didn't need my extended senses to know that Glad was not the type to have made a mistake. Having come so far, though, I was determined to be sure that Harlen had not gone to Shaletown High. It wasn't hard to locate the library, but I was immediately stopped by a librarian demanding to know what I thought I was doing. She had restless eyes and smelled like burnt potatoes, so I obeyed my instincts and launched into a dull, slow explanation of a project I needed to research before she had the chance to ask who had sent me. It worked. She was one of those quick, impatient people who couldn't bear to dally for more than a second on anything. Soon I was safely between the magazine racks.

It was easy to find *The Roving Eye*. I checked the contents pages for the first half of the year in which Harlen would have been there. By the time I had reached March, I was beginning to accept that he had not been to the school, but I went right through to June. Then I went back and checked the whole of the previous year. No Harlen.

I left the school feeling flat and disheartened. The whole trip had been a waste of time.

I checked the map to be sure I was heading the right way back to the station, and my eye fell on the yellow square marked Detention Center. There was easily time enough to visit it and still get the train I needed. In fact, I had to kill some time. I checked the map again, worked out a route, and set off.

* * *

The high, dingy yellow wall that surrounded the block of buildings that were Shaletown Detention Center looked even more prison-like than it had when Aya and her family had been inside. I wondered how any government could justify locking little kids and even babies in such a place. Had any of those politicians who approved it ever come to look at it? Had they tried to imagine how it would be if they or their families had to stay indefinitely in such a place? Not so long ago I had heard a female politician arguing that the women and children ought to be let out to live with volunteers while the men remained in a detention center. Even that seemed horrible to me. How would that politician have felt if it was her husband locked up while she was free; how would her children feel to be without their father for so long?

"You wonder how anyone could build something so ugly," said an old woman who had come quietly to stand beside me. She wore a rosette that announced she was a protester.

A fleeting but painfully vivid memory of Aya came to me; her satin brown hands clasped together in her lap in the brightly lit, white-painted visiting room; her huge dark eyes that had never stopped pleading. "Maybe it just reflects the ugliness of the minds of the people who dreamed it up," I said savagely.

"Do you know someone in there?" the old woman asked gently.

"I used to know a girl. She and her family were refused asylum. They . . . they were sent back." All of a sudden tears were spilling down my cheeks.

"Oh my dear, come and sit down," the old woman said. "I've got some tea in a thermos."

I went with her, unable to stop crying. Memories of Aya

were all mixed up with my disappointment about the whole long trip to Shaletown being a total waste; I would have to go back to school and be pursued by Harlen again without any idea of why my senses regarded him as a danger. By the time I managed to get myself under control, my face felt swollen and my eyes were puffy and itchy.

I felt vaguely embarrassed by my outburst, but aside from the old woman, who had introduced herself as Rose Cobb, the only other person at the protest tent was a huge, muscular young man with a strangely beautiful face and a halo-like mass of soft golden curls. He stared at me fixedly, and I might have felt uneasy except for his smell, which was a combination of baby shampoo and toffee and something that reminded me a lot of Luke's smell.

The old woman introduced him as Davey. I was afraid he would want to shake my hand, but he just stared at me even harder, as if he were trying to look through my face and into my head. Then he gave a funny bending nod that seemed a bit like a bow and announced that someone called Simon had said he should go home. Watching him lumber away, I realized he was slow-witted. Rose Cobb said gently that he lived close by in a trailer on the industrial park. "He's a lovely boy," she added.

I drank the tea she poured and told her my name as I sat down gingerly on one of the little fold-up stools. "It's ages since I came here last. I didn't realize I would feel so . . . angry."

Rose Cobb sighed. "Anger is a powerful force. I ought to

know, because I spent most of my life being ruled by it. I was angry at my parents for bringing me to this country, angry at my friends for not loving me as I thought I should be loved. Angry at my husband for not being what I thought he should be and at my children for preferring their own lives to mine. The people here taught me about the futility of anger."

"The refugees?" I asked.

She shook her head. "The protesters. I live across the road, you see. I'd see the protesters coming with their placards and petitions, and I would glare at them through my curtains—a bunch of scruffy, drug-taking hippies and welfare cheats, I used to think. Max would say they were just people protesting about something that troubled them. I daresay I had some smart, nasty answer for him. The truth was that I didn't understand why they were there, because I didn't think of refugees as people."

"So what happened?"

She sighed. "Max died. I was angry at him over that, too. A month or so after his funeral, I was sitting here feeling angry about everything, as usual, and all that lifetime of rage seemed to boil up in me and turn me into a lightning bolt that needed earthing. So I went across the road to give those hippies the edge of my tongue." She laughed. "Oh, how righteous I felt. But before I could say a word, some young mother pushed her baby into my hands and asked if I wouldn't mind holding him because she had to pour the tea. She'd mistaken me for one of them, and I was so taken aback that I just . . . well, I held the baby." She laughed. "It was winter and very cold.

The baby was sneezing and sniffing, and I was struck by how insubstantial he was. It made me think of my own children. I felt such a tenderness for them in that moment that it was like a little earthquake inside me. It was as if I hadn't understood how much I had loved them until that second." She laughed again. "When the mother took her baby back, she handed me a mug of tea. Then one of the young men asked the woman with the baby about a letter she'd received from someone she visited in the center. She got it out and read from it. It was so . . . well, I am sure you had letters from your friend, so you know. I found myself for the first time imagining how it must feel to have traveled here fleeing famine or drought or political upheaval or persecution, and all at once I understood why a woman with a baby would stand out in the cold to protest. It was because she had the imagination to empathize with the refugees.

"I have heard so many stories since then, many far worse than that of the person who wrote that letter, but it is that one I remember best because it broke down the wall of my ignorance and raked open my heart." She shook her head with a prim little tightening of her mouth.

"Doesn't it make you angry, though?" I nodded toward the detention center. "Doesn't that?"

Rose Cobb studied the yellow wall for a moment. "A lot of volunteers do feel angry to start with. Being powerless to make the authorities see or care fills them with rage and frustration and makes them want to smash something just to get someone to listen. Maybe it is because of a lifetime of anger that I know there is no good in anger, least of all for the person who feels it. Anger is a sickness that afflicts anything and anyone it touches."

"You think of anger as a sickness?" I asked, thinking of Serenity.

"I think it is a sickness of the soul," the old woman said. I was disappointed, and maybe she saw it, for she said, "I'm not talking about religion, Alyzon. When I say soul, I mean no more than your essence."

I shivered, because I had got into the habit of thinking I could smell people's essences, but it seemed too prideful and eerie to think I could smell people's souls.

Rose Cobb sighed. "Poor Max. He deserved a better wife than he had. I would change that if I could. Go back and be a kinder and more compassionate partner. But that's the one thing you can't do, is it? You can only go forward and be the best person you can."

"I'm sure he loved you," I said.

"Oh, he did, but that was more due to his sweet nature than mine." She poured herself another half cup of tea and offered me more, but I remembered that I had a train to catch. Before I left, Rose Cobb pointed out her house, telling me to drop in if I came back to visit any of the refugees.

* * *

Gilly was waiting for me at the station, and I asked worriedly if she'd mentioned my doctor's appointment to her gran. She shook her head and, seeing my relief, asked why.

I took a deep breath. "Because I didn't go to Remington

and there was no doctor's appointment. I didn't tell you the truth this morning because I didn't want you to have to lie if Harlen asked where I was."

"But . . . where did you go, then?"

I told her about going to the detention center in Shaletown and about meeting Rose Cobb, which led into the story of Aya and my belief that whatever was wrong with Serenity stemmed from what had happened to Aya and her family. As I hoped, Gilly jumped to the conclusion that visiting the detention center had been the only reason I'd gone to Shaletown.

Then she said, "Harlen did ask about you. He said you hadn't mentioned any doctor's appointment to him, and I asked why you should have." She frowned. "It's weird how possessive he acts about you." She hesitated, then she added, "He said he had a date this weekend with you."

"He sort of cornered me," I said wearily. "I made it for the middle of Saturday in Eastland Mall."

"I don't get it," Gilly said. "Why are you so nervous about just telling him straight out that you don't want to go out with him? Oh, I forgot, there was a notice about the holidays." She began to rummage in her bag. After a minute, red-faced and muttering, she gave up, saying she must have left it in her locker. "I am so disorganized! I swear it's my natural state! I keep thinking when I do this or that I will finally be able to get organized, but of course then there is always something else to get in the way."

I grinned sympathetically. "The thing is to tell yourself this is life and chaos is part of it."

"You sound like some sort of wise guru. Maybe that's what you're gonna be when you grow up."

I grinned. "All right, so I was raving on."

"Yeah, but in a good way," Gilly said, and we both laughed.

"That was great last night when you came to dinner," she went on. "You had this amazing effect on my grandmother. Usually she is so stuffy and disapproving."

"I didn't have an effect," I said. "We did. The three of us. I think that the dynamics between the three of us produced the right chemistry for her to talk."

"Yeah, but it has been the same ever since." Gilly shook her head. "I mean, we actually talked over breakfast this morning and . . . she made me laugh!"

"She made me laugh, too," I said. "Spooky."

"Idiot!" Gilly retorted.

* * *

Mrs. Rountree and Da were eating sponge cake and drinking tea in a pretty little conservatory I had not seen the night before.

"Hello, Alyzon," Da said. Then he held out his hand to Gilly. "We meet again, Gilly. I'm not sure if I mentioned how much I enjoyed your playing the other night. You have a fine technique."

Gilly reddened with pleasure.

"It is lovely to see you again, Alyzon," her grandmother told me warmly. "Macoll has been telling me that your mother is a painter." I stifled a grin to see that her cheeks were pink. Da has visible swoon range.

* * *

"Oh, Da! You kissed her hand!" I laughed when we were driving off down the road. "That's so old-fashioned!"

"Millicent Rountree is an old-fashioned type of lady," Da said with dignity. "And she liked it."

"She loved it," Gilly said, and flushed scarlet when she heard the wistfulness in her voice. That broke me up, and I laughed until Gilly forgot to be mortified and elbowed me hard. Da pretended not to notice any of this, and only when we had quieted down did he look sideways and ask how school had gone. Which wiped the smile right off my face.

Gilly told him about her own day, making it sound as if she was speaking for both of us and without her ever actually uttering a single lie. It was pretty impressive, and I told her so when we got home and went upstairs to my room.

"I'm not sure I want to be congratulated for being a good liar," Gilly said primly as we came through the door, then she saw Serenity's half of the room and her mouth fell open.

"Serenity's side of the bedroom," I said.

Gilly gazed about, then finally she said, "I see now why you're so worried about her. This is . . . a bit much, isn't it? You really think that business in Shaletown is behind this?"

"I don't know, but . . ." I stopped because Jesse was yelling for us to come and eat.

We had a great dinner, with Da telling jokes and stories about gigs, but I saw Gilly watching Serenity speculatively throughout the meal.

21

I slept badly and woke with a blurred memory of a dream that refused to be recalled. I felt depressed and uneasy in the knowledge that I had to meet Harlen Sanderson in Eastland Mall.

On the way downstairs I heard Neil Stone's voice, but the pleasure I felt in anticipation of seeing the big musician faded when I entered the kitchen and saw his face, and Da's.

"Don't be a mug," Neil was saying. "It's money and you need it, man. None of us would stand in the way of that. You've got to eat and take care of your family. Just do it! It's not like you're signing a recording contract."

"But we're a band," Da said.

"So we are, and who says this changes that? Christ, I was playing at my sister's wedding a month ago, and you didn't see me agonizing over leaving you guys out of it."

"She wasn't paying you!" Da protested.

"Well, that's true. Bloody cow." He said this so fondly that Da laughed and suddenly the tension dissolved. "That's more like it," Neil said. "Just take the job, Macoll. Pay some bills and get Jesse the computer he needs."

But they were still talking about the gig when I left twenty minutes later.

* * *

I decided to walk to the mall instead of taking a bus. It was a crisp, bright day, and I set off on a route that would bring me down one of my favorite streets, lined with enormous old cypress trees, their twisted trunks and branches agonized-looking.

I was halfway along it when I spotted Sarry coming out of a shop with an ice-cream cone. She was wearing luridly tie-dyed skintight jeans and a tie-dyed camisole over the top of a lacy T-shirt, and had an enormous flowered shawl wrapped around her shoulders.

"Hi, Alyzon! Isn't it a great day?" she said.

"Blissful," I agreed. "Where are you headed?"

"Going with the flow," Sarry said languidly. "Currents flow all around us, even though we don't see them. If you don't fight them, just, you know, hang loose and relax, they'll sweep you somewhere interesting. Or even somewhere you're supposed to go but you don't know it."

For some reason, her words brought back into focus my elusive dream of the previous night. I had been in the street in front of the detention center. The enormous, simple-minded protester I'd met through Rose Cobb had been with me, but in the dream his eyes had been less sweetly vacant and his golden halo of hair had shone with its own light.

"I can smell the wrongness," he had said. "You can smell it, too, can't you?"

"No," I'd said.

"Yes, you can. You smell it in people. The wrongness is inside them, making them sick and bad." Then he had vanished.

"Are you OK, Alyzon?" Sarry's soft voice broke through the glassy screen of strangeness that the memory had evoked.

Davey, I thought. *Davey was his name.*

I looked at her. "Sarry, do you think a person could visit you in a dream?"

She tipped her head to one side as if studying a painting and said tranquilly, "I think there is this country made up of all the dreams people have when they sleep, and it's constantly changing and reshaping as people wake or dream something different. And if you were . . . what does Harrison call it . . . oh yeah, lucid dreaming. Do you know what that is?"

"When you know you're dreaming?"

"Yeah. So if you were lucid dreaming, you could visit a bit of that country formed by other people's dreams."

It was a strange, lovely idea, although I didn't seriously think that Davey had visited my dreams to tell me he knew I could smell wrongness. Like the dream of Harlen whispering that he knew what was inside me, it was no more than a prod from my subconscious. But what had it been trying to tell me? Something about Harlen and how he smelled? On impulse, I asked Sarry if she thought wrongness could have a smell.

"You mean like an orange gone rotten inside where you can't see it?"

I was struck by a thought. If Harlen did smell like

something rotten, what did it mean if the smell came not from a specific memory, as I had been imagining—but from his essence?

It means his soul *is rotten,* Rose Cobb's voice whispered.

I shivered. "Imagine if you could smell that there was something wrong about a person just like you could smell the rot in an orange." I looked at Sarry and found her staring at me, her eyes wide and frightened. I was shocked to see that she had crushed the ice-cream cone in her grip.

"You can smell it in me?" she whispered. Bewildered but wanting to comfort her, I stopped on the verge of touching her, but, without warning, Sarry caught hold of my hand. Images flashed into my mind: a young ginger-haired man smiling, sliding his arms around a pretty, laughing woman. She smiled flirtatiously, and then her face changed to fright. She turned to me and cried out in a queer muffled voice, *Run and get help. Please!*

The terror in me—Sarry's terror—grew until I felt faint. But the images kept flying through my mind. I saw the man injecting something into the woman's arm. She was struggling and crying out, but he was stronger. She weakened and became passive. The man smiled at me, his face greedy and triumphant.

Then Sarry let me go. She backed up against the window of a salon and clawed at her face. I noticed people inside staring out at us. Shamed and alarmed, I stepped closer to Sarry and, without any warning, she started to scream.

I reeled back as Sarry went on screaming, letting each terrible, long, piercing shriek unwind to a thin, shrill note before she hitched in a raggedy breath and screamed again. After a few seconds, she slumped to her knees, and her screams became grunting, gasping sounds. There were livid bloody scratches down both cheeks where she had raked them with her nails. I had never been more frightened or felt more helpless in my whole life.

"What the hell is going on?" A red-faced man in an apron came out of the salon. "I'll call the police if you two keep this up. Go somewhere else and take your filthy drugs."

I fought to gather my wits. "Sir . . . we didn't . . . my friend is having some sort of fit." I gestured to Sarry and he saw, as I had, that a white froth was beginning to bubble from her mouth. His face changed. "I'll call an ambulance. Try to calm her down and don't let her bite her tongue."

Sarry had hunched forward and began to rock and groan and mutter in between gasping cries. I was afraid to touch her, so I stood where I was, babbling anything I could think of that might calm her down.

After an eternity I heard the sound of an ambulance.

* * *

"We were just talking," I told the medic as he thumbed her eyelids open. She seemed to have fallen into some sort of stupor now and sat trance-like and limp on the pavement.

"Had she taken any drugs?" the other medic asked me. Before I could answer, the first medic said, "Not drugs. Shock."

They both looked at me, and I couldn't think of a thing

to say. The medic with the notepad asked me her last name and the names of her parents, none of which I knew. Admitting this, I seemed to make the two medics deeply suspicious, although of what I couldn't imagine. They took my name and address down but refused to let me ride in the ambulance. They half lifted Sarry to get her in, and her hands flopped down their backs as loosely as the arms of a rag doll.

After the ambulance had driven away, I went to a phone booth and called Da. Then I called Gilly, but the housekeeper said she had gone out with her grandmother. She asked if I wanted to leave a message, but I decided against it. I said in as calm a voice as I could manage that I would call back later.

* * *

At the hospital a nurse told us that Sarry was under sedation but that we could wait and talk to the doctor when he came on his rounds in an hour. They wouldn't let us go in and sit with her because we were not relatives.

Da stopped me when I would have argued with the reception nurse, telling me that she was only doing her job and that we would wait. He went to get us some cold drinks, and that was when I remembered that Harrison had given me his phone number. I dug it out of my wallet, called him, and told him what had happened.

"Oh, hell," Harrison said. "Listen, I'll get a cab down, OK? Can you wait?"

I tried to get the number for her parents, but he just reiterated that he would come, and hung up.

I went back to the waiting room. Da handed me a cold

box of juice. I took it and burst into tears. Da gathered me into his arms and held me. Instead of being overwhelmed by his feelings, I felt only his love for me, as warm and soothing as a hot bath.

"What happened to your friend is not your fault," Da said gently. I heard his words as a warm vibration against my cheek. It felt so safe in his arms, but I knew that if I stayed for a few more moments, his concern would begin to give way to other thoughts and feelings, which would cause me discomfort. So I moved reluctantly out of the circle of his arms, using my need for a tissue as an excuse.

"How do you feel?" Da asked gently.

"I'm OK." I looked up at him, wondering suddenly if I *was* OK. I seemed to have done a lot of crying the past two days.

22

Harrison wanted to know in detail what had happened.

"The man who called the ambulance thought she had taken drugs," I said.

"She doesnae take drugs," Harrison said dismissively. "What were you talking about before she started screaming?"

I told him, and when I got to the bit about the dream, he nodded decisively. "That's it."

"That's *what*?" I asked, feeling irrationally angry.

"The trigger," Harrison said, sympathetic despite my snappy tone. "I guess Gilly might not have mentioned it, but Sarry . . . well, the doctors say she's schizophrenic. They claim the attacks occur because of something that triggers a chemical imbalance that makes her imagine things."

"I'm sure once she is given drugs to correct the imbalance she'll be fine," Da told me.

Harrison frowned, and it was not the frown of a boy but the frown a doctor might give someone who disagreed with his diagnosis. "I've read a lot of literature on schizophrenia, and I've talked on the Internet with some people who suffer from it and people who live with them. Sarry doesnae fit the bill. Even her doctor admits there are anomalies."

"What do you think is wrong with her?" I asked.

"Something bad happened when Sarry was very small, tae do with how her mother died. She believes that whatever it was caused her tae be . . . infected by a sickness. Not a sickness of the body, but a sickness of the spirit that she calls 'wrongness'—a sort of contagious metaphysical corruption." He switched his calm gray gaze to me. "When you asked about people smelling of wrongness, Alyzon, Sarry would have taken that tae mean that you smelled the wrongness in her."

"She said that, but I didn't," I burst out. They both stared at me. "I . . . I mean, that wasn't what I was saying."

"Of course not," Da said. "You were just talking about a dream. Harrison is only saying that what you said made your friend imagine that her sickness was apparent to you, and this set off her attack."

"It's called an episode," Harrison corrected gently, with the same mild authority as before. "But there is something more. You see, Sarry has this sickness she carries under control, but she has tae fight tae keep it that way, so that it cannae infect anyone else. When Alyzon talked of smelling wrongness, Sarry would have believed the wrongness had become active without her being aware of it. Her greatest horror is that she will infect someone else, you see. That is what set off her episode."

"You talk as if you believe she *is* infected," Da said.

Harrison pushed a wedge of straw-colored hair from his forehead. "It's easy for the doctors tae dismiss what Sarry believes as delusional. But it could also be that Sarry's delusion is a genuine perception, just one other people dinnae have."

"Like in the H. G. Wells story 'The Country of the Blind'?" Da said with a strange certainty, and Harrison nodded.

"Exactly. It was seeing how useless conventional treatment with schizophrenia drugs was tae Sarry that made us—me, Gilly, and Raoul—decide tae try simply believing that she had a sickness other people couldnae perceive. It might interest you tae know that since then, Sarry has had far fewer episodes, despite Dr. Austin's insistence that she should be on drugs all the time tae control her episodes."

"Dr. Austin," I murmured, remembering the short-tempered man—and his stink.

"He's Sarry's doctor," Harrison said. "He has been treating her since she was a child. Sarry dislikes him because he insists on medicating her after an episode, which weakens her will and makes it harder tae control the sickness. We dinnae bring her tae the hospital anymore, because after drug treatment she's like a zombie for weeks, sometimes months, until she has wrestled the sickness back intae submission."

"I . . . I didn't know," I whispered, understanding that in calling for an ambulance I had sent her to Dr. Austin. A chill stole through me, because if anyone smelled of wrongness, it was him.

"Alyzon, what happened isnae your fault, and Sarry will

tell you that when she can. But right now the most important thing is tae offer her belief. I'll wait here until she wakes. And Raoul will come and, with luck, we'll be able tae talk tae her before Dr. Austin arrives. If she's calm, we might be able tae insist he give her a smaller dose of drugs." He hesitated. "It might be better if you leave visiting her until another time."

"All right," I said, getting to my feet. My voice sounded jerky.

* * *

On the way home I kept seeing Sarry's horrified face as she had backed away from me, understanding only now that she had not been afraid of me, but of infecting me with the wrongness she believed that she carried. Except it wasn't she who smelled of rottenness.

I stifled a gasp at the realization that I had completely forgotten about meeting Harlen at the mall. There was no chance that he would still be there, even if I had been willing to ask Da to drive me back there, and I couldn't call Harlen to explain because I didn't know his phone number.

I was still worrying about it when I crept into bed an hour later, but I was so tired that I quickly fell asleep and slipped bonelessly into the dream of being a wolf in a dark, crumbling city that smelled of rot. At one point in the dream, I came upon a human: a poor frail, terrified thing she seemed to my wolf senses, and yet I had the overwhelming feeling that it was my job to protect her and her kind. Yet how could I protect her from a sickness of the spirit?

* * *

The first thing I saw when I came downstairs in the morning was a note on the fridge telling me to call Gilly right away.

"I didn't imagine in a million years that Sarry would have an episode when she was alone with you," she said apologetically. "If only one of us had been there with you!"

"Harrison said you all believe she's infected with some sort of sickness."

"I suppose you think we're all mad?" Gilly guessed. "When Harrison said we should try believing her, I was afraid we might be doing her harm by encouraging a delusion. But Raoul was all for it. He says people see him as sick because he's in a wheelchair, even though he's perfectly healthy. He said getting treated as if you are sick makes you *feel* sick, and maybe the only thing wrong with Sarry was that people didn't believe her. It's Raoul that Sarry goes to when the wrongness is getting stronger."

"She stays with him?"

"That wouldn't be allowed. But she spends a lot of her days there, and Raoul drives her home at night."

"He drives?" I said, then wished I hadn't.

Gilly just laughed. "He has a specially made car. It cost a fortune, but he makes a lot of money from his work testing games and building Web sites. It used to amaze me that he would want to drive. That's how he got so hurt. A car accident."

I blinked at the receiver, wondering how much courage it must take for Raoul to get into a car when it had so savaged him. Then I wondered how I could think of a car in the face of what we had been talking about. As if she felt the same, Gilly's voice went serious.

"We're going to see Sarry tonight." A small pause. "Do you want to come?"

"No," I said. Harrison had been right to steer me away from seeing her so soon after what had happened. But I wanted very much to talk to her when it was possible.

After I had put the phone down, I thought about Gilly and the others believing Sarry; choosing to believe that she was the carrier of a contagious spiritual sickness that could not be detected by medical science. What would they say if I told them that, like Sarry, I could perceive things other people could not? Including, perhaps, the very sickness that Sarry carried.

Except I hadn't smelled anything on Sarry, which meant either that her sickness was not what I had smelled on Dr. Austin or Harlen, or that Sarry was not infected.

My reflections were too confused and contradictory, and I knew that the best way to sort out the muddle was to just leave it for a bit. So I managed by a supreme effort of will to immerse myself in homework for almost an hour. But finally thoughts of Harlen and Dr. Austin and Sarry began creeping back in. I gave up trying to concentrate and threw myself into housework. I changed the sheets on my bed, sorted out a pile of dirty laundry, and swept the bedroom.

Finally I decided to take a walk. I had no particular destination in mind, but when I came to a reserve where Jesse, Mirandah, and I used to ride our bikes when we were younger, I went into it, feeling nostalgic.

As I set off down the longest trail, I remembered a game we used to play there. Like all our games, it had grown out of hide-and-seek and involved pretending the wilderness was a maze-like subterranean network of caves through which we were being pursued by bears. For me these were the under-bears that had come creeping out of the cracks in the earth. We could only escape their fangs and claws by being utterly still whenever Jesse, who was always in charge of them, said they were near. I remembered how exquisite the terror had been when occasionally Jesse had decided to become one of the bears and had come lumbering and snarling toward us. We had frozen and tried not to move or react to anything he did as he snuffled and butted at and sometimes even licked us.

I smiled, remembering that, right alongside knowing it was Jesse and wanting to giggle at his antics, I had been genuinely aghast that the bear would rend me and eat me.

It's funny how you can do that as a kid; totally believe something and know at the same time that it isn't real. But maybe it's because a kid's life is full of unknown things and imagined things and real things all blurred together.

The sky had been darkening almost imperceptibly, and all at once it started to rain. I ran, but after a minute I slowed down again, because it wasn't that cold.

By the time I got home, I was soaked to the bone. But I felt good because somewhere on the walk, without ever really thinking about it, I realized that I had made up my mind to tell Gilly and Harrison and Raoul the truth about myself.

23

Mirandah was busy cooking vegetable pastry puffs for dinner, so after I had a hot shower and changed, I came down to help her, and we listened to an interview she'd taped for school. It was a man talking about the AIDS epidemic in Africa and how many people were infected. The figures were shocking, and I found myself imagining a country where half the population was sick and dying. If it was America or Australia or England, it would have been on the news every night, and the whole Western world would be mobilized to help. But because it was Africa, you hardly saw or read anything about it. The man called it a secret epidemic, although it was less a secret, he said bleakly, than something from which the Western world had simply turned their eyes.

When the tape clicked off, we grated vegetables in silence for a bit, then some impulse made me say, "Sometimes people do horrible things for no reason at all. A while back, a journalist told my class about a guy not much older than us who killed his younger brother. He didn't hate him or anything. He just decided to do it, planned it, and did it."

Mirandah stared at me. "He must have had some reason. Or maybe he was crazy."

"That's what the court decided," I said, but I found myself wondering if the guy who had done the murdering had been infected with wrongness. Because if Dr. Austin and Harlen Sanderson were infected by a spiritual sickness that could not be detected by conventional science, why not others as well?

After dinner, I called Gilly, but there was no answer. When I finally got to bed, I didn't dream about Sarry or Harlen, but about Aya being held prisoner inside the detention center. I clambered up the wall, which had grown three times higher but had also developed jutting rocks that could be used as handholds. When I got to the top I stared down incredulously, because inside the walls were not bland concrete block buildings but the ruined city I often dreamed about.

All at once, I was a wolf again. I jumped down and padded along, sniffing at the greasy black cobbles until I caught a horrible smell. Rather than being repelled, I lifted my muzzle and howled in triumph, then I began to follow the fetid spoor. It brought me to a tiny room in the side of a crumbled building, and here I found not Aya, but Serenity, huddled in rags and smeared with unspeakable filth.

"Why are you following me?" she snarled. Only then did I realize that the terrible smell I had been following was coming from her.

* * *

I woke deep in the night to find Mum in the bedroom. I wasn't frightened, because she had a long habit of drifting through our rooms in the night, and more than once I had opened my eyes to find her looking down at me. Somehow her presence almost seemed like an extension of my dream, because she was staring at Serenity.

In the morning I felt tired and headachy but I resisted the temptation to beg a day home sick because if Da called the school, they were bound to mention my absence on Friday. Besides, I wanted to talk to Gilly. I dragged myself out of bed, groaning at the way my bones ached, and carefully faked a sick note from Da for Friday.

But Gilly wasn't in homeroom. I felt depressed, both by her absence and by the knowledge that I would be alone when I finally faced Harlen's wrath. But when he came into English a few minutes after the bell, he didn't even glance at me. He went straight to the back of the class to sit with some of the tougher boys. I heard him laughing and, all at once, my idea that he was infected by a spiritual disease seemed utterly fantastic.

Mrs. Barker thwarted my reluctant plan to confront and apologize to Harlen after class by holding me back to tell me I'd passed my tests.

I couldn't find Harlen at lunchtime, so I went to the office to see if the school knew why Gilly was absent. The woman at the reception desk said no one had called in, and she suggested kindly that Gilly might have caught what I had on Friday. I felt myself flush guiltily.

Afternoon recess came, and I slipped out of school to call Gilly from the pay phone down the road. Standing in the booth, listening to the phone ring, I noticed the clouds clogging the sky were dark. There was also a tense feel to the air that made me wonder if a storm was brewing. I was about to go back to school when it struck me that the ringing of the phone had sounded odd. Besides, wouldn't there be an answering machine if there was no one home?

I dialed again, listened, then called the operator. A man tested Gilly's number and agreed that there was something wrong with the line. He suggested I call back later to check the status. The end-of-recess bell had already rung by the time I got back into the school yard, so I ran to get the books I needed for next period. The locker passage was empty except for Sylvia Yarrow pushing books into her locker and swearing violently.

"Are you OK?" I asked, picking up a notepad she had dropped and holding it out to her.

She gave me an unseeing look as she reached out for it, and some impulse made me shift my hand and make physical contact. Immediately I felt hatred flow through me, thick and greasy-dark as a tide of oil. A nightmarish vision of hands pushing a white cat into a bath of water flashed into my mind—unmistakably Sylvia's hands, because of all the rings she wore.

I gave a cry of horror and jerked my hand away from her.

Sylvia gaped at me, then she turned and fled down the corridor as if all the demons of hell were after her. She had left her locker door hanging open and, as I stood there, some books slid out and crashed to the floor. Shakily, I picked them up and stacked them inside, shutting the door to the locker with trembling hands. Then I got my own bag, knowing I couldn't just go and sit in class after what I had seen.

I left the school, telling myself it couldn't be a real memory I had seen. Sylvia had only been imagining killing the cat. But even to imagine such an awful, cruel thing was unthinkable.

* * *

I'd just made it across the street from school when I heard a familiar voice call my name. I turned, staring in disbelief as Harrison approached. "What are you doing here?" I asked.

His brows lifted. "I'm here tae follow your sister."

"Oh God! You shouldn't have worried about it. Sarry—"

"Would be the first tae say I should do what I promised," Harrison said firmly. His eyes narrowed behind his spectacles. "Are you all right, Alyzon? You look a wee bit strange."

I tried to find something to say, but all I could see was the white cat, struggling and clawing the air, desperate and dying. All at once it seemed that the world I had lived in for fifteen years was an illusion, cracking and breaking away to reveal a strange, dark world in which good-looking young men smelled of rot and girls murdered cats. It was as if the underbears of my childish nightmares had finally escaped.

"No," I heard myself saying in a thin voice. "I'm not OK. Listen, Harrison, it's almost an hour before school gets out, and there's a cafe just a few streets away. Can we go and get a drink? I really need to talk."

"OK," he said equably.

* * *

"So what's up?" he asked. We were sitting at a sticky plastic-covered table with two glasses of orange juice between us. The girl who had served us was cleaning the counter nearest us meticulously, but I doubted she would hear what we were saying because of the humming and wheezing of the drink fridge.

I took a deep breath. "First, tell me about Sarry. Is she OK?"

Harrison said soberly, "She was pretty depressed tae start with. But Dr. Austin is on holiday, and after Raoul pointed out how long it had been since Sarry's last episode, the doctor taking his caseload is willing tae drop the dose."

"Did Sarry say anything about me?"

He nodded, frowning slightly. "She is still convinced you can smell the sickness in her, but Raoul managed tae convince her that, even if you could, it was only because the sickness must be in a stronger phase. He couldnae tell her that she had just misunderstood you when she's half off her head with dope."

I took a deep breath. "At the hospital you said you and the others had decided to believe Sarry was sick even though she had no way of proving it to you. Can you do the same for me? Believe something even though I've no proof of it?"

"I'll try," he said calmly, and there was something in the

222

combination of mildness and firmness that reassured me more than a truckload of words.

I took a sip of the orange juice, which was too sweet, and blinked hard to stop a sudden hot gathering of tears behind my eyes. I wasn't sure why I had the impulse to cry. Maybe it was just shock at having arrived at the moment of telling. I collected myself and told him as concisely as I could about waking after the accident to find my senses had changed. Harrison did not interrupt to ask questions, and he looked intensely interested. But when I told him about my encounter with Dr. Austin and how he had smelled, Harrison's brows climbed into his blond fringe and he said, "Are ye saying Sarry's right and ye can smell wrongness?" His accent was suddenly much thicker.

"I don't know if it is wrongness that I can smell on Dr. Austin," I said slowly. "Sarry didn't say so, did she?"

"Sarry cannae perceive wrongness in anyone but herself," Harrison said. "And she never said anything about *smelling* wrongness until she was talking about you. She always talks about feeling it getting hungry or strong. But what does it mean that Dr. Austin wanted tae drug you both? He cannae be out tae infect Sarry, since she's already infected."

"Is she?" I asked. "Because that's another thing. She doesn't smell like Dr. Austin."

"It could be . . . But wait, are you saying it was just coincidence that you started talking about the smell of wrongness tae Sarry?" Harrison sounded incredulous.

I shrugged. "Is that any weirder than anything else we've been talking about?"

He gave a short laugh, then he glanced at his watch. "Damn, I'll have tae go, but we need tae talk more about this. What happened just now in school, anyway? You looked upset."

I told him about Sylvia.

"You actually had a vision when you touched her?" Harrison asked eagerly.

I nodded. "I can't figure if I was seeing a memory or some kind of wish." I meant to tell what I had seen when Sarry had grabbed me during her attack, but he was getting to his feet.

"I'd better head back tae the school or I'll miss your sister."

"But you believe me," I said uncertainly.

"Of course I believe you," he said. I was so relieved that I felt myself blush. He went to pay, refusing my offer of money. When he came back, I got up and we went out together.

"Did Sarry ever say how she got infected? I mean the actual process?"

Harrison shook his head. "It's like I told you and your da at the hospital. It happened when she was too young tae take it in clearly, but she always connects it with her mother's death. She would have been too young tae resist anything then, so I guess it must take a while before the sickness becomes contagious. From what Sarry said, it seems tae get stronger in cycles, so maybe it is only contagious at certain times." He looked at me, hesitating. "How would you feel about telling Raoul and Gilly?"

"I mean to tell all of you. But speaking of Gilly, you don't happen to know why she didn't come to school today, do you?"

He shook his head again, then told me I had better not come back to the school with him in case Serenity saw us together. I agreed to go another way and we said goodbye. But just as I was about to leave, Harrison stopped me and suggested we meet the next night.

"I can tell you what happens with your sister, and maybe we can talk more about your extended senses."

"That'd be great," I said, meaning it.

24

I cut through backstreets until I came out along the bus route. I could have walked home, but I felt really tired, so I boarded the late bus, which I knew would be half empty. It wasn't until I got off that I realized Mirandah had also been on the bus.

"How come you're getting home late?" I asked.

"Art," she said. I stifled a yawn as she launched into a description of a printmaking process she had been learning. "So?" Mirandah suddenly turned and poked me in the arm.

"Pardon?" I asked, realizing I had phased out completely.

Mirandah gave a huffing sigh of exasperation. "Honestly, Alyzon. You are as bad as Serenity."

That woke me up, because it made me realize that none of us talked to one another about how Serenity had changed. "How come you're so down on poor Serenity?" I asked to provoke a reaction.

"I'm not down on poor Serenity," Mirandah said indignantly. "She's down on us, or hadn't you noticed? We're part of the great silent mass who fail to act decisively to stop injustice. Or are you telling me you haven't had the 'we are as guilty as the guilty if we don't act' lecture?" Mirandah said sardonically. "Or what about 'cruel times need cruel measures,' or maybe the most recent? 'The sleepers awake' diatribe? That one's a doozy."

I stared at her. "Serenity doesn't lecture me. She doesn't speak to me."

Mirandah gave a short laugh. "Yeah, well, maybe she thinks you're too far gone. Lucky you."

"So what does she expect us to do? Does she say?"

"Who knows. Blow up the government, maybe."

We came around to the back door and I stifled a groan at the sound of Rhona Wojcek's voice. Mum was in the kitchen placidly feeding Luke a shiny blob of mushed-up banana in his high chair, her head swathed in clouds of blue and silver.

Mirandah dropped her bag and sat down to watch Rhona with apparent devotion. I had to suppress a smile, because I knew that she was merely gathering material for an increasingly accurate and hilarious Rhona imitation she was developing.

I slipped out the kitchen door, intending to go upstairs and change, but to my surprise, Da was sitting on the bottom step, his coffee-ground scent overlaid with a confusion of other smells—new rope, tobacco, perfume, pine needles, detergent—but stronger than all the rest was the heavy reek of ammonia.

"Rhona?" I said sympathetically.

"She wants your mum to exhibit in a gallery that will cost an arm and a leg."

"I thought galleries just took a percentage of what sells." I sat down beside him.

"They do, but Rhona wants a big opening, and we'll need to pay for it."

"So don't do it. Mum won't care."

"She won't, but maybe Rhona's right about the need to attract buyers and gallery owners. . . ."

I clamped on my senses hard enough to see the effect Da had on the air. Somehow it didn't surprise me that the distortions were weaker than usual. "Are you OK, Da?" I asked. *Tell me what is wrong,* I thought at him.

He turned his handsome face to me. "I guess it's that for once I have the potential to earn the money we need. Only . . ." He shook his head.

"Only what?" I pressed.

"I did that big charity function for Aaron Rayc this afternoon, and it turned out not to be a solo job after all. I ended up fronting another band, and afterward Aaron asked if I would like to do a second gig with them. So what we're talking about now is a gig fronting another band."

"He lied about today's gig," I said.

"Well, no," Da said. "The lead singer was ill, and Rayc asked me to fill in. It made no sense to switch halfway through to a solo act, so we did the whole show together. Afterward Aaron offered another gig with the band because the singer is going to be out of commission for some time. It's a big gig with a good paycheck. . . ."

"Didn't you like the band?"

"It's not that," Da said. He laughed. "I guess I just feel that by taking these gigs, I'm slipping further and further away from Losing the Rope. In the end, I told Aaron I'd pass, but he told me to think it over. Then I get home and find Rhona talking about a big, expensive gallery opening." He winced as the agent's laughter rang out.

"Oh, Da," I said.

He smiled fondly at me. "I don't know why I'm so down, really. It's just one gig, after all."

Rhona exploded out of the kitchen and into the hallway, trailing fringes and silk draperies. She stopped and stared at Da and me sitting at the bottom of the stairs. But Mum, coming along behind her, only smiled at us both and ushered Rhona the rest of the way out.

* * *

I went up and lay on my bed, wondering if Aaron Rayc was really out to separate Da from Losing the Rope. Did he truly believe Da would be a better property if he was a soloist or played with some other band?

I fell asleep and dreamed one of those chaotic and troubling dreams that metamorphose slowly but spectacularly into a nightmare. I was at one of Losing the Rope's gigs, only the band seemed to be missing half their instruments. Mel went to find them, and when he didn't come back, Neil and Da sent me to get him. I ended up blundering into some sort of nightclub, peopled horribly by animated corpses.

Finally one of them noticed me and leered, baring sharpened teeth. It was Aaron Rayc. "I see you," he hissed. And suddenly the air was full of tiny creatures biting and tearing at me. I staggered back in terror, but he grabbed me and shook me and shook me.

* * *

"Alyzon! Come on. Dinner's ready." It was Jesse shaking me hard. I sat up groggily, heavy-eyed and jittery.

Over dinner, I studied Serenity, looking for clues that she might know she had been followed, but she was exactly the same as usual: pale, silent and withdrawn, pushing food around her plate. After dinner she went straight up to bed.

I didn't want to go up with her, so I hung around downstairs listening to Da and Jesse jam. Then I had a shower. As I was coming out of the bathroom, Jesse told me Gilly had phoned earlier in the afternoon. "I meant to tell you right away when you got home, but Rhona came and you know how she obliterates consciousness."

I laughed, relieved. "It's too late to call her back now. I'll do it tomorrow."

* * *

I woke to the déjà vu experience of Jesse shaking me, but it felt too early and too dark for school.

"Phone," Jesse said softly. "It's your friend Harrison, and he says it's urgent."

I dragged on a robe and slippers and hurried downstairs, my heart yammering. "Harrison? What's wrong?"

"Gilly just called," he said. "Her grandmother's house burned down on Sunday night." I gasped. "It's OK. No one got hurt. Her grandmother was at the opera, and Gilly was with me and Raoul, visiting Sarry. She only found out after she left us and went home in a taxi. She didnae call straightaway because it was totally chaotic. Her grandmother was in shock, and there were police asking questions, and they had to get some clothes and find somewhere to stay." He paused for a moment. "Whoever did it threw gallons of gasoline around to make sure the fire was hot."

"Someone did it on *purpose*?" I asked, horrified. "What about the housekeeper and the driver?"

"They have a house separate from the main residence, but they were out as well. The movies. The police think that's why it happened. Unfortunately, it also means that no one saw anything."

"But why would anyone do such a thing?"

"It could have been a robbery and someone wanting tae make sure it would be hard for anyone tae figure what had been stolen. Or vandalism. A sort of payback for the rich. There is a lot of that happening, apparently. Anyway, I'm sorry I called so early, but I didnae know what time you left for school and I thought you'd want tae know. Gilly won't be at school again today, of course."

"Where are Gilly and her grandmother now?" I asked.

"The Hotel Marceau. Would you like tae go and see her tonight? We could meet as we'd planned at the library, then go tae her hotel afterward. I think she'd be glad if you'd come."

"Of course," I said.

Only after I put down the receiver did I realize that he had not mentioned Serenity.

"What's up?" Jesse asked, passing me a mug of tea. Da came in carrying Luke halfway through the story.

"That nice, gentle old lady," he said when I had finished. "Alyzon, let Mrs. Rountree know that if there is anything she needs, to just call."

Even in the midst of my shock, I was touched by the thought of Da offering help to someone as rich as Mrs. Rountree. On the other hand, perhaps there was a kind of help someone like Da could give that no one else could. I was thinking of Portia Sting and the way Da had radiated sparks and bent the air the night of the Urban Dingo gig. Perhaps his bending of the air was some sort of positive or healing force that helped anyone within range.

* * *

I was thinking about Gilly and the fire when I got off the bus, and saw Harlen standing a little way along the fence from the school gates with the same older guys I had seen him with the day I had fled from him. I hadn't even mentioned Harlen to Harrison. This was such a strange omission that it made me wonder if my own senses had somehow subconsciously stopped me.

I went straight over to Harlen, refusing to think about anything but the apology I owed him. When he saw me, his eyes went cold and flat, but his mouth kept right on smiling. The smell of rot coming from him was overpowering, and suddenly it didn't seem the least bit exaggerated to think he might carry a contagious sickness of the spirit.

"Harlen, I'm really sorry I didn't come to Eastland on Saturday. I didn't get a chance to tell you yesterday, but I was on my way to meet you when this girl I know had a fit. I would have called from the hospital, but I didn't have your number." I said this looking right into his eyes, all the time screening so hard it was making my head ache.

"A sick friend," one of his companions said with sneering disbelief.

I glared at him with genuine indignation. "I wouldn't make up a thing like that." I looked back at Harlen. "My friend really did have a fit, and you can ask Gilly because she knows her, too. Why would I lie, anyway?"

There was a strangely long pause, and then the second guy said mockingly to Harlen, "Seems like she might be telling the truth. Too bad, eh?"

Harlen snapped at him to shut up, and then he stepped closer to me. "I was pretty mad," he said. "I thought you had stood me up for Gilly."

"I would never deliberately stand someone up," I said.

"An honorable woman," said one of the others, leering at me.

I was glad, because looking at him let me turn away from Harlen. For a moment, instead of his sick, rotting stench, I was enveloped in the boiled cabbage and dirty track-shoe odor of the other guy's essence. "Are you a friend of Harlen's?" I asked, because unpleasant as his smell was, it was infinitely better than Harlen's.

"I'm Quick," he said. "This here is Breeze. We used to go to school with Harlen until it closed down." He gave a delighted chuckle.

"Shut up," Harlen said again, forcing my eyes back to

him. "So, Alyzon, if you really didn't mean to stand me up, how about meeting me tonight?"

"Oh, I can't," I said. "Haven't your heard? Gilly's house was burned down on Sunday. I'm supposed to go and see her and her grandmother tonight."

For a second Harlen's face was so still it was like someone had used a pause button on him. Then he said, "Gilly's house burned down? Incredible. Who do the police think did it?"

The bell started ringing before I could answer.

"Time to rock and roll," Quick said, and he slouched off down the street with Breeze in tow.

"Who were those two?" demanded a teacher as Harlen and I came through the gate. "I've seen them hanging around here, and I'm not keen on it."

"They were asking directions," Harlen lied coolly, shooting me a look of smiling complicity. I forced myself to smile back, glad that the teacher was coming along right behind us.

25

Never had school seemed less relevant than it did the rest of that day. My thoughts kept jumping from Gilly and her grandmother losing everything in the fire; to Serenity, eaten up by grief and rage; to Aaron Rayc trying to separate Da from Losing the Rope; and then to poor Sarry, at the mercy of a doctor who smelled of something old and rotten. And, of course, I thought of Harlen.

It felt as if a shadow was creeping through the world, darkening all the separate threads of my life.

At lunchtime I made for the library, intending to use the computer to learn more about Aaron Rayc, but Harlen was there before me, leaning over the checkout desk and smiling at the woman behind it. I backed away hastily and headed for the computer room instead.

I sat down and got out the business card I had filched from Da's coat pocket that morning. "Rayc Inc." was printed on the heavy card in elegant gold lettering. Under it was the word "Consultants" in smaller but equally elegant script. Then in the bottom left-hand corner was an address, a fax number, and a URL. The only other thing on the card was an obscure logo that meant nothing to me.

What struck me was how little information the card offered, unless you took the luxurious quality of its production as part of its message.

I typed in the URL, and the logo came up on screen. I clicked on it, and the image flickered like a flame and vanished, leaving a coil of white smoke that wound itself into a single line of text: "Light the flame and all shall be consumed by your radiance."

It sounded vaguely religious to me, or like something from Dante's *Inferno* or William Blake. But either way, it was totally unexpected. I was still staring at the words in bafflement when they quivered and vanished.

What came up next was possibly the plainest home page I had ever seen. There was just "Rayc Inc." and "Consultants" above an old-fashioned photograph of a two-story mansion. "Castledean Estate" was written on a plate by the door, and under the picture was a Remington address. There was nothing to say what purpose the house served, but there was a paragraph explaining that Rayc Inc. had been founded decades ago, although there was no information about what the company actually did, and there didn't seem to be anywhere to go from that page.

I wondered if Rayc Inc. was some sort of charity organization. After all, most of the gigs Rayc had given Da were to do with charities, and it might explain the religious-sounding quote. But where was the plea for a donation?

I looked back to the photo and noticed that the panel with the name of the house on it looked computer-generated. I clicked on it, and the photo began to fragment and blow away like leaves in a high wind. Then I was looking at four lines of text.

The first said, "Who would teach the world, enter here." The second said, "Who would change the world, inquire within." The third read, "Who would save the world, come hither," and the last, "Who would despair of the world, come forth."

I moved the cursor to the first line and clicked. Nothing happened, nor did any of the other lines yield more than their text. I scrolled in all directions but could find nothing else.

Then all at once the screen image began to fade away. The mouse wouldn't respond, and a moment later, to my mortified horror, a bondage site came up, complete with a picture of a naked woman tied up and grimacing in pain. I was astonished, because the monitoring software the school used ought to have immediately blocked the download. I was still trying to get rid of the image when the bell rang. There was nothing to do but switch off the whole machine.

I made my way to the art room, thinking that Aaron Rayc's Web site was like a game and a virtual idiot like me was not going to crack it without help. Mirandah might manage, but she could never have kept her mouth shut about the fact that I was looking into Rayc Inc.

I was soon up to my neck in paints and linseed oil, making my usual inept mess. Whatever else had changed, I had not developed any artistic abilities, but at least the class took my mind off everything else. Because of the need to clean up after, the class always ran over, and for once I was glad because it meant I would not have to worry about Harlen waiting around for me after school. But it did mean that I had to run to make the city-bound bus that would bring me to the library in time to meet Harrison.

When the bus pulled up at the library, however, Harrison jumped on before I could get off. "This bus stops close tae the hotel, so I thought we might as well go straight there," he said when he was seated beside me. "There's a park right beside it where we can go for a walk."

I asked if he had seen Sarry again, and his face lit up. "Raoul and I went tae visit her last night, and she's fine. In fact she's more than fine, because not only has the fill-in doctor dropped the dose of drugs, he has agreed tae sign a release to allow Sarry tae enter a convalescent home in Remington. Which means she is permanently out of Dr. Austin's clutches."

His mention of Remington gave me a little start, because that was where the Castledean Estate was. Harrison went on, saying he had been thinking that we ought to check up on Dr. Austin and find out exactly when he had started treating Sarry. I opened my mouth to tell Harrison about Harlen, and this time I definitely felt a resistance to speak. Maybe it was just that we were among other people who might overhear. I decided to wait until we were in the park to try again. To my relief, Harrison switched back to talking about the convalescent home, telling me it was called Bellavie and describing its facilities. It sounded so luxurious that I wondered aloud how Sarry could afford it. Harrison said lightly that Raoul would take care of it. We fell silent then, because the bus was getting really crowded, but when we were in the park alongside the hotel, Harrison told me Gilly had said her grandmother seemed to be getting more devastated by the fire as time passed. "It's the photographs and mementos she minds most. Gilly said she seemed really lost and apathetic, as if nothing matters anymore."

"Poor thing," I murmured, wondering if the person who lit the fire had any idea or even cared about the harm they had done. "I suppose Gilly's mother will come back now?"

"She won't know what happened unless she logs on tae a local news link or gets a local paper. From what Gilly says, she doesnae make contact very often."

We came to a bench and Harrison suggested we sit for a bit. "I want tae tell you what happened with your sister last night." My heartbeat quickened.

"I spotted her easily as she came out the school gate, because she had changed out of her school uniform intae black clothes," Harrison said. "She went straight tae the city bus stop and caught the bus tae the library."

"So she does go there," I said.

Harrison ignored my interruption. "She went inside, sat down, and got out some schoolbooks. Then a whole bunch of little kids poured in for some sort of story-reading session. I was distracted for a second, and when I looked back tae where your sister had been sitting, I got the shock of my life because she'd gone."

I stared at him. "What do you mean, gone?"

"Gone. Her, her bag, her books. I raced outside, thinking she must have spotted me, but she was nowhere tae be seen. I figured she must have just gone tae the toilet. But when I got back inside, I saw her going intae one of those side meeting rooms with a bunch of other people."

"She was going to a meeting?" I could hardly believe it.

"I waited until the door shut, then I went tae the desk and asked who was meeting. The guy said it was a poetry group called the Morality Complex that meets every week on Monday nights. They've a regular booking."

"A poetry group!" I said explosively, relieved and also exasperated. Trust Serenity to make a poetry meeting so secretive! I felt like strangling her.

Harrison went on. "A pretty weird sort of poetry group. I went back tae the meeting room. I was going tae barge in and pretend I'd got the wrong door, but it wouldnae budge. There are no locks, so someone had tae be holding it closed from inside. I knocked and finally this tough-looking guy with a shaved head came out and asked what I wanted. I told him I wanted tae join. He said they werenae looking for members right now. I asked when would they be, and he said it wasnae possible for anyone tae join who'd not shown proper commitment. Commitment tae what? I asked. Tae idealism, he said. I asked how you showed commitment tae idealism, and he said that was the challenge. Then he told me tae push off. I didnae press it, because for all he was talking about idealism, he actually looked like he wanted tae ram his fist down my throat."

"A poetry club," I said. I felt stupid for having sent him on a wild goose chase, and said so.

He smiled. "I didnae mind it. The truth is I felt like James Bond, only shorter."

I laughed, lightened by his self-deprecating humor, but also by the fact that my dark imaginings about Serenity seemed to be unfounded. Harrison glanced at his watch and said we should go in. I had to lean into the wind as we came back through the park. Leaves were whipping around us and flying up into the air from the ground as if they wanted to turn back time.

Hotel Marceau was a big fancy building facing the park all along one side, and the doorman—it was that kind of hotel—gave off a disparaging smell of Drano when he opened the door for me, although his face was smoothly polite. I felt self-conscious in my shabby school uniform and scuffed school shoes and realized I ought to have had the sense to bring clothes to change into. Harrison's dark corduroy trousers and gray wool sweater and jacket were expensive and tasteful, and as he approached the gleaming desk, I saw that he was far more at ease in the surroundings than I was.

The sleek blond receptionist told us we were to wait in the restaurant. I thought her eyes flickered as they passed from Harrison to me, but when I extended my senses, she only smelled of flowers and toasted cheese, which was a lesson to me not to be so paranoid.

Nevertheless, when I saw how fancy the restaurant was, I panicked because Da had given me twenty dollars and I had the feeling that a glass of water might cost more than that here. A waiter appeared, so smooth he might have been oiled, checked a list, and said we must be Miss Gilly Rountree's guests. I felt like we had stepped into a novel set early in the previous century and tried to control a mixture of extreme unease and hysterical amusement as we followed him to a table by the window.

He took up the white table napkin, unfolded it with a practiced snap, and laid it on my lap like a magician. The waiter left after performing the same service for Harrison, then Harrison leaned close and said in a pompous voice, "Is everything in order, Miss Alyzon?" That finished me. I burst out laughing, and even though I clapped my hands over my mouth at once, the sound seemed to reverberate around the near-empty restaurant, making irises tremble in their vases.

Harrison said seriously, "Laughter is forbidden in places like this. You are permitted tae smile discreetly so long as ye dinnae show any teeth." As it always did when he was messing around, his accent had grown stronger, and I realized how much I liked it.

The waiter returned and asked if we would like to have an appetizer, and my amusement fell into the hole that opened up in my stomach. "I—I didn't realize we would be eating," I stammered. I could feel my face burn.

Before he could respond, Gilly appeared and I felt immediately guilty that I had not been thinking about her and her house burning down. But she only threw her arms around me and kissed me on the cheek. I stiffened, but fortunately all she was feeling was a rush of gladness at seeing me; it didn't hurt a bit. I hugged her back, relishing the clean sea scent of her. Then she let me go and hugged Harrison, too. To my relief, the waiter had gone away again.

"I'm so glad to see you both!" Gilly said, flopping down between us.

"Gilly, I'm sorry about your house," I said.

She sighed. "I know. Gran just can't understand why anyone would want to do such a thing. She seems so old and frail all of a sudden."

The waiter came back and asked if we were ready to order, and Harrison announced rather brusquely that he didn't have any money with him. Gilly only shrugged and said, "Well, it doesn't matter anyway, because Gran insists dinner is her treat. You have to accept or she'll be offended."

I felt Harrison look at me. Then he said. "OK, why not."

I nodded, relieved that it had been decided without my having to admit my own poverty. The waiter had stood like a statue throughout this, but he came to life as we ordered.

"What about Raoul?" Harrison asked.

"He called just now to say he'll come for dessert and coffee. He's trying to finish a job," Gilly explained.

The meal came quickly, and as if by consensus, we didn't talk about anything serious while we ate. I was surprised how hungry I felt, and the food was really good. Once the waiter had cleared the dishes away, Gilly told him with a poise I envied that we would wait for coffee and dessert because we were expecting another friend.

"What will your gran do now?" Harrison asked.

She shrugged. "We'll find another house. We're lucky that the insurance will pay. It must be dreadful if a house is burned down and there is no money for another one. But the idea of getting all the furniture and stuff for it . . . ," she sighed. "It won't be so bad for me, but poor Gran, she put that house together over her whole life with Grandad. All the furniture and paintings and rugs she bought with him or with her sister who died or with friends who are dead or far away. Or she bought them on her travels. Each bit was like a piece of her history. It's not like a house burned down for her. It's like someone burned up a whole lot of her past."

Harrison had started to tell her of an organization he had read about that decorated houses for families relocating from another country, when Raoul appeared. As he rolled across the room toward us, dark and handsome in a suit and yellow shirt, I thought that he managed to make a wheelchair look sophisticated.

Gilly's eyes lit up when she saw him and, as he smiled at her, the air between them bent first one way then the other. *So that's what love looks like,* I thought.

My neck prickled, and I turned to see Harrison watching me. I flushed, realizing he knew that I was eavesdropping with my extended abilities. Gilly began talking about Harrison's idea of how to set up a new house for her grandmother, and Raoul said it might also be possible to shop online in some of the places where Mrs. Rountree had once traveled.

"I could show her how to log in here at the hotel," he said.

"A cyber trip down memory lane with real mementos," Gilly murmured, looking excited. "I think Gran might like that."

Their talk about the Internet reminded me of my own abortive attempt to learn more about Aaron Rayc. When there was a lull in the conversation, I asked Raoul if he had ever heard of a company called Rayc Inc. He hadn't, but when I explained about its strange Web site, he looked intrigued and offered to look into it, just as I had hoped. I gave him Aaron Rayc's card and explained my misgivings about Da and the entrepreneur. Even to me they sounded vague, and finally I said weakly, "I'd just like to know what sort of man he is and what he does."

"I'll look into it," Raoul promised. "Maybe I'll have something for you when you come to my place on the weekend. I hope you'll be able to come to help us test a new game, Alyzon," he said, then he glanced at Gilly. "Of course, we can postpone if you don't want to leave your grandmother alone."

"I'll see how she is," Gilly said. "Harrison told me you've managed to get the hospital to let Sarry go to a private convalescent home."

Raoul smiled. "The papers have been signed, which means she's out of Dr. Austin's clutches."

This was the same phrase Harrison had used, and when I glanced at him I was startled to find him watching me, his eyes expectant.

"What's with you two?" Gilly asked curiously.

I was suddenly filled with doubt. "Look, I . . . I want to tell you something, but I don't know if this is the right moment. The fire—"

"Oh no you don't," Gilly said. "The fire happened and it's horrible, but Gran and I are OK and we'll get over it, because even treasured mementos are only things, not people. So spill."

"We're friends," Raoul added in his deep, gentle voice. "But being a friend doesn't mean you have to tell us what you are not ready to tell."

"Raoul!" Gilly said indignantly.

"Oh, for Pete's sake," I said, half laughing. "I do want to tell you, but it's so weird."

"Weird is OK," Raoul said.

Right then the waiter appeared. Hearing these words, he looked uncharacteristically startled. "Desserts?" he asked, resuming his bland expression.

"I have the feeling I might need a serious dessert for this," Gilly said decisively. "I'll have the chocolate mousse."

We all laughed and the tightness of the last few minutes evaporated, carrying my nervousness with it. After all, Harrison had believed me. And what would happen if Gilly and Raoul didn't? I wouldn't fall down dead.

26

Some time later, after I had told them everything, Gilly looked surprised and bemused. "What does it mean that I smell of the sea?" she asked.

"I'm not sure it means anything more than you having brown hair does. The transient smells are more revealing than essence smells, when I can figure out what they mean. When you're worried, for instance, I smell seaweed, and when you're happy, I smell cotton candy. My da smells of ammonia when he's worried."

"Worry smells different on different people," Raoul marveled.

Even Harrison had been shocked at the true extent of my abilities. "Can you smell your own essence?" he asked.

I shook my head and was about to tell them I couldn't smell Aaron Rayc's either, when Gilly gave a gasping cry.

"Harlen!" she said. "That's why you don't like him getting interested in you, isn't it? It has to do with how he smells."

I nodded, and had to fight a powerful reluctance to speak. "He smells really horrible. Worse than anything I've ever smelled. Even worse than Dr. Austin."

"Dr. Austin? You don't mean the same Dr. Austin who treats Sarry?" Raoul's voice was sharp.

I repeated what I had told Harrison, and then Harrison added our conclusions. Raoul's expression was bleak. "If you're right about the terrible smell meaning Dr. Austin has the same sickness as Sarry, it could be that she doesn't smell because she won't allow her sickness to become active."

Harrison gave me a worried look. "If that's so, this guy at your school who smells like Dr. Austin must be contagious."

"He may be," Raoul cautioned. "Remember, this is all speculation. Infecting someone else could be no more than a matter of making physical contact, although I tend to think it has to be more complicated, otherwise every second person would be infected. The point is that there are lots of sicknesses where the person, the carrier, is not aware they are infected or infectious. If you think about it, the sicknesses are served by the ignorance of their hosts, and so it may be that this sickness is driving its victims to seek situations where infection can occur."

"You're making it sound as if this sickness is alive," Gilly said, looking revolted.

"I would call it a biological imperative," Raoul said. "It might also be that the sickness is aware of people who are infected. That could explain why Dr. Austin is trying to drug Sarry. Remember how she feels that drugs lower her resistance?"

"You think the sickness in Dr. Austin is trying tae help

the sickness in Sarry tae break its host's will?" Harrison asked dubiously.

"It sounds radical, but this thing is so far outside normal that I think we have to consider it. And it would explain why Dr. Austin was trying to drug Alyzon as well. He, or the sickness in him, needed her will to be low and weak because it wanted to infect her." He shot me a look. "I assume you'd know if you were infected."

His suggestion that Dr. Austin had been trying to infect me made me feel very strange. "I can't smell my own essence, but . . . I think I wouldn't be so scared of Harlen or so revolted by how he and Dr. Austin smell if I were."

"That makes sense," Raoul said. "Gilly said this Harlen was showing an interest in you. When did that start?"

I saw at once what he was going to say. "I'd been back at school two weeks before he asked me out, but now he is asking me out all the time and asking questions about me and my family and calling me." I stopped, my skin crawling at the thought that all of Harlen's determined pursuit might be nothing more than the prompting of some malevolent virus trying to find a way to infect me. Desperate to stop the terrifying direction of my thoughts, I told them about running away like a terrified deer after seeing Harlen, and not feeling any need to do so the next time I saw him.

"That would fit with the sickness having cycles where it is stronger or weaker," Harrison said to Raoul. "It might even be that when Alyzon returned to school it was in a weak phase, so it couldn't react."

"Another possibility is that the sickness might need its host to be close for it to become aware of your extended senses," Raoul pointed out. "And maybe the reason your danger sense is warning you not to show him how you feel is because that would alert the sickness to your awareness of it."

Suddenly Gilly gasped and turned to me. "Alyzon, with the fire and everything, I forgot to tell you I saw Harlen on Saturday afternoon and he was livid because you'd stood him up. Of course, I didn't know what had happened with Sarry. I just said that I was going to see you that afternoon. He gave me this killing look and said he didn't suppose *I'd* be stood up."

I felt a strange chill at her words, and maybe I looked scared because Harrison said gruffly, "It cannae be that easy to infect you, because he would have done it already if he only had tae touch you. All you have tae do is avoid being alone with him."

"I can't keep evading," I said, feeling a stab of despair. "It feels dangerous."

Gilly said, "Maybe the reason Alyzon feels scared is because some bit of her feels that the sickness could provoke Harlen to do something about her if it saw her as an enemy."

There was a deep silence between us, then Raoul shook his head. "I'd say the sickness would have a lot of trouble directing anyone to do actual physical harm unless it was already in the host's nature, and even then, there would have to be circumstances that would allow the host to think the idea of causing harm was their own idea. Like a doctor who had a tendency to overprescribe being prompted to drug a patient."

At that moment the waiter came over to say that the restaurant was closing. I looked at my watch and was astounded to see how late it was. I asked if there was a phone I could use to call Da, but Raoul offered his cell.

"It's me," I said gingerly when Da answered. "Sorry it's so late."

"We've just finished rehearsing, and I'm sure it helped Gilly to have a good talk," Da said.

I felt guilty then, because we hadn't talked about the fire for hours. We all got up and pulled on our coats, and I noticed the waiters were standing in a group by the bar, looking bored and talking in low voices.

"I should have said I'd take you home to save your father the trip," Raoul said apologetically as we walked down the ramp with him to the foyer.

"It's fine. Da was up rehearsing anyway. I think he's going to do another gig for Aaron Rayc."

"I thought he wanted your da alone," Gilly said.

"He does, but Da is working on some new songs with Losing the Rope."

"How did he smell?" Harrison asked suddenly. "Aaron Rayc."

I shrugged. "He didn't smell of anything."

"I'll have a look at his Web site," Raoul promised. "But in the meantime, you do your best to stay away from Harlen until we can figure out how to handle him."

Comforted by how easily and naturally he used the word "we," I turned to Gilly. "Listen, I feel bad that most of the night has been spent talking about me when we were supposed to—"

"Take my mind off the fire?" Gilly asked. "I think you could say you were successful." She grinned and moved closer to give me a hug, then she stopped. "Is it bad if I hug you?"

I laughed, relieved at her simple directness. "It's fine."

"Good," Gilly declared, and hugged me hard.

* * *

Wednesday dawned warm but dark, the sky full of scabby brown clouds and the wind blowing hard in several directions at once. It was the kind of day that makes dogs howl and horses twitch their ears and break into sudden, skittish bursts of speed.

At breakfast Da mentioned that he had agreed to the new gig with the other band. He sounded cheerful, but his ammonia smell was strong. *Aaron Rayc,* I thought grimly, and I suddenly had a clear memory of him and the announcer at the Urban Dingo gig talking to the guy in green shoes, while the journalist, Gary Soloman, stood in the background watching them intently. I thought about him on the way to school, wondering if he had been doing a story about Aaron Rayc. But by the time the bus pulled up, I couldn't think of anything other than having to face Harlen again.

Reasoning that it would be better to go on avoiding Harlen than refusing him, I managed to skulk in unlikely places between classes. The day seemed to take forever.

Maybe it was that feeling of frustration that gave me the idea of going to the newspaper office and talking to Gary Soloman.

I went out of the school the back way, just in case Harlen was lurking, but I hadn't gone far before it started to rain. It was so heavy that I sprinted back to the main road, where I knew there would be a bus shelter. There was a woman standing in it already, and we exchanged rueful smiles, then stood together in silence peering glumly out at the rain. When I tired of watching the street, I turned my attention to the ads on the walls of the shelter. They were heavily defaced and I grimaced at a swastika wound about with snakes.

"You'd think no one would ever want to use that symbol again, given what it has been associated with," the woman said.

"Wasn't it originally some sort of eternal energy sign? And I think Nazis usually drew it facing the other direction," I said when we had looked at it a bit longer. A teacher had once explained the ancient origins of the symbol.

The woman studied it. "I'm not sure. But the snakes don't seem to go with eternal energy, so most likely the gang actually meant to draw the Nazi cross."

"Gang?"

"It's the emblem of a skinhead gang over in Shaletown," the woman said. "I guess they're widening their territory." She shook her head and, just then, the bus loomed up.

 27

Inside the foyer of the newspaper office, there was a line of people waiting to book advertisements. I went straight to a receptionist and asked if I could speak to Gary Soloman.

"Is he expecting you?"

"I have some important information for him," I said, trying to look older than I was. The receptionist just nodded with supreme indifference, pressed some keys on her computer console, and then talked into the mouthpiece looping out of the earphones she was wearing. She wore the earphones slightly askew so that she could hear out of one ear, and now she angled her head toward me.

"Name?"

"Alyzon Whitestarr," I said.

She repeated my name, and I extended my hearing. I heard a man's voice come over the earphones. He said my name with a note of surprise and asked if she was sure. The receptionist said I seemed to be sure of my identity, and he laughed and told her that he would come right down.

Five minutes later he emerged from the security door. His

eyes skated right over me, so I stepped closer and was reassured to discover that Gary Soloman smelled a lot like a walk through a forest in autumn.

I said, "I'm Alyzon. My class came here a few months ago, and you gave us a talk on newspapers."

"Ah!" His eyes widened in sudden comprehension. "You were with the class from hell?"

I laughed. "Not all of us came from hell. Just a couple of the boys. The rest of us come from right here on Earth."

He smiled slightly. "Fair enough. Well, Alyzon, what can I do for you?"

"You went to see Urban Dingo at the Dome."

"I didn't—" he began.

"I saw you there!"

"Yes, and I saw you," he said patiently. "I didn't recognize you at first because you weren't wearing a uniform then. I guess you went to see your . . . brother?"

"My father," I said.

"I was about to say I didn't go to see Urban Dingo, or your father's band for that matter, although it was pretty sensational. I was there because I was working."

"On what?"

His face closed up. "It's my job to ask the questions."

"So no one else should?" I asked, annoyed.

A faint impatience flowed into his features. "What was your question?"

I swallowed. "Were you at the concert because you were investigating Aaron Rayc?"

His expression hardly changed, but a sharp pickled-onion smell infused the autumn fragrance. "Let's get a coffee," he suggested. His tone implied he was bored, but his scents told me he wanted to get me away from other people.

We went out of the office and into a nearby arcade, passing three coffee places before he led me into a rather dingy Italian restaurant beside an old-fashioned barber shop. The door was open but the lights were off inside, and the big sleepy-looking Rasta man who came out at the sound of our entrance looked as if he had just crawled out of an all-night party. He just gave the journalist a wave and headed for the coffee machine.

"What will de lady have, Solo-man?" he called.

"Coffee. Espresso," I said, because I felt I needed to counterbalance the uniform.

The journalist shouted the order, then turned to give me a speculative look. "So, what makes you ask about Aaron Rayc?"

"Aaron Rayc set up the gig with Urban Dingo because he heard a song Da wrote," I said. "Ever since the concert he has been coming round and offering Da jobs, only the jobs are not with Losing the Rope. First they were solo and now they are with some other band whose lead singer just happened to get sick."

I stopped because the man brought the drinks, the silver cuffs on his dreadlocks clinking as he set two mugs down, then shuffled away.

"So let me get this straight," Gary Soloman said when he

had gone. "You're bothered because a rich, powerful businessman is showing an interest in your dad. Isn't that a good thing?" His voice was slightly mocking, and suddenly I was furious that he was using his face and voice to lie.

"I don't think it's a good thing and, what's more, I don't believe you think so either," I said very coolly.

"You figured this out from an expression on my face at a gig?" A sharp citrus smell that I guessed might represent curiosity reminded me to be careful; this guy made a living out of finding out people's secrets.

"Why were you watching Aaron Rayc?" I asked mildly, playing his game.

"I could have been looking at the other guys with him," Gary Soloman said.

"You could," I agreed.

He suddenly grinned, looking nicer. "What exactly is it that you want to know?"

"I don't like Aaron Rayc, and I want to know what he does. He's not an agent or a promoter; he says so himself. His Web site is weird because it doesn't tell you anything."

"I know about the Web site." He sipped at his coffee, although my hands around my own cup told me that it was scalding hot. Then his scents shifted, and I could distinctly smell newsprint. "I went to the concert because I wanted to get a look at him without his knowing it. I had heard a few things that made me wonder about him, but it turned out to be nothing." He was watching me over the rim of his cup.

"I don't believe you," I said flatly. "I don't see why you

257

can't tell me what you know. It's not like I'm going to steal your story!"

He sat back in his chair and laughed. "I should confide my love life to you while I'm at it, and maybe my credit card number."

His snide tone infuriated me. "Well, maybe I'll just ask Aaron Rayc why a journalist is taking an interest in him."

I hadn't meant it as a threat so much as an angry comeback, but the blood rushed to his face and for the first time his expression matched the scents he was giving out. "If you talk to Rayc about me, it might be a lot more than a news story that got hurt, girl. Your father is not the only person involved here."

I felt ashamed but also triumphant. I said, "I'm just worried about my da. I wouldn't tell anyone anything you told me, not even him."

A nerve beat at the journalist's temple. "Are you a girl of your word, Alyzon Whitestarr?" he asked at last.

"I am," I said gravely.

"Then I will give you this: Aaron Rayc is bad news to artists. He ruins their lives or their careers or he turns them into something that is the opposite of everything they cared about before they met him. I'd like to know why, and that's why I'm digging. So far I haven't found out anything that makes sense, but I have learned that bad things happen to people who poke their nose into Aaron Rayc's business. Very bad things."

I felt the blood draining from my face. I didn't know what I had expected, but it wasn't this. "My da—"

"Look," Gary Soloman interrupted forcefully. "If your dad comes into the paper demanding to know what I'm on about, I'll deny this conversation and my friend behind the counter there will swear on a stack of Bibles that you came in here with a lot of crazy talk and he threw you out. End of story."

"I said I wouldn't say anything," I said quietly.

He calmed down. "I'm sorry to get so heavy, but this is a heavy guy and he has ears in places you wouldn't imagine. Don't tell anyone about this talk, and if you've got any sense, forget about Aaron Rayc. Your dad looked like a pretty bright guy, and he can probably take care of himself a lot better than you could." He got up. "Go home, Alyzon Whitestarr." He reached into his pocket to take out a five-dollar bill and tossed it on the table.

I stood up, too. "Thank you for talking to me."

He opened his mouth as if he wanted to say something else, then he shook his head and left. I was still standing there staring after him when the Rasta man glided over. I don't know what he saw in my face, but he said, "Eh, gal, don' look so down. Solo-man is a good guy. If he huntin' a story, he gonna get dat story and he gonna protect his sources. He infamous for it, eh?"

I looked at him, and let the warm chocolate smell of his kindness soothe me. "Thanks," I said.

* * *

I walked back to the library, determined to do a search for every online mention of Aaron Rayc, but all of the computer consoles were booked. Since I was in an investigative frame of mind, I went to the outdated phone books. Harlen's friends had indicated that his previous school had closed, so I reasoned there might be an old listing for a private school in Shaletown. Talking to the others about Harlen the night before had made me feel more than ever that I needed to know what made him tick, and it might be worth visiting the neighborhood where the school had been. It was a long shot, but maybe someone would remember him.

It turned out there had been a Shaletown Boys Academy. I wrote down the address, then I went back to check the computers, but they were all still in use. I gave up and went outside. There were five minutes to kill before the bus, so I went to the phones and called Harrison. It wasn't until the phone was ringing that I remembered I had promised not to say anything about the conversation with Gary Soloman.

A man answered the phone, sounding drunk. Before I could do more than say my name, he swore and hung up. I stared at the phone, thinking I must have dialed a wrong number.

* * *

That night when I slept, I dreamed again that I was a wolf. I woke feeling tired and out of sorts, and the only thing I could think was that the dream was my subconscious trying to deal with the input from my extended senses. In particular, from my sense of smell.

When I got downstairs that morning, Da was dressed to go out and checking his duffel bag.

"What's happening?" I asked.

"Got a gig in Remington," Da said.

"Remington?"

"I told you about it," Da said, easing the zipper past the worn bit that always caught. "The gig with the other band." There was no sign of the doubts he had shown days before.

"What is it?" Da asked, catching the look on my face.

"I just don't much like Aaron Rayc," I said lamely. I wanted to tell him to cancel the gig, but even if I had broken my promise and told Da what Gary Soloman had said, it wasn't concrete enough to make him break a commitment.

"He's not our kind of person," Da said. "But that doesn't make him a *bad* person. He's doing me a favor funneling work my way right when we need it for your mum's show." He zipped his bag fully and went upstairs to say goodbye to Mum and Luke.

The phone rang and I snatched it up. "Yes?"

"Yes tae you, too," Harrison said.

"Harrison. Hang on," I told him, and gave Da a hug on his way out.

"See you in a couple of days," he said.

I grabbed up the receiver, registering what Da had said with a sinking heart. "Sorry, Harrison. What is it?"

"Did you call last night?" He sounded tired and tense.

"I did, but I thought it must have been a wrong number. There was a man—"

"It was my father," Harrison said brusquely. There was a crash in the background. "Look, I have tae go, Alyzon," he said hastily and hung up.

I put the receiver down, wondering what had happened.

I was more than glad to see Gilly waiting for me at the school gate when the bus pulled up. She hooked her arm through mine as we came into the school, enveloping me in the lovely freshness of her sea scent. I knew she was there waiting in case Harlen had been waiting, too, but he was nowhere in sight.

At lunchtime I had booked a spot in the computer lab for the first half hour, the maximum time slot, and Gilly agreed to come with me. There was a note on the computers warning students to be careful about what they downloaded because a virus had recently infected the system, corrupting much of the school's network of computers.

I typed Aaron Rayc's name into a search engine. A list of entries came up, and I clicked on the first. It turned out to be a luridly overdecorated gossip site as famous for its bitchiness as for its raunchy photos. Of course, the latter set off the school's cyber nanny and blocked the connection, so I backtracked and tried the second item on the list, a who's-who-type monthly magazine with photos and stories of people with a pedigree.

The mention of Rayc came in an article at the top, which talked about him being at a charity ball for Hunger Relief with Dita and singer Angel Blue, who had recently won a major music industry award.

"Angel Blue?" I asked Gilly, who shrugged but made a note of the name on a scrap of paper while I clicked on the next entry. This time a longer article appeared, describing the opening of a club for billionaires. The luxury of the rooms made the people lounging in them look unreal, and I felt slightly sick thinking of these same men and women attending balls to raise funds for starving nations. How many thousands of people could have been fed by the money squandered on decorations in each of the ballrooms, let alone the amount spent on clothes and jewels for the occasion? And how much of the money raised actually got where it was supposed to go?

Aaron Rayc was in a photograph with Dita; she was wearing daffodil-yellow silk chiffon. With them, according to the caption, were Lord and Lady Harmigan. The couple looked like an astonishingly ugly elderly father and his exquisite daughter, but they were described as recently married.

"I think she used to be some kind of radical artist, but I can't remember her real name," Gilly murmured, tapping on Patricia Harmigan's glowing face.

I searched the article to be sure there was no other mention of Rayc, then clicked on the next item listed. Another magazine, another article, another charity fund-raiser, but my neck prickled because this one was at the Castledean Estate. Aaron Rayc's name appeared as the owner of the venue, but the article focused on the guest headlining the concert program for the night, a rock star so famous that even I recognized his name, although he had died about three years before.

"Didn't Dawed Rafael—" Gilly began.

"Commit suicide," I said.

Gary Soloman's words floated through my mind with chilling emphasis: "Aaron Rayc is bad news for artists."

"Now I remember," Gilly said. "Everyone was calling Dawed Rafael the new Bob Dylan, because he'd brought the protest song back. But then he went into leather and chains, and his songs got a lot tougher and more violent, and people said he was outrageous and he must be on drugs. I'm sure it was him that did a concert with real blood smeared over his face, and then there was that time he used a water gun to squirt red stuff at the audience and they went crazy because they thought it was blood. A girl got badly hurt in the stampede, and it wasn't long after that—"

"He killed himself," I said. "Write his name down."

The next item was from a serious kind of art magazine, an interview with a man called Oliver Spike. He was a writer talking about technique and philosophy and about his underprivileged youth in the UK. I searched for a mention of Aaron Rayc and found it right at the end of the article, where Oliver Spike called him "a close personal friend."

Gilly wrote his name down, too, then pointed at the clock.

"One more," I muttered.

The next article was about a poet called Zarbra. There was a picture of her with Aaron and Dita Rayc, a small, plain woman with short graying hair and drab gray clothes. The article said that she was one of a number of writers to receive a coveted humanitarian award for her cycle of poems on the theme of inhumanity. The award, the article said, was the initiative of Dita Rayc, and the caption under the picture mentioned that Zarbra had won several other awards, but that this was the first with a lot of prize money. The journalist added that Zarbra had received her prize at a ceremony at the Castle-dean Estate in Remington.

Castledean Estate again, I thought.

"Oh, hi," Gilly said with such false enthusiasm that I knew at once who was behind me. I closed the browser and turned to see Harlen Sanderson leaning in the doorway in a way that suggested he'd been there for some time. My heart pounded as I tried to remember if we had said anything important out loud.

"Sorry to hear about your house, Gilly," Harlen said. He sounded sincere, but he smelled ghastly.

"At least no one was hurt," Gilly said.

"Your grandmother is lucky she had insurance and money." Harlen's voice was pleasant, but Gilly bridled.

"Money can't replace photographs and mementos from a lifetime."

"I guess not," Harlen said. He switched his gaze to me, and his smile widened to show his teeth. *Like a shark,* I thought, and wondered if it was my imagination that I could now see a cold wariness behind the warmth in his eyes. It was all I could do not to shudder, thinking of something alien, hungering to infect me. I forced a smile, but it felt thin and brittle.

"I've been looking for you all day, baby," Harlen said.

I tried hard to look pleased and coy. "I've been around," I said.

"So let's arrange that date finally," he said, then he flashed a mocking look at Gilly. "If Gilly can spare you."

Before I could answer, the computer teacher came in and

shooed us all away, saying there had been enough problems for him without having students hanging around. He seemed unusually flustered, and even Harlen's gleaming smile didn't soften him. Then the bell rang.

"Catch you later," Harlen promised, winking at me and vanishing into the stream of students.

"Not if we can help it, baby," Gilly muttered.

 **28**

We didn't talk about Harlen as we made our way to science. Instead, I said, "Did you notice that all of the people in those articles had stopped working? Patricia Harmigan married, Dawed Rafael suicided, and have you ever heard of Zarbra or Angel Blue?"

"So what?" Gilly asked.

"It's just..." I stopped, realizing I could say nothing clear without breaking my promise to Gary Soloman.

Gilly looked puzzled. "You think Aaron Rayc is responsible for those people not working?"

"He might have had something to do with it."

"I don't see how. I mean, Patricia Harmigan probably stopped because she married a rich old man, and Dawed Rafael's suicide happened at a gig when there were thousands of people watching. That poet could still be working, for all we know. And what about that Oliver Spike guy? He's still working. I saw his name in the paper just the other day."

I frowned, realizing she was right. Then I shrugged. "I just have this feeling."

Gilly gave me a long, measuring look. "I bet I'm going to hear that phrase from you a lot. But I guess I have to get used to the fact that you have more resources than the average bunny."

* * *

At home that night it was quiet because Da was away, Serenity had gone upstairs early with a headache, and Mirandah was out with Ricki. Jesse and I had beans on toast for dinner. We had just finished when Luke wailed, and Jesse went up to fetch him.

"I think he might have a bit of a temperature," he said, nuzzling one bright red cheek. "I'll give him some baby aspirin, and we'll see how he is a bit later. He's hungry, though."

I volunteered to feed Luke, and I was still spooning mushed vegetable into him when Jesse got a preoccupied look and said he had to go up and write something down.

"Sure," I said, but he had already gone out. "That is one possessed brother we have," I told Luke, who fixed me with an adoring look and spat a great gob of mush onto my hand. "Erk," I said, laughing. I felt so safe and peaceful feeding him. It felt as if I was in another world from the one with Aaron Rayc and Harlen and Dr. Austin.

After Luke finished eating, I played with him on a mat in the living room and saw little sparks and flickers in the air around him. We were building a tower of blocks when Neil came in, saying he had knocked but no one had heard.

"Everyone's out or in their bedrooms. And Da's not here, but you knew that?"

He smiled and nodded. "Yeah, I just came to borrow a mike. Mine's on the blink."

"Have you got a gig?"

"Losing the Rope has a gig tomorrow. It's only a little thing, and we've got someone to fill in for your da." He ambled out to the shed and then came back fifteen minutes later with the mike and leads.

"Have a coffee?" I urged, pointing to a plate of his favorite cookies that I had put out. Luke was in his chair hammering on the wall with his battered rabbit.

Neil sat and made faces at him while I made coffee. "So what's on your mind?" Neil asked when I slid a mug to him and sat down opposite.

"Did you ever meet that big rock star Dawed Rafael?"

"The Welsh guy that took a high dive? Yeah, I met him a couple of times when he was an up-and-comer, but then he moved into the stratosphere."

"Do you know why he killed himself?"

"Common knowledge. A girl was crippled because of some crazy stunt he pulled during a show, and he couldn't handle it. He was an idealist, see, and idealists take it pretty hard when they fall short of their own ideals."

I frowned. "He doesn't sound as if he was much of an idealist. Wasn't he shooting blood at his audience and smearing it on his face in performances?"

"Shock tactics. He was political, and somewhere along the way he lost faith in the power of music and lyrics to make an impact. He said people had to be made to see the truth of the pain other people felt, no matter what it took."

"I wonder what made him change?"

Neil shrugged. "The thing about idealists who want to change the world is that they can get pretty messed up when the world doesn't show the slightest interest in changing. I prefer your da's brand of idealism. He never tries to force anyone to do anything. He just quietly does the best he can and never seems to get angry when things don't work out. He gets sad sometimes, I think. But he doesn't savage himself and turn bitter. I've never thought it out before, but being around him is . . . well, you find yourself wanting to live up to him. Be like him." He chuckled richly. "I tell you, you feel a right git if you lose your temper around him."

"I know," I laughed. "What about a singer called Angel Blue? Have you ever heard of her?"

"Angel Blue." Neil ate another cookie absentmindedly. "She's a pop star, isn't she?"

"What about a writer called Oliver Spike?"

At that moment Mum came in, ravishing in blue draperies. "Oliver Spike. I knew him once. Hello, Neil." She kissed him and then scooped Luke out of his chair.

We both stared at her.

"You knew Oliver Spike?" I asked.

"His real name is Oliver Spinek," Mum said, going to the bench and setting out a bowl with Luke on one hip. "He was studying literature at the same time as I was doing art. He wanted everyone to call him Spike. He felt it was more serious than Oliver." She laughed gently and tipped muesli into the bowl. "Poor Oliver. He was just beginning to win prizes when there was that scandal with an underage girl. It was silly, of course. Oliver was not interested in sex. His writing changed afterward and he made a lot of money, but I doubt it would have made him happy." She went to the fridge for soy milk, poured some into the bowl, then drifted out, leaving Neil and me gazing after her in wonder.

I looked back at him. "What about a poet called Zarbra?"

Neil began to shake his head. Then he stopped. "Lesbian poet who retired to a squalid mansion in England with a bunch of stray cats. Hey, what's with the twenty questions? Am I being milked for an assignment?"

I decided to tell him the truth. "All of those people were connected to Aaron Rayc, and none of them are the same as when they started out."

"You think Rayc had something to do with changing these people's lives?" Neil asked skeptically.

"Not just people—artists."

Neil shrugged. "OK, so the guy is into artists. A lot of rich cats are. But the same question applies. Why would he want to change their lives?"

It was a good question. "I don't know, but I just don't like him. I wish he would leave Da alone." I sounded sullen and childish to my own ears. "How do you and the guys feel about this stuff Da is doing for Aaron Rayc? I mean, doesn't it bother you even a little?"

Neil drank some coffee before answering. "I'm OK with your da doing other gigs, solo and with other bands. The truth is, if he wanted to go solo or get together a better band, I wouldn't feel anything but sad for myself. Because your da is something special. You know that, of course, but I mean he's musically special. Mel and Tich and me are just damn competent, and we're lucky to play with him. Now, Aaron Rayc is playing his cards close to his chest but it's clear he has his sights on your da. Mac knows it. He also knows that he has a vision when he makes music, and that Rayc has a very different vision, and that some differences can't be made right."

I began to feel less wound up.

Neil went on. "Mac's taken these gigs strictly as one-offs, to make ends meet. In my opinion the association with Aaron Rayc is strictly temporary. I know your da can take care of himself." He threw down the last of his coffee and heaved his bulk up, patting me on the shoulder as he lumbered out.

* * *

Gilly called before school the next morning to tell me that Sarry was being moved to Bellavie in Remington later that day. I felt a surge of relief because a bit of me had feared that Dr. Austin would come back from his holiday and stop the whole thing.

"I don't know if I'll get to school today," she said. "The policemen are coming back to see Gran. Apparently there was an eyewitness to the fire."

"Wow. OK."

We decided we would meet at Gilly's hotel the next day and go to Raoul's together. I went to school, consoling myself that it was Friday, and the next day I would see the others and we would come up with a strategy about Harlen. To my intense relief, there was a quiz in English so Harlen had no chance to speak to me. I completed my paper as fast as I could and then spent recess in the front office pretending I had lost something. When the bell rang again, I headed for the computer room, figuring I could spend my study period there. But the computer room was locked and there was a sign up saying no students were to use the computers until further notice as there was a virus in the school system.

I scowled at the door, knowing that if there was a bug in the system, it would probably be in the library terminals as well. Then I had an idea. The editor of the school magazine was Jezabel Aster's older sister, Rianna, whom I knew a bit. I was pretty sure Jezabel had once told me her sister had her own server for the magazine, so if there was something amiss with the school system it ought not to have affected her computer. I knocked at the door of the magazine office and Rianna frowned at my request over her glasses, but agreed that I could use her computer for twenty minutes while she went to make photocopies.

Once alone, I closed the door and did a search for "Angel Blue." Three items appeared, detailing the career of the singer, who turned out to be a soloist with a reputation for changing her band members more often than she changed her underwear. There was nothing to suggest to me that her career had taken a dive or had become suddenly successful. But I came across a paragraph in the last article that said her real name had been Mallory Hart. This made me think of Serenity wanting to change her name and, on impulse, I typed her real name into the search engine. I was startled to find another whole set of entries, and even a fan site that claimed she was one of the greatest songwriter-activists of her generation. None of the articles mentioned her transformation into Angel Blue, and they were all dated before the Angel Blue articles. There was a photograph of her that contrasted strongly with those on the more recent sites.

As Mallory Hart, she was younger, plumper, her hair messier, her teeth crooked, but there was something striking and vivid in her expression that was absent from the perfect and bland beauty of Angel Blue, who had smiled out from the other photo with her hand hooked through Aaron Rayc's elbow.

I studied the photograph and decided it was her eyes that had changed most of all. Here they were warm with laughter and intelligence, and kindness sparkled in them, but in the more recent photo there was indifference. I read the bio and was startled to find that she had been born in Shaletown. The date of birth told me that she would be about forty now.

I decided to use the time remaining to listen to one of Mallory Hart's songs, some of which were on the fan site. It was a ballad about people who lived ordinary lives with heroic courage that would win them no awards or recognition. The song was basically saying that this was the best kind of courage because "it did not admire its reflection in other people's eyes." I liked it very much, but I cut it off to listen to the next song. This was a ballad about an old man mourning his wife, and again there was a sweetness and gentleness to the lyrics that touched me. I wondered suddenly how her music had changed when she became Angel Blue, and made up my mind to visit the big music store in the mall on the weekend.

Twenty minutes had gone and it was almost lunchtime, but there was no sign of Rianna. I typed in "Oliver Spike." There were about sixty hits. I clicked on the first and did a quick scan. The article was about several contemporary writers and implied that, of them all, Oliver was the most highly regarded. I clicked on the next entry and skimmed a review of a recent book, which said that his "merciless eye and savage pen cut through the facades of his culture to reveal the bones and innards of humanity." I grimaced, thinking it made him sound more like a butcher than a writer.

The next item was an article about writers who had longish careers and who had suddenly been lifted to fame. I was struck by one quote in which Oliver Spike said his life had been "simpler and perhaps happier before I became very successful because I was blind to the faults of humanity. I actually believed in all sorts of extraordinarily naive things such as that people are intrinsically good and will do good in most cases, or that one must be honorable, or that friendship is worth dying for. Having my eyes opened to what people are really like has been a painful business, but I can't wish to be blind to the truth."

I studied the unflattering photograph that accompanied

the article: Oliver Spike with a cigarette drooping from his lips, his eyes like dull brown river stones in pouches of sagging flesh. He looked like a picture of decadence, sitting back in his purple dressing gown and squinting dispiritedly through a gray haze of smoke.

Had it been the scandal about the underage girl Mum had mentioned that had "opened his eyes"? I had no doubt of his innocence, because while Mum seemed hardly to exist in the real world most of the time, what she did see of it always scoured through pretense or lies. Maybe Aaron Rayc had set up the scandal. But as Neil had asked, why? Unless Rayc had thought that changing Oliver Spike would make him more successful. And hadn't it? One article all but said his cynical worldview was the reason for his success.

I heard a step in the hallway and my heart started to hammer, but it was only Rianna. She put down a pile of papers and went out, saying casually that I could have ten more minutes. Elated, I hit on the next item and up came another article in a prestigious magazine. It said Oliver Spike's writing had begun as a miraculous celebration of the real and was raw in its message that humans ought to clean up their act and start realizing they were part of the world instead of above it. His later work, while more technically accomplished, had become both more obscure and darker in its message. "I am not sure I can say my work contains a message these days," Oliver Spike had said, "because a message implies meaning and I don't seem to find much meaning in the world or in life."

I shuddered. Deciding that I had had enough of Oliver Spike, I typed in "Patricia Harmigan" and came up with the article I had already seen. I typed in "Dawed Rafael," and again there was a long list. I clicked one at random and skimmed, searching for a mention of Aaron Rayc. There was nothing, and I went on following links until I came upon an interview in which Dawed Rafael spoke of being asked to perform for a charity benefit at the Castledean Estate, saying this had been his entry into the big time. Then I found a Web site for "Castledean Estate." It had the same picture as I'd seen on Aaron Rayc's Web site. The blurb under the picture said that the Castledean Estate was an unparalleled venue for corporate and private functions as well as being a retreat for artists of all kinds. Then there were some details about the number of bedrooms and bathrooms and ballrooms and function rooms and tennis courts and pools. I was still reading when Rianna came in again.

"Time," she said. I closed the window, thanked her, and left.

* * *

I spent lunchtime skulking in an empty classroom, determined Harlen would not corner me again until I had spoken with the others. The next-to-last period of the day was history, but when I got to the room, I found Mrs. Barker collecting test papers from another English class. As I helped her collect them, it occurred to me to ask if she knew anything about Oliver Spike. I was startled at the revulsion that flashed into her eyes, but she only said mildly that he had recently won an important literary prize, but that she did not much like his work.

Of course, I asked why.

"It is unnecessarily cruel," she said.

"What about a poet called Zarbra?"

She brightened. "Her work is marvelous. I read it when I was in college. I remember that it made me literally tremble with delight. She had a way of conveying ordinary life as if it were astonishingly beautiful. She made you see that a blade of grass was no less beautiful and complex, no less vital, than a human being or a deliberate work of art." She laughed. "You could even say that she is one of the reasons I became a teacher. I was fascinated by the power her words had to move and thrill me."

"Why did she stop writing poetry?" I asked.

"No one knows, because when she retired, she declined to give interviews. But how is it you came across her?"

I mumbled that someone had mentioned her to me and I had become curious.

"If you are interested, I can lend you one of her books. It is very precious to me and irreplaceable because her work is out of print now, but I think it would be safe in your hands."

I told her I would love to borrow the book, and she promised to bring it to class Monday. Then other kids started arriving, so she left.

Jezabel Aster sat next to me, saying her sister had mentioned I had been in the magazine office. She asked if I was thinking of joining the committee. I hedged, enjoying her spicy scent as much as her wit. Toward the end of class, she finished taking notes from the board before me and started doodling. I glanced over and was startled to see that she was doodling a perfect copy of the swastika and snakes that I had seen on the wall of the bus shelter!

29

"What doodle?" Jezabel stared at me, uncomprehending, in the hallway after class.

"I told you. You drew it right at the end of history. A swastika and some snakes. You must remember!"

"I don't know what doodle you're talking about," Jezabel insisted.

"Give me your history book and I'll show you."

She sighed and decanted her books onto a windowsill. I grabbed the notebook and flipped through until I reached the page. "There."

She gazed at the drawing. "Jesus, how gross. I don't even remember doing it. But so what? You think it means I have subconscious Nazi tendencies?"

"I'm not saying anything about your subconscious. In fact the Nazis usually had it face the other way. And I don't think they ever had snakes around it. I was just wondering where you saw it."

"I don't know. I mean, I feel like I did see it somewhere, but I don't remember where. You know how images sneak into your mind like advertising jingles. But why are you ask-ing about it?"

"I saw it at a bus stop and some woman told me it was the symbol some gang used," I said.

She shrugged. "Maybe I saw it at the bus stop, too."

* * *

That night Ricki brought over a movie to watch. It was a pretty impressive effort, because he also had to lug over a TV and a DVD player. It was about two extremely stupid men searching for some valuable artifact, but I couldn't seem to get the cleverness that Ricki claimed it showed. Halfway through, I drifted to the kitchen to do the dishes so Da wouldn't come home to a mountain of them. I was restless, because I was actually just waiting for him to come home and prove to me that he hadn't been hurt or changed by working for Aaron Rayc.

Ricki had also brought his dog over, a dog he had saved from death, as he often told people—usually after Nelson (named for Nelson Mandela) had chewed a shoe or some other item of clothing to pieces. Nelson had been relegated to the kitchen after having tried to eat the arm of the sofa, and now he was watching me fill the sink and giving off a strong pea-soup scent that communicated wistful longing.

"What do you want? Food?" I asked and also thought at him.

Nelson tilted his head and gave off an incense smell, which I understood as expressing astonishment at the clarity of my question, and a mint smell that expressed cautious hope. I laughed aloud and repeated my question. This time he responded promptly with the smell of the garden outside.

All right, but don't run away, I thought firmly, and opened the door to let him out. The night air was enticing, so I followed him out and gazed up at the stars. They were diamond bright in the moonless night.

Nelson began to growl and give off a distinct gunpowder scent of warning. I looked out into the street, where pools of bluish light lit a line of cars parked by the gutter. Beyond them, a figure was coming along the street. I watched until the figure became Serenity, her eyes dark-shadowed and tired. She reached the gate before she spotted me, then her preoccupation became instant hostility. "What are you doing?" she demanded.

"Letting a dog have a pee," I said with mild coarseness. "Library again?"

She glared at me. "None of your business." She looked down at Nelson, who was standing on the path between us. I noticed that he was not wagging his tail. "Get that great brute out of my way," she said coldly.

"He's Ricki's. At least, he came with Ricki."

"Get it out of my way," she said again.

"Is something wrong?" I asked as mildly as I could.

She sliced a look at me, and the contempt in her eyes shocked me with its intensity. "You don't get it, do you? Being in this family is an accident. Nothing more. There's no reason I should feel anything for you just because you're my sister, and I despise it that you can worry about me and yet not give a shit about people all over the world who are starving and dying and desperate. And when you do decide to sit up and care about someone who isn't from your family or your country, you feel it so deeply that when she and her family disappear you just go on with your life. People like you make me sick. What would it take to wake you up to how pointless your life is?"

"I didn't just forget about Aya, Serenity. I—"

"I am Sybl," Serenity gritted out between clenched teeth. She turned and went inside, and I stood there staring at the closed door with my mouth open, feeling as if she had spat into my face. Only then did I notice that Nelson was growling deep in his throat again, his face turned to the door through which Serenity had just gone.

* * *

I spent the first half of Saturday babysitting Luke, cooking pumpkin scones, and making yellow Play-Doh as I worried about Serenity and Da. He had left a message on the answering machine saying he would not be back until late that night, and Serenity was still in bed. I didn't know whether to be glad or not. I didn't want to face her, but at the same time the things she had said the night before seemed to confirm that what had happened to Aya was at the heart of her anger, so maybe I should talk to her. But what could I say? I couldn't get out of my mind how Nelson had growled at her, but when I had tried to get him to tell me why, he had only offered me a watered-down version of Serenity's licorice scent, as if this were the answer.

I gave some of the Play-Doh to Luke, but he was too little to do much more than squish it and try to eat it, so I had to keep an eye on him as well as on the food. It was all a bit of a balancing act, especially since, for some reason, Nelson had stayed over even though Ricki and Mirandah had gone out. I had tried to have another conversation with the dog, but he had not seemed to want it. In fact, his attention was on Luke, and I had to keep pushing him away so that Luke would not grab an enthusiastic handful of his rather loose and floppy face.

Don't worry, Nelson's scents assured me. *He smells good, but I won't eat him.*

By the time Mum returned with Jesse, who had driven her to meet Rhona at the gallery where she was to have her show, I was ready to go. I handed Luke over and set off for the mall, determined to listen to Angel Blue at the music shop before I caught the bus to meet Gilly at the Marceau. I wanted to see if Angel Blue's work had taken the same turn as Oliver Spike's and Dawed Rafael's, becoming harder, colder, less hopeful. I still had no idea why or how this could be Aaron Rayc's doing, but there seemed to be a pattern.

It was cloudy and looked like it might rain, but I walked anyway. Unfortunately, the music store didn't have any Angel Blue CDs in stock, but the older woman behind the counter told me she was grim, for all that kids loved her. "All that death and gloom and life's-shit-and-then-you-die." Which was as good as saying Mallory Hart had changed for the worse after getting tangled up with Aaron Rayc. Oddly, I felt reassured by this, because if Aaron Rayc was making people change by hardening them and turning them cynical, he had picked on the wrong person in Da.

Just as I got to the hotel it started raining hard, and I was congratulating myself on my luck until I got inside and the receptionist handed me a note from Gilly asking me to meet her in a cafe a few streets away. I thanked the receptionist and went back outside, sighing. There was nothing to do but make a run for it, and fifteen minutes later I arrived at Medusa's Tearoom drenched to the skin.

A bell tinged delicately as I entered the cafe, which had low coffee tables surrounded by mismatched but comfortable armchairs and sofas, all covered in lurid purple plush. There were no other customers, and an open fire made it just about perfect. The woman behind the counter noticed me and looked horrified. I promised hastily to stand in front of the fire and dry before I sat on her cushions. "It's not the cushions I'm worrying about, dearie," she said kindly. "You'll catch cold if you stay wet through like that. I'll get you a towel." When she brought it, I dried my hair and arms and face gratefully, and pressed some of the wetness out of my clothes. The woman then made me sit close to the fire on a stool and insisted on bringing hot buttered crumpets and tea. The funny thing was that her essence also smelled of crumpets. I panicked a bit when I saw the lovely silver tray with a delicate white china set and pretty doilies, but a hasty examination of the menu calmed me, because I could afford to pay.

I was impressed by this woman's kindness to a bedraggled teenager. Most adults seem to see any teenager as a walking time bomb waiting to explode. When the fire got too hot, I shifted to a seat by the window and sat contentedly watching people running by with sodden newspapers tented over their heads until Gilly arrived.

"Sorry I'm late," she said, hugging me and then grimacing at my dampness. She had an umbrella, of course.

"How is your grandmother?"

"She's just a bit shaken still," Gilly said. The woman who owned the cafe came over, and Gilly said that we would both have hot chocolates.

I protested, but she said I must have one because drinking hot chocolate alone was like drinking alcohol alone and it was her treat. Then she asked how school had gone, and I told her that I had managed to avoid Harlen the whole day. As we drank the chocolate, I told her what I had learned about the various artists. It was hearing that Mum had known Oliver Spike before he had become famous that really got her attention.

"Let's just call him," she said eagerly, pulling out a cell phone. She tapped in the number for information and gave them his name before I could stop her.

I mouthed that he was famous and wouldn't be listed, and she mouthed back that you never knew. I shrugged, but to my horror a moment later she was asking if she was speaking to Oliver Spike. Too late, I realized that she had been directly connected by the operator. Worse, before I could get the receiver from her, she had told him my name and said my mother knew him.

My danger sense was going crazy, and I grabbed the phone from her, terrified she would mention Aaron Rayc as well.

"Zambia Whitestarr?" Oliver Spike was saying in a flat, boneless voice. "I don't know the name. Was that her maiden name?"

My danger sense was going absolutely nuts.

"I think I've m-made a mistake," I stammered, hoping he wouldn't notice the change of voice.

"Zambia . . . wait, there was a girl at school," Oliver Spike went on in his weary, wintry voice. "What was your name?"

My danger sense was reacting so strongly now that I was feeling sick. "Forget it," I said and thought as hard as I could. *Forget this call. Forget the names. It was a wrong number.*

"A wrong number?" Oliver Spike said, sounding confused.

I could hardly believe I had done it again, and over the phone! *It was a wrong number,* I thought again, very deliberately. *It's a nuisance. Erase the number.*

"Just be more careful," Oliver Spike said after a moment. "It's a nuisance, because now I'll have to erase this number." There was a click as he hung up.

I handed the phone back to Gilly, who was staring at me in complete bewilderment. "What happened? You changed color about ten times on the phone, and what on earth were you saying about a wrong number? I gave him your name."

"I just felt I shouldn't be talking to him," I said inadequately.

Thunder cracked loudly, and a flash of lightning lit the room.

"Storm must be right overhead," Gilly said quietly, as if speaking loudly would attract its wrath.

Harrison burst in through the door. "Come on, you two. I've got a taxi waiting. If we dinnae take it, there'll be an hour's wait for another in this."

We paid hastily, and I was glad of the bustle because it stopped me thinking about what had happened on the phone. The figure on the taxi's meter made me feel sick all over again, but in a less eerie way. I would just have to swallow my pride and ask Gilly if I could owe her. But as the taxi sped through the rain-streaked city, Gilly announced that she would pay because her gran had given her the money. Harrison began to argue, saying he would pay for his bit, but then he glanced at me and suddenly gave in. I was startled to find his essence scent infused with lavender. I had no idea what it meant, of course, and I wasn't about to ask and have them start feeling self-conscious about my extended senses.

Once the question of who would pay had been resolved, Harrison told us about Sarry's transfer to Bellavie. He had called her already and she was deliriously happy, saying it was the most beautiful place she had ever been and she couldn't wait for the weather to get better so she could go outside.

At last the taxi pulled up to the front of a stone church.

I couldn't see the houses on either side because it was raining harder than ever, but when the taxi door opened Gilly tumbled out and ran up the walkway to the church door. Harrison did the same, and when I saw him hammer at the door, I gaped.

"You planning to set up house or what?" the driver grumbled.

I mumbled an apology, got out, and did my own splashing dash to join the others. The immense wooden door to the church opened as I reached the top of the wide stone ramp, and there was Raoul looking more casual than I had ever seen him, barefoot in jeans and a dark sweater. Behind him was a wide hallway with a very high roof and low wall lighting, stretching away to the rear of what I now realized must be a renovated and privately owned building. For a long startled minute I had actually thought Raoul might be some sort of priest.

We entered, our footsteps instantly swallowed by the muffling softness of thick dove-gray carpet. The door swished closed and cut off the sound of the storm as Raoul led us down the corridor, past a series of black-and-white photographs showing blown-up details of stonework that I guessed were bits of this very building before it had been altered.

Raoul stopped by the door to an enormous white and seaglass green bathroom and invited us to dry off. Harrison got towels from a cupboard with the ease of familiarity, and Gilly took out a hair dryer from a drawer. Ten minutes later we were all dry, if tousled, and Raoul asked if we were hungry. When we shook our heads, he wheeled the rest of the way down the hall to what he told me was his computer room.

When the door at the end of the hall swung open, I gasped because we had come to a vast room that took up the entire back portion of the church. The roof was very high and sharply angled, and on either side there were stained-glass window inserts that must have been original, transforming the dulled light of the day into jewel-bright smears of yellow and crimson and glowing indigo on the polished floorboards. The entire back wall of the house was glass and looked out into what appeared to be a minor jungle inside a huge greenhouse. The glass roof of the greenhouse was a smooth extension of the roofline of the church, and I gazed in wonder through two layers of glass to where soundless lightning flashed and forked in a bruise-dark sky.

Raoul's wheelchair gave its soft hydraulic hum, and I turned to see that there was a bench running right along the wall through which we had entered. It was laden with more electronic equipment than I had ever seen in my entire life, even in a store. There were at least six computer monitors with keyboards, at least nine cameras, a movie camera on a tripod, a scanner, a DVD player, amplifiers, recording equipment that would have made Neil's mouth water, and a hundred other bits of stuff that I couldn't even identify. Under the bench there were shelves stacked with CDs and DVDs and books.

Raoul had installed himself at a gap in the bench, and he was booting up a computer. Harrison grinned at me, acknowledging my wide-eyed wonder. He and Gilly opened a door in the side wall and brought out three folding chairs, arranging them around Raoul. I sat down, still lost for words but no longer startled at the idea that Raoul would pay for Sarry's convalescent home or have a specially modified car. Gilly's grandmother was well off, but Raoul's wealth was of another order entirely.

Raoul said, "Before we do anything else, I just wanted to show you this." We watched silently as the screen came to life, revealing four enigmatic lines of text.

"You've gotten deeper in?" I guessed, my heartbeat quickening. I felt Harrison and Gilly stir as they realized what they were looking at.

Raoul shook his head. "That's the interesting thing. I haven't. I have never come across such complex protections, but what I have been able to figure out is that to go any deeper into the program, you have to have certain code words and numbers. That means no one is meant to enter it but those for whom it was created. Now, companies do this all the time, for the sake of privacy, but why would a Web site open to the public work in this way?"

"Could it be for secret agents who might have to link in from an Internet cafe?" Gilly asked. She flushed and laughed when we all looked at her, saying she had spies on the brain because she had watched an espionage movie the night before.

But Raoul said she might be right. "Though I doubt it would be political spies. It is more likely to be connected to industrial espionage. I can't think what else it could be, unless this Aaron Rayc is some sort of master criminal. In which case from what you have said, he is following in the fine tradition of crooks who love to hobnob with stars."

"You think he is a criminal then?" I asked, disappointed because I couldn't see any way to fit this in with the pattern of artists' careers.

"All I am saying is that he has something to hide," Raoul said.

Gilly interrupted to urge me to tell them what had happened when we had called Oliver Spike.

"You felt endangered by talking to him?" Raoul asked me.

"I think it was because he could mention my name to Aaron Rayc, who would straightaway think of Da."

Gilly's face fell. "Oh God, I didn't even think. I'm so sorry."

"It's OK," I said. "He won't remember."

"But what if he does?" Gilly asked worriedly.

"He won't. I know."

Harrison was watching me closely. "You know?" he repeated.

I bit my lip, then I said, "I know because I made him forget the whole conversation."

30

"It's something else I can do that I didn't get to tell you the other night." I stopped and drew a breath to calm down. "Sometimes I can . . . make people do what I want just by willing it. By saying the words with my mind. What I've figured out is that, when we think things, we give off those scents that I can smell, and just as my senses have changed so that I can smell better, I can now also shape smells by thinking. Twice, I've willed people to forget things, and both times it worked, but it doesn't work all the time so I think it also has something to do with the strength of mind of the person I am willing."

"Like hypnosis," Gilly murmured, looking fascinated.

"But you were on the phone tae this guy," Harrison pointed out.

I nodded. "I know. I only did it because I was desperate, and I have no idea how it worked. Maybe I've got this whole scent thing wrong, because I thought it was possible only when I was looking at someone."

"It might be that being afraid activated some new ability,"

Raoul said. "The important thing is that you dealt with the danger. Figuring out how you managed it can come later."

"I'm sorry I didn't tell you this before. I guess the truth is that it feels kind of horrible doing it. Like mental bullying."

Raoul said firmly, "You were protecting yourself, that's all."

"Did you ever try willing Harlen tae leave you alone?" Harrison asked.

I stared at him, realizing that it had never occurred to me. But Raoul was shaking his head. "Maybe it would be better not to try that just yet. If the sickness Harlen carries is attracted to the possibility that your senses are altered, the last thing we want is to confirm it."

"You know, I've been thinking about Aaron Rayc," Gilly said, gazing at the computer screen. "Your being so scared and suspicious about him would make a lot more sense if he smelled of wrongness, too."

"But he doesn't, and anyway, it would be a bit of a coincidence that two infected people were after different members of the Whitestarr family," I said. "I just wish Da was home from his gig in Remington."

"Remington," Raoul said thoughtfully. I wondered if he was going to mention Sarry and the convalescent home, but instead he tapped at the keys and in a few minutes we were looking at the same site for the Castledean Estate that I had looked at in the school magazine office.

Raoul said he had come across the site earlier that day but had not looked into it. He tapped a key and we read that although it was owned by Rayc Inc., the majority of events staged there were organized by the international charitable organization ORBA, which also funded the artist residency program on the estate. Three- and six-month residencies were available to emerging and established artists from all disciplines. I felt cold at the thought of how many bright young artists might be drawn to the Castledean Estate, and what might happen to them there.

"Let's see what you need to get in," Raoul said, and tapped on the icon to download the application form. Immediately the screen began to shudder and fuzz.

"What the hell?" Raoul said, because the fuzz had vanished and now something was downloading. Then we were all staring, shocked, at a naked man.

"Oh no!" Gilly said, horrified.

"It's a porn site," Harrison said flatly.

"This is impossible," Raoul muttered, tapping the escape button to no avail. He tried returning to the previous page, but the camera panned sideways to show a child. Raoul swore softly and switched the whole computer off. I stared at our ghostly reflections in the blackened computer screen and thought about the note on the computer-room door at school.

I chewed my lip. "Raoul, when I called up Aaron Rayc's Web site on the school computer, a creepy bondage Web site came up. I couldn't get it to go away, and now there's a notice on the door of the computer room saying no one is allowed to use the computers because of a virus."

"That is . . . weird," Gilly said.

Raoul said, "It sounds as if the virus was either in Aaron Rayc's Web site and migrated to the Castledean Web site, or vice versa. But where did it originate? I'd like to look into it. Why don't you three test the game for me in the meantime."

I didn't feel the least like playing a computer game, but neither did I want to look at child porn or maybe something equally disgusting, so I agreed. Harrison and Gilly must have felt the same, because they agreed, too. Raoul settled us in front of another screen and gave us joysticks and earphones that were amazingly comfortable and therefore probably amazingly expensive. Then he explained that the game offered realistic human problems in a fantasy setting, saying that it was to be a teaching tool for psychology students.

I wasn't much of a games person as a rule, but it was fun playing with Harrison and Gilly because once we had got into the game, they played their roles imaginatively and with great flair. I felt like a lump of wood between them. Gilead, Mistress of the Flame, had a host of sometimes invisible pet salamanders and the ability to turn rock into lava, in which she could then swim; and Prince Har was Lord of Harfeld City. I was Zonda, who had the amazing ability to communicate with animals, which was ironic considering I had not told the others I could do so in real life. I was beginning to feel embarrassed about the things I kept revealing.

By the time we had finished the game, I felt refreshed and energized. I looked at my watch and was astonished to discover we had played for over an hour.

"Dinner," Raoul said decidedly, and he wheeled ahead of us out to the kitchen.

I expected to be given a hard-boiled egg and toast or noodles, but dinner was gourmet pizza made expertly by Raoul in his state-of-the-art black and white kitchen. We all watched appreciatively. When it was cooked, we carried it out and ate it at a long trestle table set up on a mosaic-covered square at the heart of the indoor jungle.

It felt incredible to be eating pizza by candlelight, bare-armed because the enormous greenhouse was heated for the tropical plants, with rain pelting softly down on the transparent roof overhead. Dessert was baked pears with rich chocolate sauce.

"That was sublime," I told Raoul when we had finished. We hadn't talked about anything but the game during the meal, and Raoul's questions had made it clear that he was really using us to test it. But then he asked Harrison and Gilly if they would carry in the trays and load the dishwasher. They both glanced at me before going inside.

"There is now a virus in my computer system, and it looks as if it has affected all of my terminals," he said. "So far as I can make out, the virus causes random links with pornography sites, then freezes a system so the link can't be broken. If you switch the computer off, the link is immediately reestablished when it is switched on again."

"Oh, I'm so sorry," I said contritely.

"You're not responsible for a virus," Raoul said dismissively. "But I want to know how it got through my firewall and

297

virus protection. To track it and to clean up my system, I will need to call in some expert help. By expert I mean a hacker. I'd like to see if she can also get some more information about Aaron Rayc. How do you feel about that?"

I knew he meant how did my danger sense feel about it. "I think it would be better if Aaron Rayc doesn't know anyone is interested in him," I said slowly, wishing I could just tell him what Gary Soloman had said. The truth was I was beginning to resent the promise that he had exacted.

Raoul nodded. "You needn't worry about Daisy on that count. She is fanatically careful. The other thing I'd like to do is to call into the headquarters of ORBA. I want to see how they are tied up with Rayc Inc."

I licked my lips, thinking I had to warn him. "Raoul, I . . . I want to tell you something about Aaron Rayc, but I made a promise."

"Promises ought to be kept," Raoul said simply.

"I know, and I *am* keeping it, but I have to tell you that . . . someone warned me that it could be dangerous to be caught prying into Aaron Rayc's business."

"This . . . person who warned you. Are they a friend?"

I shook my head. "Just someone I met while I was trying to find out more."

"Well, you needn't worry. I won't mention you or Aaron Rayc. In fact, I will present myself as a possible future donor."

I bit my lip, then I said, "Raoul, why are you going to so much trouble to help me?"

He smiled. "Partly because what I've learned has made

me curious. But I have thought a lot since we talked at the hotel, and I can't help but wonder if this wrongness—this sickness—could be responsible for much of man's inhumanity to man and beast. Imagine if all cruelty and ugliness came down to this sickness. That means humanity might be capable of being healed, if we could learn enough about it."

"But Aaron Rayc—"

"Isn't infected," Raoul completed my sentence. "But you think there is something wrong with him, and given what else your senses perceive, I mean to find out what it is about him that makes you so uneasy."

Harrison and Gilly had come back, and Harrison said, "I have tae say I feel pretty much the same way as Raoul. But I think our first priority has tae be tae protect you from the sickness. That is, from Harlen Sanderson."

Raoul stretched, and the movement made me realize how stiff I had become. I was also feeling strange because of what he had said about the sickness being behind the awful things that people had done in the world. That meant hundreds of people might be infected, and not just in our time. I said that I had better go, and Raoul suggested we all have a hot drink in the kitchen before heading our separate ways.

As Gilly put the kettle on to boil and Harrison and I assembled cups, I finally asked Gilly what had happened the previous day with her grandmother and the police.

"Not all that much. A neighbor saw two guys hanging around the place. The police just wanted to know if Gran had seen them. The weird thing is that when they were reading the description, I had the feeling I had seen them, but I can't imagine where."

"How did the neighbor describe the guys?" I asked, sipping my tea.

"One was a skinhead. The other might have been, too, but he was wearing a hoodie. Anyway, the police reckon they're part of a gang who have torched a lot of different places."

That snagged on something, but the doorbell rang. It was Jesse, and I had to go before I could drag it out of the depths of my mind.

* * *

"What's up?" Jesse asked curiously. We were halfway home, and I realized that I hadn't said more than two words the whole way.

I looked at his handsome round face lit up by the ghastly blue-green light from the dashboard.

"Jesse, what if you had the power to help humanity change for the better? Would you feel like you ought to do it?"

"Depends."

"On what?"

"On lots of things. On what I had to do to make them change, for one. I mean if you said I had to run over some kid or he'd grow up to be a monster and kill a whole lot of people, I'd say no. But if you said I had to stand by a dam and stick my finger in it to save a village, even though the whole bank might break open and kill me, I hope I'd say yes. But it's also the old power question in disguise, isn't it?" Jesse added.

"Power?" I echoed, puzzled.

He shrugged. "If you have power and use it, and power inevitably corrupts, then by using your power, you would be allowing yourself to be corrupted. But would the corruption be worse than the harm you could prevent?"

"Do you think power *always* corrupts if it is used? Might there not be a way to act and not be corrupted? Let's say you have some trusted advisers and you listen to them."

"A devil's advocate would say that they would then have power and would be corrupted by it to the extent of the power you gave them."

I sighed. "So what is it? No action is best or action is best?"

"I don't think you can make a rule. I think it has to be that you decide these things in the moment on a case-by-case basis."

"Wouldn't you still be corrupted?"

"There is always the danger, but I think if you are aware of that and make your goals humble and never let yourself get really sure or certain about anything, and if you also have trusted friends whose advice you listen to, then you're less likely to be corrupted." He flicked me a look. "That must have been some video game you were playing tonight."

I laughed.

31

On Sunday I was in the living room doing homework when Jesse came in and asked me to tell Serenity to run to the store for something he needed. He was babysitting Luke, and weekend Luke-sitters were always assigned a gofer for the day. If I hadn't been in the middle of a train of thought in an essay, I might have offered to go instead. As it was, I was only irritated slightly at having to run upstairs.

I padded barefoot up the stairs, still inside my own head when I pushed open the bedroom door and saw Serenity on her knees by the bed. My first absurd thought was that she was praying, but then I realized she was pushing something under the bed. Then the door creaked a little and she spun round.

"You're always spying on me," she snapped. "Why can't you just leave me alone?"

"I wasn't," I said indignantly. "In case you've forgotten, this is my bedroom, too! But I only came in to tell you that Jesse wants something from the store."

Serenity's eyes blazed with a loathing that shocked me and made me step aside as she stalked past, leaving me enveloped in a waft of licorice and burning hair. Shaken, I resolved to tell Da that I thought she needed help. I heard the front door slam and crossed to the window to watch her go out the gate and up the street, a string shopping bag dangling from her hand. Turning away from the window, my gaze fell on her bed and, without thinking, I crossed the room and knelt down to look. All I could see under the bed was a thin book with a yellow cover. I pulled it out. The title of the book was *The Way,* and from its size, it looked to be a poetry book. The first page had a list of what I thought must be poems, only when I ran my eye down them, they didn't sound much like poetry. The first one said, "The Way to Proceed," and turned out to be a chapter heading. The chapter began by saying that it was impossible to know one's true path if one's life was full of attachments. "The first step in learning one's path," it went on, "is to divest oneself of connections to humans and to material things. Only then is one truly naked in body and soul."

The language reminded me a bit of the stuff I had read about the *bushi,* and as I read on, it seemed to me that this was a kind of code, too. The next chapter was titled, "The Poetics of Thought and Action." Racy, I thought with a jab of humor, but at the same time I crossed to the window to keep an eye out for Serenity, knowing she would be incandescent if she caught me snooping. I did feel guilty, but my curiosity overrode it.

"To act is an expression of thought," the book said. "To act on an ideal is to live an ideal rather than merely talking and thinking about it. Courage is shown when we act upon our thoughts. Courage is making thought a reality. An ideal which is not acted upon is nothing. It is less than nothing, because it is a hollow thought with no intent. Those who profess ideals and do not act upon them are cowards and deceivers."

The last sentence jolted me a bit because it was the sort of thing Serenity had been saying, and it had the same venom I had seen in her eyes as she had stormed from the room. I flicked through the book, reading a sentence here and there and finding more of the same oddly religious-sounding philosophy with the occasional unexpectedly sharp accusatory passage. Then I came to a bit that struck me as having a different tone from what had gone before. I went back a little and read it more slowly.

There are some situations that demand action from any human being who encounters them or learns of them. That we do not act is our shame. Those who watch and do nothing while evil is allowed to exist and operate are more guilty than those who commit the evil.

History is full of such cowardice and indifference, of these watchers who did nothing. They are the dogs that did not bark, and they prospered by their silence and bred more of their kind, who see nothing and hear nothing and do not speak out against evil; who feel safe and pure because they commit no action that is evil.

Are you such a dog?

Are you one who sees evil and does not protest against it? Are you one who watches as nations slaughter one another and then turns cold-eyed to your favorite television program? Do you see the obscenely wealthy spend billions on clothes and jewelry and retaining their youth while thousands of children die agonizing deaths for want of food or clean water or shelter, and feel no desire to protest?

Somewhere in the house a door banged, and I gave a start and nervously listened, but there was no sign of Serenity. There was another bang, and I guessed that she must have left the screen door unlatched.

I knew I ought to put the book back before I was caught, but I turned to the last chapter, wanting to get some sense of what the book was leading to. The chapter heading was "Commitment."

A coldness crept through me, because hadn't the bouncer type who had stopped Harrison from going into Serenity's poetry meeting said something about commitment? And the name of the group—the Morality Complex—almost sounded like it could have been a chapter heading in the book. I read some of the last chapter.

That we must protest against evil and wrongdoing, against cowardice and avarice and cruelty, is obvious to anyone who can think or feel and who professes to be human and the bearer of a soul.

But there come moments in every life when we could do far more than merely protest or stand against evil. In these moments, it is possible that a single action may cause a beacon of light to blaze out, which would illuminate and inspire all who see it, and change the world forever.

You say that single actions do not change the course of the world? Look at history and see that it is not so. A person with the courage to act in the right moment could change the world. But most people fail the test of such moments. Their vision is dim or nonexistent and their minds clouded with doubt and fear or with inappropriate attachment to people or to material possessions.

Do not fail to grasp the moments of destiny that come to you and in which you may be a true and decisive force for change. Make your mind and spirit strong and resolute enough to reject the doubts that will rear up in your path like snakes.

Commit to the moment and act, for in this moment, by acting, you reveal your deepest self.

The door slammed again. Suddenly panicking, I dropped to my knees, but in trying to close the book to put it back under the bed, I managed to flip open the last page.

What I saw made me freeze in disbelief, for here was the swastika with snakes that I had seen before. Only this one was not graffiti or a doodle. It was printed.

And there were words under it: "Beyond this point there is only action."

"How dare you touch my things," Serenity hissed.

I spun around in fright, leaving the book on the ground. Serenity darted across the room and snatched it up.

"Jesus, calm down," I said, my words languid enough to belie my pounding heart. "What is it, anyway? Your diary?"

She actually looked as if I had hit her. The blood drained from her face and she looked deathly ill or else terribly old, except for her eyes, which seemed to go from molten dark blue to stony black hardness. "You have no idea, do you?" she asked in a low, passionate voice. "You're like some cow in a field, chewing on its cud."

"You need help, Serenity," I said.

"Fuck you," she said, and walked out, closing the door behind her with contemptuous care.

I stared at the closed door for a long time, shocked by her swearing. Not by the word itself, but by her use of it.

As a family, we didn't swear. It was not forbidden so much as regarded as dull-witted. Da had gently drummed into us that a person with a good vocabulary could say anything and everything with great precision and emphasis. A swearword was like throwing a lump of dung at someone by comparison. It might connect, but it was dull and imprecise and you got dirty using it. I had grown up, as we all had, to see swearing as a form of stupidity.

But something more frightening than stupidity was going on. What did it mean that Serenity had a book with a swastika in it that was supposed to be the emblem of some violent gang in Shaletown? And what had the book to do with the poetry group at the library?

"A pretty weird sort of poetry group," Harrison had said after following Serenity that night, and I cursed myself for wallowing in premature relief. What sort of poetry group had tough-looking skinheads minding the door? What sort of poetry group demanded commitment to ideals from its members?

* * *

Da still hadn't returned by dinnertime, so we ate his celebration dinner without him: me, Jesse, Serenity, and Mirandah, who had made pumpkin ravioli stuffed with spinach and ricotta cheese. I barely tasted the food. I was desperate for Da to come home, not just because I wanted to see he was safe, but because I had to talk to him about Serenity.

I had expected to smell rage on her, but her face was wiped clean of all emotion. Her thin pretense of eating seemed to come from habit rather than from any real desire to seem normal. When she got up from the table, I didn't go up after her, because I was determined not to go to bed until I had spoken to Da.

But it got later and later, and my thoughts swung from worrying about Serenity to worrying about Da. Close to eleven, Mum drifted into the room, looking fresh and alert. She kissed my cheek and said, "He'll be here before morning." Just as if she had read my mind.

"Mum," I said, hardly able to believe I was going to say it, "I'm worried about Serenity."

She nodded, and the movement sent her glorious red curls tumbling softly about her shoulders. "I am thinking of painting her, my darling."

I felt a surge of anger toward her. I wanted to scream at her to pay attention to the real world for once instead of only ever seeing it in terms of her paintings. There were things going on that needed taking care of, and people—Da and Serenity, and me too, maybe. I wanted to ask what kind of mother she was if you could never have a proper conversation with her. What good, I wanted to rage, was all that beauty and talent to us?

My brief fury faded, because what would have been the use of my rant? Mum would probably just suggest painting me.

She touched my cheek as she went out, and I saw a fleeting vision of flames that frightened me until I realized they were only painted. I went up to my room, feeling depressed and anxious. Serenity was already in her bed, of course, and turning to face her humped form, I focused my hearing on her breathing and heartbeat to reassure myself that she was asleep. But it was a long time before I slept.

Madness, I thought, and realized that it was the first time I had allowed myself to think the word, and yet it was what I had seen in Serenity's face when she had snatched up the book earlier. Madness or something very close to it.

* * *

That night I dreamed of myself as a wolf, but for the first time I felt myself hunted, or at least watched by hidden, malevolent eyes. And for the first time the unease I had occasionally

309

felt during the wolf dreams coalesced into the distinct feeling that time was running out.

Time for what? I wondered upon waking. Then I remembered Da and hastened out of bed with fear drubbing through me to find out if he was home. He wasn't in the kitchen as he usually was, having a cup of tea in sweaty clothes after his morning run, and my heart sank. Then I saw Serenity in her school uniform standing by the window and staring out.

"Serenity, is Da home?" I asked. She turned and looked at me as she calmly picked up her bag and went out the door.

Only then did I spot the note propped against the toaster. I tore it open and read that he was sorry he had missed what looked to have been a memorable welcome-home dinner. But we shouldn't wake him for at least a hundred years, whereupon we were to have shaving cream and a razor at the ready. It was so Da that I laughed aloud, and suddenly all my dark imaginings seemed absurd. What an idiot I was. Of course nothing could change Da.

* * *

On the bus I went back to thinking about the yellow book. To begin with, the statements in it had seemed strident but plausible. People ought to act on their ideals and stand up for what they believed in; and it was true that some of the most terrible things in the world had only been able to happen because good people stood back and did nothing. But there had been something ugly under the words, a sense that someone was being blamed; a hectoring accusation that erupted only occasionally into the open with vicious diatribes against those who failed to act.

And was that the aim of the harangue? That a reader should prepare herself to act? But to act how? Harrison had said the thug who stopped him going into the meeting room at the library had spoken of the need to prove his commitment. But what did that mean? It was like there was a haze of pompous and impressive words obscuring something harder and more sinister.

The bus pulled up at the school, and I hung back to avoid being jostled by a couple of younger boys trying to see who could punch the hardest as they got out. These were the sort of kids a gang ought to be recruiting, I thought. What use would a gang have for a reclusive, troubled girl like Serenity, with her pacifist ideals? She was more like someone they would choose for a victim.

* * *

I could feel Harlen's eyes boring into my back as we did a term test in English, and I felt sure he would say something after class about me avoiding him. I knew I should stay around and defuse his anger by letting him corner me, maybe even agree to another meeting somewhere very public, but I was in too much turmoil about Serenity. If I could, I would evade him again.

There were three essay choices, and I was relieved to see that one focused on *The Lonely Passion of Judith Hearne*. I settled to work, and did not stop until forty minutes later when Mrs. Barker called time.

As we lined up to turn the papers in, Gilly whispered into my ear that Sylvia Yarrow had left school. I turned to stare at her, and she nodded solemnly.

"Why?"

"No one knows. I heard some kids talking about it before you got here." We fell silent as we got to Mrs. Barker, and she smiled briefly as she took our papers. As we left the classroom, me hustling Gilly so we would be out of sight by the time Harlen got out, she asked if Da had got home safely.

"He came home late last night," I said, getting round a corner and out of sight of the classroom door with relief. "Let's go into a room," I said as the bell rang. "I have to tell you something." I glanced around, and Gilly finally figured out that I was worried about Harlen. So she looked around with blatant furtiveness that made me want to laugh in spite of everything. We found an empty room, and I drew her to sit at a desk that could not be seen by anyone glancing in as they passed the door. I told her, then, about finding the book under Serenity's bed and about the swastika. Suddenly she gave a gasp and bit her lip.

"Alyzon, you've just reminded me. That neighbor who saw those two guys hanging around Gran's house . . . but it can't have any connection . . ."

"What?

"Well, the policeman said the neighbor thought they were some sort of neo-Nazis, because one of them had a swastika with yellow snakes around it tattooed on the back of his head!"

I felt winded. "Did they say anything else about them?"

Gilly shook her head. "The neighbor didn't get close enough to be able to describe anything in too much detail. But, Alyzon, how could guys like that have any connection with some poetry group? It must just be a coincidence that they're using the same symbol."

"Maybe," I said. But I didn't believe it.

"What were the words?" Gilly asked. I stared at her blankly. "You said there were words under the swastika in the book."

"Beyond this point there is only action," I told her, thinking sickly of Serenity being somehow involved in the house fire that had deprived Gilly and her gran of their home. But at the same time it was absolutely ludicrous to imagine Serenity setting a house on fire, or even approving it.

It just didn't make sense.

 **32**

The next class was a slide presentation from a kid who read in such a slow monotone that I had to struggle not to fall asleep. I was glad of the cover of darkness, though, because it left me free to think. I had made up my mind that I would go to the city library that night, and after Serenity's meeting, I would follow whoever looked most like the leader of the group. I didn't know what it would prove or reveal, but I wanted to see them and get my own scent impressions, if I could.

I would have told Gilly what I intended at lunchtime, but a girl from our science class came hurrying in at the end of the slide show to say that she was wanted urgently in the science lab. Gilly grimaced resignedly as she went, but I knew she loved science and was pleased that Mr. Stravin relied on her so much.

Left alone and seeing Harlen heading outside with some other guys, I went to the school library determined to learn the correct name for the reverse swastika. I sat down at a table to draw it so I could show the librarian without a lot of explanation. On impulse, I drew in the yellow snakes in case they meant something to her. Then I noticed Harlen standing on the other side of the desk. He had not yet seen me, but I could tell that he was searching.

I was certain he had gone outside deliberately to make me think the coast was clear, and I had fallen for it. Since there was no way out of the library but past the desk and he would spot me at once if I moved, I forced myself to calm down. I might just as well stay where I was, wait for him to notice me, and play along.

Harlen saw me, and I smiled and raised my hand. He looked really startled for a second, then he came toward me. To my astonishment, my danger sense went berserk. I clamped hard and tried frantically to think why it would react so violently when it hadn't that morning in English. Fortunately, the librarian called out to ask Harlen something and, flustered with panic, I folded my drawing and stuffed it into my pocket. Like a switch being thrown, my keening danger sense fell silent. Curious, I took the drawing out again and at once my senses began to shrill. I stuffed the paper quickly into my pocket again and the shrilling died away, even though Harlen was approaching, his smell as hideous as ever.

"Hello, stranger," he said. "Glad to see you without your watchdog."

"Hi," I said, sounding stiff to my own ears and wishing I was a better actress. But I intensely disliked him referring to good, kind Gilly as a watchdog.

"I'm not letting you out of my sight until you name a time

and place for our date." His voice was caressing and amused but determined.

I crossed my fingers and said brightly, "That would be great! We could meet after school one night in the mall. I love that cafe we were going to meet at before."

"I was thinking more along the lines of a drive-in," Harlen said.

"Drive-in?" I echoed, startled. "I didn't think those things existed anymore."

"There's one out on the back road between Shaletown and Remington. There's a retro cafe attached to it," Harlen said. "I can have a friend drive us there in my mother's car."

Even though I was casting about desperately to find a good excuse to refuse the arrangement, a bit of me couldn't believe how arrogant Harlen was assuming that his friend would chauffeur us around. But maybe the arrogance was just another symptom of infection.

I said diffidently, "I don't think my da would agree to a drive-in. I can ask him, though."

"Tell him it'll be a comedy," Harlen instructed. "And tell him I'd take very good care of his little girl."

I managed with great effort not to shudder. When he left, I took the drawing out again, and this time when I smoothed it flat, my senses were quiet.

I played devil's advocate with myself. Maybe it wasn't that Harlen was connected to the Shaletown gang. Or maybe he was, and the swastika emblem was just a recycled logo like Jezabel had suggested. In which case there might be no connection between the Shaletown gang and the book under Serenity's bed.

But Harlen had gone to school in Shaletown, and hung around with at least one skinhead. And Serenity's problems seemed to have begun in Shaletown. And the gang with the swastika logo was based in Shaletown. And besides all that, why would my danger sense go crazy at the possibility that Harlen would see the drawing I had made if there was no connection?

Then a memory slid into my mind: Harlen giving me an unlabeled CD for Serenity.

I realized then that I had to go back to Shaletown. I didn't know how all of the stuff with the gang and the swastika connected to Harlen, but I wanted to find out. Because the thing I feared most was that Harlen, who carried a contagious sickness of the spirit, was involved with my spiritually wounded sister.

The remainder of the day, I spent my time uselessly willing classes to go faster. I was like a dog tied to a stump, wanting nothing more than to be free to follow my own desires. But at last the school day ended. I couldn't tell Gilly what I meant to do, because her grandmother was in their car waiting with Samuel. I hadn't seen the old woman since the night I had gone to her home after my visit to Shaletown, and she looked startlingly frail and old. But she smiled warmly and told me to come and see them soon. Gilly was touchingly protective of her, and as I waved them off, I was glad I had said nothing about my intention to spy on Serenity's poetry group. She had enough on her plate without worrying about me as well.

I spent an hour doing homework in the school library to give Serenity time to get into her meeting. Harrison had said she had worked for a while before going into the meeting room, and I didn't want to risk lurking in the city library where she might spot me. The other advantage of hanging around was that there was less chance of bumping into Harlen, though I felt as if our meeting in the library had taken the pressure off me a bit.

There were only two older kids waiting for the city bus, and in a short time I was getting out at the city library. I was fairly sure I had left enough time for Serenity to get into the meeting room, but just in case I came into the entrance hall warily. There were six meeting-room doors, and the two nearest the front door were shut. I sauntered past them, but even with my hearing fully extended, I couldn't make out more than that there were people in both. That meant there was soundproofing in the walls, like in Da's shed.

I checked my watch and then went through the library doors, which were opposite the meeting-room doors. I wanted to find somewhere I could position myself so that I could see everyone coming out. The best spot was the magazine racks, because if Serenity happened to come into the library after the meeting, she would never go there, and from behind them I could see through the doors and into the hallway. The shelves were waist high so I would have to squat the whole time, but being close to the door, I would be able to get out quickly to follow my quarry.

I checked my watch again and then went to the checkout desk and asked the pimple-faced guy on the other side of the counter if my stamp-collecting club had begun their meeting already.

He frowned and said he didn't think there was a stamp-collecting club scheduled in any of the meeting rooms. He pulled out a ledger to check and ran his finger down a page. Then he shook his head, saying I must have got the day wrong as there were only a regular poetry group meeting and some people trying to organize funding for a jazz festival. I asked when those meetings would end, and the guy said both meetings had booked an hour slot, so they would both end in about ten minutes.

I pretended to be puzzled, and he suggested the meeting I wanted might be at the East Library on the other side of the city. I wandered off trying to look disconsolate, but a backward glance showed that my performance was wasted. He had already forgotten me in the process of checking out a great pile of books for an elderly couple.

I went to squat down beside the magazine rack, but I had been there barely five minutes when a whole bunch of people lined up at the checkout desk, blocking my view completely!

Cursing myself for not anticipating this, I knew I had about five minutes to find another spot. There was nowhere else in the library, I realized, and the only other choice was to wait outside. I would just have to hope Serenity didn't see me. But when I came into the hall, I had a brainstorm. I could hide in an empty meeting room!

I ducked inside a darkened room just as I heard the door

to one of the other meeting rooms open. There was a hum of voices as people came out, and I was about to stick my head out to look when a voice behind me said softly, "I wouldnae bother."

My heart gave a great bound of fright, and I swung round to find Harrison sitting on the table closest to the door. His pale hair glowed and his spectacles reflected rectangles of light from the door, with me arrested in them like an ant trapped in amber. I was so shocked I couldn't speak. Harrison got to his feet and came over to me. "That's the festival people," he said softly.

"Wha . . . what are you doing here?" I gasped.

He grinned, a slice of white in the dimness. "Same thing as you, I guess. Thought it might be interesting tae take a second look."

"Why?" I asked.

He shrugged. "Watching a person once isnae enough tae get a clear picture of anything. You need tae watch a few times tae be able tae establish patterns." We heard the sound of another door opening. "That's them," Harrison mouthed and put a finger to his lips.

I nodded, and we both turned to look out into the hall, although we couldn't see anything without leaning out of the doorway. I extended my hearing until I could detect people moving into the hallway and down the passage, some going into the library and others going through the front door and down the steps. I didn't move, because now that the door was open, I could hear the sound of chairs being stacked and desks shifted. Someone was straightening the room, and I hoped it was the person I meant to follow.

At last I heard the light snap off. Footsteps came into the passage and stopped. I strained my hearing, wondering what he was doing. Again I heard footsteps on the terra-cotta tiles—a flat, heavy man's tread, I thought—then registered in horror that they were not going away but coming toward the end of the hall where we were hiding.

My senses instantly screamed of danger. I turned in silent panic to Harrison, who had grown rigid beside me. He stared at me for a split second, then he took off his glasses. His gray eyes looked silver in the dim light, and I had time to note there was no fear in them as he reached out and pulled me into his arms. Before I could protest, his mouth was on mine.

Of course, I realized immediately what he was doing. I clamped hard on my senses and, at the same time, I made my body passive and leaned into him just as a man came to stand in the doorway, watching us. I saw him out of the corner of a slitted eye. He smelled of burnt rubber, gasoline, and the sharp chemical stink of formalin.

Then he was gone, and so was the smell.

The danger sense faded at once and I ought to have stepped away, but the minute Harrison's lips had touched mine, I had felt his feelings: anger, determination, and a powerful curiosity. Then I had become aware of a second level of feelings, fiercely repressed. Harrison knew what this contact would mean and was trying to keep his deeper feelings from me.

But the kiss was too intimate and too prolonged, and even though some bit of me registered that the man had gone, I did not let go and step away. Instead, my clamp seemed to dissolve and I was filled with a hungry heat and the intoxicating smell of storm and lavender and wet leaves. I wound my arms tightly around him, pressing myself against the whole length of him, and pushing my fingers into hair that was astonishingly soft. My whole body seemed to want to merge with his, and at the same time I felt my senses penetrate his, wanting whatever was being withheld.

I let my tongue touch his, demanding access to the sweetness I sensed. He groaned against my mouth, then violently wrenched away from me. I stared at him, shocked, yet a potent residue of all that I had felt was churning and boiling through my veins, urging me back into his arms. Harrison's face was chalk white, his cheekbones standing out under eyes that were mercury-bright rings around huge dark pupils. He looked . . . appalled.

Mortification flowed through me like a tide of lava. "God, I . . . I'm so sorry. I don't know why I acted . . ." I heard the agonizing shame in my voice and lifted my hands to my cheeks. They felt ice cold and feverishly hot at the same time.

Some of the starkness seemed to go from his face. "You didnae . . . ," he began urgently, but he checked himself and shook his head hard. Then he put on his glasses and said in a voice striving for calmness, "Look, we'll talk about this later, but we have tae go or we'll lose him."

I felt sick. I ached. I felt like crying. I nodded. Harrison stepped past me and looked out. I stayed where I was, leaning against the open door and trying to get control of my body. A few minutes passed, or ten hours, then Harrison said tersely, "He's gone out. Let's go."

I made myself follow. My legs felt unsteady, and I had to bite my lip to keep the tears back. I had never felt more confused in my life.

Harrison stopped abruptly at the entrance to the library and looked out. I guessed that Serenity must be waiting for Da, but when I looked past him, I saw with a stab of alarm that there was a guy standing with her. He was not a skinhead, though his hair was very short, and he was older than I had expected. Maybe thirty. I extended my senses, but neither of them was speaking just then. Serenity was looking through her bag and then, wordlessly, she drew out a book and gave it to the man. The yellow book.

He nodded and reached out to clasp her shoulder. Then she turned and went away down the street. The guy watched her for a long moment, then he crossed the street and went in the other direction.

"Come on," Harrison said decisively.

We hurried down the library steps, and as we reached street level, I glanced back in the direction Serenity had gone and saw that she was some distance away, walking swiftly. Harrison had already set off after the guy and I hurried to catch up, but when I made to cross the street, he shook his head. "We can follow less conspicuously from this side of the street."

I nodded, ashamed all over again at what had happened in the meeting room. What must he think of me turning a clever ruse to protect us from discovery into some sort of impassioned embrace?

The guy we were following was walking swiftly and with purpose, and he didn't look back once. "He's headed for the highway," I said. Once we reached the road that ran parallel to it, I felt immediately exposed because there were no trees and few cars. If our quarry glanced back, he would see us.

But he had vanished.

"He's taken one of the underpasses," Harrison said urgently, and broke into a run. At the underpass entrance, I stared at a sign in dismay, because it said that the underpass split in two. One path would take us to the bus station and the other to the mall.

"He'll be too far along for us tae see which way he went," Harrison said. "Choose."

"Eastland Mall," I said. I would have raced down the steps, but Harrison pointed to the highway. I understood at once. If we crossed over it, we would arrive at the mall first. We scaled the concrete barrier and dodged across the highway, which was crammed with traffic. Luckily there was so much of it that it was virtually at a standstill. Beyond the barrier on the other side was an enormous parking lot. We wove through the cars, and by the time we reached the fountain in the square where the underpass came out, we were both panting hard. I sat on the damp stone rim, positioning myself so that the water would screen us from anyone coming out of the tunnel. Not that the man would recognize us if he did see us, because I had been plastered too close to Harrison for anyone to have got a good look at our faces back in the meeting room. Firmly I shoved down the embarrassment that coiled up in me like a snake.

"Was that the guy who warned you off last time?" I asked. I was surprised how normal my voice sounded.

"No," Harrison said. "This guy is older, and the other one was bulkier and he had a shaved head."

"Did you see them all go into the meeting?"

"They were going in when I got there, your sister and about seven others. All young and all loner types, I'd say. Hard tae see why they would belong tae a group."

"Did you see the book Serenity gave the guy?" I asked. Harrison nodded, and I told him about it. He looked blank when I described the symbol in the back, so I had to tell him about the swastika being the symbol of a Shaletown gang. "It might be that the symbol is just one of those recycled images that starts cropping up everywhere, but . . ."

"Your instincts say not?"

"Well, it was also how you had described the guy that stopped you going into the poetry meeting. He sounded like a thug."

Harrison nodded. "That's exactly what he looked and acted like. But why would a gang tough be messing with this yellow book and a poetry club? Unless it's propaganda and they're recruiting. But what sort of gang sets up a poetry group tae collect members?"

I hesitated, and then said what I had barely allowed myself to think. "What if it's not members they're recruiting, but victims?" I told him what had happened in the library with Harlen and the drawing I had made. "It's like my senses were telling me it was dangerous to let him see it, and why would that be, unless it was connected to the sickness in him?"

"There could be other reasons, but . . . are you saying you think he is part of this gang in Shaletown?"

"What if he is, and he—or the sickness in him—is using it to find victims?"

Harrison looked grim. "Jesus. If that's true, it means your sister . . ." Then he stood abruptly and looked over to the underpass outlet. "It's taking too long. He must have gone the other direction. Let's take the underpass tae the bus depot and see if he's waiting for a bus."

We sprinted down the stairs and through the long, green-painted, urine-smelling tunnel with its flickering, insect-filled fluorescent lights. There was a lot of graffiti on the sweating walls, but no reverse swastikas with snakes. We came out right at the door of the depot terminal and stopped, again panting hard. There were six concrete islands lying parallel like fish left to dry on a rack, and four big buses disgorging or boarding people and luggage. Announcements coming through a loudspeaker mounted on a pole by the underpass outlet were advising that one of the buses would depart in ten minutes.

We ran frantically about for five useless minutes, then Harrison said we ought to calm down and look methodically. After fifteen minutes we gave up. Either our quarry had caught a bus or he had cut through the depot to the suburb on the other side, and was long gone.

"Let's see if any buses have just gone," said Harrison.

I felt suddenly drained of purpose and energy, and my stomach ached hollowly although I did not feel hungry. Harrison led the way across to the terminal, which was a great barn of a place with a high roof of glass arching over a metal frame made to look, for some reason, like a giant fish skeleton. There were restrooms and seats and a kiosk and, above a row of glass-fronted desks where you could buy tickets, a big board where white numbers and letters on black squares flipped and clicked over to reveal bus destinations and times of departure and arrival.

"Earlier departures have gone off the board. Let's ask," Harrison said. He went forward to one of the counters and I hung back.

Harrison came back to me. "Guess what?" I shook my head, unable to see how anything the guy behind the counter could have said would have got him so electrified.

"A bus tae Shaletown left five minutes before we got here," Harrison said.

# 33

We were sitting in the bus station food court under a blare of fluorescent lights having hot chocolates out of thin plastic cups that buckled with the heat. Harrison spoke softly. "If that poetry group is a way of collecting potential victims, it means your sister might be in a lot of danger. Which is what your senses have been telling you all along?"

I nodded, feeling cold and afraid. "You know, when I was first back at school after the accident, Harlen gave me a CD for Serenity. That's the first time I was close enough to smell him, and it wasn't long after that he started asking me out."

"Maybe he had got close enough for the sickness tae pick up your reaction tae how he smelled," Harrison said.

"But what is the book for? I mean, how could it have anything to do with Serenity being a possible victim for the sickness in Harlen?"

Harrison pondered this for a while, running his fingers through the blond lock of hair that fell over his forehead. "Maybe . . . maybe the book is part of preparing someone for being infected. Like you're more susceptible tae the flu if your resistance is low; the poetry group is first of all a way of luring in people whose spirits might be weakened, and then the aim is tae weaken them further."

"But, Harrison, that yellow book wasn't just a computer printout that anyone with a bit of savvy could put together. It was a proper printed book. How could some gang make such a thing?"

"It doesnae sound very likely, but maybe 'gang' is a misnomer. This group might be a lot more organized than it seems. Maybe this Shaletown gang is an actual club with sponsors and members and even a headquarters. They would have the means tae produce a proper book."

"You're saying a club of people like Harlen, all infected, aren't you? But those guys I saw with Harlen were not infected. They smelled bad, but not like he does."

"That's a good point. Unless he has infected them and the sickness hasn't matured enough tae become active yet, so you cannae smell it. Or maybe he couldnae infect them because they were not able tae be infected. Maybe a spirit needs tae be wounded tae be vulnerable tae infection."

I shuddered. "The thought of a group of people like Harlen plotting to get victims is horrible," I said. And the idea of Serenity at the mercy of such people filled me with fear, but what could I do? I could hardly tell Da or the police or even Serenity what we suspected. I would sound like a maniac.

"We have tae find out more about this Shaletown gang,"

Harrison said. "You mentioned that Harlen went tae a school in Shaletown, so I think we should start there."

I told him about my abortive visit to Shaletown, and my later discovery that Harlen's school had closed down. "The only other thing I thought of was going to the neighborhood where the school was and talking to the neighbors. I got the address from an old phone book."

"Clever girl," he said, looking impressed. "OK, so we go there. Can you take another day off without the sky falling?"

I nodded at once, then I told him something else that had occurred to me. "I think the Shaletown gang had something to do with the fire at Gilly's place. Remember how angry she said Harlen looked when she ran into him the day I had stood him up?"

"You think he put the gang up tae it?"

"I don't know," I said. "But he was annoyed at her always being around." A wave of remorse flowed over me. "If it's because of me that her gran's house was burned down . . ." My fingers were plaited together so tightly that they were hurting, but before I could loosen them, Harrison had put a hand over them. It was done instinctively on an impulse of pity and sympathy, which I felt when our skins touched. But then Harrison snatched his hand away, almost as if he was remembering what had happened when he had touched me before.

I felt my cheeks redden, and I wanted the ground to swallow me up. I wanted to say something light and offhand, but I couldn't seem to speak.

"Alyzon, look at me," Harrison said. His voice was warm and gentle, and so I did. "Alyzon, listen. Back there in the library when I kissed you—"

"I know," I said, cutting him off. "I know you did it to stop that guy seeing us and getting suspicious. I don't know why I acted like I did. . . ."

"Alyzon, you dinnae need to feel bad about how you reacted because the way you acted . . . well, it wasnae you."

I stared at him, bewildered. "I felt—"

"What *I* was feeling," Harrison ended my sentence flatly. "You see, I did kiss you tae stop that guy getting suspicious, but having a girl in my arms . . . Well, Alyzon, what can I say? I'm a guy, and there is just this inevitable biological reaction. Only in this case, your senses thought that what you were getting from me was coming from you."

Relief flooded through me, and it struck me that he had been both kind and courageous in saying all this to me. I said shyly, "They tell us all the time that boy hormones are pretty strong. I guess I am the first girl in history to know it firsthand."

"So we forget it happened?" Harrison asked. I nodded, but of course I would not forget. How could I? In a sense it had been my first real kiss. And what a kiss! If anyone had asked before, I would have said that Harrison was probably as inexperienced as I was, but there had been no awkwardness or hesitation in how he had held me.

It was getting late, so we finished our cold hot chocolates and Harrison offered to walk me back to the bus stop. We walked in silence for a while, then Harrison shot me a look, his face pale in the harsh spill of light from a street lamp. "I dinnae suppose . . ."

"What?"

"Well, I was just wondering if it might not be your sister who brought your da to Rayc's attention. What if that CD Harlen gave you tae return tae your sister had your da's song on it? Maybe she took it tae that poetry group for some reason, and knowing Rayc's interest in celebrities, someone passed it along tae him."

"Why would Serenity talk about Da in a poetry meeting?" I asked.

"You said yourself she is angry at him, and I bet there would be every invitation and encouragement in those poetry meetings for people tae wallow in all the negative things in their lives," Harrison said.

I shivered, because it seemed likely he was right. Harrison shrugged off his coat and draped it around my shoulders. I didn't protest, and as his warmth and woody scent enveloped me, our gazes seemed to snag. Harrison took off his glasses very purposefully, and my heart began to hammer because I thought that he was going to kiss me again. Then a car roared by and blatted its horn at us, and he just polished the lenses and put the glasses on again.

We made our plan to meet at the train station the next day, and Harrison offered to get Raoul to call the school pretending to be Da, and say I was ill.

"What about your parents?"

"There's just my dad, and he won't care. My mother died when I was born, and he kind of lost interest in life after that." There was something in his tone that made me think of the barrier I had come upon inside him. It struck me that none of us, Harrison or Gilly, me or Sarry, had normal mothers. It was one of those significant-seeming details that didn't add up to anything.

* * *

I felt a powerful rush of relief and gladness to see Da sitting at the table reading a book when I entered the kitchen.

I ran to him and hugged him, without remembering what the consequence might be, but I only felt a warm lovely envelope of love enfold me. "Hey, I missed you, Aly Cat," Da said, smiling. It was something he'd called me when I was about five and had spent half the time pretending I was a stray cat that had wandered in, pestering everyone for pats and bowls of milk and hissing when I was ignored. "I wondered where you'd got to."

"I was with Harrison," I said, sliding onto a stool. "So what happened with the gig?" I kept my tone carefully light.

"It was . . . interesting."

"Interesting?" I persisted, not liking the word.

"Well, it was unusual because as well as a lot of artistic types in the audiences, there were dozens of musicians, some of them pretty big. I've never performed for so many performers before. It was an honor, in a way."

"I thought it was a charity function."

"Oh, it was, but it wasn't a fund-raiser. The performers

and the sponsors were being thanked by the charity for their help throughout the past year, and there were a lot of speeches in between performances about future projects, so I guess everyone was being nicely warned that they'd be needed again."

"Was Aaron Rayc there?"

Da nodded. "He gave one of the speeches about an annual fund-raising event coming up at the Castledean Estate, which is his property."

My skin prickled. "He didn't happen to invite you to perform at it, did he?"

Da laughed. "No, he did not, but I wouldn't have minded if he had. Provided he asked me with Losing the Rope. I all but said as much, as a matter of fact."

"Good for you," I said. "Who else performed?"

"Lots of people. There were a couple of rap guys called Neo Tokyo who were pretty good. Nice guys, but very young. The biggest name was the Rak."

"I don't like their music."

"I don't much like it either," Da admitted. "It's not that their musicianship is bad. In fact, the guitarist is brilliant. But their lyrics are so savage and judgmental." He laughed and shook his head. "I must be getting old."

"Being angry isn't the same as being young," I said.

He gave me a surprised look. "Well, no, I guess it's not, but a lot of the time it does seem to be the same thing, doesn't it?"

"Maybe kids think that's how they're supposed to be because musicians and writers keep telling them so."

Da said thoughtfully, "Now that you mention it, maybe that's why the Neo Tokyo boys seemed so confused to me. They have a great energy, but it's as if they're trying to push it into this angry, edgy stuff like the Rak does. I suspect that they have something different to say. Or they would, if they made the effort to figure it out rather than just emulating the Rak."

"I bet Aaron Rayc loved them," I said.

"I don't know if he liked it, but he did say that the Rak's music expresses an anger that people feel but can't show. That it offers an outlet that doesn't hurt anyone." He paused. "He asked me to play a couple of numbers with them."

"And did you do it?" I asked.

He laughed at my expression. "I told them I couldn't do their music or songs, so they suggested using a couple of my songs. I was taken aback because I would have thought my music would be anathema to them. We spent a whole day rehearsing and adapting the two songs we had decided on. It was interesting, but a little disturbing, too. I also did a couple of Losing the Rope songs with Neo Tokyo. They were nowhere near as polished as the Rak, but I have to say I enjoyed it a lot more. They seemed to understand the music better, and when they altered it, they just added something new to it rather than turning it on its head." He smiled.

I smiled, too, because although I was sure Aaron Rayc was out to change Da to make him marketable in a certain way, seeing him made me feel he was too complete, too grounded in his honesty and beliefs to be manipulated.

Mum came in wearing a drifting green shirt over tight black pants, her hair a cloud of red floating around her shoulders. She looked stunning, and I saw the adoration in Da's eyes. For some reason the look that passed between them reminded me of Harrison's kiss, and I got up abruptly. But as I reached the door, I heard Mum tell Da that she was painting Serenity. I turned in time to see a troubled look on Da's face.

"You're painting Serenity?" Da repeated.

"I have been wanting to paint her for some time," Mum told him gently. She reached out and touched his cheek.

A little puzzled by the exchange, I went to have a shower. I had been determined to tell Da about Serenity the moment I saw him, but what had happened that night with Harrison had changed my mind.

Lying in bed a little later, I felt heavy with tiredness. But on the verge of falling asleep, I found myself vividly reliving Harrison's kiss. It roused in me a restless heat, and even though I told myself it was just an echo of boy hormones, it felt very much like longing.

* * *

I set out to meet Harrison the next morning as planned, managing to make a quick call to Gilly before I left home to explain I wouldn't be at school. I told her only that Harrison and I were going to Shaletown to see if we could learn more about Harlen. If he asked about me, she could say she didn't know where I was, which would be true in the most specific sense.

"I believe that is what my gran would call splitting hairs with the devil," Gilly laughed, then Mum came in yawning and I had to end the call. I told Mum that I would be with my friend Harrison after school and would come home late, and she nodded. She would forget to mention it to Da, of course, unless he asked her.

I had left early enough to change into casual clothes at the station, because a uniform was identifiable and we didn't need any nosy neighbors calling the school to ask what was going on. The train was already at the station when I got out of the washroom, and I was pacing up and down the platform anxiously when Harrison arrived late, looking heavy-eyed and flustered. "Sorry," he said briefly. "Did you get your ticket?" I shook my head. "Good. Raoul's going tae drive us."

I stared at him. "All the way to Shaletown?"

Harrison nodded. "It'll give us more time there. But we have tae get the bus over to his place, because it'll be quicker at rush hour than for him tae drive over and collect us."

"Is everything OK with you?" I asked once we were on the bus. He glanced at me, and I read his awareness of my extended senses.

"Just home stuff going on," he said. "How did it go with your da and that Remington gig, anyway? I gather he's OK?"

"He was so much the same as usual last night that I feel a bit stupid for being worried," I admitted. Just the same, I told him what Da had said about the gig, and Harrison said finally that maybe Aaron Rayc just liked exerting his power and influence and seeing what happened. Because neither of us could figure out how it could possibly benefit Aaron Rayc to have Da play a couple of songs with the Rak. Harrison knew of them, too, but like me he didn't care for their music.

"I guess we're not angry enough to like it," he said.

His words made me think of Rose Cobb, and I wondered aloud if there would be time to stop in and say hello while we were in Shaletown.

It took us almost an hour to get to Raoul's house, and he opened the door at once as if he had been waiting for us. He wheeled straight down the dove-gray hall to a garage that was not visible from outside the house. There we got into Raoul's car.

We had just got to the highway when it started to rain. Raoul switched the windshield wipers on, and I watched them, half mesmerized, as Raoul made Harrison go over everything that had happened the night before.

I dozed a bit. Soon after I saw the familiar sign welcoming us to Shaletown. Raoul pulled the car into a lot behind a comfortable-looking bluestone pub, which turned out to have a ramp entry and widened doors for wheelchair access.

"How lucky," I murmured, but Harrison said sardonically that he doubted luck had anything to do with it. Raoul gave him an amused look and said he had found the pub via the Internet.

"You got your computers cleaned up, then?" Harrison asked.

Raoul shook his head, maneuvering into the pub. "I had a third telephone line installed and bought a new computer." He saw my horrified look and laughed. "It was a good lesson not to rely totally on one system," he said. "Daisy will repair the rest when she comes later this week. Now, let's have a quick lunch before you head off."

Once we had given our orders to the waitress, Raoul spoke decisively. "All right," he said, "you'd better have these." He took out a map of Shaletown and showed us where the private school had been: Carmine Street. "As you see, it's not far from the detention center." Raoul put a cell phone on the table. "My number is stored in it. Just call or text when you're ready to be collected." Then he put down two clipboards with paper, saying a survey would be a good reason for us to go from house to house asking questions.

"What are you going to do?" I asked him.

"I have an appointment at the Shaletown office of Rayc Inc."

I gaped at him, and Harrison asked, "He has an office here? Isn't that kind of weird?"

Raoul laughed. "I thought that would get a reaction from you both. Yes, he has an office here, and yes, it is odd. Apparently his wife was living in Shaletown when he met her, and the office building belongs to her. She inherited several holdings when her previous husband, a self-made Shaletown man called Jamie Makiaros, died. The property is tied up so Rayc can't sell it, and I suppose he decided he might as well make use of it."

"Where did you find out all of this?" I asked worriedly.

"Just some clever Internet snooping on my new computer. No communication with human beings and no downloading, so don't worry. I rang the office this morning to say I had heard Rayc Inc. would be able to give me some advice about finding some more meaningful way to donate money. I said that I was driving through today and would like to discuss the matter. His secretary asked who had given me the name of the office, and I told him I had heard it at a cocktail party."

"You can't ask him about Da," I said, still not completely reassured.

"Of course not. I doubt very much that the man himself will be there, though. I'd just like to get a feel for what the organization actually does. But you two had better go."

I hesitated, then I reached in my bag and got out my journal. "I've been writing stuff down since the accident, and I thought maybe you would like to have a look. The last bit is a copy of what I read in that yellow book."

Raoul took it, looking pleased, and by the time our food came, he was already leafing through it.

* * *

"It's lucky the rain stopped," I said as we walked briskly along the street. Harrison, map in hand, was doing the navigating.

Carmine turned out to be a wide street with beautiful, well-established trees on both sides and a glistening carpet of red, brown, and yellow leaves lying beneath them. It was a residential street, and most of the houses were enormous redbrick or sandstone mansions with beautiful well-kept gardens and gleaming Range Rovers or Volvos sitting in their driveways. The households' second cars, Harrison guessed. He reckoned the primary cars would be BMWs or Mercedes.

"Just the right setting for a private school," Harrison added. But although we walked the street from end to end, we saw only houses. "Nothing that could have been a school," Harrison said. "You're sure you got the street right?"

"I am," I said. "Maybe there's more than one Carmine Street in Shaletown."

"No, Raoul would have checked."

We began to make our way back along the street on the other side. "Maybe it's been turned into a house since it closed," I said.

"None of these is big enough tae have been a school. Hey!" He had stopped and was gazing back along the street. "That park we passed at the other end of the street. Was it actually a park or could it have been a vacant block?"

"But . . . they wouldn't pull a whole school down and then not build anything in its place," I protested, following him back.

The lot was a huge grassed expanse with nothing to suggest there had ever been any building there. But there was no sign saying it was a park either, and around the corner we found a "For Sale" sign with the phone number of a real-estate agent.

"This must have been it," Harrison said.

"But why would it have been taken down?" I asked.

"There could be any number of reasons. It might have been a bit of an eyesore."

"In a neighborhood like this?" I asked.

"It might just have been a white elephant, hard to sell, so they figured grass would do better. On the other hand, it's not sold and I wonder why." His eyes lit up. "I've an idea." He got out the cell phone that Raoul had given us.

"Hello, is this Kernes Real Estate?" Harrison made himself sound older and slightly bossy. "I'd like tae speak tae someone about the large lot on the corner of Carmine Street." His eyes widened and he gave me a pointed look. "Yes, the big one that used tae be a school. I don't suppose you know anything about . . . Well, can someone else help me? OK, I'll call back. Thank you. Yes, thank you." He pressed the end button. "The woman who handles it is out tae lunch. Let's go canvass the neighbors."

We pulled out the clipboards and marched up to the house closest to the vacant block. Harrison rang a doorbell shaped like the head of a lion. No one answered. We tried a few times, and then moved to the next house. A cleaning woman answered, saying that the owners would be home after five.

"Have you worked here long?" Harrison asked. "Maybe you can help us. It willnae take long."

The cleaning woman sighed and shrugged. "OK, why not. I've worked here for two years."

"That block back there on the corner; it was once a school?"

The woman frowned. "It was some sort of school. Why?"

"We're doing a project on land use," Harrison lied smoothly. "We're looking at how it's changed, and why. Whether land has always been vacant or what used tae be on it. What happened tae the school, anyway?" It was neatly done. The woman was diverted from her momentary suspicion.

"There was some kind of explosion, I heard. Or maybe it was a fire."

I was glad she was looking toward the lot just then, because I couldn't control the jump I gave. But Harrison simply asked why it hadn't been rebuilt.

The woman shrugged. "Mrs. Callow, she's the owner of this place, she was sure it had been bombed; it was all she could talk about. Some people have too much money and too little sense to fill all the time they have on their hands." She glanced at her own reddened hands complacently. "She was real disappointed when the police found it was an accident, because she couldn't go round anymore telling her friends that she had lived next to violent criminals." She laughed derisively.

"What did the police think had happened?" Harrison asked with the sort of flattering eagerness that storytellers love.

"I can't say I recall. It was the boiler that blew up, or maybe a furnace or something. Then there was a fire, and I think some people were killed. Or maybe somebody was only injured." The woman frowned at me. "Is she all right?"

"I'm fine," I said huskily. "I think that pie I ate for lunch might have been a bit off."

"We'd better go. Thanks," Harrison told the woman. I felt her eyes following us as we passed on down the street and out of her sight. Harrison made me stop and sit on a fence, saying I was as white as a ghost.

"Did you hear what she said?" I demanded shakily. "There was a fire and someone was killed."

"She said *maybe* a fire and *maybe* a boiler accident and *maybe* a bomb. And *maybe* someone or a whole lot of some-ones were *maybe* killed or injured," Harrison said.

"Harrison, you don't understand. When she said there had been a fire, I . . . I remembered. That day I told Harlen that Gilly's house had burned down, he asked who did it."

"So?" Harrison asked, looking baffled.

"Don't you get it?" I cried. "That was the first thing he said. But I didn't *say* anyone had burned it down. Why would he jump to the conclusion that it wasn't an accident? It's proof that he was involved in the fire."

"If you're right, it's also proof that this sickness can pro-voke people tae pretty extreme actions." He glanced around and said we had better get on. We could talk more later about the fire.

Three "no answers" and then, at the fourth house, an el-derly man with a foreign accent came to the door. His scent was nice and friendly, and there was none of the impatience that I had smelled in the cleaning woman. Harrison explained about the survey, then he asked about the school.

"There was a school that burned down. I had not emigrated then, but my sister wrote of it to me," the old man said. "She did not say it was a private school, but that difficult children went there. What is the word you see in the newspapers all the time? Delinquents. Yes, it was a school for delinquent boys. But it was a school where the parents are very rich, and so the school was very fine with many facilities."

I exchanged a glance with Harrison. "Do you know how the school was destroyed?" he asked the man.

"My sister said that it was an accident. Some kind of boiler explosion and then a fire."

"Was anyone hurt?" I asked.

"Yes! You have reminded me. It was a terrible thing. An inspired music teacher died, my sister said. An accomplished violinist. She called him the heart of the school. A wonderful man who had given his life to helping difficult young men and boys," the old man said.

"Your sister seems tae have known a lot about the school," Harrison observed.

He smiled. "My sister is the sort of woman who makes it her business to know a lot about everything. Besides, I think there were occasions when the school invited the neighbors to performances and concerts. To assure them that they were not at risk, I suppose."

"Was there . . . was there any suggestion of the explosion being deliberate?" Harrison asked.

The old man frowned a little at the question. "My sister would certainly know if there was such a suggestion. And she would have told me. What makes you ask such a question?"

"I was just . . . curious," Harrison said lamely. "We heard there used tae be a gang of kids at the school that caused a lot of trouble."

This was a straight-out lie, and I felt myself blush, but Harrison held the old man's gaze as he considered it. At length he shook his head. "I doubt gangs would have been encouraged or indeed permitted at such a school. The authorities would be trying to prevent such things, I should imagine." He shrugged. "I do not know who would have spoken of gangs. Perhaps they were thinking of the gang that set fire to the bakery a few weeks ago."

Harrison shot me a look and then said, "A gang set fire to a bakery?"

The old man shifted from one slipper-clad foot to the other and I smelled the faint mustiness of his fatigue. "It was madness. There was no money to be stolen, and the woman who ran the place is not the sort of person to have alienated anyone. Indeed, she is a wonderful woman and gave work to young people whom no one else would employ." He sighed.

Harrison held out his hand and thanked the man for his time. The door closed as we walked down the street and Harrison said, "What do you make of all that?"

"I don't see how a gang that vandalizes a bakery would have anything to do with the rest of this."

"Unless the vandalism is some sort of initiation rite. 'Proof of commitment,'" he added with emphasis.

I didn't say anything. I was thinking of a woman who had employed difficult young people, whose bakery had been burned; and a musician whose work had inspired delinquent boys, killed in a fire. Almost as if they had been harmed for their goodness.

34

We tried several other houses, but the occupants either did not want to speak with us, were not at home, or had moved to the street since the school had closed down. The sky had gradually darkened, and now Harrison eyed the clouds looming overhead and said we might as well give up and go see Rose Cobb.

It took twenty minutes to reach the detention center, and the wind was buffeting us by the time it came in sight. I noticed a small group of protesters, set up on the lawn beside the entrance, hurriedly pulling plastic bags over their placards and loading them into a dark green van. As we drew level, they got into the van and drove away.

"Which house?" Harrison cried, as thunder rumbled.

"This way," I called. Lightning flashed overhead, and as if it were a signal, it began to pour. We broke into a run. In moments we were standing on Rose's front porch, rain lashing at our backs.

"Hope she's home and doesnae mind letting in a couple of drowned rats," Harrison said ruefully.

I knocked at the blistered green door with a sudden stab of doubt. I had only met Rose Cobb once, however well we had got along. What if I had misunderstood her invitation? What if she had forgotten me? Before I could voice my apprehensions, the door opened and Rose stared out at me blankly. But at once, to my great relief, her face folded into the warm, kind smile I remembered.

"Alyzon! My dear girl, how lovely to see you! Come in, you and your friend. This house faces right into the teeth of the wind, so the veranda is all but useless as any kind of shelter." She stood back and the wind seemed to push us through the door and into her little hallway. Harrison caught hold of the door and wrestled it closed, and we all laughed.

Rose made us take off our coats and, after I introduced Harrison, told us to go in and sit by the fire while she made some tea. Harrison grinned at me, and I grinned back. With his damp and wildly tousled hair and half-fogged glasses, he looked cheerful but slightly demented. It wasn't until we got into the living room that I realized Rose had another visitor. It was the same young man who had been with her before: Davey.

He rose and stared at us both. I was startled to see his hands were stained black to the wrists.

"Uh, Davey?" I said awkwardly. "This is my friend Harrison, and I'm—"

"I know who you are," Davey said, not even glancing at Harrison. "But you shouldn't say your name because the air remembers it and some people can read the air. Sniff the names out of it like dogs sniff up each other's pee words," Davey said earnestly.

Rose Cobb bustled into the startled silence with a tray, and Harrison sprang up to help her set the table. "What awful weather it is, but that's winter for you," she said. It was only after we each had tea and a scone with jam that she asked what we were doing in Shaletown.

"We had some stuff to do," I said vaguely. "I actually thought you might be across the road. Silly, when it's raining."

"We try not to let rain stop us," Rose said. "But today there were some of the other protesters there and . . . well, sometimes things get rough when they're there, so I don't go over on those days."

"Other protesters?" I asked curiously.

"Oh, there are all kinds of protesters, not that I would have known that once upon a time. There are the ones like Gwenny and her friends, who are peaceful protesters, and then there are those who are determined to make a point no matter what it takes. Angry protesters," she added, looking to see if I remembered our last conversation. I nodded. "The ones over there today seem to be what I call political protesters. I like that sort least, because what they want never seems to have much to do with helping people."

"They are bad," Davey said.

Rose took his hand. "No, Davey, they are only a bit exclusive." She looked back at Harrison and me and added, "I'm afraid they were rather rude to me when I went to offer them some tea and scones, and it upset Davey." She patted his hand.

"Simon says they are bad," he told her, patting her hand back in exactly the same consoling way and leaving no mark despite the stains on his hands. "Simon says Davey needs to go home soon."

"But it's still raining, dear," Rose objected.

"Davey will not get wet," Davey said serenely.

"You know what, we have a friend with a car, and we were supposed tae call him tae pick us up," Harrison said. "We can give Davey a lift home."

"What a good idea. What do you think, Davey?" Rose asked.

"Davey must go in the car and show the driver where to go," Davey said complacently, as if repeating instructions.

Harrison called Raoul while Rose told me with some pleasure that one of her daughters had sent a lovely long letter. "But tell me now, what other errand did you have in Shaletown?" she asked with sudden curiosity.

I glanced at Harrison, who had put the phone away. He said, "We've been trying tae find out about a private school that used tae be here in Shaletown."

"The Boys Academy at Carmine Street?" Rose asked.

We both stared at her, and I realized what a fool I was not to think she would know about the school. Shaletown was relatively small, after all, and she had lived here for a long time.

"I remember when it opened. It was called Shaletown

Institute, and a grim place it was back then, with very serious ideas about discipline. It closed down for a time, and then it was opened up as the Shaletown Boys Academy and set out to target wealthy families with problem sons. It was run along very military lines to start with, but then the management changed and the school seemed to go through a sort of renaissance. Instead of fierce exhausting sports, the boys were introduced to the arts. Music in particular. There were a great many concerts in those days, and it was a real pleasure to attend them. In the end the place became rather a model school."

"But it burned down," Harrison said.

Rose sighed. "Yes. I remember thinking at the time what a pity it was."

"Why didnae they rebuild if it was so successful?" Harrison asked. "There must have been insurance."

"There was a great deal of damage to the school buildings, but I think it was more that there seemed no heart to rebuild. You see, one of the music teachers—actually the man who had really been responsible for the school's renaissance—died in the fire. A terrible tragedy." She sighed.

Suddenly there was the sound of a horn from outside. I explained quickly about Raoul so Rose would not think him rude. We pulled on our damp outer clothes in the tiny entrance hall, Davey's size making it even more cramped.

"Davey, you can show them the way," Rose said. "He knows it very well," she added reassuringly to me. Then she gave me a hug and said, "You come and visit again with your young man here." I blushed and didn't dare to look at Harrison, which caused Rose's sharp eyes to narrow speculatively so that I was quite glad to get out into the rain and wind again.

But when we were all squashed in the car, I saw that Harrison looked unperturbed and realized that her teasing would probably mean no more to him than kissing me had meant. I felt rather aggrieved that I had made so little impression on him, then wondered at my own contrariness. I ought to be glad that his kiss and my reaction to it hadn't marred our friendship!

Raoul greeted Davey, who only said, "Davey came so he could show you the way." Then he proceeded to point out the way to the industrial park where he said he had his trailer. The area lay beyond the straggling residential edge of the town, over a stretch of barren hill paddocks. The road brought us around the hill and past a group of enormous warehouses rising above the shabby clutter of little shacks and sheds that made up the rest of the industrial park. Most of them looked to be closed up and derelict.

Then Davey cried out that Raoul should turn into a driveway leading to a small gray-timber shack with a dribble of smoke coming from its chimney. It was surrounded by a herd of half-rusted and disassembled relics that might once have been cars, and there was a sign on a post that said "Dolen Spare Parts." Under it, so faded that it was barely discernible, was "Scrap Metal Supplies." I wondered if Davey operated the business. His blackened hands seemed to suggest it, but how could he make a living from this run-down shack when it looked as if all the other businesses around it had failed? Then I realized Davey was probably on some sort of disability payment.

"Davey lives in the trailer in back," Davey said cheerfully. "You park here." Raoul pulled up in front of the shack as he had been directed, and Harrison and I got out to let Davey out. It was still raining, but not as heavily as before. Davey went round to say "thank you" to Raoul and shake his hand.

"I'm sorry, Davey, I can't get out because . . . ," Raoul began.

"Davey knows. Legs no good. Davey once had a cat with legs that didn't work. They shot that cat, and Davey cried."

"I guess he was a good cat," Raoul said gently, as if there was no hurry, though the rain saturated his shoulder and wet his cheeks.

"Davey loved that cat," Davey said sadly. Then, seeming to cheer up, he said, "Simon says go that way now." He was pointing in the direction of the warehouses.

"Thank you, Davey," Raoul said. "Maybe we'll see you again sometime."

"Oh yes, you will, Simon says," Davey told him. He tapped the hood of the car with his black finger. "You got something in there needs replacing. That'll be a good reason to come back. Davey will get a new one for when it breaks."

He pumped Raoul's hand again with his huge black hand, then Harrison's, but when he came to me, his smile faded. He looked at me with his guileless blue eyes, his sweet scent filling the air. "You gotta be careful here, Alyzon Whitestarr.

This is one of their places, and they're stronger in their own places." Then he turned and trotted over to the hut, waving before he entered.

Harrison had got into the car and I followed, trying to shake the unease that Davey's nonsense had made me feel.

"Did he just tell you that you should be careful?" Harrison asked me.

I shrugged. "It's probably what people tell him all the time, and he thinks that's just how you say goodbye."

Raoul started up the engine and drove back onto the road, the headlights picking up little more than the rain slanting down. He headed the way Davey had indicated, but a few minutes later we came to a dead end: a cul-de-sac with the enormous metal warehouses on all sides.

Raoul began to turn the car around, but there was not much space so he had to go back and forth a few times. I was wondering how trucks managed when Harrison let out a cry that startled Raoul so much he stalled. We both followed Harrison's gaze to a warehouse door with a security light angled toward it. It looked no different from any of the other warehouses around us, and I looked at Harrison in puzzlement.

"Look at the name above the door," Harrison said. "It's the name of the guy you said was married tae Dita Rayc—her first husband."

"Second," Raoul corrected. "And you're right. Makiaros Inc. This must be one of the properties he left her."

"It's on the other warehouses, too," I said, squinting back

through the rain. In fact, it turned out to be on all of the ware-houses; Harrison insisted on getting out and looking.

"What an odd coincidence that we should just come upon them like that," Harrison said as we were driving back along the road.

35

On the way home, Harrison asked Raoul about his visit to Aaron Rayc's office. It was still raining steadily, and the wipers were on high.

"Dita was definitely a wealthy woman before she married Aaron Rayc," Raoul said. "The office building turns out to be the highest building in Shaletown, with gold-tinted glass windows and a foyer that wouldn't be out of place in New York. I know from my research that Makiaros practically made a religion of keeping business in one's own backyard, but the building seemed overdone. I commented on it to the woman who spoke with me. I was told that the man who built it—she meant Makiaros, I'm sure—believed that Shaletown had the potential to be a major industrial city. I suppose that is why he had so many warehouses built. Other than the showiness of the office, the only thing I noticed was the amount of electronic security in the building, but it was very inconspicuous. I doubt I would have noticed if I hadn't been looking."

"Why would a charitable organization want so much security? They must be hiding something," Harrison said.

"For all I know, half of it may not have been operating. Or it might just have been more grandiose planning on Makiaros's part," Raoul said.

"Did the woman say anything about what Rayc Inc. does?" I asked curiously.

"Not specifically. Apparently neither Rayc Inc. nor its international associate, ORBA, operate in the same areas as such organizations as Oxfam, World Vision, or Community Aid Abroad. Their interest is in trying to change society so that the sorts of problems these other groups deal with would cease to exist. I said that I thought this was admirable though ambitious, but that I was definitely interested if I could be convinced that a donation of mine would effect some specific and concrete change for good in the world. The woman who spoke with me suggested I meet with someone more senior who could explain some of their projects to me. I said I was a busy man, and we left it at that, but I don't have any doubt they will contact me. But now it's your turn. Tell me what you learned about Harlen Sanderson's old school."

I left it to Harrison, and let myself be lulled by the sound of the rain and the rhythmic *slap slap* of the wipers. Raoul listened, then finally shook his head. "So we don't have any real proof that the explosion was the work of a gang, or even that this bakery fire was the work of a gang. In fact, there's no true indication that a gang even exists."

I roused myself to say that the woman in the bus shelter had mentioned a Shaletown gang.

"That could still be a rumor," Raoul said. "I wonder if it

would be possible to track down a teacher who worked at the academy. It shouldn't be that difficult. I have a friend in the education department."

It wasn't until we were close to home that Raoul mentioned the journal, saying he had read part of it but wanted to finish it, if I would let him keep it for a while longer. He suggested that I come to his place for dinner with the others the following night, and he would return it then.

"Just one thing puzzles me. Who is Professor Kirke?"

That made me smile, and when I told him I'd addressed my journal to a fictional character, he laughed.

Raoul insisted on dropping me at my door. I had told him I would be fine catching the bus, but getting out of the car into the wet, cold evening, I was very glad to know that a warm kitchen and a hot shower were only a few steps away.

* * *

There was no one in the kitchen when I entered, although the room smelled of cooking. I went upstairs, glad there was no one around to wonder why I wasn't in school uniform. Ten minutes later I had filled the bath and was neck-deep in hot water. I sank down into it and indulged in sheer mindless pleasure for a while.

But eventually I found myself thinking about Shaletown Boys Academy. A chill crept into the bath as I realized what a perfect place a school for delinquent boys must have been for a sickness that preyed on wounded spirits. And then along had come the music teacher, lifting those boys up, inspiring them. If the sickness had led Harlen to get his friends to burn down Gilly's house just because she had gotten in the way of his pursuit of me, what might it do to remove someone like the music teacher? Could it have prompted Harlen to get the teacher permanently out of the way?

I told myself I was going too far. After all, the explosion had closed the school down. The sickness could not have wanted that.

Suddenly Mirandah hammered on the door, saying that dinner was nearly ready. I got out and scurried to the bedroom to dress. Serenity was laid out on her bed, but she didn't look at me or in any way acknowledge that I was in the room. I wanted badly to tell her what I suspected the poetry group intended for her. But what could I say that would not make me sound like a nutcase?

I went downstairs, thinking that I could do nothing until I had proof of some kind.

Mirandah and I were serving the spinach quiche Jesse had made when the phone rang. It was one of the members of Mirandah's jazz group. Jesse took over serving and passed me Luke's bowl of mush. I spooned it to him absently, making faces to distract him when he looked to be getting bored with the concept of dinner. I had just finished feeding him when Da came in the back door, shaking his head a little. I thought he looked tired.

"Bad pupil?" Jesse asked.

Da laughed. "Brilliant pupil. No talent." He sighed. "It ought to be that when a person works hard and is dedicated, he receives his just reward. But talent is capricious, and it can appear in the lazy as well as the dedicated. How do you tell someone prepared to give his soul that it won't be enough?"

There was a knock at the back door, and before Da could turn back to open it, Rhona Wojcek burst in, clad in painfully bright fluorescent orange and green stripes, complaining bitterly about the wet path, as if we had watered it just to spoil her lime suede boots. Da sent Mirandah up to get Mum and poured Rhona a glass of red wine. She grimaced after tasting it, but still drank it pretty fast.

I retreated upstairs, feeling only slightly guilty because Rhona really was bad for digestion. I was lying back drowsing when I heard her leave, but I was too warm and lazy to go down. I roused myself enough to peel off my jeans and slide under the covers.

I dreamed of Davey the mechanic, riding on the back of a dog the size of a small elephant. As in the previous dream, the slow gentleness of his expression had given way to an alertness that made him look like a different person, despite the fact that in all other ways he looked like Davey. He called to me to climb up behind, saying that I could travel with him, but I told him rather sharply that I couldn't. He quirked his brow sardonically and said I could do more than I knew, and then he laughed.

* * *

By the time I got downstairs the next morning, Serenity had left and Mirandah was feeding Luke. Da came in from his run, saying that it was wet as hell everywhere, but at least the rain had stopped. Mirandah lifted Luke from his chair and put him into Da's arms, and Da put him right back in the chair.

The physical handover of Luke was a tradition dating back to a time when he had been left on the grass in his bouncy chair for over two hours, with each of us thinking that someone else was taking care of him. Luckily he had been in the shade, but we were all horrified when Da came in with him crying his eyes out. These days, the rule was that you physically handed Luke to the person who was to be in charge of him next. That way you could never be in doubt about who was supposed to be watching over him.

Mirandah dashed out in a flurry. I was about to leave, too, when I remembered to tell Da I was going to dinner at Raoul's that night. "Can I get a lift home after?"

"I've got a late rehearsal tonight for a gig, but maybe Jesse can do it." Da looked at Jesse, who had just come downstairs, and he nodded.

"A gig with Losing the Rope?" I asked.

He shook his head. "It's with those two guys I met at that last gig. Neo Tokyo. They've asked me to guest with them in a show called the Big Sleep. Funny name for a gig, but it's supposed to be quite big."

"Jeez, Da," Jesse said. "Even I've heard of the Big Sleep. It's going to be huge. More than two thousand people in a field with a gigantic stage that will be especially built for it."

"Two thousand. Can that be right?" Da asked.

Jesse shrugged. "The same crew did a similar thing last year called the Big Eat. Two thousand expected, but three thousand turned up. There's more than one band, and it's for charity, right?"

Da nodded. "Aaron Rayc said there would be a number of bands. We'll play one of the last slots before the night winds up. I didn't realize it would be so big an audience, though. Well, it doesn't make any difference really."

"Neo Tokyo are rap, you said," Jesse commented, reaching out to take Luke from Da. "I didn't think that was your thing."

"Rap's not as attractive as some other music is to me," Da admitted. "But these Neo Tokyo guys have an interesting approach, and they're superb musicians."

I had to ask. "Da, how come Aaron Rayc keeps organizing things for you? I mean, what does he get out of it?"

Da studied my face. "Alyzon, I'm afraid I've given you the wrong impression of Aaron Rayc. I had a good talk with him and I realized that he only suggested working with other bands so that I could stretch myself as a musician. He doesn't get anything out of helping me or anyone else, except that he likes doing it. And that's a good thing in a world where just about everything is for sale. You know how rare it is that someone like this comes along in the life of a musician? Someone who can really make a difference?"

Make a difference how? I wanted to ask darkly, but didn't. "I think he likes manipulating people," I said rather primly.

Da smiled. "And you think he's playing chess with me? To what end?"

"Well, that's the big question, isn't it?" I said, thinking of what Harrison had once said. "Maybe he just likes the power."

Da shook his head. "Oh, Alyzon, that might be the motivation of a character in a book or in some Hollywood movie, but real people's motives are far more complex. There are always layers to our decisions and actions that even we can't read. And think about this: There were artists of all kinds I met during the three days I've just done, and none of them had a bad word to say about Aaron. They all talked about how helpful he had been. Many of them only got a break because of him using his influence on their behalf."

"It sounds too good to be true," Jesse said.

Da grinned. "Never look a gift horse in the mouth. Besides, it wasn't Aaron's idea that I do this job. The Neo Tokyo guys asked me off their own bat. Aaron doesn't really have a lot to do with the Big Sleep. His focus will be on a private invitation-only parallel event. The great thing is that we'll get paid that night, and the fee will cover Zambia's gallery opening and leave enough for me to finally get some emergency money socked away."

"I thought that was what the last gig was for," I said.

"That money won't come in for a bit."

* * *

I barely managed to get to the bus stop in time, and dropped into a seat clutching my side and puffing hard. Serenity had got on, too. I wondered how Mirandah had made the earlier bus, when Serenity had missed it. Maybe she had gone for a walk. Of course, I couldn't ask; anyway, she had taken a seat at the very back of the bus. I felt her eyes on me and wished I could just go back and speak with her. But the gulf between us was a great deal more than could be bridged by a walk from one end of the bus to the other.

36

The school day dragged as if every minute was shaped out of treacle. What made it worse was that Gilly had not come to school again. I wanted to call her at lunchtime, but the class before ended up with a long detention and when I raced to the public phone in the few minutes remaining afterward, I found someone had cut the cord. Then when I got back to school, the hall monitor spotted me, wrote me up for going offgrounds, and gave me a detention. It was that kind of day.

The only good thing was that I managed again to successfully avoid Harlen by hiding shamelessly in classrooms, avoiding the lockers, and taking cover in detention.

* * *

"You're late," Harrison said when I arrived at Raoul's place.

"Detention," I said wearily. "Is Gilly here?"

"She was here when I got here," Harrison said, and ushered me to the kitchen, where Gilly and Raoul were sitting with their hands wrapped around mugs of hot chocolate. Gilly looked pale, and her eyes were red.

"Gilly, what's wrong?" I asked. She got to her feet, and her lovely sea scent enveloped me as she hugged me.

"I couldn't go today," she said. "Harrison told me what you think about Harlen and the fire."

"I felt like she ought tae know," Harrison said to me apologetically.

"I'm so sorry," I told Gilly, feeling my eyes prick with tears.

"No!" she said, sniffing hard. "You are not to be sorry, because how could this be your fault? In a way it's not even Harlen's fault. It's this thing inside him. This sickness. That's the enemy."

Raoul set his mug down firmly and said, "There is something I need to show you, Alyzon."

He turned his chair and wheeled out of the kitchen, leaving us to follow him. Gilly and Harrison exchanged puzzled looks that told me they had no idea what we were to see either. Instead of going right to the back of the house, Raoul wheeled through the last door before the end of the hall, into an enormous living room lined with floor-to-ceiling bookshelves. The only furnishings on the cream-colored tile were two long, pale curves of modular sofa and a big square coffee table made of white wood. On the few bits of wall without books, there were black-and-white photographs of winter-bare trees framed in the same wood as the coffee table. The books and blue cushions set at regular intervals along a deeply recessed windowsill provided the only color in the room. Through the window I could see a Japanese maple growing out of an intricate swirl of bricks.

Raoul had wheeled to a desk set up in the midst of the bookshelves, where there were another computer and a few other pieces of equipment. I went over to stand behind him with the others as he booted up the computer, then turned his chair to look at us. "I received a message from Rayc Inc. this morning, inviting me to an ORBA fund-raising event at the Castledean Estate. I responded by e-mail. Confirmation came back almost at once, with the same logo as on the invitation, and I don't know why, but I started fiddling to see if I could decode the image."

He turned back to the screen and opened a file on the desktop, and then we were looking at the digitized logo I had first seen on Aaron Rayc's card. "Now watch," Raoul said, and he tapped at the keyboard. "This is a simulation of what I did with the image, without all the dead ends."

The logo began to shimmer and shiver, the dots moving closer together in tiny rigid jerks, subtly rearranging themselves and overlapping until an image came into focus.

"What is it?" Gilly asked with a grimace of distaste.

"It's a swastika with yellow snakes," Harrison said in a stunned voice, and I felt his eyes on my face. "It's the symbol that was at the back of Serenity's book, isnae it?"

I nodded. "And supposedly it's the emblem of a gang in Shaletown. But what does it mean?" I stared at the image on the screen again, feeling stupid with astonishment.

"It's the sickness," Gilly said. "It has to be."

"But Aaron Rayc doesn't smell of the sickness," I protested.

"Neither does Sarry," Raoul reminded me.

"You think Aaron Rayc is infected but fighting it?" I demanded.

Raoul shook his head and said, almost dreamily, "Actually I've been thinking in a different direction completely. What would ultimately happen to a person who was infected and didn't resist? Maybe it's like when an animal dies and rots. Bacteria begin to break the organism down, and there is an awful stink while that's happening. But once the process has run its course, there is no smell. In Aaron Rayc's case he might smell of nothing because there is nothing left to be corrupted. Of course, it's not a physical sickness, so he doesn't die. His body and mind go on, but what was essentially him is gone."

His soul, I thought.

"And you think he's trying tae infect her da?" Harrison asked.

Raoul shook his head. "I'd say he's gone beyond the capacity to infect."

"Then why is he always coming around?" I asked.

"I don't know, Alyzon, but try this for a theory. He can't infect anyone, but he still has the same voracious drive to perpetuate the virus, so his desire to infect evolves or mutates into a desire to enable infection." He pointed to the logo still glowing on the computer screen. "I decided to check out a hunch once I saw that, and it wasn't hard to find out that Rayc Inc. owns a printing press in Shaletown."

"You think he's printing those books?" Gilly whispered.

"I'd bet my life on it," Raoul said calmly. "I bet he's behind them, and the poetry group, which lures in discontented and spiritually wounded people who might be made vulnerable, somehow, to infection."

"But how could Aaron Rayc do all that and not know he's infected?" I asked.

"I think he would know he was infected by this stage, because in a way all that would remain would be the virus in a human receptacle," Raoul said.

"How does Alyzon's da fit in, and all these artists and musicians whose lives Rayc messed with? Do you think they're all infected?" Harrison asked.

"I think the arts might be a good trawling ground for victims. A lot of painters and writers and musicians create out of the wounds to their spirit."

"You think he set up the poetry group and published those books and arranges charity functions and patronizes artists to give the virus more targets?" Gilly said doubtfully.

"There's no reason to suppose Rayc would not be as ambitious and creative and diverse in serving the virus as he would be as a successful businessman."

"Maybe it's not your da he's interested in, Alyzon," Gilly said. "Maybe he comes around to keep an eye on Serenity."

It made a kind of sense, especially when I remembered how eagerly Aaron Rayc had said her name the first time he came to the house.

"What I'd like to know is how he met Harlen Sanderson," Harrison said. "Do you think Rayc infected him before he stopped being able tae infect anyone?"

"I think it must have happened like that," Raoul said. "Harlen went to school in Shaletown and Aaron Rayc was courting a wealthy widow there, so there is certainly a possibility that they might have met."

Raoul broke off and insisted we eat then, even though it was clear that no one had much appetite. It felt so sane and good to wash and shred lettuce and chop spring onions, and I realized Raoul had suggested eating as a way of drawing us out of the nightmare dimension we were creating with our speculations. Maybe that was why, when the lasagna and garlic bread came out of the oven, they smelled so wonderful. Once again, we ate at the jungle table. Raoul even insisted we light candles, and that reminded me of Gilly's gran, talking about making things beautiful as a sort of response to all the ugliness in the world.

As we loaded the dishwasher, Raoul told us the names of the directors of ORBA were listed on the confirmation e-mail, and Aaron Rayc's name was among them.

"I'd say that is why ORBA ended up funding residencies and running events at the Castledean Estate."

"So what are we going to do?" Gilly asked suddenly. "We have to do something about Alyzon's sister."

Raoul nodded. "Obviously we can't warn her that a boy at her school is trying to infect her with a sickness of the spirit. Which leaves us with only one option—watching over her. Alyzon, do you know where she is now?"

I nodded. "She's with my mother tonight, sitting for a painting."

"Good. She's safe for now. But in the future, she must not be left alone if there is any chance she will go out. And when she does, one of us must follow her."

I bit my lip. Keeping tabs on Serenity would mean dealing with her fury if she spotted me trailing around after her. But it had to be done; Raoul was right.

"It is possible that infection isn't something that happens all at once," Gilly said hesitantly. "Could there be something happening in those poetry groups—a slow process of infection?"

Raoul shook his head. "Of course, we don't know anything for sure, but from the little Sarry has said, I'd say infection would occur all at once. I'd also suspect that at the moment of infection, the spiritual wound that makes a person vulnerable would need to be reopened or deepened."

Peeling a kiwi fruit, Gilly said, "Alyzon told us those guys who were with Harlen didn't smell infected. Why wouldn't they be, if this virus is so hungry?"

"I think infection cannot be so simple a matter, especially if, as we have reasoned, the infected person does not know what they carry," Raoul said. "I think only certain types must be naturally vulnerable, and they have to be set up for it."

"You think Alyzon is that type?" Harrison asked.

"We don't know what attracts the virus. It may be something quite random, like a certain scent or something else that we can't identify," Raoul answered.

I thought of the way the air churned between Rayc and Da and wondered if it was simply that the sickness in Rayc was drawn to something in Da's scent that it identified as a weakness; the ammonia scent, maybe? Or the smells that expressed his love for his family?

Raoul began to dish out fruit salad, and dimly I registered that the others were talking about how infection might take place, but I shut out their voices and focused on my train of thought, sensing that it was carrying me somewhere.

Aaron Rayc had stopped or altered the output of those artists he had been involved with. I just didn't believe that could be an accidental side effect of whatever else was happening. And such a fortunate side effect it would be, because the dark stuff they produced after getting involved with Rayc was enough to wound anyone's spirit.

My mind made a quantum leap, and I stood up so abruptly that the chair I had been sitting on crashed to the ground.

"Oh God!" I whispered. "I know what Aaron Rayc wants from Da! He wants to change him so he can use him to reach people, soften them up so that they are easier to infect. That's why he messes with all those artists! Some of them must work fine just as they are—ones like the Rak who produce bleak, dark, and hopeless stuff of their own accord. He'd only need to promote them and make sure people hear and see what they do. Then there would be others he just manipulates until they are broken enough to produce the sort of art he wants from them. And the ones that won't change, he stops from working."

"But your da won't change," Gilly said soothingly. "He's too strong and kind and good."

I sat down, because of course she was right. Aaron Rayc had manipulated Da, but he could not change Da's essential nature. Put him with two confused and angry young rappers, and he would help them to build on their strengths and lift their spirits. Give him someone like Portia Sting, who was wounded in spirit, and his instinct was to heal her.

I had a sudden vivid image of the way the air around Aaron Rayc bent inward while the air around Da pushed out. The first time I had noticed the effect, I had thought it looked as if they were opposing forces. And now I saw that this was exactly what they were. Aaron Rayc carried a sickness that urged him to wound and break and darken people, and Da carried something that lifted and strengthened people.

Raoul's last words were that we had to find some way to break Aaron Rayc's influence, since we could not go to the police. We needed to learn something about him that could be used against him, and maybe the activities of the Shaletown gang were his weak point. If we could establish a real connection between them, all we would need then was a way to publicize it.

I thought of Gary Soloman then, and told them I knew just how to get publicity, if we came up with something.

37

The next day Serenity caught the early bus to school and I did as well, having set the alarm to make sure I was up in time. It was early enough that once I had seen her go into the school, I was able to double back out of the school yard and call the newspaper office. I didn't expect Gary Soloman to be in, and I had written out a message for the receptionist to leave, but she insisted on putting me through to his voice mail. I hate leaving recorded messages, so I just read out my note, asking that he meet me at the Quick Brown Fox so that we could discuss matters of mutual interest.

I felt a bit pompous saying those last few words, but I hadn't wanted to be specific. The time I had given him was when Serenity would be with Mum in the studio for at least a couple of hours. Keeping tabs on her at lunchtime and recess was no small feat, and I had little time to talk to Gilly. She would have come with me, but that would have made us too conspicuous. The one good thing about tracking Serenity was that it brought me face to face with Harlen's old friend Cole at a moment when I knew that Harlen was on the sports field with the rugby team.

"Hi, Cole," I said, stopping him with a bright smile. "Listen, I was just wondering if you've always lived here."

"I have," he said, looking puzzled. "Why?"

I feigned disappointment. "Oh, I'm just doing this project and I need to interview someone who used to live somewhere else. Someone said you used to live in Shaletown."

There was no mistaking his reaction. He paled and looked sick. But at the same time he seemed to brace himself. "I never lived there," he said.

"Oh, damn," I said lightly. "Do you know anyone who did?"

"Live in . . . Shaletown?" The faintest hesitation, but again unmistakable. It was as if he disliked saying the word.

"Not just there," I said airily. "Anywhere other than here. It wouldn't have to have been for long, but it has to be living there, not just visiting or vacationing." I was babbling, wanting to allay any suspicions.

He mentioned a few people I might speak to, and I muttered as if I were fixing the names in my memory. I thanked him and at the same time I reached out and lightly tapped his hand. Then I walked away without looking back.

My heart was hammering from the jolt of electricity I had got from the touch, but I had been expecting it so it shook me a lot less than the accidental touches. I had wanted to know something in particular, and for a second I had gotten a flash of something. Cole standing on a white sandy road blazing with reflected sunlight except where the blocky shadow of a building fell over it. Some long grass by the road, shimmering in the heat. Not enough to guess where it was, but enough to tell me that it was a place Cole had been, which he associated with Harlen Sanderson.

Next period I was separated from Gilly by one of those teachers who seem to think close friendship in class is a bad thing, and made to sit next to Marilyn Bloom. I would have been annoyed except I suddenly remembered that she had a younger brother named Karl who was in the same year as Cole. On impulse, I asked if she knew him.

"He came round a couple of times," she said. "He was a hanger-on type who'd do anything to belong. You couldn't like him no matter how slavishly he tried to please you. I don't think the teachers like him any better than the kids, even though his aunt's a teacher here."

"His aunt?"

"Mrs. Barker," Marilyn said. "Her sister is Cole's mother." I stared at her. Could what had happened between Cole and Harlen be the reason that Mrs. Barker had acted so strangely about Harlen?

* * *

Back at home that afternoon, once Serenity was in with Mum, I changed out of my uniform, shoved some homework into a shoulder bag, and set off, calling out to Jesse that I was going to the mall. If Gary Soloman didn't come, and it was a definite possibility, I would simply do my homework at the Quick Brown Fox.

I reached the mall at ten past five, and twenty minutes later Gary Soloman strode in, frowning. When he sat down in the booth, he emanated annoyance. "All right, what is it? I don't have time for these sorts of games," he said.

I lost my temper a little. "Fine, then I won't take too much of your valuable time. I just wanted you to know that I am investigating Aaron Rayc with my friends, and we have found out some things you might like to know. I haven't mentioned you to my friends because I promised not to, but I want to suggest we give you what we've learned, and that would mean breaking my promise."

His expression tightened as I spoke. "Alyzon, I warned you to be careful. . . ."

"I *have* been careful," I said firmly. "We all have."

"Who is 'we'?"

Two could play the secrecy game. I looked into his eyes, smiled, and said, "That's none of your business."

He smiled, too, briefly. "Well, you are discreet, I'll give you that. And you keep your word. Look, I'm sorry I was so sharp just now. It's just that it was a hell of a job to get here, and I was afraid that you were going to tell me that . . . well, anyway, what have you found out?"

"I can't tell you until I talk to the others."

"Can't or won't?" he asked, offering me his handsome prince's smile.

"Won't," I said coolly.

He shook his head with amusement. "All right, you can tell them. When will you talk to me?"

I considered for a moment. "Next week maybe." After Raoul had been to the ORBA function, and after Daisy found out what she could about Rayc Inc.

Despite his avowal that he didn't have time to spare for such meetings, the journalist spent another twenty minutes trying to talk me into giving something away. Then he switched tack and began asking me about myself and my life and my interests. He was being so nice and smooth and friendly that alarm bells rang, and I thought of a film I had seen a while back.

"You can't romance it out of me," I said bluntly.

For a moment he looked astounded, then he burst out laughing. His eyes were so admiring that I flushed with pleasure in spite of myself. He offered me a lift home, but I said I'd call my brother. The truth was that I wanted a few quiet moments to think before I headed home. Ten minutes later I rose and turned to leave—and was shocked to find myself face to face with Harlen Sanderson!

"H-Harlen," I stammered. "What are you doing here?"

He smiled coldly. "Looking for you."

I knew he must have called the house and spoken to Jesse, and I prayed that he hadn't seen Gary Soloman, because he would certainly remember that Gary was an investigative journalist and wonder why I was meeting him.

"I needed some time out of the house," I said, trying not to sound guilty. "My sister is acting so crazy these days, you wouldn't believe it. You know her, don't you? You gave me that CD for her?"

"I was just passing it on," Harlen said lightly. But his thick rotting smell deepened and became momentarily more horrible. I swallowed hard, because the faint scent of violets and licorice had been mixed up in that dreadful stink. Which meant he knew exactly who Serenity was. I wished I dared reach out and touch him, but even the thought of it made my danger sense go off.

"You want to go for a walk?" Harlen invited.

I didn't need any warning from my danger sense to refuse. "I've just called Jesse to come and get me," I lied.

"So," Harlen said, leaning across the table. "Any news on who torched Gilly's place?"

Fury clawed at me that he could mention it so casually, when the smell of smoke and gasoline wound so revealingly through his awful smell, but I held his gaze guilelessly and shrugged. "I think the police are putting it down to vandalism."

"Useless bastards, the cops," Harlen said pleasantly. "So what about the drive-in?"

"I still have to pin down Da," I said.

"Your da," Harlen mocked. "Well, OK, let's go ask him now. I'd like to meet the famous Macoll Whitestarr."

"How do you know his name?" I asked.

"Everyone knows his band outdid Urban Dingo," Harlen said easily.

He had given me an opening and, without thinking, I took it. "It's funny you should mention that gig, because ever since, Da has been getting a lot of work through this guy called Aaron Rayc."

Harlen's smell altered, but rather than becoming darker and stronger, I had the weird impression that it drew back and faded. Then my danger sense began to scream, and I had the utterly strange and dreadful impression that something dark and ancient was looking at me out of Harlen's eyes.

I clamped on my senses to stop myself giving way to screaming hysterics and bent to suck childishly and loudly at the froth in the bottom of the tall glass. Harlen got jerkily to his feet and said he had to go. His eyes were like fogged green pebbles. He sketched a stiff, unnatural-looking wave and went out.

I stayed sitting there until my legs recovered, then I did call Jesse. It was only after I got home that I cursed myself for not having called Harrison from the mall when I had the chance, because I arrived right at dinnertime, when there was no possibility of making a private call. I ate veggie moussaka distractedly, sitting between Serenity, who sat dissecting her meal in stony silence, and Mirandah, who had clearly had another fight with Ricki and ate with tears trickling down her cheeks.

It was lucky that Da and Jesse were talking intensely about music or there would have been dead silence at the table. The only time my ears pricked up was when Da reminded Serenity that she had a dentist appointment straight after school the next day. He said he would collect her with Mum and Luke, and they would all visit the dentist on the way to look at Mum's new gallery. His voice was light and friendly, but I saw how he watched her and I smelled the ammonia sharpness of his concern for her. Then Mum called down to Serenity, her voice croaky with weariness as it always was when she stopped being nocturnal for a while.

I escaped upstairs as soon as Serenity had gone up, taking Luke with me and playing with him on my bed until Da came and got him for a bath. Then I went down to the kitchen to call Harrison, but Mirandah was sitting by the phone staring at it pitifully. I sighed and went back upstairs and did some homework.

I fell asleep without realizing. It was nearly midnight when Da came in to say Harrison was on the phone. I went to the kitchen, where Neil and Tich were eating doughnuts and drinking coffee.

"Alyzon!" Harrison almost shouted.

"Is something wrong?" I could feel Tich and Neil listening and struggled to keep my voice low and calm.

"Is something *wrong*?" Harrison growled, his accent strong. "Christ, Alyzon. Ye scared me half tae death. I called hours and hours ago, and yer brother tells me you've gone out tae meet Harlen Sanderson! And ye dinnae call back!"

"Oh, Harrison! I didn't get the message. My brother can get . . . distracted. And I wasn't meeting Harlen. I had gone to the mall, and he called here and found out where I was going. We only talked for about ten minutes in a coffee shop, and then he left."

"What did he want?"

"Same thing as usual," I said carefully.

"Someone's there?" Harrison guessed.

"Of course. Maybe we could meet tomorrow after school?"

"What about your sister?"

"That's fine," I said guardedly.

"All right. I dinnae get it, but I get it. After school it is. You can come with me tae Raoul's."

I agreed, then hung up to find Tich and Neil looking at me sympathetically.

"Boyfriend problems?" Tich asked.

"Of course not," I said, feeling myself blush annoyingly. "He's just a friend."

"A pretty good friend if he called this late to ask about another man," Neil said, grinning coyly at me. Despite everything, I couldn't help smiling. "There, that didn't hurt, did it?" he said. "Despite what the world says, love is a laughing matter."

"I am not in love!" I laughed.

"Laughter is the best medicine," Tich said wisely, which cracked Neil up. Tich regarded him with wounded amusement. "I read that in *Reader's Digest*!"

Neil nearly convulsed with laughter. His big belly wobbled like jelly. Da came in carrying some music and looked at us all in puzzlement, which made it even funnier.

On the way up the stairs a few minutes later, it struck me that it had been ages since I had laughed so hard; I noticed how light it had made me feel for a moment. But when I was back in bed, wakeful now, my smile faded at the memory of my conversation with Harlen and the queer certainty that for a second the sickness he carried had been fully awake and fully aware, because I had mentioned the name of Aaron Rayc.

38

Despite my increasing feeling that school was irrelevant, I was glad on Friday to be plunged into a day that turned out to be full and demanding, even if half of it was taken up with making notes for holiday homework. Gilly told me at recess that she and her gran were going house-hunting that night. She said they were both sick to death of living in a hotel and eating in the restaurant or ordering room service. I told her about Harlen finding me at the mall, and her eyes widened in alarm.

"Do you think Harlen will tell Aaron Rayc you mentioned him?" Gilly asked.

"Maybe, but it came up naturally enough. And it was worth the risk to see how Harlen reacted."

* * *

At the end of the day I hung around after class, helping to tidy up because I had the feeling Harlen would be waiting to find out if I had asked Da about the drive-in. When I judged that enough time had passed for it to be safe, I slipped out the side door and made my way through the backstreets to meet Harrison at the same cafe we had sat in when I had told him the truth about myself. We had planned to meet inside in case of rain, but the sun was shining and he was waiting outside, leaning against the wall. He had a complicated expression of sadness mingled with resignation on his face before he noticed me, and I wondered if he was thinking of his father. Then I called his name and he swung round and smiled.

"I'm sorry about worrying you last night," I said.

"What happened with Harlen, anyway?" he asked, setting out for the bus stop.

I asked if he'd mind if I waited until we were with Raoul, because I had already told it once to Gilly that day.

"OK," he said. "So who was listening last night?"

Some reckless daring prompted me to say lightly, "A couple of Da's musician friends. They thought you must be in love with me because you were calling so late."

Harrison gave a strangled laugh that sounded both alarmed and embarrassed. All at once, desperate to shift the subject before he said something that would cut me to the quick, I asked if there was something wrong with his father.

Harrison lifted his eyes to the sky and gave a sort of muted Tarzan cry.

I gaped at him in astonishment, and he looked down at me and burst into laughter. "I'm not going mad," he said when he had got control of himself. "It's just that . . . ah hell. I might as well tell you. My father is an alcoholic. That's what I meant when I told you before that he tries tae hide from things. He's a binger. That means a lot of the time he's fine and he doesnae drink at all. But about once a fortnight he goes on a bender and drinks until he falls down wherever he is, then he wakes and drinks again. When the binge is over, he somehow gets himself home. Last night was the first night he'd been home for three days, and he was a mess. I had tae clean him up, and at the same time I was worrying about what had happened tae you."

"Oh, Harrison," I said, full of pity. "Can't he get help?"

"There's not really anything anyone can do," Harrison said. "He's a pretty good father when he's OK, but we try to keep the binges tae ourselves because otherwise welfare would be ontae us and there would go all of my freedom."

"I didn't know," I said softly.

He shrugged. "How could you? You can do a lot but you cannae read minds, thank God." He said this so harshly it jarred me. He gave me a quick look. "I dinnae mean that how it sounded. It's just that I wouldnae want anyone reading my thoughts."

When we got on the bus, we were both silent. I was thinking about how it must feel to have to take care of your father instead of the other way round. I looked at Harrison out of the corner of my eye, but his expression was intensely private and gave away nothing of his thoughts.

* * *

"Hello," Raoul greeted us, looking pleased. "You're just in time to try some of this hot chocolate I've made. They serve it like this in Italy; it's made with melted chocolate instead of powder. I've got some croissants from the bakery in honor of it."

So there we were half an hour later, eating croissants and

drinking hot chocolate that was the most delicious thing I had ever drunk in my life. But then Raoul asked what had been happening and Harrison turned to me expectantly, so I set the cup aside and told them about Harlen. I expected them to reproach me for the risks I had taken, but Raoul said he thought my extended senses would keep me from doing anything that would endanger me.

"You say you felt this virus was looking at you out of Harlen's eyes? Like it was alive?"

"Maybe not alive exactly," I said. "Just . . . roused."

"It could be," Raoul said thoughtfully. "In a way, every cell in our body is a separate life-form with its own motivations, responding to different stimuli." Raoul absently poured us all some more chocolate as I told them about Cole. They both looked interested when I told them of the brief vision I had experienced.

"It sounds a lot like he was thinking about where he was when things went wrong between him and Harlen, and if you are right about their falling-out, then there is a good chance you saw the place where the infections happen," Raoul said. "It's a great pity the vision wasn't clearer."

Harrison drew in a deep breath. "It's a long shot, but when you talked about what you saw, Alyzon, it made me think of those warehouses on the industrial park in Shaletown. Remember the ones owned by Rayc's wife? There was long grass by the side of the road, and if it wasnae raining, that sandy surface could look white. And a warehouse would cast a blocky shadow."

"It's worth taking a look," Raoul said. Then he got a

strange look on his face and he said in a halting voice, "You know what? It's an odd thing, but my car is acting up."

"We could take a train there this weekend and have a look around," Harrison offered.

"You don't understand," Raoul said. "That young guy we drove to the industrial park? He said that something in my car would break, and it would give me a reason to come back."

Harrison nodded. "I remember. But it could just be that he's a good mechanic."

The hair was rising on the back of my neck as I told them what Davey had said to me.

"He mun be able tae see or sense people who are infected, too," Harrison said, his accent growing stronger with his excitement. "That has tae be what he means by 'them' and 'they.' And I've just thought of something else. Ye ken how he said he'd got tae show us the way, and it sounded like he'd got his tenses muddled. Well, what if he meant exactly what he said? That he was showing us the way tae them. Tae the place where the gang meets and where the infections happen. The warehouses! And he directed us there! Ye ken what this means?"

"I do," Raoul said softly. "But I wonder if you do."

"What do ye mean?" Harrison asked, frowning at him.

"I mean we are talking about rather more than extended senses if Davey really was directing us to Them. Because how did he know he was supposed to direct us? Who told him? And if no one told him, then how does he know? And how did he know my car would need repairing? He couldn't . . . unless he can see into the future."

Now it was my turn to gape.

"He is part of this, somehow," Raoul said. "And I believe he knows we will see him again, and why. Tomorrow morning I'm going to drive to Shaletown and find out what he knows. And I'm going to take another look at those warehouses."

"You ken what I think?" Harrison said, looking from Raoul to me. "I think both you and Davey are a natural response tae this sickness. If we think of humanity as an organism, it stands tae reason there'd be a response tae an attack."

"A response by whom? God?" I asked.

"By the organism as a whole. Just like each individual body produces antibodies when a dangerous organism invades."

"You're saying we're some sort of antibodies?" I was glad to laugh at the absurdity, because I had begun to feel a little like we were floating off into the ether.

But Harrison said quite seriously, "In a metaphysical sense, yes, that's exactly what I think."

The telephone rang and Raoul went to answer it. He came back looking worried. "That was Bellavie. Dr. Austin has just been on the phone demanding to know by whose authority Sarry was removed from his care. He's planning to go to Remington."

"He mustn't be allowed near her!" I said, appalled.

"My sentiments exactly. The trouble is that as her previous doctor on record, he does have some authority. I've just called Dr. Abernathy, the doctor who's been caring for Sarry at Bellavie. It's her day off, but she has agreed to come in when Dr. Austin arrives. She wants me to meet her at the hospital."

"We'll go, too," Harrison said, half rising, but Raoul shook his head.

"I need you to stay here and wait for my hacker friend, Daisy. She's to come this evening, and I don't want to spend the time right now tracking her down to postpone."

"I can stay," Harrison said, glancing at me.

"Me too. At least, I can stay until the last bus."

"Don't worry about the bus. I'll be back in time to drive you home," Raoul promised. "Help yourself to anything you want, and use the computers or TV or whatever."

"OK," Harrison said. "But are you sure?"

"I'm sure. Daisy's not the sort to take kindly to being stood up. Even by someone who can't stand. I'll leave a note for you to give her."

"I dinnae like this," Harrison said after he had gone.

"Me either," I said. "Why would Dr. Austin go all that way to see Sarry?"

"The sickness must be driving him. But dinnae worry. Raoul willnae let him lay a hand on her." Harrison suggested we pass the time by going through the articles that referred to Aaron Rayc and making a list of all the other artists he had been associated with, because sooner or later we ought to try to find out which, if any, were infected. We had only been at it for twenty minutes when the doorbell rang.

Harrison went to answer it and ushered in a scraggy old woman of about sixty, clad in skintight leather jeans and leather jacket, a white T-shirt, and black boots with high stiletto heels. She had the foulest mouth I had ever heard on someone old enough to be a grandmother; she was furious to hear she had just missed Raoul. We barely managed to stop her walking away then and there, but she calmed down when she read his note.

She shoved it in her pocket, looked from me to Harrison, and then swore some more about being left to deal with a kindergarten. Harrison looked as if he was about to say something, but I just asked her sweetly if she wanted to see the computer room. "You think I need directions, kid?" she snarled, and stalked past me into the hall and down to the back of the house.

"We need her," I hissed at Harrison, before hurrying after her. By the time I got into the back room, she was already at a terminal tapping away. Ten minutes later she shifted to the next terminal, and then to the next, tapping and huffing and swearing constantly. Now that her attention was not riveted on me, I was able to study her properly, and the strange thing was that in spite of her language and grumpy rudeness, my senses warmed to her jasmine and bubblegum scent. In reality, however, she smelled of smoke and sweat. She had set a packet of cigarettes on the desk beside her, but she made no attempt to light one the whole time she was there.

"You Alyzon?" she suddenly asked, glancing over her shoulder. Her hands continued flying over the keyboard.

"Yes," I said, realizing Raoul must have written about us in the note. She made no comment and went on tapping until

Harrison came in, then she gave him the same interrogating glare. "You're Harrison?"

"I . . . yes," Harrison said, looking startled.

"Don't sound too sure, kid. Gotta be sure of who you are in this world, or someone'll steal your identity." I didn't know if she was joking or not, and from the look on his face, neither did Harrison.

"Can you fix the virus?" he asked her.

Daisy gave him a withering look. Then she said, "It's an interesting breed. Designed to form spontaneous links to heavy porn sites, and it can circumvent the sorts of bars people use to stop their kids viewing stuff like this. Lucky Roo has such a sophisticated setup, because a normal system wouldn't let me track the originating site." She tapped for a bit more as we waited with bated breath, then she let out a hiss of air between clenched teeth.

"You've found it?"

She nodded absently. "The Castledean Estate Web site."

"But . . . but that's the Web site Raoul logged in to when—"

"There's a false loop of trails that would bamboozle a lesser hacker, but I can tell you that the virus originated at that site," Daisy said, and she gave a small smile and stretched with the languid sensuality of a cat, all the skinny stiffness in her smoothed and fluid with triumph. Then she shot us a look and said, "And this site is linked to the Rayc Inc. site that Roo asked me to check out. Doesn't surprise me. The guy's a freak."

"You know Aaron Rayc?" I asked.

"Better than his mama," Daisy said with a leer. "What I don't know about his finances and business dealings ain't worth blowing your nose on. He's a savvy businessman with a knack for making money."

"What makes you call him a freak, then?" I asked.

Daisy stopped tapping to look at me as if she had forgotten I was standing there. For a moment I thought she would refuse to tell me anything. But then she said, "The way he deals with all that money he makes, for instance. It's like he doesn't give a shit about it."

"What do you mean?" Harrison asked.

"He routes most of it to causes all over the world," Daisy said.

Harrison looked so disappointed I knew he had expected to hear that Rayc Inc. were drug or arms dealers. "He runs a charity," Harrison said.

Daisy seemed to take this as a personal criticism. "I'm not talking about the company, boyo. I'm talking about his personal fortune. He gives thousands away to noble causes," she snarled. "Leprosy Society. Mother Teresa's Helpers. Starlight Foundation. It's like he's a give-a-holic. Because dig a little deeper, and you find his giving ain't quite so discriminating. For instance, he donates to the IRA, the Red Brigade, and a dozen different religious cults with more than a nodding acquaintance with terrorism."

"Aaron Rayc sends money to terrorists?" I asked, totally confused.

Daisy glared at me. "You got wax in your ears, kid? The

guy is funding everything. Anarchists' leagues and neofascist groups, Ku Klux Klan and black-activist organizations, gun-support groups and fanatical antigun organizations. It's like he's funding both sides of just about every hot cause you can imagine. And quite a bit of Rayc's company donations wind their way to some pretty offbeat causes, too. It's all here." She got out a memory stick and set in on the table beside her cigarette packet. "Now, what about a drink?"

"Sure, uh, what would you like?" Harrison asked.

Daisy smiled, and for a second she looked like someone's sweet old grandmother. "Now I wouldn't say no to one of Roo's special Italian hot chocolates. You just toddle along and make it up, and I'll put what I brought into Roo's system."

We exchanged a look, then went out obediently. Somehow I wasn't surprised to find a jug of the chocolate in the fridge with a note telling us to heat it in the microwave for Daisy.

She came in as we were pouring the chocolate and prowled restlessly around the kitchen, picking up things and putting them down again. She came to the list of names we had been compiling, and which I had brought in from the living room, and picked that up, too.

"I remember that guy." She was pointing to an opera singer. "He was this fat bozo with greasy hair and a voice like an angel. Just hearing him made you want to wrap yourself around him, at least until he stopped singing." She cackled, and I hoped I didn't look as shocked as I felt. "He went on and made the big time. Then he just went crazy and started singing these operas written by a madwoman. People went in the beginning because of him, but the reviews stank. Ended up in an asylum, he did."

Harrison handed her the chocolate, and she slurped it up with the noisy relish of a little kid before leaving without so much as a goodbye.

"So that was Daisy," I said when Harrison came back from escorting her to the front door. We both laughed, then the phone rang.

Harrison answered it while I washed the cup and pot, wondering what it meant that Aaron Rayc funded so many causes. Then Harrison came back and I turned to ask him, but his face was white as chalk and his eyes were like bruises.

"What is it?" I whispered, frightened.

"That . . . that was Raoul. It's Sarry," he said, his eyes filling with tears.

"Harrison, what . . . ?" I took a step toward him.

"Alyzon, she . . . she's killed herself."

 39

Raoul returned at two in the morning, looking drawn and exhausted. I made hot tea for him, suppressing a little stab of horror at seeing blood on his collar.

"What happened?" Harrison asked when Raoul had a mug of tea in his hand.

Raoul sighed. "I hadn't long arrived at Bellavie. I was just speaking with a receptionist when one of the nurses came rushing along the hall shouting that Sarry had cut her wrists. She was young and frightened or she wouldn't have blurted it out like that. There would be a code she should have used so she didn't alarm any visitors. As it was, I insisted on coming with them, and short of physically restraining me, there was nothing they could do." He gave a weary laugh and I wondered how he could laugh at such a time, before deciding that he must be suffering from shock.

"It was Austin, wasnae it? How did he get tae her?" Harrison demanded through gritted teeth.

Raoul blinked at him, eyes red-rimmed with fatigue. "Austin arrived about twenty minutes before me and bullied the head nurse into shifting Sarry to a small room where he could examine her. One of the younger nurses was passing and heard her scream. She ran in and found Dr. Austin trying to administer an injection. Sarry was struggling and terrified."

"Bastard," Harrison grated.

"Dr. Austin ordered the nurse out. If he had been in whites she might have obeyed, but he wasn't so she told him to leave Sarry alone," Raoul went on. "When he didn't, she knocked the syringe from his hand. Then she rang for help, and minutes later the head nurse appeared and hustled Dr. Austin out into the hall. He was shouting that Sarry had been removed from his care without the proper authority and that he had merely been trying to administer a tranquilizer. The young nurse had been left to calm Sarry, who started babbling that Dr. Austin was 'one of Them'; that she had felt the wrongness in him. The nurse ran out to tell the head that the incident had brought on an episode. Sarry would have been alone all of five minutes, and that's when she did it. She used a scalpel."

"I cannae believe this has happened," Harrison exclaimed, his eyes blazing. "What was he trying tac do?"

"Drug her strongly enough to let the sickness take over, I'd guess. But he somehow let her feel or see that he was infected. I'm sure he thought Sarry wouldn't fight. Or it might be that the sickness was driving him so hard he didn't think. Frankly he looked a mess. His clothes were obviously thrown on without any regard for how he looked, and he was unshaven, his hair wild. If he hadn't had his ID with him, I doubt he'd have been let in at all."

I wondered how Raoul could think about clothes with Sarry so recently dead. The tragedy of her life and death seemed to me to be some terrible shadow that had got inside me. I kept thinking of her licking the ice cream and talking about going with the flow. Kept feeling it was my fault it had come to this.

But Raoul was talking again. "By the time I got there with the nurse and the receptionist, Austin was ranting that they'd killed his patient. I said that I thought we should call the police and, just like that, all the bluster went out of him. I was careful not to say who I was, and Austin assumed I was connected to the hospital. He said we'd all be sorry for our interference, then he left. After he had gone, the head let me go in and talk with Sarry." He took a deep breath. "They had bandaged her wrists to stop the blood, but there was so much of it over her. . . ."

"Ye spoke tae her before she died?" Harrison asked in a wretched voice.

Raoul looked at him blankly. "Died? What are you talking about? I've just told you they bound her wrists, and a little later, when the doctor finally arrived, they gave her a transfusion."

"But . . . are ye saying she's nae dead?!" Harrison jumped to his feet in agitation.

Raoul looked at him and then at me in dawning horror. "Oh God, don't tell me you've both spent all these hours thinking she was dead? I said Sarry had cut her wrists, I didn't say she had died! But I'm an idiot—of course that's what you would think. No wonder you both looked so shattered when I got here!"

Harrison's face changed. "She's nae dead," he said to me, as if I had not heard Raoul's words. I slumped in my chair.

Raoul shook his head, "I'm so sorry to have put you both through this. It was just so confused there, and when I spoke to you Sarry was in the process of having a transfusion. I only called in the first place so you wouldn't worry over me being so late."

"Sarry's alive," I whispered, wanting to hear the words again and again.

Then Harrison was demanding to hear the whole story from the beginning because, for him as for me, the fact of Sarry's death had been all that mattered when Raoul had told it the first time. Raoul smiled and obliged, and Harrison and I interrupted constantly and in the middle of it we realized that we were all ravenous so we phoned for pizza. Given the circumstances, we ought still to have been grim, but the news that Sarry had not died after we had spent hours mourning her was such an incredible relief that Harrison and I were elated, and Raoul ended up the same.

Later, when the pizza had arrived and we were eating it in hot slabs straight from the box, Raoul said, "I stayed be-cause I wanted to speak with Sarry before I left. She'd fainted from loss of blood and shock, and the transfusion took place while she was still unconscious. She woke very groggy and confused, but when the nurse tried to administer a sedative, Sarry begged not to be drugged. Not even the usual small dose. Dr. Abernathy decided under the circumstances to permit it. But she wanted Sarry to rest, so I was only given a few minutes with her."

He paused to take a drink, and Harrison and I waited expectantly.

"She looked so small and frail . . . and utterly exhausted. But very calm. I don't think I've ever seen her look so calm. I told her that I was sorry I hadn't got there sooner, and she said, still with this calmness, that she would rather be dead than devoured by the wrongness inside her. I asked if that was why she had cut her wrists. She said that she hadn't been able to think of anything else to do—that if Dr. Austin had succeeded, she would have been helpless because the sickness is very strong now. Ironically that poor little nurse who saved her from Austin probably ended up pushing her the final inch, because Sarry had thought when the nurse talked of getting the doctor, she meant him. But the nurse also found an unbroken ampoule that Austin had left behind, and she means to send it off to be tested. I'll be very interested to hear the results."

"I cannae believe he did this," Harrison said. "He must know he's stepped over the line legally as well as ethically."

"I doubt he is capable of caring. On the drive back it occurred to me that the sickness of spirit might erode logic and reason when it goes far enough."

I was bothered by this conclusion. "Aaron Rayc must be

a lot further gone, if we're right about him, but he doesn't strike me as anything but cool and calculating."

"I was thinking about that, too," Raoul said. "I'm wondering if Aaron Rayc isn't some sort of anomaly. It seems to me that the end result of the sickness would usually be a sort of complete mental disintegration; a hollowing out that leaves a human shell. But in Rayc's case the wrongness is able to go on operating after it has traveled its usual course."

I shivered. Raoul sounded so certain, so convinced of his theories, but the truth was, we knew frighteningly little of the sickness and what it would do to its victims. "Do you think Austin'll try to get to Sarry again?" I asked.

"She'll be safe. I've hired security for her. He'll be there by now."

"Surely Dr. Austin will be charged for what he tried tae do!" Harrison protested.

Raoul frowned. "I'd like to say yes. Dr. Abernathy struck me as a strongly ethical woman. But I think the medical profession has always been a bit of an old boys' club, and they would far rather deal internally with their dirty linen."

"He should be in jail!" Harrison said.

Raoul asked about Daisy. He sounded hoarse and he looked exhausted. After Harrison told him what Daisy had said about the virus and Rayc's finances, I suggested we ought to go. Raoul asked if we would mind if he sent us home in a taxi. As we waited for it, Harrison wondered again why Rayc would fund so many disparate groups, and Raoul said it was almost certainly just another way to sow despair and pain and discord. Once we released his weird financial dealings to the media, he would go from influential friend of the stars to persona non grata. His charity, too, would fall from grace. "He will still be what he is, but his power to cause harm will be weakened," Raoul concluded.

"But not stopped," Harrison said grimly.

Raoul didn't take that up. He agreed that we should use Gary Soloman, but said the journalist had to make absolutely certain that Aaron Rayc would not learn who had blackened his name. Because if he did know who had destroyed him, he was likely to be utterly ruthless.

I shivered. "You make it sound as if he would send someone to kill us."

Raoul gave me a level look. "I think that someone infected by wrongness would not stop at murder."

* * *

Harrison and I sat in silence as the taxi bore us away from Raoul's church house. The gliding motion of the taxi and the flickering of streetlights against dark, silent streets soon lulled me to sleep. I dreamed that I was a wolf in the ruined city, only this time a dog was running beside me, a great white-furred beast that, when I looked at it, nuzzled me on the cheek. I was startled to feel both its devotion and its desire, and my wolf-self responded with a quickening of her own desire. The shock of this woke me with a start.

Harrison was leaning over me. "Ye . . . you're home," he stammered.

"Thanks," I said, touched that he had gotten the taxi to bring me all the way home first.

Despite it being so late, Da was up with Neil and Tich, and they were in the middle of reworking a song when I entered the kitchen. The song they were reshaping was one of my favorites, a lovely ballad full of wistful hope and gentleness, but what they were doing with it seemed jarring and uneven to me. When they had finished the run-through, Neil asked what I thought and I wished he hadn't.

"I've always liked that song." My voice sounded scratchy with tiredness.

Da sighed. "So did I. Which is maybe why I don't like this version."

"Why don't you leave it as it is?" I asked.

"I need a song that Neo Tokyo can play. I can just hear Aaron saying that it's slight compared with the big topics they usually tackle."

"Slight!" I almost shouted. "Why is it that people always think bad, dark things are more real and important than things that lift you up and make you feel life is worth living? You ought to tell them *that* in a song."

"Wow," Neil said.

I felt silly then, but Da surprisingly gave me a hug, and for a minute I was immersed in his essential gentleness and smells. But I began, after a blissful few seconds, to feel other things. His worry about money, his concern for Serenity, and his inner dialogue about musical integrity. Rather than pulling away as the weight of his feelings began to press down on me, some instinct born of all that had happened that night made me hold him even more tightly, lay my cheek against his, and use the only weapons I had against the yammering of his doubts and worries—my love for him, and the lovely, radiant memory of the Urban Dingo concert.

When I let go, Da looked slightly dazed. "Alyzon. What did you—"

I cut him off, not sure myself what I had done. "I think what you and the guys do with your songs and music is really important, because it's an antidote to the despair coming from everyone else."

"Your da couldn't have found better words, Aly Cat," Neil said.

Da looked at me closely. "Are you OK, Alyzon?" I remembered then that I had called him earlier to tell him about Sarry and to explain I would not be home until late.

"Oh, Da, I should have said at once! We misunderstood when Raoul called about Sarry. He said she had cut her wrists, and we thought she was dead, but she wasn't."

"How is she then?" Da asked.

"She's had a blood transfusion and she's sleeping peacefully."

"Why'd she do it?" Neil asked, sounding baffled. "A kid your age, your da said."

"She's had a much harder life than I have, Neil. Her mum died when she was really little, and she doesn't have any brothers and sisters. She's been alone since she was about five."

"Poor kid," Tich said.

My eyes burned, my throat ached, and I felt I could sleep for centuries and still be tired.

"You look all done in, Aly Cat," Da said gently. "Go to bed. We'll talk in the morning."

I stumbled upstairs, took off my outer clothes, crawled under the bedding, and was asleep almost at once.

* * *

I woke what seemed five minutes later, my head fit to burst. I staggered to the bathroom, certain this was the result of whatever I had done to Da. I dry-swallowed a couple of headache pills, splashed water on my face, and brushed my teeth, the events of the previous night surging through my mind.

I went to the bedroom and was startled to see that it was lunchtime. Serenity was sitting up on her bed, dressed and holding a notebook on her lap. She looked calm, and although she smelled of licorice as strongly as ever, there were no gasoline or burning-hair smells. Before I could think what to say to her, there was a brief rap at the door. Jesse poked his head in to say Mum wanted to know if Serenity was ready to sit. Serenity rose and all but glided out, the same blankness in her expression.

I went downstairs to find Da on the verge of leaving to rehearse with Neo Tokyo. There was none of the weariness I had seen in his face when I had come home the night before, and, to my delight, the air around him was bending outward as powerfully as it had used to do. There were even a few sparks.

"You seem pretty happy," I said.

"*Inspired* is the word you want, Aly Cat. And you can blame yourself for it; what you said last night."

"What I said?" I echoed.

Da grinned. "You said that lifting people's spirits wasn't anything to do with telling them to be happy or sad. What was important was to lift people up so that for a little while they could get a clear view."

"I said that?"

He laughed. "Maybe I jazzed it up a little. Or maybe your words sparked it, but that's what I ended up writing a song about. I wish I had time to play it through for you, but I've gotta get traveling. Not much rehearsal time before it has its day in the sun."

"You seem OK about playing with other people now," I said.

Da shrugged. "I felt like the integrity of my music was the same as my loyalty to Losing the Rope. Then a couple of nights ago Neil tells me I'm a fool to think it; that music doesn't belong to anyone once it's made, and that no musician belongs to a single band. He reckons that if Rayc Inc. want me to play solo or Neo Tokyo wants me to do this function, then why not? After all, Losing the Rope can still play together and we'll continue to write our songs. And last night, writing this song with them for me to play with Neo Tokyo, I realized there was something exciting and invigorating in mixing it up with other people and other styles. And of course, music and songs are ageless and timeless when they are really saying something important."

He glanced at his watch and began to pull on his battered bomber jacket. Watching him, I felt that the sunshine slanting in the window was drenching me and the world with some bright warmth that made the whole dark night seem like an evil dream. Sarry was stable, Serenity seemed to have found some peace, and Da was his usual wonderful self.

"What if Neo Tokyo don't like what you have?" I asked.

Da just smiled his old sweet smile. "I have the feeling I can convince them."

I laughed aloud out of sheer happiness. "Da, I honestly think you could convince the world of anything with your music."

He looked startled and pleased, and it hit me that even though the sickness may have targeted Da, he wasn't just an empty vessel. No one was. He might not know about the black corrupting force stealing through the world's spirit; he wasn't fighting or hunting it; he was simply living. But just by living his good strong life, he was its adversary. He was the sort of person whose presence filled you up and shone beams of light into the dark corners of your mind, showing you that there was no monster under the bed or vampire outside the window.

That he hadn't needed me to save him made me feel a delicious lightness and a crazy desire to burst into song.

* * *

Jesse asked me a bit later to help him in the yard. He had made a swing, but he needed someone to hold Luke in the seat so that he could adjust the rope. We were in the middle of a maneuver that involved me holding a gurgling Luke while Jesse made a knot when I heard a car door slam and an engine start. Instinctively, I turned to wave to Da. But instead of his battered van, I saw a green van pulling away from the front of the house.

A cold hand seized my heart and I swept Luke up, ran inside, and raced up the stairs. In half a minute I was pushing into Mum's studio, panting hard. She looked up at me from behind a canvas rectangle mounted on her big easel, beautiful and tranquil as a paint-smudged angel.

"Where's Serenity?" I demanded.

"I don't know," Mum said vaguely, her face turning back to her easel as if it was compelled by some magnetism.

"But you never let a sitter interrupt a session," I almost screamed at her.

"She didn't break it," Mum said. "I've finished the portrait."

I gritted my teeth. "Where did Serenity say she had to go?"

"She didn't say," Mum murmured.

I thrust Luke into her arms, uncaring that she would smear him with paint. "Maybe you can manage to pay attention to the real world long enough to watch him," I said coldly, turning on my heel and slamming out into the hall. Some bit of me protested that I was being unfair, but a terrible fear was building in me.

I almost collided with Jesse on the stairs. "Alyzon, why in the hell did you just . . . ," he began, then he stopped, seeing my face. "What's the matter? Where's Luke?"

Mirandah came out of her room. "What's all the yelling?"

408

"Do you know where Serenity went?" I asked her.

"I saw her getting her coat," Mirandah said. "She said she was going to see a documentary. Why?"

I heard the muffled sound of Luke beginning to cry in the studio, and I felt a little like doing the same. Yet some sensible bit of me was asking what on earth I was making such a fuss over. It could easily be that Serenity had gone to a movie. Hadn't she seemed much calmer today? So why did I suddenly feel such frightened urgency?

It was the van, I thought.

"Did Serenity say where this documentary was playing?" I asked Mirandah.

She shook her head, but Jesse said, "The only place I know where they play documentaries is the theater in the mall. Alyzon, why are you asking all of these questions about Serenity?"

"I . . . I just have this feeling she might be in trouble."

"In trouble?" Jesse and Mirandah exchanged a baffled look.

I heard Mum call out, and went reluctantly back along the hall to her studio, knowing I deserved her reproaches for the way I had snarled at her. And yet Mum never reproached anyone for anything. So what did she want?

40

I pushed open the studio door and Mum was still sitting there with Luke in her arms. He was tugging delightedly on the long coils of red hair. I must have imagined him crying, I thought confusedly.

"I'm sorry I yelled," I said.

She didn't acknowledge the apology. "Alyzon, would you like to see the painting of Serenity?"

This was so unexpected that I laughed harshly. "Mum, I can look at it later. I have to . . ." But she turned the easel, and I stopped talking because the portrait was one of the best and most terrible Mum had ever painted. Serenity, dressed all in black, was standing with her hands hanging loosely by her sides gazing straight out of the canvas. Most of the bottom of her face was empty space, like in a Magritte painting, and you could see into the small cavern of her skull where a fire blazed. One eye was also a blank opening so that you could see the flames clearly through it as if it were a small window, while the other was Serenity's normal eye, staring out with the same expression that I had seen in her eyes just before in the bedroom: blind and blankly serene. A blue-centered almond floating on a sea of flame.

"What . . . what is this?" I whispered. I looked at Mum, feeling frightened and sick. "Why did you paint her like that?"

Mum answered almost casually. "Before your father came into my life, there was a darkness in me. I could feel it trying to consume me, and I thought I was going mad. Then I fell in love with Macoll, and it was suddenly easy to fight. For a time I thought I would defeat it, but then I realized that it can't be defeated. Not once it's inside you. But I found out that I could use painting to fill the gaps in my heart and mind so that there was nowhere for it to grow. Nothing of me is available to it when I paint."

My ears rang with the enormity of what I was hearing. Because unless I was going insane, and in that second it seemed a distinct possibility, Mum was telling me that she was infected by the sickness just like Sarry. That she had been infected before any of us were born. It sounded as if Da had helped her fight the sickness in almost the same way that Harrison and Raoul and Gilly had done with Sarry. Her love for him and his for her had given her something solid to hang on to. But unlike Sarry, Mum also had her painting. How ironic if creating art could be shaped to resist the sickness as well as to serve it. That was maybe why Mum did not have Sarry's mental frailty.

"How . . . how did you get infected?"

She blinked at me. "Infected? That's a good way to

describe it. I . . . I don't remember really. It happened when I was young. It was the seventies, and I was so full of anger and confusion. I had run away from home and was living in a squalid apartment with some people like me. A woman came there one night. She befriended me and invited me to stay with her. She was so attractive and compelling, and she seemed to represent something that I didn't have. A purpose or a meaning for life. So I moved in with her. I discovered then that she used and dealt drugs. It didn't make her less glamorous to me, but then one night . . ." She shook her head, almost shuddering. "Alyzon, I can't think of it. I daren't. It's too dangerous for me. I need to paint."

She thrust Luke at me and began to take the painting of Serenity down. For a long moment she held it at arm's length and looked at it. To my fascinated horror, tears spilled down her face. She looked at me with anguish in her drowning eyes. "I don't want this to happen to her. That's why I painted what I see. So that you could see what is happening. So that you will save her."

I stared at her. "Me? But Da . . ."

She shook her head. "Macoll is strong, but he can't save her."

"Mum, I . . ." I hardly knew what I wanted to say, but suddenly she turned aside and thrust the painting face-first against the wall.

"I have to paint," she muttered, and tore a sheet of paper from a rough block and began to sketch rapidly with a nub of charcoal. Even in the few seconds before I moved to leave the studio, I saw some of the rigid tension ease out of her back, but she did not turn around again.

I left the studio carrying Luke, shaken to the core by what had just happened. I hardly believed it, and yet if it was true, so much of Mum's eccentricity suddenly made perfect sense. I had always thought of her as inner-directed, but I had never, until now, known what held her inner eye. It was suddenly obvious to me that she had extended vision, despite her apparent blindness to ordinary things. How else would she have seen what she saw in Serenity and whatever it was that she saw in me? I felt an ache of pity for her, fighting a long, bitter, lonely battle against an enemy that only her death could finally vanquish.

There were a thousand questions I wanted to go back and ask, but something in her face had told me that she would refuse to talk about what had happened to her. I went down to the kitchen holding Luke as if he was a spar of wood in a wild sea. Mum had risked something to paint Serenity, I thought. Had risked herself. I suddenly remembered how Da had looked that night when Mum had told him she was going to do the painting. Anxious, concerned, troubled. He knew Mum saw things other people didn't see. That was what had always made him so tolerant of her eccentricities.

Again I had the urge to turn back and demand that she tell me more, but Serenity was missing and there was no time to waste.

* * *

Jesse and Mirandah were in the kitchen looking worried.

"We have to find Serenity," I said. My mind was sharp now, and very clear. "Jesse, find out if there's a documentary playing at the mall. Mirandah, can you think of any other places where they show documentaries?"

"There's the Historical Records Center above the library," Mirandah said as I put Luke in his high chair and peeled a banana to give him a piece. "They have a small theater where they show archival films. I'll get the number."

"Anywhere else you can think of," I said. "Call all of them."

Jesse found the number to the mall theater and called as Mirandah flipped through the phone book. A moment later he hung up and said there were no documentaries scheduled for the day. "OK. Now what is going on?"

"Serenity is in danger," I said.

"What kind of danger?" Mirandah asked, pulling the phone toward her.

Some of my certainty left me. "I don't exactly know." I felt my words were lame, but I wondered if maybe I had underestimated how deeply everyone else in the house had worried about Serenity's slow transformation. Maybe no more needed to be said.

"She acted kind of weird in the hallway," Mirandah said. "She looked at me, but I felt like she was looking straight through me."

"There's been something up with her for ages," Jesse said decisively. "All right, let's find her." He called the numbers that Mirandah gave him, but within fifteen minutes we had not found a single documentary playing that day.

"Where do you think she's gone then?" Mirandah asked.

I stared at her. "I don't know. We should try to contact Da. Where is his rehearsal?"

"It's at those guys' place. Neo Tokyo," Jesse said.

"All right. Call Neil and see if he has a number for them or knows the address." Jesse picked up the receiver, and I turned to Mirandah. "You're sure Serenity said nothing else? Did she say she was going with anyone? Or that she was being picked up?"

"As far as I know, she doesn't know anyone to be picked up by," Mirandah said. "But if you really want to know . . ."

Jesse hung up and said that Neil didn't know where Da was rehearsing.

I turned back to Mirandah. "What were you going to say a second ago? If I really wanted to know . . . what?"

She shrugged. "I was just saying maybe you ought to look in Serenity's diary if you want to know where she went."

"Serenity doesn't keep . . ." I stopped, remembering her reaction when I had wondered at the fuss she was making over my touching the yellow book. It's not as if it's a diary, I had said, and she had blanched.

Mirandah took my silence as disbelief. "She does. I came in to borrow something of yours when you were in the hospital, and Serenity was writing in a notebook. I would have thought it was homework, except when I turned away, I saw her in the mirror, shoving it between the bed and the mattress. What else could it be but a diary?"

I thought of the notebook Serenity had been cradling in her arms before she went into the studio to Mum, and ran out of the kitchen and upstairs. Sure enough, the notebook I had seen was hidden beneath the mattress. One glance told me that Mirandah was right. It was a diary.

I carried it to the kitchen and handed it to Jesse, asking him to use his speed-reading ability to see if there was any mention of where Serenity might have gone. He frowned, but then he opened it and began to read.

I dialed Harrison's number. It rang and rang, and I was just about to give up when a man answered the phone, his voice low but pleasant. Remembering the last time I had called, my voice was cool as I asked for Harrison.

"He went out just after lunch," the man said gently. "I'm his father, Jack. What was your name?"

"I'm sorry," I said, shamed by my rudeness—because alcoholism was a sickness, too, after all. "I . . . I'm Alyzon Whitestarr."

"Well, he didn't leave you any message, Alyzon," Harrison's father said. "I'll let him know you called, shall I? Does he have your number?"

I said that he did, thanked his father politely, and hung up. Then I dialed the hotel where Gilly and her grandmother were staying. The concierge told me that they were out and he had no idea when they would return. I dialed Raoul's number but got his voice mail. I left a message asking him to call and said, as I had not felt able to do in the other two messages, that Serenity had disappeared. I was aware of Mirandah and Jesse exchanging glances of alarmed puzzlement, but there was no time to explain because the phone rang the minute I put the receiver down. It was Harrison. He said in a cheerful voice that he and Raoul were returning from errands and had dropped by his house. "My father said you just called."

"Serenity has disappeared, and I'm afraid she might have gone off in a van."

"Hold on." There was a swift urgent exchange, then Harrison said they would be over shortly. After hanging up, I turned to find Jesse lifting his head from the diary. His eyes were appalled.

"She hates us," he said, sounding shattered. "Over and over again she says it. All of us, but especially Da. She says he is a filthy hypocrite because all he does is sing songs while the world falls into darkness. That's how she puts it—falls into darkness! She says Da is a collaborator because he doesn't fight anything."

"It's because of Aya," I said.

Jesse nodded. "She calls 'Song for Aya' the anthem of a coward. But what else could Da have done that he didn't do?"

"Flip to the last entries," I said impatiently.

"I'm scared," Mirandah said.

"Listen," Jesse said, and he read, " 'If I truly believe in my ideals, I must act upon them. I must show them all what is courage. It is strange and lovely how all confusion fades once you accept that you are ready to act. Let Da see what it is to have the courage of one's convictions. Will he dare to sing of what I will do? I doubt it, and yet it would be a penance. People like him must be made to see that there are those who are prepared to do anything for their ideals. I am ready.' "

"Jesus, what is she planning to do?" Mirandah cried, looking horrified.

"I don't know," I said tersely. Because Mirandah's question made me realize that it did sound as if she was preparing to do something. Had I been wrong? Was she actually joining the gang rather than becoming its victim? I said impatiently, "Read the rest of it."

Jesse bent over the pages once more, his body now tense as he scanned the lines of writing. Luke began to cry. Mirandah picked him up, grimaced, and went to change him. I hurried upstairs after her, to pull on boots and a sweater and jacket. When I brushed my hair and cleaned my teeth, my face looked grim and purposeful in the spotted mirror over the sink.

"I've got something, but there are no more dates," Jesse said as I reentered the kitchen. He read, " 'They say that I must not be afraid, but I *am* afraid. It is cowardice, of course. But I will not allow myself to bow to fear like Da and the others in my family of useless dreamers and idealists. What is the use of living a good life when there is so much evil? We have to show the politicians who make these laws that there are consequences to their actions. They think they can do anything, make any law, set any injustice in motion and no one can touch them. But soon they will not dare to be complacent. They will know that there are those prepared to dare anything for their ideals, no matter what the cost.'" He stopped reading and said, "It sounds like she's going to make some sort of radical protest against the government."

"Soon," Mirandah reminded us.

I shivered. "I am ready," Serenity had written. There was a finality to the words that fitted the possibility that she was on the verge of some extreme action. I thought of the sickness inside Aaron Rayc and knew that whatever Serenity meant to do, it would darken the world.

"Let's go through the obvious things she might do," Jesse said. "She could shoot someone, only it wouldn't help those refugees. It would just give the authorities another excuse to say refugees were trouble and the people supporting them were unstable lunatics."

I thought of the warehouses in Shaletown and wondered if there were guns there. Daisy had said Aaron Rayc supported the gun lobby, so maybe he had boxes and boxes of weapons. But the idea of Serenity shooting anyone seemed like something out of a bad action movie. "She would never hurt anyone," I said.

"Listen," Jesse said, flicking back several pages in the diary. He read: "'Sacrifice is necessary. It is most central to any ideal of honor.'"

"She's definitely going to do something illegal and get arrested," Mirandah said. "Maybe she's going to set off a bomb."

"Where the hell would she get a bomb?" Jesse asked, and I could smell a sharp peppery smell that I read as apprehension.

"Same place she'd get a gun!" Mirandah snapped.

"What about a fire?" Jesse said.

"She might light a fire," I said, thinking of the fires at the Shaletown Boys Academy, the bakery, and Gilly's house. And then I thought of the fire inside Serenity's head in Mum's painting.

"There's a government office in Eastland Mall," Mirandah said rather wildly.

"It would be pointless to burn that," I said. "There are sprinklers and smoke alarms. In the end there'd be no more than a bit of singed carpet, which would be paid for by the insurance company."

"Hang on," Jesse broke in, and he bent over the diary. "Look here. I thought it was just a doodle, but it might be a map that's been scribbled over."

Mirandah and I crowded close, but the map, if it was a map, had been pretty well obliterated by a grid of lines. The only thing I could see was a big black cross, but I couldn't see what was under it.

The doorbell rang, and I went to let Harrison in. "Raoul said he'd wait in the car tae save time," he said. I led Harrison to the kitchen and introduced him to Mirandah. She gave him a speculative look that, even in that anxious moment, annoyed me. She offered coffee, and Harrison said Raoul could probably use one as well. Mirandah looked intrigued when

Harrison said Raoul was in a wheelchair, and offered to take the coffee out herself. She did not question why two strangers should be enlisted in the search for Serenity, but I saw Jesse eyeing Harrison curiously when I handed him the diary.

Harrison read the page that was open, but before he could have read more than a line, he looked up. "You saw a van pull away, you said? Was it a green van?"

I nodded. "Dark green. I don't know why, but somehow that made my . . . made me certain that Serenity was in it. Then I went upstairs and she had gone."

"There was a dark green van parked outside the refugee center in Shaletown," Harrison said. "The protesters got intae it and drove off when it started raining. The ones Rose Cobb said were 'political.' "

I gasped. He was right. "It must be the detention center that she's going to target." I looked at Jesse. "We have to go there right now. I'll explain everything when we get back. When Da comes home, can you get him to call this number?" I had Harrison write Raoul's cell number on the pad beside the phone.

"OK," Jesse said. "But this better be good when I finally hear it."

* * *

As soon as we got into the car, I told Raoul what had happened. He drove toward the highway, but instead of saying anything about Serenity, he said, "I forgot to tell you both last night. On my way back from Bellavie, something went wrong with the car. It got worse and worse and in the end I called the roadside repair line. The guy rigged something up to get me home, but he said it would only last a day or so, then I would need to get the part replaced."

"I bet Davey will have the part," Harrison said.

"But we're not going to the warehouses," I protested. "It definitely sounds like she's going to do something, and there would be no point in doing it there."

"We'll go to the detention center first," Raoul said.

I told them then about Mum's picture and the things she had told me. The car slowed momentarily as Raoul and Harrison stared at me in disbelief.

"I wish you could see the picture," I said slowly. "No normal person could have painted it. And when Mum talked about having a darkness inside her, I just couldn't believe it."

"What seems unbelievable tae me is that this whole thing would revolve so strongly around one family," Harrison said. "But maybe it's because all of you have extended senses or at least the potential tae have your senses extended." His eyes widened. "Jesus, maybe you are the way you are because your mum was infected and fighting it when each of you was born!"

"A hereditary disposition for extended senses?" Raoul said.

"Or something," Harrison said. "I wish you had asked your mother how she was infected."

"I did. She said she couldn't remember but that it had something to do with an older woman. But then she wouldn't say any more. Talking about the infection seemed to make her especially afraid."

"It is the same with Sarry," Raoul said. "Maybe talking about it activates the sickness. But listen, I've just had a thought. There's no way your sister could set the detention center on fire. The outside wall is two stories high and made of stone, and so are most of the internal buildings, from what I've seen on TV."

"And the center has its own fire truck, so even if she did manage to set something alight it wouldn't be long before it was out," I said. "I remember seeing it there once when we were visiting Aya."

"Maybe this whole idea of some sort of political action is just a ruse tae get Serenity tae Shaletown," Harrison suggested. "Maybe the real destination is the warehouses."

Twenty minutes later Raoul turned off the highway into Shaletown. "We'll park in front of your friend's house. You can go in and see if she's seen anything more of these protesters in their green van, and that'll also give us an excuse for being there if anyone is watching. If nothing is happening there, we'll go to the industrial park."

But Rose was not home. From her porch I could see a little clutch of protesters with placards and lanterns sitting vigil, so I went over. They were not the protesters Harrison and I had seen; these were young women and elderly men and children, as well as young men with great shaggy manes of hair or dreadlocks. I asked a young woman in shabby overalls if she knew Rose. Her face was lit by a warm smile. "Of course I know the dear old thing," she laughed. "I brought her some of my brownies. I had forgotten; she's gone away to visit one of her children."

By the time we were approaching the hill between the end of the residential area and the fields surrounding the industrial park, the sky had darkened to a grayish, indistinct evening.

"You know the French call this time of day the hour between wolf and dog," Harrison said.

I stared at the warehouse roofs, feeling my skin prickle at the thought of how many times I had dreamed of being a wolf since my accident.

41

The door to the dilapidated office was open, but I couldn't see inside because there were greasy-looking multicolored plastic streamers hanging in the space.

"Anybody there?" I called, parting the streamers and poking my head in.

There was no answer. I stepped inside. It was so dim that at first I could see nothing. I extended my vision until I could make out a desk with a phone and a cash register, all half buried under paper. The rest of the space was filled with battered and oil-stained benches covered in hundreds of bits from car engines. There were more parts set along shelves that ran behind the desk from floor to roof, and through a gap between the shelves wide enough to serve as a door, I saw there was more space. The whole place reeked of grease and dust.

"Hello?" I said, and this time I extended my hearing. There was someone in the room beyond the shelves. "Davey?"

I caught the sweetness of his scent before I saw him. He stepped out from behind the shelves, and I was struck anew

425

by his strange, childlike beauty. "I . . . my friend is here with his car. He needs something replaced, just as you said he would."

"Simon said," Davey replied solemnly, and he crossed to the nearest bench and picked something up. "Davey ordered the part, and now he will fix the car of the legless man."

I drew a shaky breath, trying to think how to shape what I wanted to ask. "Davey . . . did you know we would come today?"

He nodded.

I took another breath. "The other day, you said this was one of 'Their' places. Did you mean the warehouses?" I pointed, and he looked in the warehouses' direction for a long moment as if he could see them.

Then he said, "The warehouses are one of Their places. They are not there now." His eyes shifted back to me, and for a split second I saw a flash of the same intelligence that I had seen in the Davey of my dreams. Rational or not, I knew he had somehow reached out to me in them.

"Do you know where They are?" I whispered.

"They are coming," Davey said.

"Is my . . . is my sister with Them?" The words were too sharp, and Davey blinked as if some spell had been broken.

But then he said, "Simon says a girl is with them who is not yet one of them. Simon says Davey must fix the car now, and Alyzon Whitestarr must go and look at Their place. She must be quick and not let Them see her because then They will come to Davey."

"Come here? But why?"

"They made all the other people who were here shut up their doors and go away. But Simon says someone must watch and see what is happening and that someone is Davey, so Davey does not go. Then when the moon was full, They came to see Davey. The moon makes Them hungry when it is fat. Davey was very frightened because Simon said They would try to put the wrongness in him, but it wouldn't find a way in. They hurt Davey and then They said he could stay, but he must tell if anyone comes and especially if someone asks about the warehouses, or They will hurt him again. Davey wanted to close up Daddy's door and run away like the others, but Simon said be brave and be one of those monkeys."

"Monkeys?" I echoed.

Davey lifted one blackened hand to his mouth and covered it, and a slyness flickered over his soft features, but it was the innocent slyness of a child. Then he shifted his hand to one eye and then to one ear, and I understood. The three wise monkeys. See no evil, hear no evil, speak no evil. He tapped his nose and smiled, and there was such sweet mischief in it that, despite everything, I found myself smiling, too.

I went back outside to where Raoul and Harrison waited in the car. "Davey was expecting us. He has the part you're going to need. He says no one is at the warehouses now, but that They are coming and that They have a girl with them. I need to go and have a closer look."

"We can take the cell, and if it looks like Serenity is in

danger, we'll message you, Raoul," Harrison said, smiling at Davey as he approached with his tools.

But Davey did not smile back at him. "Simon says Alyzon Whitestarr must go alone."

Harrison began to argue, but although my mouth felt dry with dread, I managed to say calmly, "It's OK. I'll go alone." Raoul put the spare phone on silent and punched some buttons, then handed it to me, saying I had only to push the send button if I needed help.

Davey suddenly lifted his head like a dog hearing something humans could not. I extended my own hearing and made out, very faintly, the distant hum of an engine.

"They are coming," Davey announced.

I shucked off my backpack and handed it to Harrison. "Dinnae do anything stupid," he said brusquely, but there was anxiety in his eyes and for a moment the smell of lavender was overpowering.

I turned to Davey, who reached out and grabbed one of my hands in his silky black grasp. A wave of shining childlike confidence surged into me, and I saw clearly the image of the wolf that I became in my dreams; only in Davey's version, beams of white light shone from my eyes!

Then he released me and told me to go.

There was no time to marvel at what had taken place. I set off at a run, knowing the warehouses' bulk would hide me from the cars I could hear coming. Instead of going along the road to where it ended in a cul-de-sac, I fought my way through waist-high weeds to the triangular, weed-choked no-man's-land between the first two warehouses. My extended vision allowed me to avoid a mound of overgrown construction rubbish, but not the thick, black ooze of mud puddled at its base. Grimacing at the filth I could feel squelching around my sandals and between my toes, I realized the best position I could achieve without putting myself in danger of being seen would afford me a view of the entrances to only half the warehouses. It would have to do.

Knowing I might be there for some time, I found a slight depression close to the wall of the first warehouse and squatted down. Only then did I realize that I could no longer hear any vehicles. I puzzled at this until, after a good ten minutes, I heard the sound of a car starting up. I recognized it as the deep purr of Raoul's car, and I listened as it headed back along the road. Then two more engines roared to life, and I heard them coming closer. They must have spotted Raoul's car and stopped at Davey's place. I wondered worriedly what had happened, then headlights indicated the two vehicles had swung into the cul-de-sac and grated to a stop. I could hear the Rak playing from one of them, and when its door opened, the noise hit the night like an explosion. The metal wall of the warehouse shuddered with the thumping violence of the bass. Barely audible under the racket, I could hear people getting out of the van and the other vehicle, slamming doors and talking in an overlapping murmur.

It took me a good two minutes to calm down enough to lift my head clear of the grass. When I did, I was dismayed to realize that I could only see the front of the green van, not the doors; the other vehicle was completely out of sight, which meant it had probably been parked behind it. .

I focused my hearing on the voices and distinctly heard a familiar girl's voice. I tried thinking about Serenity to focus it more acutely, but the Rak kept gnawing into my attention. I willed her to come around the back of the van so I could see her, but nothing happened. Then I heard the sound of rattling metal—keys at the door of the warehouse I was leaning against.

I leaned sideways and pressed my ear to the corrugated metal of the warehouse. The voices were muffled enough that I knew the warehouse must be lined, and that in itself was strange. Who would go to the trouble and expense of sound-proofing such enormous warehouses in the middle of an all-but-deserted industrial park?

Collecting my wits, I pushed my hearing until my head began to hurt. The sounds of conversation I could hear were too fragmented to make sense of. I caught the high pitch of a female voice again and homed in.

". . . don't understand why . . . there will be dozens of better cameras . . ." I frowned, because all at once the voice seemed too high and clipped to belong to Serenity.

"You need to prove your commitment and courage," a male voice said, so distinctly that I knew he must be right on the other side of the wall.

When she answered, the girl used a plaintive and sulky voice. "I don't understand how filming can—"

"You don't need to know all of the details." The male voice was coldly dismissive and, just like that, I recognized it.

Harlen Sanderson.

I gasped. And then I heard Harlen say with perfect clarity: "What was that?"

I held my breath, because although common sense said he could not have heard me, my danger sense was thrumming hard, reminding me that people infected with wrongness seemed also to have their senses extended.

"What was what?" I heard another male voice ask.

"Shut up." Harlen bit the words out. "Switch that music off!"

Suddenly my danger sense began to scream. I had a mental image of Harlen silently signaling his companions to go outside and circle around either side of the warehouse. Forcing myself not to panic, I turned and stepped back until I reached the pile of rubble. I climbed over it and, without hesitation, lay down flat in the black sludge. I rolled back and forth in it, then I swiftly smeared it over my face and neck and hands. Then I rolled against the side of the warehouse, pressing my face to the wet earth.

My danger sense began to roar, but I turned my mind away from it and made my flesh still, my breath slow, my heartbeat a whisper.

And I listened.

For a long moment I heard nothing, but then I caught the shifting glow of a flashlight. I prayed that whoever held it would not walk down into the dark cleft, or would not come far enough for the light to find me. I prayed that I would not hiccup or sneeze or cough.

Then I smelled him. Harlen.

Fearing that the sickness he carried would allow him to scent my terror, I turned my mind to scouring rain falling onto the gray-dimpled skin of the sea. But behind my tight-closed eyelids, the light grew brighter as Harlen came closer.

Then I heard a quick, light step. "I don't know what you think you heard. I didn't hear anything." The girl's complaint grated against the night, and at last I recognized whose voice it was: not Serenity's but Sylvia Yarrow's.

Harlen ordered her to shut up in a savage voice, and then he swooped the light around one more time and came another step into the cleft. Knowing he must be at the mound, and literally standing over me, I burrowed into the stillness of my mind until I found a place where it was quiet and safe and clean, and where I could not sense the world.

* * *

Harrison was half-dragging, half-carrying me through the door of Davey's shack. I stared at him in utter confusion, because the last thing I remembered was lying beside the warehouse.

I tried to speak, but my lips were numb and I realized I was trembling uncontrollably.

"You got close," Davey whispered. "Almost too close . . ."

Only then did the white-faced Harrison notice that I was awake. With an exclamation of frustration, he drew me over to a seat by the stove and asked Davey to fetch warm water and a cloth and towel.

"There were two green vans," he said abruptly. "They both stopped here by the side of the road. The bouncer type from the poetry group got out of one and came over tae Raoul's car. Luckily I was inside the hut monitoring the cell in case ye called for help, because otherwise he'd have recognized me for sure. He wanted tae know what Raoul was doing on the industrial park, and Raoul said his car had been acting up and Davey had been recommended by the roadside assistance people. Then Raoul asked why the guy was asking so many questions. The bouncer said there had been some trouble at the park and he was one of the people keeping an eye on things. He told Raoul he'd better watch out because some people had been hurt pretty badly. Raoul did a good job of looking unnerved as he paid Davey and drove off. The bouncer guy watched him go, laughing, then he told Davey tae watch himself, got back in the van, and drove off."

Davey had come in with water, and Harrison began very gently to mop my face clean of filth as if I were Luke's age, as he continued his story. I gave myself over to the combination of the cloth strokes, the pervasive scent of lavender, and Harrison's voice.

"We climbed ontae the roof of the hut after the van had gone. Simon suggested it, Davey said. We saw the guys and the girl from the vans go intae a warehouse, then after what seemed an age, they all came out again. It was obvious they were searching for you. I was all set tae call Raoul, but Davey . . ." Harrison glanced at the big man, who had a peaceful, almost absent expression. "Davey told me it would be all right; that you would be able to stop them finding you. A little later they seemed tae give up searching. They set about carrying out some stuff tae the van, locked up, and drove away. Then Davey told me I must go and get ye. It took me ages tae find ye, and when I did, I near had a heart attack because you were lying there so still. I couldnae seem to rouse ye proper. Ye stood and walked, but I had tae lead ye. It was like ye were in a trance."

"Harlen Sanderson was there," I said. "And Sylvia Yarrow."

Harrison's dark blond eyebrows lifted. "The girl who drowned the cat?"

* * *

Harrison and Davey left me alone to change into some dry clothes Davey had unearthed from a goodwill bag that had been wrongly delivered there some time before.

"What a coincidence," I thought when the bag contained jeans and a sweater in my size. I shoved my own filthy, mud-sodden clothes into a plastic bag, thinking I would have to find some way to wash them without anyone at home seeing them. Then I remembered what had happened before we had left for Shaletown and groaned at the thought of having to explain myself to Mirandah and Jess.

I looked up to see Harrison regarding me with a queer look on his face.

"What's the matter?" I asked.

"Nothing," he said almost tersely. "At least, Raoul just called to say your sister got home hours ago. Your brother had to wait until she was in her room before calling. He said they'd put the diary back and that you shouldn't mention it. I guess he feels guilty about reading it."

"Jesse would," I said. But I wondered if he would so easily put away his memory of Serenity's scalding hatred.

"Aren't you relieved?" Harrison asked.

"I ought to be," I admitted. "But it feels like I'm waiting for the other shoe to drop. Because they must have come to get her, and they took her somewhere before coming here. That's how we managed to get here before them. Well, at least we can go home."

Harrison nodded. "Raoul is waiting for us on the other side of the field. Davey says it's better for us tae go tae him."

"You will be careful, won't you?" I said to the gentle man, hating the thought of leaving him there. It was like leaving a puppy in a lion's den. And yet he had been there all along, keeping watch.

"Simon says, 'Be a monkey,' " Davey said very seriously.

* * *

"That's a good look on you. Sort of advanced street wear," Harrison said as we crossed the field.

I bit back a sharp response as I tripped for the tenth time on the hem of the coat that Davey had given me. I hitched it up, feeling ridiculous. Of course, in fairy tales the prince only had to kiss the princess or scullery maid to realize that he was crazy about her, never mind the soot or mud or ragged clothes. Unfortunately, in my case the kiss seemed to have had the opposite effect on the hero.

"That's real life for you," I sighed.

"What?" Harrison asked.

But we had reached the end of the field, and as we climbed over the fence, a car parked on the opposite side of the road flashed its lights. In five minutes we were seat-belted in and on the way home. Harrison told Raoul everything.

"Are you OK?" Raoul asked me.

"I feel stupid getting everyone so worked up and then nothing happens," I said.

"Nothing!" Harrison said almost indignantly. "We know for sure now that Harlen is linked tae the Shaletown gang, and indeed from what you say, he might even be its leader. And we know that another girl from your school is involved."

"But involved in what? Making films is hardly a criminal activity. And we still don't know what Serenity did tonight, or what she is going to do. And what on earth am I going to tell Mirandah and Jesse?" My voice had a ragged edge to it.

There was a silence, then Harrison said. "I've been thinking. You say that Serenity wouldnae hurt anyone by shooting or bombing. But what if she's been set up tae do something she doesnae realize will hurt people? What if she's tae be given a gun and told it's not loaded. Or told tae set fire tae someplace that is empty, only it isn't? Wouldnae finding out she had really done something dreadful wound her again, in just the way that would be needed for infection?"

I stared at him, feeling sick.

"I made some calls while I was sitting in the car just now," Raoul said. "It turns out that a politician whose portfolio includes immigration is scheduled to visit the Shaletown Detention Center on Monday afternoon. It seems to me that this would be the perfect occasion for your sister to make some radical statement that goes wrong."

"We have to stop her from hurting anyone," I said. "Harrison's right. It would destroy her."

"You know," Raoul said thoughtfully, "knowing where and when something is going to happen might offer an opportunity we shouldn't ignore."

"Opportunity?"

"I wonder if your journalist friend would respond to a tip. Imagine if he was there to witness what was happening, and knew that Aaron Rayc owns the warehouses nearby and funds the gang that meets there and produces books that prime kids like Serenity to do harm. It might even be that we could set it up so that *he* could stop your sister. That would make a dramatic story, and once he had access to the stuff Daisy dug up . . ."

"That's brilliant," Harrison said. "Raoul, you are a genius."

Raoul laughed at his enthusiasm. "Not quite. But it does seem the perfect way to save your sister and discredit Rayc without any of us getting in the limelight. After the ORBA function tomorrow night, we might even have more to offer him."

"I've just had an idea," Harrison said. "Alyzon, you have tae go with Raoul tae this ORBA thing. If there are going tae be a whole lot of celebrities there, you could smell any who were infected and we'd have a list that would take weeks of checking tae compile otherwise."

"It's up to you, but it might be a good thing," Raoul told me. "The only thing is that Aaron Rayc will be there, so we'd have to keep you away from him."

* * *

By the time Raoul dropped me home, the house was night-time quiet, with only Jesse up reading in the kitchen.

"Where's Da?" I asked, shrugging off the derelict coat and my backpack. I had no fear that Jesse would comment on my clothes because he never noticed anyone's clothes—not even Mirandah's.

"He's not home from the rehearsal yet," Jesse said, and I heaved a sigh of relief. "Look, Alyzon," he went on, using his rare stern-big-brother voice, "it's time you did some talking."

I sat down. "I'm sorry about causing such a fuss tonight, but Serenity is mixed up with some weird people, and when she just went off . . ."

"Weird people?" Jesse asked.

"On Monday nights she meets these people in the library. They're supposed to be meeting about poetry, but I think the group has been set up to suck in people like Serenity."

"What do you mean by 'people like Serenity'?"

"Angry, hurt, mixed-up people," I said. "You read her diary."

"I did, and I'm ashamed to have done it."

"Jesse, Serenity is our sister, and whether or not she hates us or thinks she does, I love her and I'm scared for her. I'm scared of what she might do."

"As far as I can see, you don't know that she's going to do anything," Jesse said. "That diary stuff might be nothing more than a sort of cathartic purge. Tonight she went to see a documentary, just as she said. She seemed perfectly calm and composed when she got in. I asked how she had got there, and she said some friends gave her a lift. You had me and Mirandah half convinced she was going to shoot someone or set something on fire."

"You read her diary. You tell me if that was written by someone calm and composed."

"All right," Jesse said with sudden decision. "You tell Da all of this by tomorrow night before his gig, or I'll tell him."

I gaped at him. "He has a gig tomorrow night?"

He nodded impatiently. "The Big Sleep gig is Sunday, didn't you hear Da say?" He gave me a narrow-eyed look. "Why?"

"I just . . . I just didn't realize it was so soon." I collected my wits. "Look, I can't drop this in his lap before an important gig. I'll tell him Monday night, I swear."

Jesse gave me a level look. "You better, Alyzon." He got up and said he was going to bed.

I sat there staring at the vase of fiery chrysanthemums, trying to take in the fact that the function to which Raoul had been invited was on the same night as the function where Da would play with Neo Tokyo. I was an idiot not to have put the two things together sooner. Then I realized something else. Raoul had said the charity function would take place on the grounds of the Castledean Estate—Aaron Rayc's own property.

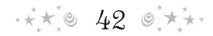

42

It was my turn to watch Luke the next morning. I had volunteered, partly because it meant Serenity would have to stay home with him all afternoon while I was at the charity function. She hadn't complained or seemed to care, which reassured me that Raoul was right in thinking it was Monday night we had to worry about.

When I handed Luke to her, I noticed that she still smelled densely of licorice without even the merest trace of violet. That further convinced me that she had suppressed the old Serenity almost out of existence, in preparation for what was soon to happen.

Luke giggled and touched her face with his fat little starfish hands, and for a moment her face twisted as if love for him knifed through her. I left them, praying that an afternoon with Luke and his wonderful radiant innocence would bring her out of the darkness she had woven for herself.

* * *

It took over an hour to get to Raoul's because the Sunday buses came less often, and I was startled and pleased to find both Harrison and Gilly there. I barely had time to greet everyone before Gilly announced that she had come to ensure that my own father would not recognize me. Without giving me a chance to protest, she all but dragged me down the hall to the bathroom, where she bade me undress, shower, and wash my hair. I protested that I was perfectly clean, but she insisted, saying a canvas had to be properly prepared. I could see how happy she was, so I gave in.

I came out in a towel, and Gilly examined me like a doctor about to make an incision, then alarmingly asked if I minded her trimming my hair. Before I could do more than stammer a weak answer, she whipped out scissors and began snipping vigorously.

"Have you done this before?" I asked, horrified by the amount of hair raining down.

"I've done it to my Barbie dolls for years," she said blithely. Swallowing hard, I told myself that my hair, unlike that of the unfortunate Barbies, would grow back. At last Gilly laid aside the scissors, painted some horrible-smelling brown mess onto a few strands, and wrapped them in foil. I wanted to ask what she was doing to me, but then she took up tweezers and began plucking out eyebrow hairs. This was so excruciatingly painful that I screamed. She nearly poked my eye out, and reacted to the news that I had never plucked my eyebrows with Mirandah-like superiority. Several painful minutes later I offered to sell her Da if she would stop.

"Pathetic," she said, leading me back to the bathroom. She proceeded to wash the brown stuff out of my hair, at the same time running water into my ear so that it gurgled. The whole time, she was rubbing sandpaper-like gel onto my face and arms and neck, then washing it off. Then she puffed some foam into my hair and rubbed it through.

"What is the point of putting all this stuff on me if you're only going to wash it off four seconds later?" I protested.

"Feel how soft," she said, pointing to my bare arm. I rubbed it and marveled. Then, before I could stop myself, I wondered if Harrison would think so.

"You're blushing," Gilly accused. That made the blood in my face get even hotter. "Wow," she said. "What were you just thinking about?"

"Nobody. I mean, nothing. What now?" She gave me a skeptical look but only began to wipe pale brown stuff on my face. "Ugh," I said, looking at her fingers.

She said loftily, "It'll make your skin feel like silk."

"Dirty silk," I muttered.

She started doing things to my eyes, and I flinched until I realized she wasn't intending to pull anything out. Even so, when she got to the mascara, she ordered me severely not to make my eyes water.

"Like I can stop them," I said, cringing.

She told me to shut up and then started drawing on my mouth with a pencil. Crimson, I saw. I wanted to tell her that I didn't think I'd look good with lips the color of blood, but she had a ferocious look that told me she'd stick the pencil in my mouth if I opened it. I wanted to look when she was finished but she wouldn't let me.

"You have to get the full impact." She regarded me critically, then dusted enough powder over my face to flour the bottom of a dozen cake pans; then she went to the door and took a zipped clothes bag down from the hook.

"Oh no!" I said, pointing to the mini she drew out, which looked like she had got it off one of her Barbie dolls. "I'm not wearing that. I brought my own clothes."

"You can't wear your own clothes. They'll make you look like you. The whole point is for you to look like someone else."

"God," I said. But I pulled on dense black tights and then the skirt, which came to just above the knees and was stretchy, so not as minuscule as it had looked. She got out cherry-red boots that Mirandah would have changed colors for. They were a size too big, but Gilly told me just to put my socks back on over the tights to make my feet bigger. Then she handed me a cherry-red and black striped top made out of stocking material. I put this on and then a sort of slick tank top over that, then a dark red tailored riding jacket. Then she sat me down on the edge of the bath while she blow-dried and fluffed my newly shortened hair. I could see the ends curling up and my head felt light. But maybe that was my state of mind.

At last, she let me look.

I gaped.

I looked about ten feet tall and beanpole lean. My hair had been cut into a sassy bob, and there were two flashes of indigo color in the very short straight bangs, another two slashes of purple in one side. My face, far from muddy, was milk pale, and my lips looked like someone had cut them out of a magazine. I appeared, I thought, about five years older. Maybe more.

"You look like a French rock star," Gilly said, admiring her handiwork. "Perfect. Let's go show the guys."

"Wait!" I said.

"Stage fright," Gilly pronounced. "Come on. Into the deep end is best. You look hot."

I was actually shaking as I walked slowly down the hallway behind Gilly, although I told myself it was the boots, which still slipped around on my feet a bit.

"Ta-da!" Gilly said in the doorway, and she waved me in with a theatrical flourish.

I swallowed and stepped into the room. I made myself look at Raoul, because I was scared to look at Harrison. What if he thought I looked horrible?

Raoul gave me an admiring once-over. "Well, you don't look like a schoolgirl," he said.

"Doesn't she look French with those short bangs?" Gilly asked, delighted. She had gone over to Raoul and taken his arm in her pleasure.

I looked at Harrison because it would have seemed odd if I hadn't, and struck a pose to hide my nervousness. "What do you think?"

"You look different," he said in a peculiar flat voice.

"Different good or bad?" Gilly asked. I could have strangled her. I stopped feeling like a French rock star and started feeling stupid.

"Different," Harrison said.

"Boy, don't go overboard with flattery," Gilly teased, but I could see puzzlement dawning, and it would be one step from that to her remembering how I had blushed.

"Time to go?" I asked Raoul. He nodded, and I noticed that he looked very cool in a dark gray suit so velvety soft it was like liquid.

* * *

"You OK?" he asked once we were on the way.

"Fine," I said, and heard the false brightness in my tone. I was hurt by Harrison's reaction, and yet what else had I expected? Then I told myself sternly that this was a serious and maybe even dangerous quest for information and I ought to be concentrating on that.

"I really do doubt your da would recognize his little girl right now," Raoul said. "But he might remember me, so I will have to be sure to be gone before his gig finishes. It would be most unfortunate if he arrived and mentioned to Rayc that I was a friend of yours. The wheelchair makes me look harmless but very distinctive."

"Well, I think you'd look distinctive with or without the wheelchair."

He gave me a warm look. "That's a nice thing to say, Alyzon. I guess a lot of the time I feel the wheelchair is pretty much all people see when they look at me. It defines me."

"Maybe people who don't know you," I conceded. "But I have to say that I never saw anyone make a wheelchair look more cool."

He laughed out loud. "So I define the wheelchair? Not bad."

I asked how Sarry was then, and he sobered and said that she was beginning to remember whole slabs of her childhood that she had forgotten. "Some of it is fairly harrowing, but Dr. Abernathy says it's a positive sign that she is remembering instead of keeping it locked up. But she's pretty fixated on Austin, and that's not good. She keeps thinking he was around even when she was small, and that he knew her mother." He paused. "The main thing from Sarry's point of view is that they are no longer drugging her. Dr. Abernathy says it would be counterproductive, given that she is phobic about drugs. And no wonder. One of the things she's been remembering is seeing her mother shoot up, and it looks like she might have been an addict."

I thought of the flash of vision I had seen when Sarry had grabbed me, and wondered if her mother's drug use had been forced. I told Raoul what I had seen, and after a whole lot of questions, we decided that this must have been close to the time Sarry had been infected, and that perhaps what she had seen was the drugging of her mother prior to infection. When we had talked this subject to death, Raoul asked if Serenity had seen the painting that Mum had done of her.

"I doubt it. She doesn't show anyone what she's painted for ages and ages, and sometimes she doesn't show it at all. She just takes it out to the backyard in the middle of the night and lights a bonfire, and Da helps her. I wonder how much he really knows."

"Maybe he just loves her and trusts her," Raoul said. "Like we do with Sarry."

* * *

447

We hit signs pointing the way to the Castledean Estate five miles before Remington, and turned off the main road. There were no streetlights on the side road leading to the estate, and the clouded sky made it dark, but the headlights shone over car after car parked along the side of the road, and clots of people walking toward the gates. By the time we got to the parking lot entrance, Raoul had to crawl along because there were people all over the road. I was guiltily glad of Raoul's disabled sticker, which enabled us to enter the packed lot and weave through hundreds of cars to the disabled parking spaces right by the entrance to the estate. Men and women in white fluorescent suits were directing people, looking like nothing so much as officials dealing with atomic fallout.

Raoul's wheelchair lurched over the loose gravel in the lot, making me nervous that it might tip over, but I wasn't much safer, tottering along in my boots, and twice it was Raoul who caught my hand and steadied me. We made it without mishap to the line of people waiting to enter, and when our gold-edged tickets were scanned by a man roaming along the line, the man's face changed and he ushered us out of the line.

"Welcome to the Big Sleep Gala Party, sir," he told Raoul effusively. "Your entrance is this way." He led us to the front of the line, but instead of sending us through the main gate into what seemed a seething tide of people intermittently visible under roaming colored lights, we were taken to a smaller gate. Beyond it waited a woman who told us her name was Klara. Raoul introduced me as his niece, Tanya, and the

448

woman offered me a professionally brilliant smile before turning her attention to Raoul.

We followed Klara along a well-made path. It led us away from the enormous stage, which in the distance looked a bit like a landing pad for a spaceship, surrounded by all that country darkness. We were headed for a cluster of large white tents linked by covered walkways hung with holiday lights.

Two security men were standing at the door to the first tent, wearing black suits that accentuated the unnatural breadth of their shoulders. They nodded unsmilingly at the woman and stood aside to let us into the perfumed and candlelit interior, which had been made to look like a ballroom in some palace. The furniture was all beautiful heavy wood and looked as if it was antique. On every table, amid an incredible array of food, were enormous, beautifully detailed ice sculptures of birds, surrounded by dry ice that gave off a mist of pale smoke. There were also giant vases of flowers set about: lilies, bird-of-paradise flowers, and blazing bursts of gerberas, irises, and tulips. A woman in a white dress was playing a white harp, and there was also a white grand piano, although no one was sitting at it. The men and women standing around were dressed in expensive suits and magnificent, lavish gowns. It was attire for the Academy Awards, not a marathon of bands in a field, and I wondered for the first time what the point was of holding the two events simultaneously.

"See anyone you recognize, Tanya?" Klara asked me coyly, coming close enough for me to perceive her strong burnt-onion smell under the hair spray. I instinctively stepped back from her. "Are you all right?" she asked, and there was a speculative look in her eye that made me regret bringing myself so much to her attention.

"Everyone's like a million years old," I said, putting on a sullen adolescent look. I cast a glance of disparagement at the harp player, and Klara smiled brilliantly.

"Now, Tanya," Raoul said in an avuncular sort of voice. "Maybe you can get yourself a drink and something to eat."

That was my signal to cut loose. I sighed and shrugged and slouched off, playing my role with a certain relish. I went to a drinks table, and a man in a white suit with a startling orange-looking tan poured me mineral water with a twist of lemon. I tried to look as if I were drying out after a hard night as I accepted it and walked over to the food table. I swallowed a couple of grapes and looked around the room, pretending boredom. In fact, I was anything but bored.

As Klara had tried to point out, there were a lot of famous faces: musicians and singers and actors I had only ever seen before on the covers of magazines or at the movies. There were also hundreds of unknown faces, and the crowd was getting thicker minute by minute. I began to look for the artists I had seen associated with Aaron Rayc in the many articles I'd read about him.

The first I spotted, ten minutes later, was a very beautiful woman with old-looking eyes that I recognized as Angel Blue, once known as Mallory Hart. I drifted close enough to smell her and recoiled at the rotten stench of infection she gave off. Five minutes later I saw Oliver Spike, but I didn't go near him because my danger sense reacted so sharply at the sight of him. I passed a heavyset man in a business suit talking in a loud voice to a group of starlets I recognized. He didn't smell of infection, but the three girls he was speaking to smelled overwhelmingly of rotten meat.

I felt myself scrutinized, too, but it was the sort of occasion where people came to look and be looked at, and it meant nothing. I did feel embarrassed a couple of times when men and once a woman gave me frankly admiring looks that invited me to come up and talk to them, but I pretended not to see.

By the time I had been circulating for an hour, I had managed to identify only two more people who were infected, but I didn't recognize either of them and could think of no way to learn their names save by asking. Most of the guests had bad essence smells, though, which suggested that their spirits were weak or corrupted; I wondered with a chill how many of them had been earmarked by Rayc for infection.

Then I saw Raoul, and my heart caught in my throat because Klara was introducing him to Aaron Rayc. Dita was with them, too, wearing a diaphanous ice-green dress that frothed about her shining limbs like foamy waves. Her glossy black hair was pulled back and dressed in an elaborate cluster of the palest pistachio-colored pearls and white flowers, and both she and Rayc were smiling brilliantly down at Raoul.

Dita reached out to stroke Raoul's hand as she said something, and my skin crawled. Then she turned away and beckoned to a young man who emerged from the crowd dressed in cream moleskins and a pale suede jacket. He kissed her hand and cheek so intimately, and his hair shone so like hers, that I realized they must be related. He turned to Aaron Rayc and bowed rather than taking the older man's hand, and I began to wish he would turn my way so that I could see his face.

Then Dita went to introduce him to Raoul, and I was shocked to the core—because I saw that it was Harlen Sanderson.

Without warning, Harlen whipped his head in my direction. Fortunately, despite my incredulity, I had the wit not to turn hastily away. Instead, I simply shifted my gaze slightly and tried to relax into the strange, deep stillness that had stopped him finding me the night before. I felt his eyes rake the crowd, skating over me, and then the pressure was gone. I waited another full minute before daring to think of him or glance in his direction again, and found that he had vanished. Aaron and Dita were still speaking with Raoul, so I could not go over to him. My heart pounded with fear at the thought that Harlen was somewhere nearby, trying to find who had been staring at him.

I had to get out of the tents, but how? Raoul had said it was permitted for guests of the gala to cross to the main venue, but he had the tickets and I dared not go and get mine from him now. The obvious answer was to just sneak out, but I couldn't even think how to get away from the bracelet of tents with all the security around. Frightened of being out in the open any longer, I made my way to the toilets, following discreetly posted signs. My legs felt stiff and the boots awkward. The hair on my neck prickled the whole time I wove through the crowd at the thought that I might come face to face with Harlen at any moment. I told myself it was silly to feel so frightened because there would be nothing he could do to me among so many people. But the awful essence scents of so many of the people I passed—bad eggs, spoiled milk, burning gasoline—made me wonder if that was true.

I was sweating with tension and fear by the time I reached the toilets, which were deluxe portables in a side tent clamped onto the main tent. Unfortunately, there was no other way out of it. Once in a stall, I felt safer, and if there hadn't been an attendant who had seen me enter, I might have been tempted to stay there. I replayed Harlen Sanderson kissing Dita Rayc and felt again my shocked realization that they must be mother and son. No wonder Dita had seemed familiar to me. But why was Harlen's last name Sanderson when Dita's previous husband had been Makiaros? Then I remembered that Makiaros had been her second husband. Harlen must be the son of her first marriage. I shuddered in revulsion at the thought that Rayc might have infected his stepson.

I had a moment of fright, thinking that Harlen must have seen Raoul at Davey's. Then I remembered Harrison had said that only the bouncer had got out of the van, so Harlen would not have got a good look at him. Suddenly I remembered the cell Raoul had lent me. I fished it out of Gilly's shoulder purse, but after typing out a text message, I noticed there was no signal. I thrust the phone back into my purse as someone knocked on the door. Then the attendant asked if I was all right, and I realized that I had groaned aloud.

"Fine," I called out chirpily, flushed, and then opened the door. The attendant was a young woman only a little older than I was. She had returned to her position behind a table upon which rested bowls of perfumed water sprinkled with rose petals. She smiled at me, and when I smelled her fragrance of hot waffles, I had an idea.

"You don't know when the bands are supposed to begin playing?" I asked in a girlish, confiding tone.

Her smile turned rueful. "You're in the wrong place if you think you're gonna hear any real music in here. The walls of the tents have been especially treated to make them sound-proof."

I stared at her. "But . . . why did these people come if they don't get to hear the music?"

"Most of them are showbiz and arty types and socialites who come to be seen and to see what other people are wearing and who they're with. The rest are money men and women who would probably have a heart attack if they heard the music they get rich from."

"Wow, that's pretty cynical," I said, a little startled.

She sighed. "Sorry. This job sort of washes the stars from your eyes, you know? But how come you're over here instead of over there, anyway? I mean, you're not trapped behind a washbasin."

"My uncle is in there hobnobbing," I said glumly. "My boyfriend is in one of the lesser bands, but I can't find a way to slip this mausoleum and go over to see him without being questioned by one of those goons in suits."

She giggled. "They're awful, aren't they? But can't you just ask your uncle? You can go over if one of the hostesses escorts you back to the main gate."

"My uncle will insist I stay here." I leaned closer. "He doesn't approve of my boyfriend. I thought I'd be able to go over and see him and then sneak back."

"Ohh," she said. I smelled her curiosity when I mentioned my boyfriend.

"His name is Macoll, and he's with Neo Tokyo."

"I saw his picture," she said to my surprise. "He's hot, but isn't he kind of old?"

"I'm into father figures," I said with a straight face.

She hesitated and then suggested that I could try going through the catering tent. It was open at the back so chefs could go out for a smoke. I could then just go over the fields and through the performers' trailers. There was sure to be a way, because the bouncers would be at the front gates.

I thanked her and went warily back into the main tent after getting directions.

Again I threaded through people, keeping my eyes peeled for Harlen. Conversations about the music industry, the publishing world, this or that gallery or agent swirled about me. The room boiled with conversation and loud bursts of laughter, and it seemed to have grown hotter and somehow tenser.

Then I saw that some huge screens had been unveiled or brought in, or maybe they had been there all along and I had not noticed them because there had been nothing on them. But now they were glowing with life and movement, and I realized they were offering a view of the enormous stage being watched by thousands of people a short walk away. It seemed weird that there were visuals but no music, only the harp and then the piano playing something light and vaguely classical, which bore out what the washroom attendant had said about the people at the function not caring about the music, only the prestige of being special guests at the Big Sleep Gala Party.

I was almost to the catering section when I spotted Klara. Before I could turn away, she noticed me, so I stopped and told her to tell my uncle I was bored. I was as rude as I thought Tanya would have been.

Klara regarded me for a moment out of her wide beautiful eyes. Then she said, "You seem very strung out, Tanya. Are you on something?" It took me a thick second to figure she meant drugs. She was smiling approval.

"What's it to you?" I asked, my mind racing.

She smiled a catlike smile of satisfaction. "Do you have what you need?" she asked. "I have a friend who might be able to help you if you don't."

"I've got my own friend over there listening to the music, if I could just figure out how to get out of this place," I retorted, wondering if I could manipulate her into getting me over to the Big Sleep.

Klara's wet red smile widened. "I'll tell your uncle you would like to go and see the bands as soon as the formal part of this occasion is over, shall I?" Her eyes glimmered like fluorescent lights on pools of oil.

Cursing her inwardly for not offering to take me over at once, I shrugged ungraciously, and watched her vanish into the crowd. She would report to someone that Raoul's niece took drugs, I was sure. That made me realize that such a gathering as this, with its endless supply of wine and food and its svelte army of Klaras slithering about and suggesting a refill or a little shot or a pill, would be a perfect way to gather information about people. Was that what this was all about? A gathering of intelligence to be used to manipulate people?

I shivered and followed the next waitress with an empty tray into the catering tent, refusing to stop when someone called out, certain I would be sent back if I did. As I had hoped, no one came after me; everyone was too frantically busy. I burst out of the back of the tent into the cool bite of the night. I looked up and saw that the sky must be totally clouded over because not a single star showed.

I set off at once through the darkness, making directly for the back of the huge stage. Oddly, I could hardly hear the music, although I could feel the ground pounding with the vibration of it. I supposed it must be that all of the music was pouring away from the tented area, and out into the audience and beyond.

It was hard to walk on the tufty, uneven grass, and after tripping twice on the rough clumps, I stopped and pulled off my boots, socks, and tights. When I got to the trailer city behind the main stage, I hesitated, wondering if it would be all that easy to go through to the main performance area. There would be dozens of bouncers guarding the fences to stop fans getting over to mob the Rak or other musicians.

As I walked along the makeshift street between the caravans, it gave me a little shock to realize that Da must be in one of them with Neo Tokyo. For one instant I wanted desperately to go and find him and tell him everything. I wanted to feel his arms around me and be enveloped in his reassuring warmth and his goodness and kindness. I wanted, I realized, to be his little girl, only somehow all that had happened had taken me out of the realm of childhood. I hadn't realized it until that moment, and I felt a pang of almost unbearable grief.

"What are you doing back here?"

It was a bouncer, but a lower form of the breed than the suave and suited men back in the tent area. He grasped the back of my jacket and propelled me firmly where I wanted to go before I could stammer more than a few incoherent words.

43

From not being able to hear the music, I went to being nearly deafened by it, because the bouncer had pushed me out virtually in front of an enormous phalanx of speakers set up to the left of the stage. There were more speakers on the other side, and a wire fence ran between them to create a no-man's-land between stage and audience. There were a lot of bouncers here, all wearing black T-shirts with "The Big Sleep" and a moon stencilled on them. The band onstage was the same one I had seen playing silently within the tent. The set must have been almost over, because the lead singer was beginning to smash his guitar to pieces.

I was watching in bemusement when a girl bumped into me. I turned to look at her, and she beamed at me vacantly, emanating a candy and new-plastic smell, tinged with something sharp and unpleasant. She was drunk or on drugs, I thought, and wondered if she had brought her own, or whether there were people busily distributing stuff to the eager crowd. This chilled me because of Sarry's claim that drugs lowered your resistance to the sickness.

Suddenly I felt frightened, because what if this was not just a concert to raise funds or an occasion for directors to schmooze, or even a means of gathering information that could be used to serve the sickness, but a cover for the sickness to feed and spread? There had been a rapacious anticipation in the air back in the tents, which I had been too close to recognize when I was in the midst of it; an expectancy that electrified the air. And I had left Raoul back there!

I reminded myself that, like Da, his spirit was strong and unassailable. Besides, there was nothing I could do to help him now unless I fought my way to the main gate and made enough of a fuss that someone would fetch Klara to admit me. But that would only bring me back into danger. I had to trust Raoul's intellect and capability.

I looked at my watch and was astonished to see that it was a quarter to ten. Raoul and I had agreed to leave before eleven, because of him wanting to avoid being seen by Da, so I ought to make my way out. But it had to be nearly time for Neo Tokyo's set, and a bit of me wanted to stay and see them, in spite of everything. I wanted to see how Da would affect all of these thousands of people; whether he would do what he had done at the Urban Dingo gig. There was no chance of him spotting me from the stage, of course, but without cellphone reception there was no way to let Raoul know I wanted to stay.

Someone tapped my shoulder, and I turned to find myself looking at Gary Soloman. As luck would have it, the guitar was totally obliterated at that moment, and the applause that swelled and broke all around us was loud but nowhere near as loud as the music had been.

"I almost didn't recognize you," he shouted. I was a little startled to sense his admiration. "You here to see your dad?"

I nodded and asked what he was doing at the concert. He tapped his nose, and I knew I wouldn't get anything out of him. "You do realize, there's something wrong with all of this?" I tried anyway. "Something ugly and dangerous under the fun and music and people laughing."

The journalist frowned. "Alyzon, you haven't taken anything, have you? I know there's a lot of stuff circulating. Booze and drugs and weird cocktails. I wouldn't touch any of it."

I wanted to laugh at the thought of doing anything so dumb, but it was a timely reminder that I couldn't tell him the whole truth about what was happening—he didn't know me at all.

Suddenly there was an ear-piercing spike of sound from the system, and everyone fell silent. An announcer began to scream that we were about to experience the incredible sound and talent of the Rak, who were the voice of their generation.

"The Rak!" he bellowed, and screams and applause rose in a thunderous wave; an apocalyptic storm of sound and adulation swelled, which would drown me if I did not find a way to rise above it. Then the music began. Earwig music full of hate and blood and violence. I clamped savagely on my senses, so that the air hissed with whispers and people became pale as ghosts, their screams no more than a faint wind.

I was only dimly aware of Gary Soloman bidding me

farewell and pushing away through the frenzied gyrations around us. A guy in a T-shirt spoke to me. I couldn't hear his words, but he seemed to be talking slowly and carefully as if he were underwater. The whites of his eyes were threaded with veins.

"Incredible," I said when his mouth had stopped moving. He beamed and upended a water bottle into his mouth. I sidled away from him, smiling and mouthing apologies. There seemed to me to be a madness skittering over the faces of the people I saw, tainting scents that ran the full gamut from sweet to horrible. But there was no smell of rot. No sickness. At one point, unable to move, I looked up at the stage. The Rak were clad in dark jeans and T-shirts with splattered blood prints over the front. Their faces were so pale they looked dead—even after I unclamped my senses by a fraction.

The lead singer began to make horribly realistic vomiting noises into the microphone. The people around me shrieked and stamped and cheered. He gave them the finger and closed his hand over his groin. His face was a vicious leer of triumph. He was the conquering hero of this roiling country of music and darkness.

"Isn't he incredible?" a girl beside me screamed.

"Incredible," I said softly, wondering if she would feel like this if she wasn't in the midst of a crowd. I could smell the way the essence scents and the smells of excitement and madness were forming a single enormous crowd essence smell, which the Rak's music was drawing up and shaping.

The Rak's bass guitarist began to hammer out a screaming riff, and I cringed as if it were an attack. But everyone around me screamed and jumped up and down, begging for more. *More,* they screamed. *More!*

I tried to push sideways, but I was still caught in the press of bodies. Too late I realized that I ought to have worked my way along the stage to the other side, where the entrance gate was, in the lull between bands. The only way to move now was to dance, so I did, glad that I had taken my boots off.

I had given up the idea of waiting for Da; all I wanted to do now was escape and await Raoul at the car. He might even be there already, I realized, if Klara had let him know what I had said.

I had managed to work my way a little deeper back where the press of the crowd was not so tight, but I was sticky with sweat, my toes hurt from being stomped on, and the soles of my feet felt cold and abraded. I was now sorry I had taken off the boots, but there was no way to put them on again here; besides, if I tripped in them and fell into this sea of madness, I would be lost.

The Rak finished their song and went on to sing another. This time I managed to unscreen long enough to discern that they were singing about how Hitler and guys like him had it right because the world was full of darkness that needed letting out. I shuddered and was suddenly sure that, like Angel Blue and Oliver Spike, the Rak were infected.

Pushing and fighting and struggling to get free of that crowd, I felt as if some monstrous beast had me, and as the essence smell of the crowd darkened and thickened, I began to feel more and more afraid. I wanted Da, and I wished Gary Soloman had stayed with me, but most of all I realized that I wanted Harrison. The warm strength of his arms and the beauty he had made me feel when he had kissed me were so much the opposite of the ugliness seething through the crowd. For a wonderful second, thinking of that kiss made me feel his mouth on mine, and this drove back the fear, reminding me that I had come tonight to see what I could learn; it was cowardly to run away when my sister's life and maybe the safety of my family depended on me.

I turned to face the stage and saw the Rak's lead singer gyrating and spasming in a dervish dance, his face a mask of demented hatred. Gritting my teeth, I unclamped my senses and forced myself to listen to what he was doing, because I wanted to feel what the crowd around me was feeling. The song, if it could be called a song, was all about the power of hatred, and the right of people to feel it and act it out rather than repressing it. He was sneering at love and kindness and gentleness. He was screaming that people who felt those things were fools. He asserted everyone's right to hate and hurt and dig to the dark parts of their soul.

I looked about me and saw with a chill that people in the audience wore his expression as if he had somehow transferred it to them via the music. Eyes glittered with malice and people bared their teeth in vicious, glimmering smiles that approved every bit of pain and savagery he described. Those smiles were so like grimaces of agony that they made me flinch. People snarled and laughed and screamed for more and more. They turned to one another to bellow how incredible, how totally, incredibly right it was. They danced in place, isolated and facing the stage, shaking their fists and raking the air with their clawed hands.

I had the surreal feeling that I was in a crowd of people going through some sort of werewolf-like change into animals, except no beast but the human beast could hate so powerfully, so deeply, so creatively.

The Rak played three more songs and then ended with a crash of sound. They were off the stage so swiftly that the audience seemed startled. Then a murmurous sound of discontent and irritation and anger rose. The announcer came on with a squall of feedback to announce Neo Tokyo.

It could not be by chance that Da had been set up to sing after the Rak. I had a sudden feeling of premonition, which my danger sense affirmed, and I began to fight my way back to the front of the audience. Pushing through, I risked becoming an easy target for the aggression rippling all around me. But Da and the two young men who must be Neo Tokyo came onstage, drawing everyone's attention.

"Da . . . ," I whispered.

He walked in his long, loose-limbed way to the mike at the far left of the stage, and Neo Tokyo took the other two mikes with the same casual grace that they had to have learned from Da. They bent to rearrange several other instruments at their feet and I held my breath as they took up their first instruments; Da his guitar, and Neo Tokyo panpipes and a flat drum. There was a gentleness and a simplicity in their movements that made me think of the old Vietnamese grocer packing his fruit away and I felt my anxiety fade. They were so different from the pounding, dizzying, nightmarish quality that the Rak had brought to the stage with their grinding, savage music, showers of sparks, gusts of fire, and puffs of smoke all lit by the frenetic whirling of laser lights. There were no special effects now. Just three men in a white light.

"Who the hell are these guys?" someone nearby asked.

I held my breath as the music began and felt a burst of relief that it was not Da's, because offering one of his songs to this resentful, aggressive crowd would be like waving a red rag at a bull. The song was edgy enough not to oppose the potent mood the Rak had established. It was, I understood after a little, a song about confusion and the rage that comes from being lied to and kept in the dark. It was a good solid song with clever, sharp-edged lyrics and it drew up perfectly and naturally the threads left hanging by the Rak. The beast crowd calmed down and began to listen.

Athough the lyrics spoke of anger, they were analytical and clever, and the audience had to think in order to get them. I was fascinated to see how the song took all of the churning fury and aimless aggression that the Rak had woven and unwound it, seeking for the center.

Ultimately the song was about discovering the core of fury, the molten heart, and I began to understand exactly what Da liked about Neo Tokyo. It was angry but there was not a mindless rage in it, nor any desire to blame anyone. At its center was puzzlement and honest confusion.

I looked around me. I could smell and see that people were still unsettled from the Rak's music, but the song was sucking up their raggedy energy, turning it cool and sending it back into itself. When it ended, there was a good swell of applause, although nowhere near the frenzied mania that had erupted after the Rak played.

The next song began at once without the band making any attempt to draw out more reaction from the crowd. The lyrics were about a woman trying to find a way to live in a world full of paths that all seemed wrong, and with no idea what a right path was because all ways were hemmed by rules that she did not agree with and could not obey. Again it was a song about confusion, but it was specific and compelling and veined with a yearning for something beyond confusion.

It was not one of Da's songs, but this time he sang with the two younger men, and his influence was in the way the words came out. His older, deeper voice was the kindness and tolerance that gentled the sharp, angry voices of the two younger men.

The band played a long, looping instrumental break of competing sounds, which reiterated the theme of confusion and longing, somehow suggesting that the woman's story was a story that was repeated again and again.

I looked around and extended my senses. Tension and aggression were still flickering in people's faces, but there was puzzlement, too. I felt a stab of triumph. If Aaron Rayc had set the crowd up to reject Da, then he had miscalculated both the malevolent power of the Rak and Da's own radiant ability. Because even without singing any of his own songs, Da had brought Neo Tokyo to the point where they could defuse the anger and aggression wrought by the earlier band.

And yet, even thinking this, I felt unease snake through me. Because Aaron Rayc had seen Da perform the night of the Urban Dingo gig. He knew what Da could do to an audience. He must have realized that Da was likely to affect Neo Tokyo in a positive way. So why had he allowed them to invite Da to join them?

I had come far enough forward that I was only two-deep from the wire barrier keeping the crowd out of no-man's-land and away from the stage. That was when I saw her standing in the fenced-off area between the stage and the audience. Sylvia Yarrow. There were security guards close enough to make it clear she had permission to be there. She was just standing still and watching, but my danger sense went mad.

The night suddenly got brighter, and through the three-story-high scaffolding that had been set up to back the stage, I saw that the clouds clogging the sky had parted and the moon was shining down.

Then it hit me. It was a full moon, and Davey had told me that this made those who were infected hungry!

I looked back at Sylvia and saw her lift something to her face. My heart gave a great sickening lurch of terror, because it was a video camera.

I began to fight and shove my way toward her.

"Watch out!" someone said indignantly.

"I'm going to be sick," I shouted. Miraculously, the crowd parted. But even when I reached the wire fence and shouted her name, Sylvia did not hear me. I threw a leg over the barrier and half fell over into the ground on the other side.

"Hey!" someone cried.

I ignored them, making for Sylvia; again I shouted out her name, but the noise from the amplifiers obliterated my voice.

At last I reached her. I grabbed her shoulder and wrenched her round to face me. "Sylvia, why are you filming my father? What is supposed to happen to him?"

"Your father?" She looked so baffled that I had to believe she didn't know that Macoll was my da.

"What are you supposed to film?" I yelled, beginning to feel frantic. "Tell me before it's too late!"

Sylvia stared at me like a person waking from a ghastly, compelling dream. The blood drained from her face and she turned her head down to look at the camera she was holding. She looked at the red record light, glowing like a ruby. The horror in her eyes was no less than if she had discovered she was holding a severed head.

"What the hell do you think you're doing?" a voice growled, and one of the security guards was pulling me away from Sylvia. Released, she reeled back toward one of the enormous amplifiers and I saw the camera fall from her hand. I screamed out to her to tell me what was supposed to happen, but she was staring down at the camera.

I twisted in the guard's grasp and saw he was a burly older man with sandy hair. He smelled of soap and fresh tomatoes.

"Please, you have to help me," I yelled over the music.

"That's my da up there on the stage. He . . . he's going to be hurt. That girl was supposed to film it."

"You've seen too many movies, girlie," he said. "Now you just calm down and maybe I won't throw you out."

"Please!" I screamed. "I have to get to the stage."

"OK, out you go," the guard said decisively. I struggled in his grip like a mad thing, trying to focus enough to use my mental voice on him. I dug my toes into the soggy earth but he was too strong and his hand was against my wrist, forcing his weariness and boredom and disgust into me. Desperately I thought of Harrison, seeking the courage I had found earlier in the memory of his kiss. But it was too hard with the guard touching my skin.

"Harrison, help me," I screamed, and wrenched my arm to stop our skins touching. I felt my thought form about the shout and fly out into the dark troubled night. The guard's grip had slackened in surprise and, taking the only chance that might come, I wrenched myself out of his grasp and ran back toward the stage. But I tripped over one of the snaking lumps of cord on the ground and fell hard. I was still gasping and winded when the security man dragged me roughly to my feet and shook me like a rag doll.

"One more stunt like that and you'll be sorry," he snarled.

Then I heard Da's voice coming from all around me, saying softly that the next song had been inspired by one of his daughters and written for another. For Serenity.

I turned to the guard. "Please," I said into his face. "Help me. That's my father and he's in danger."

He frowned. "Girlie, if that is your dad, which I doubt, he won't thank you for interrupting him right now."

"But you don't understand. . . ." I stopped because Da had begun to sing without any instrumentation, and his voice was so strong and strange and pure in that first soaring note that even the guard turned to look at him.

"It is our soul that makes us yearn," Da sang, little shimmers of light beginning to drift from him and hover above the crowd. "That spark in us which cares not for what is but only for what might be, what could be, what should be. That dreaming spark which, if it is not extinguished, will blaze and sing to the universe, the song it sings as painfully beautiful and ephemeral as life."

"Now that man has a voice," the security guard said. He sighed and began to shepherd me away.

"Let her go!" Harrison ordered, and suddenly he was there, pulling the guard's arm away, freeing me. I didn't stop to wonder how or why he had come there. I ran toward the stage, dodging cords and security guards, trying not to move too fast in case one of them instinctively grabbed me. Trying to get close enough that Da would hear me.

He was singing now about the courage that lay at the heart of the soul spark that made us all yearn for love, for happiness, for beauty, for purpose, for immortality in a world that seemed sometimes to be so dark and hopeless. I waited, knowing that there would be a break any moment, and that I must make him hear me. But midsentence, midword, his voice faltered. I looked up and saw that he was looking up, too, and back.

Then I saw her. Serenity, standing high in the web of scaffolding that was both the backdrop to the stage and the support for most of the effects and light boxes and cables. The ominous white eye of the moon had gone behind the clouds again and she would have been invisible against the blackness of night and shadow, if not for the lights trained on her, revealing a too-thin girl in black with lank, heavy hair hanging in rat's tails around her shoulders.

"Serenity?" Da's amplified voice filled the air.

"My name is Sybl," Serenity hissed.

I could hear her perfectly, although she spoke in a low, venomous voice.

Please, I thought. *Please don't hurt him. Don't hurt all of us.*

"What the hell is this?" someone cried near me. I turned to see that it was another security guard. "How the hell did that kid get up there?"

"What is she doing?" one security guard asked another.

"Maybe she's part of the act," someone on the other side of the barrier suggested.

That stopped all the guards.

"A stunt?" someone else said. The guards nodded, but they kept their eyes on Serenity.

I looked at her, too, and noticed what I had not noticed before with a swooning rush of relief. Her hands were clenched into fists, but she had no gun and nowhere to conceal one. Mad as it seemed, my first thought had been that she meant to shoot Da. But maybe she only meant to make some sort of accusing speech that was supposed to humiliate him.

"Come down, honey," Da called softly.

The crowd beast listened, half enchanted by the gentle plea and love in that deep, beautifully textured voice.

But Serenity shook her head, and that was when I realized her hair was not just lank. It was wet. Her clothes were, too. But how on earth had she got so wet?

Serenity laughed, a high, cold sound without mirth or brightness. "Come down to what, Da? To this filthy, ugly world full of hate and cruelty? To you and your cowardice? Your stupid, pointless songs that don't help anyone? Your fiddling while Rome burns? I don't think so. I don't think there are many people my age who would want to come down to that. And you know what? Maybe we won't. Because we have a choice. We can accept you and your foul world and become like you. Or we can have the courage to turn our backs on it all. Wasn't that what you were just singing about, Da? Courage? I don't think you know the meaning of the word. Well, I will show you what it is, and maybe I will be the first of many to show it to you and to all of those people like you. We will show you what we think of your world, your dreams, your failures!"

I was confused. She had no weapon, but there was a terrible threat in her voice.

Without warning, a hand closed over my mouth and someone pressed their face to mine, their skin against my cheek and bare neck. I almost fainted then, because the touch opened me up to some sliding black force that oozed at me and sought to pour itself into me. It was Harlen. I saw the torn fragments that were all that remained of the Harlen that had once been, all that had not been devoured by the sickness that drove him now. And then I felt the sickness itself. The wrongness, Sarry had called it. I felt the vast screaming hunger that motivated it and I clamped myself shut, rejecting it with every ounce of my being. But it was like a hurricane, battering and tearing at my defenses.

Distantly, I heard Da telling Serenity he loved her and asking her again to come down so they could talk, but I dared not turn to see what was happening for I was locked in a deadly struggle. I had never imagined that the sickness would be so strong, so powerful, so voracious.

And then I saw what I was doing wrong.

I summoned all of my will, all of my extended senses, all of the parts of me, known and unknown, and relaxed into Harlen's grip.

He had not expected it and he staggered a little and loosened his hold, letting me turn so that I could see his face. It was no longer handsome. It was distorted with what I read as madness. I pressed my hands to his face and called to Harlen with my mind and voice. And for one long minute visions snapped and fluttered into me like bits of paper shredded by the wind. Harlen as a small dark-haired boy, weeping at a funeral beside a cold-faced, beautiful mother; Harlen trying to hug Dita, who pushed him away and told him to be a man. Then he was smiling at an older man with dark hair and a hawkish nose. The man was in a classroom, surrounded by boys with instruments. The music teacher from Shaletown Boys Academy! I was startled to feel Harlen's love for him, and then I saw Aaron Rayc, smiling too, offering admiration and gifts. Then his mother kissing Rayc and the boy's scalding jealousy. Then Harlen was older, creeping along a corridor and entering a boiler room. He was altering settings on the instrument panel, looking over his shoulder with a mixture of bravado, fear, and anguish. Then he was in court, his face blank and cold. Aaron Rayc was smiling at him, and his face grew larger and larger, distorting and swelling.

Then the visions that were all that remained of Harlen were swept aside by a dark tide that flowed inexorably toward me: the thing inhabiting him, hungering and vast.

I was afraid, but I knew what to do. I did not try to pull away or close myself to it. I stayed open and I let the radiance of my love for Da and for Luke and Harrison and Gilly and for Serenity and Mum blaze out at it.

Somewhere in the depths of my mind, I seemed to hear the howling of a wolf.

Harlen screamed and flung me away from himself. There was blank terror in his eyes. He fled into the crowd. I swung back to the stage and my mind reeled to find that Da was standing there still, looking up into the scaffolding where Serenity stood. The deadly struggle with Harlen had taken only seconds.

"What do I care about your love for me!" Serenity demanded of Da. "I will show you what true love is." She smiled at Da, an empty curl of bloodless lips. She brought her two hands together. She was holding something, fumbling minutely. I saw a tiny orange light flare and die.

In my mind's eye I saw Mum's painting. The blank eyes floating in flames.

"Oh God," I whispered. I opened my mouth to scream out to Da, to warn him. But Serenity had lit another match, and as she brought it toward her, she said distantly, "Why don't you sing now, Da? Sing while I burn."

There was only one thing I could try to do, and I did it.

"Catch her!" I screamed and thought as hard as I could. I saw Da throw down the mike and begin to run toward the scaffolding. Then I turned my will on Serenity and pushed her as hard as I could. The push hurt me more than anything I had ever experienced. I tried to resist the great sledgehammer of darkness that was descending on me, but I had nothing left to resist with.

I fell like a stone into utter blackness, my last sight Serenity falling, flaming.

44

I dreamed of flames leaping and crackling all around me. I dreamed of people crying out and of a gelid, yawning emptiness that gloried in the screams and fear and anguish and the terrible smell of burning flesh.

"Alyzon . . ."

I heard the urgency in the unfamiliar voice and part of me wanted to respond to it, but beyond the light waited some unimaginable pain that I could not bear to face.

"Alyzon." Another voice, and one I knew. I let it draw me up until slowly I became aware of my head and body. I groaned and retched because I was aching all over. I felt as if I had been savagely battered.

" . . . blood around her mouth could mean internal bleeding," said the unknown voice, a woman's, calmly.

I opened my eyes and saw flames leaping high and exultant in the darkness. Had I simply climbed from one fiery dream into another?

"Careful," the other voice said swiftly.

I became aware of the salty metallic taste of blood in my mouth. "My . . . father . . ."

"Shh," said the woman authoritatively. "Where is that orderly with my bag?"

I saw now that the speaker wore white. Then quite suddenly, I remembered Sylvia lifting the camera, the moon glaring out of the night sky like a baleful, unforgiving eye. I saw the snarling terror of the sickness when I opened myself to it, and felt the terrible sucking drain of energy it had taken to push physically at Serenity.

I tried to sit up in my agitation, but hands held me down gently but firmly.

I shuddered. I had tried to save Serenity by pushing her off the scaffolding, with the slim hope that Da might have got to her in time to break the fall and to put out the flames, but she had been so high. And she had been burning as she fell.

I tried to speak, but the paramedic had risen and was speaking to two security men now, pointing away into the fitful darkness.

I realized when darkness fluttered its wings around me that I was not far from drifting back to unconsciousness. I willed it away, but doing so brought the hovering headache down to roost. It sunk its claws so deep into my skull that I moaned and lifted both hands to my head to stop it from bursting apart.

"Alyzon! Alyzon, ye have to resist it. We'll find a way tae heal ye. I swear . . ." It was Harrison, kneeling beside me, his face taut with fear and revulsion, his accent stronger than I had ever heard it. His words told me that he had seen Harlen holding on to me, and thought I was infected. Before I could summon the energy to reassure him, someone gave a shout, and we watched as a high bit of burning scaffolding gave way with a metallic creak, folding slowly sideways. There was a loud twanging sound, and a severed cord flicked up and began snaking dementedly, hissing and shedding sparks. The sudden brightness illuminated Harrison's eyes as he looked down at me.

"I love you," I said.

"What did ye say?" Harrison asked.

"I'm not infected, Harrison. What happened to Da and Serenity?"

"You're not . . . that's . . ." He drew a long breath and visibly collected himself. "They're fine. They've been taken tae the hospital. We can go after them as soon as the paramedic gives ye the OK."

I lurched up into a sitting position with a violent effort. I could not bear to think about the numbness in my mind. "I . . . I'm weak. Help me up."

He obeyed, and when I was on my feet, he asked, "What happened? I saw Harlen—"

"He tried to infect me," I said. I couldn't talk about the rest yet, because I was beginning to understand what the night had cost me. "Harrison, what happened when Serenity fell?"

"Your da grabbed some tarpaulins and broke her fall, and then he smothered the flames, someone said."

"You didn't see it?"

He shrugged ruefully. "I was being dealt with by your bouncer friend. But once the fire got into the scaffolding and the wiring he had tae let me go, because there was a stampede for the gates. A lot of people were hurt, which is why the place is crawling with paramedics and police."

I swayed against him. "You're not OK," he said, looking alarmed.

"Don't let me go," I whispered.

His arms tightened.

Around us the scene seemed even more chaotic now that I was upright, and the firelight gave it all a nightmarish quality. There was the scaffolding and stage consumed in flame, white jets of water from a fire truck parked to one side, the firemen invisible except for the fluorescent stripes on their hard hats and coats. Some of the trailers behind the stage were also in flames, and I could see the shapes of people silhouetted against the light. There were lots of people around us, too. Some were clearly audience members who had not yet left, but there were also uniformed police, roadies, bouncers, and people in service uniforms. In the distance I could still see the cluster of tents, and I wondered what had happened to Aaron Rayc and all of the wealthy, famous people who had been there.

"Raoul!" I cried, remembering.

"It's all right," Harrison said soothingly, but at that moment the paramedic returned with her bag.

"You're up," she said with resigned disapproval. "Well, let's have a look at you." She opened her bag and shone a small flashlight into my eyes, then she pressed my head gently and asked some questions before telling me I was lucky that I had a hard skull. Another paramedic came hurrying by and asked her to come and help him with a couple of kids who looked as if they had overdosed on something behind the stage.

"I think there were a lot more hard drugs than you would usually get at this sort of thing," I told Harrison, after they had hurried off. "One guess who supplied them, or at least made sure they were available."

Harrison steered me gently in the direction of the tents. "Come on. Let's find your brother."

"Jesse's here?"

"How do you think I got here?" Harrison asked.

I hadn't wondered, I realized. It had seemed so right and natural that he would be here when I needed him.

Harrison explained. "Jesse called Raoul's cell tae tell you that Serenity had disappeared again. It was out of range, so the service routed the call tae his home phone. Gilly and I answered, of course, and he told us your sister had gone off in a green van. It was Jesse who figured out that Serenity was headed here. Gilly and me were all for driving right tae Shaletown, but Jesse said we had it all wrong. It wasnae the government or the detention center Serenity wanted tae hurt. It was your da. He figured she would attack him."

"I thought that, too, when I saw her in the scaffolding. But she never meant to harm Da physically. She was supposed to sacrifice herself in such a way that it would destroy him in front of all those people. And everyone who saw what happened would have been wounded by it."

"Jesus," Harrison muttered.

"What happened when you arrived?" I asked.

He laughed. "Your brother just railroaded the heavies at the gate, saying it was an emergency. Talk about determined. He didnae lose his temper, but he just went on and on and he was so smart he sounded like a lawyer pleading a case in court. Maybe that's what they thought he was, because in the end they let us in tae see Raoul. As soon as we were in, I sneaked off. I was supposed to warn your father. Jesse and Gilly were going tae find Raoul and you. We had no idea you were over here already."

He stopped, seeing Raoul and Gilly coming toward us, Jesse with them looking pale and frantic. "Alyzon," he said. "Thank goodness you're safe." Then he did a double take, obviously getting close enough to see the blood. "What the hell happened to you?"

"It's just a bloody nose," I assured him.

Jesse gave a distracted nod. "Where are Da and Serenity?"

"An ambulance took them away," I said. "Jesse, did you hear what happened when—"

"Hear it!" Jesse exclaimed. "I saw it. We all did. It was on screens all around us. The classical music stopped and the sound went up so you had no choice but to look and listen. Da and Neo Tokyo were onstage playing, but we could see Serenity in the scaffolding—"

"You saw her before your father stopped singing?" Harrison asked.

"In close-up. Thank heavens she fell and Da could get to her in time," Jesse said fervently.

"You definitely saw Serenity in the scaffolding before Macoll stopped singing?" Harrison asked again in a queer, urgent voice.

This time it was Gilly who answered. "She was just standing there staring down at your da. He didn't know she was there until people in the audience or maybe some roadies noticed her and started reacting. Then he looked up and stopped singing. You could see because the camera angle changed and we were looking at Alyzon's da from over Serenity's shoulder. God, the look on your da's face when she was talking . . ." She shivered.

Jesse said, "It wasn't until she lit the match that we understood she must have doused herself with gas. God, I still can't believe it!" He shook his head. "Alyzon, I have to go home and get Mum and Mirandah and Luke. I'll take them straight to the hospital. Maybe you could go there now if Raoul . . ." He glanced back at Raoul, who nodded gravely.

* * *

We were in Raoul's car when Gilly said, "Why do you suppose the fire caught the stage and scaffolding so well? I mean, you'd think it would have been mostly metal. . . ."

"I think the scaffolding was doused in gasoline," Harrison said. "That's why the bouncers were so fanatical about keeping people back. They must have been given orders tae make damn sure no one got past the barrier. No one wanted the audience to get burned. Not physically, anyway."

"But why would anyone put gas on the scaffolding?" Gilly asked.

"Tae make sure there was no proof that the whole bloody thing was stage-managed for maximum impact. You realize there was a camera rigged to film Serenity burning herself. There had tae have been a mike as well. How else could we have heard her so well? And what about the lights on her?"

"But the police—"

"Wouldnae think of looking for evidence that there was some sort of setup," Harrison said. "After all, it was a stage, and they wouldn't think twice about seeing cameras and mikes. Police'd blame the whole thing on your sister, and that would be that. So long as the evidence was destroyed and no one stirred up any questions. If anyone thought tae wonder about how they could see or hear Serenity so well, they'd probably dismiss it, thinking the stage mikes must have picked up her voice, and that she was illuminated by incidental lighting. Because why on earth would anyone want tae film such a thing?"

That made me think of Sylvia Yarrow. I needed to tell them what I had figured out about her filming. But first, I had to do something else.

"I have to go back," I said.

"I'm coming with you," Harrison announced.

"No. I saw Gary Soloman back there, and I can tell him what you've just said. He'll talk to the police, and that'll make them look for proof while it's still there to be found. And he'll write about it." I looked at them all: Harrison with his cut and bruised cheek, white-faced Gilly, and stern Raoul emanating strength and purpose. I realized how much they meant to me, how their strengths had given me strength. "I don't want them to get away with this. This is part of what will destroy Aaron Rayc."

"Alyzon, do you realize that Harlen—" Raoul began.

"Is the son of Dita Rayc and her first husband. I figured it out when I saw them together."

"He'll be back there," he said. "What if he tries again?"

"He won't," I said. "I don't think he will ever do anything much again." I felt a stab of pity for him.

Harrison's eyes widened as he understood what the others did not. I said to them all, "I have to go back alone because we don't want Gary Soloman to know who you all are, remember?"

"She's right," Raoul said.

"Soloman might have gone," Harrison protested.

"He's a journalist," I said simply. "And this is a big story that links to something he has been investigating. Would you leave if you were him?"

"What if Aaron Rayc is back there?"

"It doesn't matter. He can't infect me."

"We dinnae know that for sure," Harrison said flatly. "Besides, a man who would set up a thing like this is capable of anything, and ye might have special abilities, but you're still flesh and blood."

"Harrison, I have to go back."

* * *

485

I ran into the muddle of light created by fire engines, flash-lights, and flames. The wire barrier had been trampled flat at the center, and I stepped over it. There was a lot of smoke drifting from the stage, and I found myself walking back into a shifting darkness. I coughed and gagged and squinted, try-ing to make out the faces of people in the red-brown light.

I had figured a journalist would be at the heart of the chaos, and I was right. I found him by the stage talking to a burly policeman. I waited until the officer had turned away, then spoke his name. Gary Soloman turned and stared at me. "Alyzon," he said, almost uncertainly. "I'm sorry about what happened to your sister."

"She did what she did because she's sick, but she would never have got this far on her own," I said, wanting him to understand. "Someone convinced her to do what she tried to do tonight. And someone helped her. How else did she get all the way here in the middle of nowhere if someone didn't drive her? How come she managed to get up on that scaffolding without anyone seeing her, with all those security guards? And why were the lights and cameras on her before she spoke, but no one gave the alarm and tried to get her down?"

His gaze had narrowed. "Are you saying someone wanted a disturbed teenager to kill herself in front of a two-thousand-strong audience?" I looked at him levelly. "All right. Who?" I let the silence force him to answer his own question. "Aaron Rayc?" His voice was tinged with incredulity.

"I doubt he set all the stage stuff up personally, but he has a stepson who goes to our school. He was here tonight."

"Why?" he asked, with the same urgent curiosity as when he had asked why a boy would kill his little brother. But the truth was too fantastic and required proof I did not want to give—could no longer give. So I gave him a question.

"Why would a wealthy businessman interest himself in artists of all kinds, and twist their lives out of shape?"

Gary Soloman nodded slowly. "I don't know the answer to that, and there is no clear proof that Aaron Rayc deliberately set out to change people or harm their lives. And there is no clear proof of what you are saying about tonight."

"You can interview people. Ask them about when the lights went on Serenity, make it clear in your story that the lights and camera and sound were all set to capture the action."

"My editor will refuse to print the story. He'll call it libel. If you want a reputable paper to cover this, you need proof," Gary said.

Then I remembered. "I saw a girl filming the stage from behind the barrier. I bet she got Serenity climbing up into the scaffolding, and maybe she even got a shot of whoever was helping her."

"So what?" the journalist said. "It's no good if some anonymous person has footage—"

"She dropped the camera over there," I pointed, wondering if it was possible that it was still there; that it hadn't been trampled or destroyed by water or falling debris. "If you could find it and show it to the police, they'd have to find out who gave the orders to have the microphone and camera set up in the first place."

I was sure the camera would contain footage that would incriminate Harlen, but I also had a strong unfounded certainty that it might show Aaron Rayc, too, because the sickness in him would want to watch, would not be satisfied to see it on a television screen.

I took Gary Soloman to where I had seen Sylvia Yarrow, and he got out his key ring and switched on a tiny flashlight. Then he began searching. I looked, too, but it was the journalist who found the camera, miraculously intact, and held it up with a cry of triumph. I could see that the record button was still glowing like a little red eye and wondered if it was possible it had fallen in such a way that it could have captured all that had happened.

Gary Soloman trained his flashlight on it and began examining the mechanism.

I took the chance to slip away. He had the scent now, and he would run with the story. If we were lucky it would tear Aaron Rayc and his reputation to pieces and maybe even put him away. And if the camera didn't contain anything that Gary Soloman could use, next week I would send the stuff Daisy had unearthed.

I had just about reached the ragged outer rim of the light from the fire when someone stepped out of nowhere to bar my way.

Aaron Rayc.

His eyes reflected the flames behind me, and to my horror and revulsion, he was smiling widely, his teeth oddly long and yellow-looking in the queer light. I had never seen a sight more frightening in my whole life, because it was not just the bloated, consuming sickness that he carried looking at me, but a man who had accepted and embraced it.

"Alyzon Whitestarr," he said.

"What do you want?" I asked, terrified despite my brave words to Harrison.

"I want nothing," he said. He gave a soft whispering laugh that made my skin crawl, and I realized it was true in some ghastly way. Whatever he—it—was wanted to devour all light and life and love and hope until there was nothing.

"What is it that *you* want?" he asked me, and now there was a black mindless savagery in his eyes.

"I want to go and see my father and sister," I whispered.

"Then what are you doing here," he asked, nodding over his shoulder without taking his eyes from mine, "talking to that journalist?"

My heart gave a great lurch. I glanced away toward the fire to give myself time to think. Then I shrugged. "I saw him when my class visited the newspaper. I was just telling him he should find out how come the security guards didn't stop Serenity from getting up there." I let a petulance tinge my voice; let it come out thin and childish.

"Journalists have their place," Rayc said after a long pause. "Well, I daresay our journalist friend will do his job." Again he gave his weird giggle that made the hair on my neck stand on end. Then he held out his hand.

I forced myself to take it, because it was a test. I put my hand into his with a strange feeling of sorrowful triumph.

Because he suspected that I was able to perceive the sickness, and that was no longer true: what I had done to save Serenity had killed the extended parts of my senses. Once again, I was just ordinary Alyzon Whitestarr.

Aaron Rayc released my hand, his face a bland mask. "I understand your father and sister have been taken to Baron Central Hospital in town. I can arrange for a car. . . ."

"No, thank you. I came with . . . with my brother," I said evenly, resisting the urge to wipe my hand on my clothes. "We wanted to surprise Da, but . . ."

He blinked once, slowly, like a lizard sunning itself on a rock, then he said, "Go."

It was a dismissal, a release, a signal of disengagement.

I went past him into the deeper darkness beyond the dying fire glow and the blaze of lights that had been rigged up on poles to light the area so that the firefighters could aim their hoses. I was walking away from the light, but it seemed to me that I was walking away from some greater and more irrevocable darkness.

* * *

In the car on the way to the hospital, I told the others what had happened.

"Then he knows what you can do?" Gilly asked fearfully, and I saw from her expression that she was thinking of the fire that had destroyed her grandmother's house.

It was so hard to say it out loud. My voice came out in a whisper. "He felt nothing, because there is nothing to feel." And I told them.

There was a long silence after that, with only the sound of rain patting on the windshield and the tires swishing along on the wet road, the sound of the car heater humming industriously. No whispers. I looked out into the darkness and prayed that I had not lost my extended senses for nothing. Prayed that Da and Serenity were all right.

The others began to talk about what had happened before Da had sung, and I forced myself to listen, to add what I knew or guessed to their speculations, because it distracted me from the gaping emptiness inside me, and from the terrible flatness of a world seen through normal senses.

"It's a battle we've won tonight, not the war," Raoul said at length. "We may have lost Alyzon's powers, but we will have Sarry and Davey, and I am certain there will be others. It is not over."

Harrison leaned over and asked softly, "Are you all right?"

"No," I whispered, and he reached out and drew me into his arms. I could not feel his emotions, only his great, mute warmth and the strength of his embrace.

I buried my face in his woolly gray sweater and wept for what I had lost.

45

At the hospital the first person I saw was Dr. Reed, who had treated me all those months ago when I had fallen into a coma. To see her was like coming full circle in a weird sort of way. It was so strange and sad not to smell her essence.

"Alyzon," she said. "My poor dear girl. I've just been to see your father, but he's sleeping."

"How is my sister?" I asked.

"They're both up in the burn ward. I'll take you," she offered with the brisk kindness I remembered and had once been able to smell.

Harrison caught my arm as she pressed an elevator button, saying he would go back and find Raoul and Gilly and they'd wait in the foyer downstairs. I nodded.

I was too frightened to ask how Serenity was. But I kept seeing Mum's painting. The blank, dead eye in the burning cavern of her face.

Dr. Reed brought me to a desk on the fourth floor and talked with the nurse who was behind it. Then she pressed my shoulder and said she would come back later if I wanted to talk. The woman behind the counter suggested kindly that I wash my face before going into the ward. She showed me a washroom, and I stared at my white-, black-, and red-smeared face, feeling tired and heavy and sad. Then a nurse ushered me along a hallway in her squeaky shoes.

"This is the ward where your father is, Alyzon," she said. "He'll be a little groggy because we've given him some painkillers for his hands."

"His . . . hands?" I saw his fingers on the guitar strings and felt sick.

"He'll be scarred but OK."

"My sister . . . ," I began, dreading the answer.

"She's had some surgery, so she is still recovering from the anesthetic. When she fell, two of her ribs broke and punctured her lung." She caught me as I swayed and brought me to sit down on a hard plastic chair by the door, peering professionally into my eyes. "Your sister will be all right, love. A punctured lung is serious, but she got here in time and the bones will heal."

"The burns—"

"Are bad, but they will heal, too, in time, and she can have plastic surgery. They were both very lucky. But now, why don't you go in and see your father?"

I went into the ward. Dimly I registered that there were other men in the other beds, but I had eyes only for Da, who lay in the bed nearest the window, farthest from the door. His hands were fatly bandaged in white and lay on either side of his long lean shape under the white hospital coverlet. His eyes were closed, and he looked so tired that my heart ached, because I loved him so much and I hadn't been able to stop the awful thing that had happened.

Fighting tears, I stumbled to the side of his bed and looked down at his hands; I couldn't bear to look into his face. "Oh, Da," I whispered, half suffocated by grief. "I'm so sorry."

"Sorry about what, my sweet, brave Aly Cat?" Da rasped. "We saved her."

I looked at him in astonishment and found him smiling his wonderful, kind, radiant smile. I felt a burst of joy that seemed to split my heart. Because that smile told me that the unbearable *hadn't* happened. The sickness hadn't won. Da hadn't been broken.

I did cry then. Such a wild storm of uncontrollable tears that one of the other patients rang for the nurse, who came hurrying in and wanted to give me a sedative.

I collected myself and looked at her. "I'm sorry. I'm fine. You can't imagine how fine I am." I laughed and burst into tears again.

"She's fine," Da said.

"Well, I'm glad everyone is fine. Do you think you could be fine a little more quietly?" the nurse asked with asperity.

Da promised we'd be good, and then he told me to sit on the bed close to him as she marched out.

"Your hands—"

"Will hurt if you sit on them," Da said earnestly, and I laughed and sniffed and scrubbed at my cheeks before pulling myself onto the bed carefully.

"Da, I'm so glad you're all right. I was so frightened."

"So was I, my love," Da said, understanding that I had not meant his burns.

"Serenity didn't mean what she said up there. What happened with Aya hurt her, and she got more and more sick. Only we didn't see because she kept it locked up inside of herself."

Da was nodding. "I should have got help for her, but I guess I thought, given time, I would find a way to unlock the hurt and help her. My arrogance almost brought us all to disaster. When I looked up and saw her there tonight . . ." He stopped for a bleak moment. Then he looked at me. "If you hadn't called out to me to catch her, I'd never have realized that she meant to jump. I'd never have got there in time to break her fall and put out the flames. . . . I still can't imagine how I could have heard you above all that noise."

I swallowed. "Da . . . I . . ."

"Da!" It was Mirandah's voice, and I turned to see her coming toward us, makeup smeared blackly around her eyes. Behind her were Jesse and Mum carrying Luke, the agitated nurse flapping in their wake and trying to say something about the number of visitors.

I slid off the bed. "I'll go out for a while." I looked back to see Mirandah fling herself on the side of the bed and begin to cry. But when I tried to pass Mum, she caught my hand. I looked up into her eyes and thought of what lay inside her, the darkness that she had been fighting for longer than I had been alive, which she was fighting even now.

"Oh, Mum," I said.

"My darling girl," Mum said. "You did it. I knew you could, and nothing else matters but that Serenity is fine and so is your da." She kissed me and then let me go.

* * *

I went out into the hall and asked to see Serenity then. The nurse told me that she was still unconscious, but I asked if I could see her anyway.

She was in a small room, alone, surrounded by green and chrome hospital equipment. There were tubes protruding from her nose and mouth and chest, and parts of her neck and face were swathed in bandages along with both arms. Her hair lay in lank burnt clumps, and there was a singed smell coming from her that made me feel ill. And what would I have smelled if I had still possessed my extended senses? I wondered. Because we had saved her life, her body, but what about the invisible parts of her? The spirit that had been wounded by our failure to save Aya from heartless bureaucracy, and which had been brought so low that she had been ready to kill herself? And most of all, would she be able to recover from what she had almost done to Da, the dreadful scalding hatred that had taken her to the top of the scaffolding with such a ghastly intent? Could anyone recover from that?

If she was like Sarry and Mum, and had the courage to fight, I thought. Given time and lots of love and people who she could talk to, who might be able to bring her to understand how she had been manipulated . . . maybe.

It might even be that what Da had done in catching her and beating out the flames would help her to recover. Because it was something to know someone loved you that much.

But whatever else happened, when Serenity woke, she would be questioned by the police, and what she said would add to what Gary Soloman would reveal, and seal the doom of Aaron Rayc. I thought of Harlen and wondered what would happen to him, because he had been a victim, too. Only he had no one to save him. No family to love and be loved by.

I reached out to touch Serenity on the cheek, feeling a stab of anger at the dreadful game that had been played with her life. She had been nothing more than a poor little pawn to kill the soul of a king.

My head ached as I instinctively tried and failed to reach into her. I sighed, leaning to kiss her cheek and thinking that simple human warmth was still a pretty powerful thing.

"I love you," I told her softly, and her eyelids fluttered but she did not wake. "We all do, and you better hurry up and come back home to us." I kissed her again and crept out.

* * *

Harrison was waiting outside the room, and I went into his arms as easily as if they had been made for me.

"How did you know where I was?" I asked in a voice that was husky from all the tears I had shed and from the yelling I had done a million years ago back in a dark field.

"I always ken where you are," he said softly, and I felt his breath in my hair. "But I heard you call my name at the concert. I heard your voice inside my head."

I pulled back a little so that I could look up at him. "I think some sort of connection formed between us that day at the library when you—"

"Kissed you?" he said. He smiled at me. "Well, it was some kiss."

"It was," I said shyly.

His smile faded. "I thought I'd forced you tae respond, and that you were horrified by it."

"I was . . . I mean, I was horrified that you might be horrified." I laughed, and then we were both laughing.

Harrison said, "I really did kiss you tae stop that guy figuring we were spying on the poetry group. But when you responded, I . . . I couldnae help myself."

"I know. A guy reacts that way to any woman in his arms," I said tartly.

He grinned. "I couldnae just tell you I reacted like that because it was you in my arms and that I had dreamed of kissing you like that a million times," he said softly but without embarrassment.

I swallowed. Licked my lips. "Afterward there were times when I thought you might kiss me again. I . . . I wished it."

He laughed softly, shaking his head. "I wanted tae kiss you breathless every time you looked at me. I thought I was turning intae some sort of sex maniac, and I was terrified that you would pick up what I was feeling because of your extended senses. That's why I was always so careful not tae touch you."

My own smile faded, and his arms tightened. "I'm sorry

your senses are back tae normal. But you know, maybe it's like Goethe said: 'Great powers come tae those who need them.' If it wasnae for them, your sister would have done what she tried tae do. She would have destroyed herself and your father, and it would have been a terrible victory for the sickness."

"But it's not over."

"No. Like Raoul said, it is a battle we won, not the war, but you've done the main thing. You've made us see the sickness and understand a lot about how it works. We've just been talking about it downstairs. Eventually we'll figure out exactly how transmission of the sickness happens, and then we can really fight it."

"I know how it happens," I said quietly. "I figured it out when I saw Sylvia at the concert with the camera. That day at the shed, Harlen insisted that she had to film something."

"I suppose they intended tae use the footage tae hurt even more people," Harrison murmured.

"Maybe, but that wasn't the main reason he wanted her to film it. You see, we were right in thinking a person has to be wounded spiritually in order to be opened up deeply enough to be infected. But we were wrong in thinking that someone else had to hurt them. Because the deepest wounds aren't the ones we get from other people hurting us. They are the wounds we give ourselves when we hurt other people."

Harrison drew in a long breath and leaned back to look down at me. "Jesus, you mean they wanted Sylvia Yarrow tae film Serenity burning herself tae death—"

"Because to film such a thing instead of trying to stop it would be so terrible that it would slash your spirit open to the core. Harlen was right there, hanging around, watching like a hawk, and he tried to stop me interfering with her. I think he was waiting for it to happen, and when Sylvia stood there and filmed Serenity burning herself, he would have infected her. He would only have to touch her. When Harlen tried to infect me, he just grabbed hold of me and put his skin against mine."

We stood for a while in silence, and I thought about Mum and Sarry and what they might have done to open their spirits to such a devouring darkness. But I did not wonder for long, because whatever they had done, they redeemed themselves each moment that they lived by fighting the corruption that they had allowed into their souls. I knew how hard it must be, and how frightening, because the sickness had touched me as well. But there had been no wound by which it could enter me, and I had been able to fight it just by showing it my spirit.

And I would go on fighting with the others. It didn't matter that there was no longer anything special about me. I had shown myself that a whole spirit was all it took to drive off the sickness. That was worth knowing.

"For goodness' sake!" Gilly said, and Harrison and I sprang apart guiltily. She burst out laughing. "Oh, very subtle. I hung around for at least fifteen minutes waiting for the kiss, but since you still seem to be working up to it and I'm starving, I just wanted to tell you that Raoul and I are going to get the pizza that Harrison came to ask you about half an hour ago."

"Och, the pizza . . . ," Harrison said as he flushed and ran his hands through his pale hair.

"I guess your mind isn't exactly on food right now," Gilly said kindly. She walked off, tossing me a look of delighted mischief as she passed around the corner. I looked at Harrison, and all of a sudden we both started laughing. We laughed so much that we wound up leaning against the wall.

Then Harrison said. "About that kiss . . ."

"Oh . . . ," I said.

He rolled slowly sideways so that he was facing me, leaning lightly against me and pressing me against the wall. He looked into my eyes, refusing to let me look away or close my eyes as he moved closer. I felt the heat of his lips and the warm rush of his breath, and then he did what he had promised to do, kissing not only the breath but all the laughter out of me.

"Oh," I said when he let me go.

"Very profound," Harrison said, grinning. And he kissed me again.

And this time, oh this time, I smelled wood smoke and lavender and chocolate.

Acknowledgments

My thanks to the real Alyzon Whitestarr and her family—strangers, then, whose names I borrowed after an extraordinary dusk encounter.

Thanks also and perhaps most of all to Nan McNab. Grace in life is rare and friendship more rare still, so I count myself twice blessed in having both in such a brilliant editor.

I also want to thank the ever-present and gently vigilant Janet Raunjak at Penguin, and Miles Lowry. Last but far from least is Adam Totic from the Internet café in Veletržní Palác Gallery in Prague, without whose help and tolerance I would never have managed to get this book edited between countries.

About the Author

Isobelle Carmody began the first of her highly acclaimed Obernewtyn Chronicles while she was still in high school, and worked on it while completing a Bachelor of Arts and then a journalism cadetship. The series and her short stories have established her at the forefront of fantasy writing in Australia.

She has written many award-winning short stories and books for young people. *The Gathering* was a joint winner of the 1993 Children's Book Council Book of the Year Award and the 1994 Children's Peace Literature Award. *Billy Thunder and the Night Gate* (published as *Night Gate* in the United States) was short-listed for the Patricia Wrightson Prize for Children's Literature in the 2001 New South Wales Premier's Literary Awards. Isobelle's most recent works include the Little Fur series for younger readers, which she also illustrated.

Isobelle and her family divide their time between their homes in Australia and the Czech Republic.